what
we
set
in
motion

A NOVEL

stephanie
austin edwards

Novel Ideas by SAE
P.O. Box 1064
Beaufort, SC 29901
www.novelideasbysae.com

(This is a work of fiction. Names, characters, businesses, places, events and incidents are either the products of the author's imagination or used in a fictitious manner. Any resemblance to actual persons, living or dead, or actual events is purely coincidental.)

Library of Congress Catalog Number: 2015912276

Publisher's Cataloging-in-Publication data
Edwards, Stephanie
What We Set In Motion: A Novel
p. cm.
Ebook: ISBN 978-0-9965719-1-3
Paperback: ISBN: 978-0-9965719-0-6
Hardback: ISBN: 978-0-9965719-2-0

1. Fiction-General. 2. Fiction-Literary. 3. Fiction-Inspirational.

First Edition

Printed in the United States of America

This book is dedicated to
Lowcountry Women Writers,
my husband and best friend,
Paul Coffman,
and our perfect, four-legged children.

CHAPTER 1

August 1969

 Choices are the hinges of destiny.
—PYTHAGORAS

I T WAS THE BRAVEST DECISION I'd ever made.
I walked into the perfectly appointed living room of our historic Lowcountry home as if on a scouting mission. Across the room, Daddy sat in his burgundy leather chair, his feet on the ottoman, reading *The Beaufort Gazette* and sipping his afternoon Jack Daniels on-the-rocks. His blue oxford-cloth shirt and tan chinos, almost a uniform for him, looked fresh and starched in contrast to the humidity hanging in the outside air.

"Hey, Daddy," I whispered, testing his mood. The light from the table lamp shone off his balding head.

Silence was his response.

Motivated and driven like my daddy, I was about to graduate in December, finishing college one semester early. According to him, I lacked nothing in my twenty years. By adding a diploma to my compulsory training in etiquette, cotillion, equestrian and sailing, he often boasted to whoever would listen that I would be among the most polished young girls in the rural South. As a member of one of the few families able to regain their empire after the "War of Northern Aggression," maybe I should have realized sooner that Samuel Preston Barnwell had plans for me the minute I stepped off the stage.

At the fireplace, I adjusted the cluttered pictures on the mantel to steady myself and search for the man I used to know. Daddy had once been my hero and carried me with him everywhere. On boat rides to the far reaches of the South Carolina Sea Islands and up the brackish creeks inland to Colleton County, he taught me to fish, crab and shoot. In Savannah and Charleston, I attended the symphony and visited art museums. In Columbia, I watched him work his keen business sense.

My hand reached for a picture of Daddy and me when I was about seven, standing beside his '57 black Ford pickup, each holding fishing rods and stringers of spot tail bass. Next to that was another picture of us, this time in a field. I was eight, pointing my first rifle toward the sky. Wearing a camouflage shirt and pants, Daddy grinned brightly at the camera under a full head of sandy blonde hair, his arm wrapped tight around my shoulders.

I set the picture back and searched for other familiar ones. *When did my recital pictures leave the mantel?* Mama always displayed my ballet pictures right in the center, but they weren't there now.

"So, have you decided if you're going on to graduate school at that fancy college of yours?" Daddy barked into his newspaper, breaking the silence but still not looking up. "Or can I count on you coming home where you belong and back to work with me?"

I braced at the question and his tone. His temper came through clearly, and all I said was, "Hey."

2

After spending three years at the University of South Carolina, about a three-hour car ride away, coming home and back to work with Daddy was not what I wanted. Early in high school when Mama's health forced her to quit working with him, I'd taken over and learned her job. Afternoons and summers I helped manage Daddy's considerable portfolio of real properties, collected current and back rent and showed the available buildings for lease. While he was away on hunting or fishing trips with his buddies, I showed parcels of the land we owned to prospective buyers, usually Yankees looking for a steal from a local. I encouraged them to move their businesses to our town, but by the time negotiations were underway, Daddy made the prices and the restrictions so high, the buyers usually left in a hurry and a huff.

As he grabbed his sweating highball glass, the right corner of his newspaper fell in toward the center. Beside the coaster, I saw my final tuition check. *It's now or never,* my mind repeated. Once my body finally heard the command, I pulled my shoulders back and lifted my chin, as if entering the stage from the wings and walked over to pick it up.

While sitting in the high-back chair across from him, I calmly announced, "After graduation, I'm not coming home." Knowing my next statement would be truly hard for him to take, I sat up taller like a perched bird, hands in my lap. "I'm moving to New York City."

My daddy was such a diehard Southerner that he once canceled a January trip to Vermont to celebrate the birthday of the governor, an old college roommate, because he feared he and his pregnant wife could get snowed in, and a child of his just might be born a damn Yankee.

"New York City," he repeated through a laugh. His face lifted from his newspaper on to me for the first time. "And do what?"

"I am going to dance." I reveled in saying those words.

"Why in the world would you want to do that?"

"To become a professional dancer. This is what I want–more than anything."

"A dancer? In New York City? With all those hippies? I'm not paying for any such thing, young lady." His eyes narrowed and his mouth tightened as he stared straight at me. Then his focus dropped back to his newspaper.

"I've been offered a scholarship to study dance at the Leland Lemire Studio. They don't give these to just anyone." In college I discovered the unbridled freedom of modern dance and never picked up my toe shoes again. "Daddy, I know this is hard for you to understand, but I want to be part of a professional dance company, so I have to do it now, while I'm young. I may never have this kind of opportunity again." I yearned for his understanding, something I once had and took for granted.

"You are not cut out for such a life. Look around, Nadine. Do you think you could survive without all this?" He gestured as if to point out to me for the first time the elegance of our house. "You wouldn't last ten minutes without my support or the Lowcountry." He pointed toward the glass doors and the view leading to the river.

My eyes followed his arm to the view I took in only an hour before.

Returning from my final appearance at the weekly "Ladies Member Lunch" at the club, I couldn't wait to get home to change out of my least favorite attire and prepare myself for my last talk with Daddy before going back to college. I kicked off my white leather pumps and threw my matching purse on the bed. When one shoe landed at the base of the double windows framed with sheer tieback curtains, I laughed at my sorry aim and padded over to pick it up.

Outside, afternoon sunlight edged the giant oaks near the weathered dock of our historic and waterfront home. From the marsh, an egret fluttered its wings in slow motion and lifted into the air. The smaller birds, smartly tucked in the shade of the palmettos, called out to whoever listened, but like my kind of people, remained rooted in place. In the brutal August heat, even the squirrels seemed to run listlessly. A wayward goose searching for his mate crossed the rising pluff mud, waddling from one foot to the other as the seven to eight-foot tide passed from slack toward low on the Beaufort River.

Just like Mama used to tell me as we shared the best parts of our day on the porch, this magnificent landscape resided in the deepest part of all of us. When goose bumps scurried up my arms at the thought of leaving, I turned away before I caved. I unzipped my navy blue A-line shift dress and let it drop to the floor. I gently laid my mother's pearls in my silver baby dish that I kept on the dresser. Still in my slip, I unsnapped the barrette from the back of my head and let my wavy curls float down around my shoulders. Once a few strands of hair covered one eye, I struck a pose in front of the mirror like Cyd Charisse in *Silk Stockings*. Mimicking what I saw in the movie, I danced around my bedroom for several minutes channeling Cyd's best choreography. After taking my bow to an imaginary audience, I sighed, pulled my mop of hair back into a low ponytail, dropped my slip and stepped into clean, but permanently fish gut stained shorts and an old white polo shirt. *That's better.*

When I turned to pick up my scattered clothes, I saw the contradictions I grew up with: teddy bears mixed with air rifles, tutus with fishing vests. My bedroom was a shrine to the good times.

"Everything you need is right here." Daddy broke my thoughts. "This is where you belong," he added as he set his drink down and turned a page.

Where I belong? Those words felt so wrong. "No, it's not," I said, too loudly. "You don't understand." Lowering my head, I fingered the check. I never argued with Daddy before, but this time sadness rushed through me, and I couldn't stop. "You never understand. Anything would be better than this." I felt the redness in my face rise, an embarrassing and uncontrollable trait I inherited from my mother.

He looked up. A mixture of sorrow and pain flashed across his eyes, something he hadn't shown since Mama died. The look disappeared so quickly, I didn't understand if it reflected my wanting to leave or his need to control.

Because I was carefully sheltered from the political and social changes of the world beyond my geographic entrapment, my unspoken mission growing up was to be all that my father's heart desired. Until I went away to college, my life resembled his vision: student council and class officer, National Honor Society and Merit Scholar, cheerleader, and even homecoming queen. It was the sixties and for a Barnwell girl, still an idyllic time in the South. I spent my summers playing tennis, swimming and competing in Sunfish sailing regattas in the river. On some evenings, I gathered with high school friends at Hunting Island on the beach over open fires, playing guitars, singing *If I Had a Hammer, Scotch and Soda, and This Land Is Your Land* at the top of our lungs, not worrying whether we could carry a tune. I glided through my teens on the wings of success and lineage and never imagined going against Daddy—on anything.

Gathering every scrap of courage, I stood on an inhale lengthening every muscle and bone in my body, as if preparing for a solo. "I am going, and I'm going with Frank, right after graduation."

He stared at me for a few seconds before his already booming voice rose to a new crescendo. "With Frank? Like hell you are!"

Meeting Frank opened up a whole new world for me. He made me aware that I could live my dreams too. Although a true Southerner from Columbia, South Carolina, Frank was not from a lineage my daddy recognized. He told me many times Frank had ideas that weren't quite right. After finding out what he was studying, Daddy hadn't hesitated to tell either of us how he felt.

"You're majoring in what?" Daddy asked the first time I brought Frank home.

"Drama, sir. I'm going to be an actor." Frank stood erect and proud. He winked at me.

"Acting, as a career, is for children and ne'er-do-wells," Daddy said, puffing out his chest. "You need to find yourself a real profession, son." He flicked the side of his cigar. Cinders fell into and around the ashtray next to him. Frank didn't react. He focused on his goals no matter what my daddy or anyone else said.

Now in a lowered voice, Daddy continued, "I've told you before, Nadine Carter Barnwell. You can dance in your spare time all you want at that fancy college. But when you're done, you're going to come home and work with me. Your family has led this town for generations. I didn't spend all these years building up a business for nothing. As my only child, it's time for you to prepare to take the helm. I don't know what has gotten into you, but that is all I am paying for."

I got up and moved to the patio doors which led to Mama's prized camellia garden. Staring out, I felt an urge to lift my body into an arabesque, a pose of power and control. My legs naturally stopped in fifth position in preparation. But in my frustration my arms belied my training, and rather than lifting out from my center they folded tightly across my chest.

In the murkiness of the glass doors my image began to form. My reflection suddenly reminded me of my beautiful mama, at least the last image I remembered. Although different heights, we had the same red hair and oval shaped face. Since her death, I focused so much on Daddy's needs that, sadly, Mama's image was fading for me.

"It's your high cheekbones and eyes," Aunt Amelia used to tell me. "Your father sees your mama in you." I loved hearing that I looked like her, but the eyes and the hair may have been where our likeness ended. She was soft spoken, porcelain-skinned and tiny boned like a bird. I was five-feet-six inches, slender, but muscular and with too much energy. Until illness took Mama over, weakness of spirit was never a part of her character. I like to think that I inherited those strengths. I always loved hearing the story of how Daddy and Mama met. Daddy had been so impressed with the tiny woman with the large spirit that he knew he would marry her after their first meeting. In May of 1938, two clans, both considered the mainstays of their community, joined when Samuel Preston Barnwell married Lorelei Benton Carter.

Now, I missed my mama more than ever. She would have known what I needed. She would have helped me make Daddy understand that dance was a huge part of my spirit. She wouldn't have liked it either, but she would have known that leaving them and Beaufort was vital.

Daddy's reflection appeared in the patio door behind mine. The temperature in the room rose as his body turned toward me. "I've told you, Nadine; my daughter is going to be the best damn young woman in this town. Hell, not only this town, the whole Lowcountry, maybe even all of South Carolina. There is no way I am going to help you or your hippie friend move to New York City to squander your talents, no matter how noble you think dancing is." With his newspaper in one hand, he leaned over the drop-leaf table beside the door and pounded his fist on it with his other. "What are they filling you with at school? You are not that talented. I promise you, you will be laughed right out of there!"

I stepped back as though slapped across the face. "They will not!" I shouted back. "You've no idea what you're talking about. They already think I'm talented. You haven't bothered to see me perform since–I can't even remember when." Anger, which I was taught to control as a Barnwell, rippled from my head down my body like swells generated from the wake of a speedboat. I swayed trying to keep it inside.

"Get rid of that boy, Nadine Barnwell. You are not moving to New York City, and that is final."

Before I could say anything else, he snapped his paper closed and walked out of the room.

I turned and clenched the back of the chair to try to keep from exploding. Then, spewing out of me like hot lava, I heard myself say what I had never let myself say before, "You're not going to hold me here like a prisoner to your view of life. There's a new world out there beyond the South, and I'm going to dance whether you like it or not!"

His fading footsteps stopped. "No, you are not!" he shouted back. Then, as if invisible, hidden or omnipotent, he called out from the shadows, "If you go anyway, don't ever come back!"

I wanted to throw that same chair at him, but didn't. Instead, I picked up my bag, slipped through the patio doors and hurried across the manicured lawn. On the dock, I stopped, bent over and took several deep breaths. The whole float rocked as my black lab, Bear, raced down the ramp and screeched to a halt at my feet. I felt and smelled his warm breath in my hair, heard his nails clicking as he stepped up and down in excitement. Then I lifted myself up and with Bear at my heels, paced several lengths of the splintered planks, trying to push away my anger. A tightness settled in my chest and neck muscles blocking my thinking. But after a few minutes, my focus returned and as clear as a lightning bolt in the night sky, I knew what to do. I needed to get to Aunt Amelia right away and tell her what Daddy just said, what I said. Ask her to help me figure out what, if anything, I could or should do next.

If Daddy didn't care if I ever came back, I didn't care if he knew where I was going. But I did follow one more rule. After writing my destination on the covered chalkboard, a mandatory requirement for all boats leaving our dock, I quietly untied my bateau from its cleat, stepped in and pushed off. Bear paced the dock looking for a place to jump into the boat. "No, you can't go this time. I'll be back tomorrow," I shouted as if he understood English. His sad eyes watched me float out into the creek without him.

The boat drifted silently for several minutes before I pulled the cord on the Johnson 50Horsepower Motor. There was just enough time to get to Camp Pinckney, our remote family fish camp on an island without roads or bridges, before the blackness of the Sea Islands set in.

Tears clouded my vision as I steered the bateau through a series of creeks to get to more open water. I wiped my eyes with the back of my sleeve until my sight cleared up. Because the brackish water was so cloudy, it wasn't easy to know exactly where the deepest parts of the creek were. Depending on the tide level, mudflats and oyster rakes could be just under the surface, waiting to catch a prop or a keel. Once caught, a boat could be kept firmly in place, stranded for many hours while the tide went all the way out and back in just enough to float once again. That's when I realized that if I wasn't careful, I was going to be stuck in the pluff mud forever and no tide change was going to set my boat free.

The sound of dolphin spray caught my attention. I turned in time to see four of them arcing out of the water in micro-intervals, then curving back down, nose first like a line of synchronized swimmers diving into a pool. Daddy and I used to love to come out at feeding time and watch for dolphin pods. When I first asked what a pod was, he told me they were family.

I knew what family meant to him even if he had lost his ability to show love. Whenever he and his friends got together, they always fell into bragging bouts about who was the most Southern, who was the purest Beaufortonian. According to Daddy, his grandfather, Ebenezer Barnwell, went through hell and back, determined to regain the empire he and his family built and then lost. My great-grandfather, grandfather and great uncles worked tirelessly to rebuild their lives. They had a vision and an unwavering focus stemming from an understandable fire of hatred and revenge. How many times had I heard this story? But couldn't Daddy see the war was long over, the empire rebuilt? Now he owned and managed much of the property in the town and even more throughout the county. He had what he wanted and his work suited him perfectly.

"Now it's my turn," I shouted into the wind. "I want my own life and my own vision." A seagull swooped in toward me before turning direction at the last second and landing on top of an empty dock piling stacked with other birds. Their freedom and grace pulled at my being.

Within fifteen minutes I was in the widest part of the river, headed to a place almost as far away from civilization and Daddy as I could get. Sitting on a hammock of land on a deep swiftly flowing creek, edged on two sides by green feathered marsh and to the rear by a density of coastal trees and shrubs, this camp was a refuge from the increasing demands and early signs of encroaching civilization on our quiet southern town. The camp itself was nothing more than an expanded lean-to, haphazardly upgraded over the years, closely resembling a sharecropper's shack. I came to this place with Daddy a hundred times over the years, back when we were close. Now it remained the only part of him I still understood.

A half hour after leaving home, I arrived at the fish camp.

After tying up the boat, I walked toward the house, aware of the familiar sounds of nature that surrounded me as the darkness swallowed their shapes. Aunt Amelia, my mother's only sister, and her husband, Uncle Hamp, were already there waiting for me. They were staying at the camp for one last weekend before heading to their second home near Asheville, North Carolina. This unusual couple lived only two houses down from me my whole life. I was at their house almost as much as mine, mostly because they loved and accepted me without reservation. I could tell them anything. Back when Mama still had her sense of humor, in her less oppressive years, we often joked that I was actually Aunt Amelia's child, birthed through my mother's womb.

Diminutive in stature like Mama, my aunt met me at the door, studied my face for a moment and gave me a long, strong hug. She was an earth-mother herbalist and almost always wore loose khaki pants, a long gauze blouse, and her pewter and enamel amulet necklace to keep trouble away, with a clientele who believed in her.

"You look upset," she said. "Go sit on the porch and I'll be there in a minute." I nodded.

In the kitchen I heard Uncle Hamp, a tall, gangly, jolly man about fifty years old clanging pots, dropping utensils and letting out an intermittent, "damn it" while he prepared his seafood specialty, Frogmore Stew. As her business, production, and delivery manager, he was her rock in every aspect of her life, she often told me.

Aunt Amelia soon came out, carrying cups of tea. Whenever there was something significant going on, Aunt Amelia brewed her special tea. Even if it was a hundred degrees outside, she believed in the tea's healing power. After handing a cup to me, she sat in the weather beaten rocker next to mine.

Dusk was a reverent time of the day to us, and we respected and participated in the growing darkness with our silence. Only a few hundred yards away, across another hammock of land, we heard the rhythmic movement of the ocean caressing the shoreline to the east. In the distance, the unmistakable *plop, plop* of deer hooves in wet marsh drew my attention to their outlines, as they moved single file near the maritime forest. A breeze rustled leaves in the giant live oaks that clung to the land like a mother to her child. I sensed nature settling in for the evening all around me.

But I was far from settling. I still churned from Daddy's words and mine. Each incoming wave and its retreat entered the pulse of my body.

Aunt Amelia broke the silence. "What did he say, Nadine?" she asked, still looking out into the darkness. Her graying shoulder-length hair, lifted off her shoulders by a magenta bandana, made her look more like a queen than my aunt.

"The short version? He said, 'no.'" I took a sip from my cup.

"That's all?" she asked.

"No, of course not. Sam Barnwell didn't talk long, but he was quite clear." I mimicked his voice, repeating his angry words. "First, he said I wasn't talented enough, second, that I'm not moving to New York City and third, to get rid of 'that boy'." I paused, barely able to form the next words. "And fourth, if I left anyway, not to ever come back." Feeling the slap of those words all over again, I wrapped both hands around the warm mug, put my feet up on the wood slat in the center of the screened porch and rocked.

"Oh, I see," Aunt Amelia said. She lifted her cup under her nose and breathed in the aroma. "And what did you say?"

"Some things I shouldn't have. And then he walked out of the room—again, as if I have no rights." I raised my face toward her. "In all the versions of our conversation about me leaving that played out in my head before the real one, those last words, *don't ever come back*, never entered my mind."

The cicadas suddenly ramped up their chorus, drowning out any further talk. I wondered if Aunt Amelia also directed the night sounds, giving her time to absorb Daddy's words.

While I listened I pictured her and Mama sitting on this same porch, rocking and talking late into the night. If she'd lived, Mama and I would be sitting here talking. But thankfully, Aunt Amelia's unique perspective on life helped Mama and me through her illness and death. Now I needed Aunt Amelia to help me find my way.

After the cicadas had tapered off, she said, "You're in a difficult situation. As you know, great southern families always hold on tight to their own. Because he's my brother-in-law, I've been close to your father ever since he met your mama, and I know exactly how stubborn he can be. Your daddy doesn't see life any other way."

"But if I stay much longer, it'll be too late. If I stay, get married, and live my life as he expects, I'll wither and die. I will."

"I know, Nadine." She reached over and touched my arm. "I've known that you would need to leave here since you were a small child. But it was up to you to realize it."

"But if I leave, what will happen to him? Even though I've been at school, you know I've taken care of him since Mama died. He's come to expect me to continue."

"You have to honor what your heart calls you to do, no matter what anyone else says. No matter how painful it is."

The love and understanding that I'd always gotten from Aunt Amelia and Uncle Hamp came through again. No price can be put on being understood when you feel so torn apart. We sat again in silence but this time, a comfortable silence.

A bird lifted into flight in the distance, only recognizable by the sound of the flutter of wings used to pull its legs from the sucking mud. Aunt Amelia waited a moment, then, as if cued by the bird, continued.

"This might feel overwhelming to you, but there are some things you and I can do right here, right now, if you are willing to open yourself to experiment; you know, look at an alternate solution. This decision for you is crucial because it will direct the entire rest of your life."

I'd been familiar with Aunt Amelia's rituals since I was small, participating in a spring and an autumn ritual, a full moon ritual and one for the garden harvest, but not one where I was the focus. My daddy didn't care one lick for that side of her. He called her work "voodoo," but it wasn't. The light from her amulet reflected into my eyes. "I will do anything," I said, slapping my hand on the chair arm for confirmation.

"Okay. This is what you need to know." She sat up, leaned toward me, elbows on her knees and took my hand. "When we are faced with life-altering decisions, usually stemming from an emotional crisis like this one between you and your father, we have a few options. We can do like most good southerners and turn our situation over to a very busy God, leaving our enlightenment to His schedule or like many others, consider therapeutic counseling which is meant to be lengthy. But if we don't have that much time, we can access the steps required to find out what our true life is by letting the universe and our whole being know precisely what we want through a Life-Path ritual."

"Yes, I see," I said, not really seeing this clearly yet.

"This is not a magical spell or a cure-all. It is a powerful guidance technique available to those who choose to put their faith behind it.

Then as if taking his own cue, Uncle Hamp called us in for dinner.

Before we got up from our chairs, Aunt Amelia added, "You need to understand the core issue here. It's choice. Choice is the hinge that opens the doors, Nadine. It is the be-all and end-all of a fulfilled life. What you decide to do next with this situation will be a pivotal life choice. It's important to do it right. But it is also only your first of many choices ahead, so you must pay attention well. If you can recognize what you truly want, not just what you think you want and are ready to stand by your truth wherever the path takes you, the effects of this will lead you toward not just a desired career or relationship, but something far more complete, yet rare, which I deem The Full-Hearted Life. But be really sure, because if you do this, what we set in motion is very powerful."

As we stood to go inside, I grabbed her arm and held it tight, as if she and her offer might blow away in the wind. "I'm sure," I said. "I know what I want."

After dinner Uncle Hamp and I moved into the living room area. Aunt Amelia brought out three white candles, marking pens and pieces of sheer cloth about three inches square. Uncle Hamp set out lanterns as Aunt Amelia lit the white candles and placed them on the low table in the center of the room.

When everything was set, she began. "Over the years, you've seen me work with people and their problems, but you don't know how I do it. Like the New Year's kiss at midnight or the Catholic ritual of communion, rituals are everywhere and have been for thousands of years. Rituals have lasted through the centuries because they are simple, familiar, easily repeatable and can have lasting effects. In this ritual you will write what you really want for your life on this cloth square. You can't write something vague. You have to know what you want, commit to it, and show the universe you believe it is already a certainty. Don't say the words out loud; write them." She paused to sip her tea. "Do you understand, Nadine?"

"Yes, I think I do," I said.

"Good, because we're all going to do this. Group energy is vital. It speeds up the process."

Uncle Hamp smiled. I could tell he'd done this one before.

"Now write."

I wrote the first thing that came into my mind: To have a life of my own choosing, will dance professionally in New York City. A sense of peace came over me as I put this into words.

"Are you done?" Aunt Amelia asked.

I nodded.

She disappeared into the kitchen and came back with a large metal bowl filled with water, which she placed on the table.

In the August air as candlelight reflected off the sweating bowl and the nightlife sounds quieted, Aunt Amelia began. "Nadine, you go first. Now repeat what you wrote eight times in your mind, and when you are done place the fabric square in the bowl."

I followed her instructions without asking questions, as I learned to do over the years. Once the fabric sank beneath the surface, the ink began to fade.

She continued. "By the time all the words disappear from the cloth, a new part of your life will be set in motion. If you accept this as your truth, nothing can stop it from beginning."

When the ink was totally gone, she lifted my square out and handed it to me.

Uncle Hamp and Aunt Amelia each confirmed their choice to spend less time in Beaufort and more time at their new mountain home. At the end, we stood stone silent in the candlelight, eyes transfixed by the sweating bowl, each holding our blank wet squares. I didn't know what they were thinking, but I felt the words I wrote permeate my whole body. In fact, I imagined my body as translucent, with my words like a hologram, filling the spaces that should have been bones, muscles and blood vessels.

Aunt Amelia placed the palms of her hands together and lifted them to the center of her chest. "And so it is," she said, bowing. I did the same.

Afterwards, as I sat alone on the porch holding the cloth square, breathing in the still salt air, a chill suddenly ran through my body.

What have I done? What am I giving up? My father worked hard for what he wanted, partly for his own ego and partly to have something to pass on to his children, as his family had done for generations. But there were no other children—only me. With the rising moon, light slipped through the tree trunks and I watched the darkened landscape again take form. As the magnificent world I just willed to leave behind stood still and strong before me, a pang of guilt for my ungrateful attitude grabbed me in my chest. Drawing in the comfort and beauty of the only world I knew, I blinked away the wetness that slid from my eyes.

Then everything shifted again. I suddenly understood that Daddy's precious Sea Islands, even with their changing shorelines, felt permanent to him. Like many in the Lowcountry, he didn't welcome change, and he worked hard to keep his family's lives under his control. But as I sat there I realized mine couldn't be one of the lives he controlled any longer.

Just above the tree tops a full golden moon appeared, beaming like a theatrical floodlight, enveloping the marsh and me. Its radiance filled the dark spaces of the wilderness. I wanted to bask in that moonlight forever, only what emerged was the unwavering image of dancing in New York City. I clearly saw that if I stayed with Daddy in the Lowcountry, I would never be anything more than Sam Barnwell's daughter.

Suddenly, I was overtaken with the confidence I needed to break from all I knew and let my new life begin. I couldn't wait to get back to school and tell Frank. He would be so relieved.

CHAPTER 2

August 1969

*One can never consent to creep when one feels an
impulse to soar.*
—HELEN KELLER

T HE EMPTY HOUSE I CAME back to the next day was
Daddy's way of emphasizing he meant what he said about
me moving to New York City. I packed my remaining
things, left a note and headed back to school.

Sam Cook, Bo Diddley, Buddy Holly and Patsy Cline blasted
from the radio of my car for the first twenty miles as I drove back
to school. I tapped the steering wheel and belted out the words to
every song as the engine of my '65 VW Beetle purred along. But
along the rural parts of the highway, which was most of it, radio
reception came and went. I finally turned it off. Near Columbia,
the flat land of the Lowcountry began to slowly rise all around
me, edging the highway in lanes of loblolly and longleaf pines.
Their magnificence reminded me of the corps de ballet in Swan
Lake, which then reminded me of how much I wanted to dance

in New York. This would never have been a possibility for me if it wasn't for Frank. I suppose you could say he was my first right choice before Aunt Amelia gave me the ritual to follow.

The first moment I saw Frank something stirred inside me. That September day in my sophomore year would be the last warm day at school for the next eight months. As I left my two-hour dance technique class, sweaty and still breathing hard, there he was, standing outside the door by the railing in the quad talking to Tammy, a girl I knew only slightly. In his left hand he held a black motorcycle helmet; with his right, he tucked chin length hair behind his ear. Looking at his faded blue work shirt and jeans, I suspected his clothes fit not only his body, but also his personality. As he talked to Tammy, I could almost see sparks pop off him. When he looked up and caught me staring, I was drawn into intense dancing eyes as piercing as a hawk's and as inviting as the warm summer ocean.

Without thinking, I walked right up and interrupted their conversation. "Hi, Tammy. How are you doing?"

"Oh, hi, Nadine," she said as I stared straight past her to him. "You know Frank Prescott, don't you?"

"No, I don't believe I do." I thrust out my hand, not waiting for Tammy. "Hello, I'm Nadine Carter Barnwell." My normal shyness about meeting the opposite sex disappeared.

Frank lowered his helmet to the ground, took my outstretched hand in his and placed his other hand on top of mine. "Nadine, hello. I like your name," he said, widening his mouth into a full smile.

I grinned back stupidly, drawing a blank for what to say next.

After our hands dropped, he picked up the slack. "So how do you two know each other?" His eyes shot from Tammy and back to me.

"Nadine is a dancer. She's in–I mean–we're in dance classes together."

"A dancer. I should have guessed." When he stepped back and ran his eyes over my attire, I felt self-conscious. Still in my leotard and tights under blue jeans, I wore a towel around my neck, a heavy dance bag on my shoulder and the ends of my hair were slick from sweat. I wasn't exactly the picture of a sorority coed on the way to her next sociology class.

"Nadine is one of the best dancers in the Dance Department," Tammy said. Her compliment surprised me. "And Frank, he is the star of the drama department. You two haven't met?"

Even though the school was small, I knew almost nothing about the drama students and suspected they knew even less about the dance students. Our departments were on opposite sides of the campus. I did know that the school built a new theater for the drama students a few years before that was supposedly outfitted with the latest "everything," whatever that meant. My department, unfortunately, struggled and made do with dance rooms in the Physical Education Department, spaces that hadn't changed since the college was first built in the 1930s.

"From the South Carolina Lowcountry, right? Maybe Beaufort."

"Yes, from Beaufort. But how did you know?"

"I have a thing for accents. Part of the job description. I knew it wasn't Charleston because I used to visit relatives there, but it's close, and to the trained ear it's different from the Midlands and different again from the Upstate." Frank checked his watch. "Oh, man, I've been talking too long, again. I have a rehearsal in five minutes, and I've got to run."

I didn't want him to go. I just met him.

Then he turned to me. "Will I see you again, Miss Nadine Barnwell?"

"I don't know, Frank, uh..." I pretended I didn't remember his last name.

"Prescott. Franklin—Patrick—Prescott." He emphasized each part of his name with his own drawl and made a slight theatrical bow. "Hey," he said, reaching in his pocket, "I've got an extra ticket to the final night of my play on Friday. Anyone want it?" He held it out to both of us.

"Thanks, Frank, but I can't make it," Tammy said.

"Oh, I don't know either," I said, as he pushed the ticket toward me. When I didn't take it, he took my left hand, placed the ticket in my palm and curled my fingers around it. In that instant I was his; this had never happened to me before. I moved through this encounter as if directed in a film. I didn't know the outcome, but I was willing to wait for what the writers would come up with next.

"It's *Barefoot in the Park*. I'm not Robert Redford, but I think you might enjoy it. See if you can make it, Nadine. I'd like that." He smiled like a movie star at a premier, and I felt bouncing in my stomach. Was it my heartbeat?

I held the ticket and watched him jog away.

"It's his final role before graduating," Tammy said, watching him, too. "I've no idea what he's going to do next, but they say he is really good."

I didn't respond. I had no doubt he was a star. Something seemed to radiate from him. Tammy placed her hand on my shoulder. "Earth to Nadine, hello?"

"Is he—I mean—he isn't a romantic interest, is he?" I thought she was engaged, but I hadn't talked with Tammy in a while. I had to ask.

"No, heavens no. Elliott and I are still getting married in two months and twelve days. He will open his dental practice as soon as we get back from our honeymoon in Acapulco. Frank is an old friend of Elliott's; they both grew up in Columbia." She paused for a moment before continuing. "He is good-looking, though in that rugged Steve McQueen sort of way, I have to admit; and a great actor, but he wouldn't make a suitable husband, not to me anyway." Tammy picked up her bag from the ground and tossed her head to the side and back, in an arc, flipping long, perfectly cut glossy brown hair off her face.

"I've got to get to class. Watch yourself, Nadine." She disappeared down the walkway toward the buildings to the left. I sensed Tammy wouldn't let a small thing like her love of dance divert her from a life of stability and position. What she wanted was too much like my daddy's plan for my life. I shuddered at the thought.

When Friday came, I found myself clearing my schedule for the evening to go to Frank's play. The audience of mostly drama students responded with long applause and bravos. I jumped up with the rest of them. After the last curtain call, I waited until the theater emptied before finding my way backstage. In the center of the empty stage, a line of admirers formed to congratulate Frank. Finally, he saw me standing in the wings. The same 'movie premier' smile stretched across his face and lit up his eyes. Then he mouthed to me, "Please stay," grasping his hands as if praying.

When the last person left, he came over to me, and I congratulated him just as everyone else did. But before I finished he interrupted me. "I have to go for 'notes'." He looked over his shoulder and across the stage. "Will you wait a little longer?" he asked, "I won't be long."

"Yeah, sure," I said, not understanding what he meant. He and the rest of the cast disappeared into a room off the side of the stage, and I was left watching the technical crew move the sets and props around.

After about fifteen minutes, they all came back out, and I could hear them talking about a party. Everyone, including the crew, filed out the door.

Frank walked up to me and asked, "Would you like to go?"

"Yes," I said, as if under a spell.

"Oh, wait, I forgot my sweater in the dressing room. I'll be right back."

While waiting for him again, with only a work light illuminating the stage, I began to dance for my own imagined audience. This stage was nothing like the meager dance room I was used to. What a thrill to be on a real stage, I thought as I improvised movements from one side to the other.

After one last turn, I realized Frank had come back and was standing quietly in the wings, watching me. I stopped as soon as I saw him. He came over, put his hands on my cheeks and pulled my face toward his. At first the kisses were light and short. Then his lips stayed longer, and he held me tighter. To keep from bending too far back, I rose on the balls of my feet, then put my arms around his neck. On the empty stage, the kiss seemed to last forever.

We reluctantly went to the party but only stayed long enough for him to say he showed up. After about a half hour, we disappeared out the side door and headed back to school. We wandered the campus through the night, stopping at park benches and leaning against trees, falling back into the same kiss we started in the theater. On the steps of the amphitheater, we sprawled across the cement seats. I felt myself slipping into a territory I wasn't sure I was ready for. I put my hand over his mouth and sat up. "I–I can't do this. I mean, I want to do this, but I can't; not like this, not here, not yet."

He sat up. "Yeah, maybe you're right," he said, out of breath. I didn't think he meant it, but he didn't argue. We walked in silence to the parking lot. Before I got the car door open, we kissed again, and I was pinned between the car and his body. I could have stayed like that all night, but he suddenly pushed himself away and opened my door.

"Oh, man. Not like this. Not here, not yet. Nadine Carter Barnwell, can I call you tomorrow?"

Now, as I checked the mileage sign on the side of the highway closer to Greenville, I still felt his lips. The music would come back soon, so I turned on the radio. Maurice Williams and the Zodiacs were singing "Stay," one of my favorite songs. *Oh, won't you stay, just a little bit longer. Please let me hear that you will.* I sang along with Maurice, moving my torso to the music in my seat. Once past Greenville the rise of the foothills would block the music again, so I turned the radio back off and laughed out loud at myself, thinking how quickly Frank and I came together.

After that night at the theater, I found myself looking for Frank around every corner, in every quad, in each hallway. My roommate, Deni, commented more than once that watching me around Frank was close to sickening. I didn't care. Daddy was exceedingly protective. I'd dated only a few times in high school and hadn't gone steady with anyone. No boy ever got my attention the way Frank had.

On our next date or actually our first official date, he took me to see "Butch Cassidy and the Sundance Kid." In the darkened theater, he took my hand in his but soon dropped it. He then slipped his arm around my shoulder and began rubbing his palm up and down my left arm. Touching in the darkened theater made concentrating on the movie difficult. Before the movie was over, we left.

His apartment was small, but he didn't mind. "No more room-mates for me," he said. "I've earned some time alone after four years of flaky roommates." He turned on a dim light in the corner, showing a room almost as dark as the movie theater. Dark-brown velvet-like curtains covered the windows. The couch and one armchair were also brown.

He walked over to the bookcase and turned on his record player. I heard the first record drop, and the needle make contact with the vinyl. The Lettermen began singing "Just the Way You Look Tonight," and he handed me a glass of wine. As soon as I took my first sip, he began stroking my hair. The stroking moved down to my face, my neck and my breasts.

My breath caught and then I exhaled at once. I lifted my arms, put them around his neck and pressed my whole body against his, lips to toes. His scent enveloped me, musky like the earth. I didn't protest this time.

From that night on, we were inseparable, at least whenever we weren't in class or rehearsal. In those early days, Frank talked continually about theater. I saw how deeply dedicated he was to his craft. Unlike me, he knew exactly what acting meant to him and what his opportunities were. I was swept away by his elo-quence and his dreams. I couldn't imagine his dreams wouldn't come true—for him. I envied him. Back then I still believed the most I would ever be able to do with my dance was to perform locally and teach while I work with Daddy.

By the end of that spring semester three major things happened: I finally got it, what everyone was whispering about when I lost my virginity; Frank entered the master's program, which meant he was staying with me; and I took him home to meet Daddy.

"My father wants me to be a doctor like he is," he told me in bed one night after we'd made love. His face darkened as he sat up and stared out the window of his tiny apartment. "But acting is everything to me. I can't imagine my life without it." As he began, to talk his eyebrows relaxed and his forehead smoothed. A glow began to shine through his body. "When I'm on stage, when I'm immersed in a character delivering lines, it's the most alive and wonderful experience in the world. It's also when I feel most like myself."

I felt that way about dance, only I rarely said it out loud. Frank's arms were raised above his head and bent at the elbows, so I moved closer and placed my side against his.

"Strange, I know," he continued, "how being someone else makes me feel more like myself but it does." He turned and grabbed both my shoulders and held me out from his body. "You know I love you, but I want to go to New York, Nadine. It's probably the single most important move I will ever make as an actor." His grip intensified and I started to wince, but he interrupted me. "I want you to come with me."

"Go with you? To New York?" I was stunned. Daddy cursed New York my whole life, but the thought of living there sent electrical charges through me. I tried to shake it off. "I would love to go with you, more than anything. But I can't do that," I said, easing out of his powerful hands. Even though there was change all around, a move this bold was out of the question for this southern girl.

"Okay. I'll ask again later." He got out of bed and headed for the bathroom. With the door slightly cracked, he said, "You've told me some about your mother, but tell me more about your father." Frank would meet Daddy for the first time in a few weeks. "All I know is that your father owns land and buildings and leases them out. What else does he do?"

"Daddy, I always call him Daddy. He's just a businessman. I guess he could have been a politician. He was asked to run for state representative once, and he probably would have won if he'd done it. Everyone thought the world of Samuel Preston Barnwell in those days. That was before growing and collecting money became his central focus. It was after Mama's illness that it got so bad. Everyone agreed that something changed in him. His friends tell me it's nothing to fret about, but they don't have to live with him. I do, or maybe I should say I did." I got out of bed, and as Frank came out of the bathroom, I went in.

"You still think of yourself as living at home, don't you?"

"Yeah, I guess I do. I mean it's been the two of us since Mama died. You wouldn't think anyone should have to worry about someone who has so much, but I do worry. I worry about leaving him almost as much as I worry about staying with him." When I came back out he was looking for his clothes.

"Look what's happened in this country," he said, picking up his jeans and t-shirt from the floor. "You don't have to be a hippie to see that rules are being broken; that people are changing. I think you have to ask, if you stay would you cut off something important in yourself?"

I knew what he meant but couldn't quite see it as a choice I had a right to make. What I knew was that as powerful and rich as Daddy was, he needed someone, and I was his only child. But I was also angry at him, and anger never helps in making good decisions.

Frank's argument got better and more persuasive each time the subject came up. Soon, my eyes began to open to all the possibilities before me. I saw that it wasn't my mother's world anymore, and after about a month of these conversations and love-making, I made up my mind. From that moment on, the conversation shifted to how we would get to New York, where we would live, and everything we needed to do to make it all happen.

"I'm going to study at the Actors Studio and HB Studios," he said after my announcement. "With Uta Hagen and Herbert Bergdorf as my teachers, I'll be ready to audition for anything." His confidence in his future was infectious.

"I guess I can now take that scholarship to study with the Leland Lemire School of Dance," I chimed in. "I was flattered when his dance company offered it to me while doing a workshop here, but I didn't think I could ever use it. I'm going to now."

"That's fantastic," he said, as he walked around his apartment describing our imagined life in New York City, gesturing like a Shakespearean actor. "First, we'll get an apartment, in The Village, of course. We'll find part-time jobs that will allow us to study and perform." He took me in his arms. "And, most importantly, we'll be there for each other." I fell even deeper under his spell, and he sealed his promise with a kiss.

The energy of those talks kept me up late at night when I should have been getting my dancer-required eight hours of sleep. I didn't know if it was the excitement of going or the power I felt after making my first major life choice, but I was walking on air. We were going to New York City and going together, right after my graduation only a few months away. I remember how I dropped straight back to earth when I realized that first I had to tell Daddy.

About twenty minutes from campus, I snapped out of my reverie when a truck tried to change lanes and nearly cut me off. Slamming on the brakes, I saw another truck in the rear view mirror about to make me into a sandwich. Unable to move to the right, I tapped the brakes several times, making my rear lights flash as a warning. It worked and we all slowed down in time to prevent a disaster. I relaxed my tight grip on the steering wheel, let out a loud exhale and tried to refocus my thoughts on my new life ahead. Crawling slowly uphill, I remained stuck between the two trucks until I came to my turnoff.

Our 1940s arched doorway and plaster-walled apartment only three blocks from the campus was something I would miss. The curved bay window had a seating area below and vivid green trailing plants that hung from macramé-covered pots, filling the living room with warm natural light on a cold day. It was a great place to read or people-watch.

I grabbed my bags and raced up the front steps. Once inside I headed right for the phone and dialed Frank's number.

He answered on the first ring. "Hi, I'm back," I blurted out, breathless from my dash. "I need you to come over right away."

"Hey, hi, slow down. How did it go? With your father? Is everything okay?"

"That's what I need to talk to you about. Can you come over?" I grabbed the phone's long black cord from the entrance table and circled around to the couch.

"That doesn't sound good. Did he say no?"

"No? No is an understatement. Please come over."

"Okay, give me a minute. I'll come as soon as I can."

As I put down the receiver, my roommate and fellow dancer, Denise Hansen, known as Deni, came through the front door. "You're back. Great! Tell me everything."

She threw her dance bag in one corner and herself on the opposite side of the couch. Men always did a double take around Deni. Lean and tall with long willowy limbs and unusual flexibility, she contained all the outward attributes of the perfect dancer. Her downside was that she didn't have a grasp of improvisation or choreography like I did, and she definitely didn't have the same drive as me. In my envious opinion, God wasted the package on her. Unfortunately, the package was essential to choreographers.

I usually worked harder than she did, and yet, she always looked like the star. Physical beauty is incredibly deceptive. But Deni and I really got along.

"She needs a mother and you need to mother," Aunt Amelia told me recently. "You want to create something. Deni wants to be somebody. There's a big difference. But she worships you, Nadine. Be a good example for her."

I shifted on the couch toward Deni, "It didn't 'go' at all. Daddy will have nothing to do with my plans. He says that I have an obligation to stay." Her enlivened face turned into a frown and then into a faraway glaze.

Deni and I had known each other since the ninth grade when she moved to Beaufort with her military family. Her parents separated about a year after she entered high school. When her father got orders to Camp Lejeune, North Carolina, her mother stayed in Beaufort with the kids, for some stability, she said. Deni's father tried his best to come back to South Carolina a lot. The split was low key, attempting to keep the drama down. Regardless, having parents separate was traumatic whether it was in your face or incognito. As fewer visits and less money came from her father, her mother, a trained nurse, took a job at the local hospital and tried hard to balance raising two children alone on not much money. At least Deni's father agreed to pay for her college.

"But, I am going," I said emphatically, bringing Deni's focus back into the room. "I am going to have my own life and dance in New York City." I got up to put the phone back on the table. Suddenly, I realized I just repeated my ritual words out loud and quickly added, "And live with Frank." I beamed with my new-found confidence.

"You are?" Deni jumped up to hug me. "Fantastic." Then she backed away and her face clouded over again. "I wish I was going."

It seemed my enthusiasm about going to New York rubbed off on her. I held her at arm's length. "You've got another semester before your graduation," I said. I didn't want to leave her but knew I would. "Then you can stay with us if you want, or you can come with someone else. You can do anything you want. Oh heck, everyone can come. I feel so good, so free." I got up from the couch and danced around the living room as if on stage.

I heard a knock at the door and turned to answer it. Frank stood there with his hands in his front jeans pockets, his brow lifted and pinched like he asked a question. Worry exuded from every pore. He forced a smile.

As he stepped inside the door, I threw my arms around him and blurted, "I'm going with you."

CHAPTER 3

September 1969

Passion is the trigger of success.
—ANONYMOUS

SINCE THE RITUAL, THE CHOICES I made each day became less unconscious and more intensified in my mind, as if they were holograms tinted in greens and pinks.

Because school wasn't far from my apartment, leaving early put me ahead for the day. Normally, I could beat the nine o'clock mass of students descending on the campus parking lot and get to class in plenty of time to begin my careful pre-warm-up warm-up. This kept my muscles in top shape, giving me an edge over all the latecomers.

That morning I had to hurry because Frank left a message the night before with Deni, saying he needed to talk to me about something. I didn't see the message until I got up.

I didn't know it at the time, but the next significant choice of my new life came when I backed out of my driveway. I turned right instead of my usual left. This led me to turn left at Holly Road instead of my usual right at Winthrop Avenue, where I came to a dead stop in front of a Piggly Wiggly tractor trailer trying to negotiate a turn in less space than required for its size.

As the truck finally made the turn, I looked at my watch and realized I only had a few minutes to get to class on time. If I concentrated, I might be able to pull my karmic powers together and miraculously find a waiting parking space as I entered the lot closest to Fields Gym. At the last light before the entrance, I tried unsuccessfully to scan the area. When the light turned green I eased ahead down the first row and found one empty space. But as I approached, from out of nowhere a yellow and white Volkswagen van made a sharp left directly into my space. I threw my arms up over my head and let out a yell before banging my head on the steering wheel. When I looked up, an awkward, tight-faced boy got out of the car, pulling books, notebooks, and a red sweatshirt out of his backseat. He slammed the door, made a slight hand-wave toward me and mouthed the word, "sorry" before he disappeared toward the campus.

Hoping I hadn't used up all my karmic powers, I circled the next two rows and came back around in time to take the spot of someone just leaving. An empty space was an unusual sight so early in the morning since everyone was coming to campus, not going.

I looked at my watch again. If I hurried, I still might get to class on time, but talking with Frank would have to wait until later.

As I approached the building, I saw Frank waiting under the ancient magnolia tree that marked the entrance to Fields Gym and my dance class.

"Frank, what are you doing here?" I asked breathlessly.

"Where have you been? I need to talk to you, Nadine." He leaned against the tree, both hands in the front pocket of his jeans again, making his shoulders appear close to his ears.

"I'm sorry. It's going to have to wait. I'm late to class already."
I moved my heavy dance bag from my right shoulder to my left.

"Class can start without you."

I turned my face toward his and squinted. This didn't sound
like Frank. "You know I have to get inside and warm up. Can't
this wait until tonight?"

All at once he blurted out, "I can't go to New York with you."
He stepped away from the tree, looked at the ground and kicked
a rock across the grass. "Not right now."

I froze. "What? Not go? What do you mean? You have to go."

"I've been given the job offer of a lifetime. I can't see how I can
turn it down."

"A job offer? This is what you wanted to talk to me about?" I
tried to think of what he meant. Then I remembered. "You mean
the movie you auditioned for months ago? I thought you said
they already cast it."

"Yeah." Frank lowered his eyes and chin as he spoke. "Apparently,
they changed something or someone. They offered a speaking
part to me yesterday. I wanted to think about it last night before
talking with you this morning. But you didn't show up. They
said if I wanted the job, I needed to give them an answer first
thing today."

"You've already said yes? But our plans. Everything is set; you
know that."

"Yes, I do. But a movie, Nadine. God, do you know how long
actors wait to be offered a movie? I'm sorry, but I can't pass this up."

I backed away as if he'd hit me.

He took his hands out of his pockets and reached toward me.
I stepped back even farther.

"You know I'd take you with me if I could. But a first movie
job isn't going to allow that. I don't know where exactly we'll be

filming or my hours or even where I'll be living. Probably with other actors."

"I know that. But you know I'm already committed to going to New York. I accepted the scholarship to the dance school. They're expecting me." The reality of what this meant suddenly came clear to me. "I've changed my whole life around. My father won't speak to me, let alone support me. I'm ready to go with you. I can't do this alone, Frank, and I can't stay here now." The rest of the campus faded from my view and this conversation became the only part of life that existed.

"Can't you find someone else to go with? I can join you as soon as the movie wraps."

If I hadn't turned right instead of my usual left this morning, I would have been here early enough to talk him out of this. My face and shoulders tightened to hold off my rising panic, my voice barely above a whisper. "I've got to go."

I turned and sprinted toward the dance building and straight to the bathroom outside my class. I didn't want him or anyone to see my face, which by now was red and splotchy.

By the time I got inside, class had already begun. Everyone was seated in their favorite spots across the polished rosined wood floor. Looking more serious than relaxed, all twenty or so of my classmates attempted to contort their bodies into the various configurations being called out by the teacher. Mr. Palmer, a former Cunningham dancer, paced slowly throughout the class, looking for any mis-steps or mis-shapes. To him, our bodies needed to be in perfect alignment by that point in the warm-up exercises. From the position they were in, I saw how far behind I was. The floor work was nearly over, and they would shortly move on to the standing exercises.

The class consisted of fifteen women and five brave men. No doubt these men felt comfortable taking a dance class because the teacher was male, had been checked out and determined not to be 'gay.' Maybe they already learned that dance is not for sissies.

At around five-foot-nine, and I guessed about thirty-five years old, Mr. Palmer had powerfully developed arms, shoulders, pectoral muscles, enormous thighs and sculpted buns. Although he exuded a unique confidence that appealed to the men, his body may also have had something to do with the number of women in the class.

The dress varied from the standard black scoop-necked leotard and tights to bolder colorful combinations of tops and bottoms. Some students wore T-shirts with tights and dance briefs and others, expensive hip-hugging dance pants. Almost everyone was barefoot and wore bulky, multicolored leg warmers. The floor exercises had not created enough sweat yet to show on their bodies or linger in the closed room atmosphere, as surely it would in about twenty minutes.

I moved quietly sideways, hugging the wall as best I could, given the floor was littered with dance bags, dropped clothes, shoes and books. Mirrors with attached ballet bars lined the twelve-foot southern wall from floor to ceiling. This is where, in a few minutes, the dancers would stand at attention, forced to examine what they like and didn't like about their bodies, simultaneously eyeing the bodies of others.

Then I saw Deni looking at me from under her arm as she stretched her inner thighs in 'wide sit' on the floor. She mouthed, "Where the hell have you been?" I shrugged and rolled my eyes. Since I was already in my leotard and tights, I quickly removed my patchwork jeans and white peasant top, kicked off my sandals and added leg warmers and a sweatshirt to get started.

"Nadine, class starts at 9 o'clock, not 9:15," Mr. Palmer said, breaking his corrective walking duty to single me out.

"Yes, Mr. Palmer. I'm sorry. I, uh, had trouble finding a parking space."

"The other students got here on time today. I suggest you adjust your morning schedule to get a spot in the parking lot and on this floor before class starts next time. I certainly hope this isn't the way you plan to start this semester. And I am talking to each one of you now."

"Yes, Mr. Palmer. I will."

But I didn't know where to go. I couldn't find an open space. Deni scooted over on the floor, and the dancer next to her did the same. Reluctantly, I took the spot on the back row next to Deni and began a quick 'catch-up' warm-up. I disliked the back row; I preferred being in the center of the front row. Everyone else in the class was glad to have me move to the front; that way, if they didn't remember the exercise or combination, they could follow me. I had been dancing almost all of my life, so I knew them all.

I hated not being properly warmed up more than anything, but I didn't want to upset Mr. Palmer any more than I already had. He was quite proud of his 'talent' and respected me as a dancer. He also wanted his classes run a certain way. He didn't mind pointing out our shortcomings anytime, especially if he was in one of his moods. Avoiding those moods was a skill I developed. Some called it "sucking up" but I called it "professionalism."

This morning's class turned out to be a great distraction. I remained on the floor when class ended, continuing to stretch.

"What's with you?" Deni asked, getting up. "You left the apartment before I did, and you are never late. I'm the one who usually comes 'waltzing in' late, as Mr. Palmer likes to say."

"It just took longer to get here this morning," I said as I leaned over my right leg, with both legs stretched out at a 45-degree angle from my torso.

"Yeah, and that's what made you so late?" She bent from the waist and placed her palms flat on the floor, giving her hamstrings a good stretch.

"And then I couldn't find a parking spot." I changed sides and stretched over my left leg.

"Oh, so that's your problem." Deni raised her torso back to standing.

"Not entirely."

"Hey, Nadine. You all right?" One of the few male dancers at school rushed by on his way to pick up his dance bag and books.

"Yeah, I'm fine. Just ran a little late this morning," I said. He disappeared through the crowd of people leaving through the door.

Deni toweled off and pulled her jeans on over her dance clothes. Showering and changing between classes wasn't always an option, so we carried smell-good products in our dance bags.

"What do you mean 'not entirely'?" She asked after she pulled her blouse over her head.

"It's Frank; he was waiting for me outside. He had something he needed to tell me."

"Okay. What is that, Nadine? What was so earth-shattering?"

I leaned over in arabesque and held the pose, feeling its power brace me against my anger. "He says he can't go to New York with me-not yet, anyway." I lowered myself back to standing, my eyes falling to the floor. I didn't want to see Deni's "I told you so" look. When I glanced her way again, she was leaning over, pulling on her boots and shaking her head.

It usually was the other way around and I wasn't used to being the one who needed support. A hug should have been a welcome relief but instead, I felt uncomfortable. I'd always been the strong one in our relationship, and I didn't like the vulnerable feeling taking over. My mind flashed on Daddy. I didn't want to be just like him but sometimes I found I was.

The last few people gathered their belongings, backpacks, towels and sweatshirts and left the dance room. Deni moved back toward the door, unclicked the large barrette holding the mass of blonde curls on top of her head, gave her head a couple of shakes, picked up her dance bag and flung it over her shoulder. At the door, she turned back toward me. "I'm sorry to have to run; I've got to get to English class. The timing is terrible, but is this really that bad? I mean, it's not like you can never go. Can't you go later, when he's done?"

Through gritted teeth, I said without pausing, "I don't want to go later, Deni. I want to go now. That was the plan. Don't you see? What will I do, sit around and wait for Frank to be ready? I can't do that. If I go home, Daddy won't let me leave again." I took a breath. "For me it's now or never. I won't have this opportunity again."

"Oh, I guess you have thought about this. Maybe it was good he laid this on you just before such a long workout. Let the body tell the truth and let the mind rest. Oh, shit, I'm going to be sooo late. See ya." The door banged as it closed behind her.

I turned around to an empty room. The only way to know there had been so much life around me only minutes before was the lingering odor of sweat.

I watched myself in the mirror as I did during every class. I was my own worst critic. My arms were too long, my legs too muscular. I swore that in my next life, I would have seriously long legs, thick, waist-length blonde hair and a pencil thin body. But for now, I would have to be satisfied with being five-foot-six with uncooperative wavy red hair, and always thinking I needed to lose a few pounds.

I took a moment to improvise, giving myself a brief sense of performance, an unmatched feeling of being completely in the moment, totally alive and in control as if there were such a thing. There was, though, a power in movement for me that I didn't find anywhere else; not in teaching and certainly not in the 'position and place' my daddy worshiped. For the next ten minutes, I danced as if I were at Carnegie Hall. I didn't need to be famous; I didn't need to be rich. I only wanted to dance and dance for as long as someone would let me.

As I walked into the apartment that evening, I saw Deni cooking in the kitchen.

"What's going on here?" I asked, dropping my dance bag down to the floor.

"Oh, hey, Nadine," Deni said, looking up from the pot she stirred on the stove. "I'm cooking you dinner; pasta with fresh tomatoes and mozzarella cheese."

"You are?" This was an unexpected gesture that I truly appreciated. I ached from exhaustion; it seemed I was exhausted a lot lately, and the bad news from Frank had only made me more tired.

"What's the occasion?" I didn't want to make small talk but knew I had to.

"Because of the day you've had. Because of Frank's announcement."

After dinner, we moved to the living room. I gathered the oversized orange, red, yellow and green pillows stacked beside the couch and made myself a secure little nest on the floor by the bay window.

"I have come up with a plan," Deni announced from a corner of the couch.

"A plan? About what?" I leaned back into my pillow stack with my feet outstretched on the green one.

"A plan about you going to New York."

"Oh, you've come up with a plan for me to go to New York. What is this plan, pray tell?"

"I can go to New York with you." She smiled as if she'd just solved world peace.

"You what?" I sat up from the pillows. "You mean the two of us, go together?"

"Yeah, something like that," Deni said.

I needed time to come up with a kind substitute for "no." "But I finish in December, and you won't be graduated until when, May?" was all I could think of.

"Yeah, May 15th is graduation. I thought we'd leave in early June."

She had me. Then before I could stop her, questions and answers began flying through my head. Going alone wasn't an option for me. But I wondered if Deni was ready for New York City. She would be relying on me to guide her, as I would have been relying on Frank. Would I be able to care for her and myself? Then I realized I didn't know when Frank would be able to go. I'd heard of directors doing re-shoots for months after the initial filming ended. What if he was offered another job?

I studied Deni's face to see if she was sincere or just dreaming big. In the silence, the answer back was that it was up to me to take charge of my own dream. I next thought about my destination: Leland Lemire Dance Studio. My mind kept working on this puzzle even though my mouth wanted to say, "No way." I supposed if they would hold my scholarship for a few more months, I could look for a short-term teaching job somewhere. The school being so rural, there were no job opportunities for me nearby. How about near Aunt Amelia and Uncle Hamp? *Now that's a good idea.* Living in Asheville would keep me away from Daddy until I left.

Could this work? Was this the answer?

By morning, everything was settled.

"This is great. You can go on to New York with Deni, and I'll get there as soon as I can," Frank said the next day at his apartment after I told him of Deni's idea. I think it relieved some of his guilt for changing our plans.

"Yeah, I guess I can do this without you. I hope I can do this without you."

"Of course you can. It will be great."

"Great for you. The hard part, getting a place to stay temporarily, jobs and an apartment will already be done by us, and all you'll have to do is show up." I stood by the window with my back to him. He came up behind me, leaned his whole torso into me, then swooped his arms around my shoulders. I melded back into him as he kissed my shoulders, the side of neck, then around to my cheeks. I pivoted within his arms, ready for the rest of it.

For the next two weeks, all we did was go to classes and make love as if we were not going to see each other ever again. Spontaneity superseded caution more than once. The electrifying conversations about the future were left at the doorstep. He made promises, saying he would be back with me in New York before I even realized he was gone, but I only half-listened. Plans changed and now I was the only one in charge of my destination.

My last semester was only a formality anyway. Finished with all my graduation requirements except for one class with Mr. Palmer, I kept myself busy performing in student dance concerts, finalizing graduation details and trying to find work.

I knew more certainly than ever that I needed to leave Beaufort and South Carolina. To carry out the first step of my new plan, the only thing I had to do was make sure I didn't move back home before Deni and I left. I figured Daddy would try to stop me if he thought I was moving to New York against his wishes. But if he really meant what he said about me not bothering to come back, maybe not.

And then the unthinkable happened.

CHAPTER 4

December 1969

The hardest thing to learn in life is which bridge to cross and which to burn.
—DAVID RUSSELL

THE DAY I LEARNED I was pregnant, my heart broke apart into tiny shards of mica. After the test results were announced and the doctor and the nurse left the room, I sat on the examining table, hugged my knees to my chest and rocked back and forth in a manic prayer. Instead of "Thy will be done," my mantra became, "Dear Lord, not me, not now, please, please say they are wrong." But they weren't wrong. Just outside the office several miles from campus, I stopped at a bench when my racing adrenaline slowed enough to allow me to think. Across the street, a breeze coursed through the small park, creating a wave in the tall golden grasses as if they were dancing to Debussy. Although I saw birds fly from tree to tree without a care, the pounding inside my chest blocked all other sounds.

I added up the facts; Frank had been gone for two months and ordinarily I never missed my period. This news made me feel like I hadn't slept in weeks. Slowly, I made my way back to my apartment to lie down. Deni was away so I had some time to absorb this news before she questioned any panic in my face.

When Frank called from the movie set that night, I tried to sound casual. "Hey, Frank, how's it going?"

"It's going great, Nadine. I can hardly believe I'm here. Seeing how they actually make a movie is wild. Wherever we are it's like a city within a city. These people are really professionals. They make it all happen. Man, I'm so glad I got to do this; having a movie credit on my resume will make being seen in New York so much easier." Hearing the joy in his voice, I held the phone away from my ear so as not to get pulled into his world.

"I'm sorry. I'm going on and on. How are you? What's happening at school? How are your aunt and uncle? Is everyone okay?"

"Not that much exciting going on here. Not compared to you," I said, rubbing my belly. "When do you think you'll be finished?" *What the heck will I do if he comes back too soon? Before I have time to think about this?"*

"I don't know exactly. Things happen, change so fast around here. You think you have a schedule and then you find out there's no schedule at all. They bring us in early and keep us late. But like I said, I'll join you in New York as soon as I can. I just don't know when." He paused. "It may be a little longer than I thought, though. There's, uh, talk of another movie after this one." I heard background voices. Someone asked when he was getting off the phone.

"Another movie? They're shooting another movie right after this one?" I was conflicted. I didn't like that his coming back would be delayed further, but it might also give me time to figure out what to do, or say, or not say to him or anyone else.

"Yeah, isn't that something?" He really sounded proud of himself. "It sounds really exciting," he continued, "and–don't get me wrong–working on a movie is really cool, compared to anything I've ever experienced but the truth is the hours are long and the budget is low, so I'm not exactly living the high life here. It's kind of lonely at night. I miss you, Nadine, I really do. I wish you were here with me."

I realized I had sucked in my breath, waiting for him to say something, anything involving me, us. "Me too, me too," I said almost inaudibly.

"Is that all you can say?"

I had no idea what he would do if I told him we were going to be parents. How much would he miss me then? Most actors struggled for years to get where he was at that moment. I couldn't imagine taking this wonderful start away from him. Jeez, how can I tell him a thing like this? I haven't fully absorbed it myself.

"I'm sorry. I'm happy for you and also sad, I guess. I miss you so much, I can hardly bear it."

"That's better. It's hard, of course, but everything will work out, I promise. Only, I don't know exactly when I can call you next," he added. "We're moving to a remote location without phones. I'll call as soon as I can. Where will you be? Will you be back home for Christmas?"

"I–I'm not sure where I'll be." The tension from what had and hadn't been said turned into a headache. Part of me wanted him to read my mind, realize I needed him more than ever, and come rushing back to help me solve this irreversible problem.

Then, in the distance I heard someone yell his name again.

"Oh, they're calling me to a rehearsal. I guess they think they're going to get to one of my scenes today. There's so much waiting around. I didn't know how much."

Then I heard his name called again, this time by a woman. I hadn't imagined women on the crew, except in the makeup and costume departments.

"I've got to go. I love you. Bye."

Before I could say, "I love you too," the connection cut off.

I lowered the receiver to the front of my face and stared at the phone. Thankfully, the opportunity to tell him my situation was gone. I wanted to will this pregnancy away, and telling him would make it real. The lives about to be touched went far beyond Frank's and mine. Without my mother around to buffer my mistakes, how could I ever tell my daddy? Suddenly, I thought of the one person in my life who might understand; once again, I needed to talk to Aunt Amelia.

"Oh, dear child. Now this is a complication," Aunt Amelia said over the phone.

I gave us both a moment, then unleashed my story all at once. "This can't be happening. I have to go to New York. I have to dance. I can't be pregnant, Aunt Amelia; I can't be. We performed a ritual for my life, remember? My plans are in motion, you said. I didn't say anything about wanting a baby." I banged my head on the wall near the phone as tears filled my eyes.

"I understand," she said dropping her "kind-aunt" voice and using her authoritative voice instead, "don't doubt the power of what you put into motion at Camp Pinckney. Your course is still the same. But you are pregnant. A baby is inside you. You can always go to New York later."

There were those words again: "Go to New York later."

"There is no 'later,' Frank, and I can't raise a child in New York City and pursue our careers. You have to have money. I'm caught. Daddy will cut me off if I leave. And if I go to him for help because I'm pregnant, he will make me stay. My God, I will become exactly like what I am running away from."

"So, are you going away to be a dancer or to not be like your family?"

Ouch. I deserved that. Aunt Amelia always cut through to the essence of things. Because she saw through what most people could not, she didn't pump me full of empty rules.

"Both, both are so important to me."

"When are you supposed to leave for New York with Deni?"

"In June."

"And when are your classes officially over?"

"Friday, December 19th."

"Okay then, you'll stay at school as long as possible; then go home and visit briefly with your father over Christmas, get all the rest of your things and come to live with us on December 26th. We will sort this out together, before making any announcement to the world."

Those were the words I'd wanted to hear. Words would not make my problems go away, but I would be safe with Aunt Amelia and Uncle Hamp. I needed time to find Deni another roommate and move out of that apartment. And there were some parties at school that weekend. My next steps started to come to me. I could craft an excuse for not coming home for at least six months by telling Daddy I was taking a job in the mountains near Asheville, teaching rural, underprivileged girls. I knew Daddy would be relieved I wasn't moving to New York with Frank, and he was unlikely to visit since he did not much care for Asheville or poverty.

I would explain the same to Deni who would be busy preparing for her own last semester graduation requirements. As for Frank, since the phone connections were difficult where he was filming, I would make him believe I wouldn't have access to a telephone either. He could always leave a message with Aunt Amelia if he needed to. I figured that the less I talked with any of them, the less likely I would give in to my own pressure and confess my pregnancy.

On December 26th, minutes before sunset, I arrived in Asheville. As I unpacked my car, the azure sky deepened each second toward indigo blue over the single story, red-roofed white clapboard house. Sitting atop a knoll, this wonderful house faced east and north, allowing Aunt Amelia's herb and vegetable garden surrounding it on two sides to fill with enriching sunlight each morning. I knew as soon as the last box was out of the car that I had made my next right choice.

Although totally different, my mama and her sister Aunt Amelia had been inseparable, at least until Daddy swept my mama off her feet when they met in 1937. A festival queen and an avid short story writer, Mama couldn't resist Daddy's charming personality and his undivided attention. They married a year later, and, quickly, their family expanded with a baby girl born in 1940. But that baby was sickly and when she died at two months old, Mama was devastated. Afterwards, she fell into a deep depression and only started to come out of it, my aunt told me, when I was born eight years later.

A few months after the baby's death, Aunt Amelia and Uncle Hamp bought the house next door, allowing my aunt to stay by Mama's side throughout her "long mourning," as Daddy began to call it. Amelia, too, lost a baby; a difficult miscarriage late in her second trimester. Another pregnancy never came along.

Once I was born my aunt stepped in to help raise me. Since it was just Aunt Amelia and Uncle Hamp, being next to us was a good fit for everyone.

"We have to talk about this, Nadine," Aunt Amelia said as soon as Uncle Hamp and I carried the last of my bags into the house. "When are you going to tell Frank and your daddy?"

"I don't know. I don't know anything yet," I said, frustrated at having to think about telling anyone so soon.

"Tell me what is stopping you from telling them." She led me into the living room.

"There are so many issues here." I collapsed on the couch as they all hit me at once. "It's more than just me wanting to go to New York City and live my own life. I still don't know what Frank would say or do, but I couldn't imagine he'd find this news joyful. And I don't have the money to raise a child on my own."

I picked up a magazine from the coffee table and flipped through the pages without looking at them. Then I closed it. "I'm twenty-one, and I have the right to make up my own mind about this. But once Daddy finds out, he will try to force me to raise this child, in his house, in his way. I can't do that." I tossed the magazine on the coffee table and slouched back on the couch. "Giving this baby up seems like the only solution that makes any sense. Adoption is the only way—for everyone." I had been thinking this for several weeks, but it was Aunt Amelia who instinctively knew how to get me to say it. I felt better once I said it aloud.

"If that's what you want, honey, there's this attorney in town," Uncle Hamp said, taking the chair across from me. Many times he had smoother edges than Aunt Amelia. "It's someone who would handle everything. He finds good homes for babies in need and the whole process would be private. No one would ever have to find out." I realized he had to have been thinking a lot about this, too.

"But how? How will everything remain confidential, Uncle Hamp? How can you be sure he will find a good family?" I placed my hands on either side of my belly, as if I was protecting this child from hearing the plans.

"He's a respected attorney in these parts. I learned about this side of his practice while we were on a fishing trip last summer. A few years before, he helped out a member at Kiwanis whose young daughter was unexpectedly pregnant." He shifted in his chair, leaning forward, hands on his knees as if telling a big secret. "She was younger than you, still in high school and had just gotten a scholarship to Harvard. The way it sounded, the family didn't like the boy and wanted their daughter to be the first in the family to go to an Ivy League school. Her parents kept her at home for the last six months. She didn't go anywhere. I think they told everyone she had mono and couldn't be allowed to infect anyone. Now she is through college and heading to medical school." He leaned back in his chair. "I asked him the other day if he still arranged private adoption, and he said yes. He didn't ask any other questions, just said to come to him when the time is right, but not to wait too long."

Not wait too long. Suddenly, I had to make my next choice. Aunt Amelia and I connected eyes; hers telling me I had to make up my own mind. With a sigh, I took my hands off my belly and turned back to Uncle Hamp. "If you have confidence in this attorney, then I will too. When can I meet with him?"

On a gray, damp January afternoon, after I signed the agreement and left the lawyer's office, I stood for a moment on the outside steps. Suddenly, the sun edged through snow clouds, washing my body with light. I took the moment as my next sign from God and the universe. I willed myself to settle in for the five months ahead while wishing the whole process was already over.

CHAPTER 5

January-June 1970

> *In the long run, we shape our lives, and we shape
> ourselves. The process never ends until we die. And the
> choices we make are ultimately our own responsibility.*
> —ELEANOR ROOSEVELT

O VER THE NEXT SEVERAL MONTHS, I worried about keeping this pregnancy from Frank, Deni and Daddy. But with Frank so remote, Deni so focused on graduation dance concerts, and Daddy too frugal to make many long distance calls, I got only one or two short calls from any of them. My plan was working better than I imagined. Then as the weeks passed, something began to change. Even though I tried to keep up with dance exercises in the house on cold winter days, I often felt sluggish later in the day. So one afternoon when I was around seven months pregnant, I put *The Blue Danube* on the stereo and a waltz found its way to my feet. I lifted my arms as if partnering with an elegant man in tails, imagining my floor-length ecru satin gown swishing behind me. I turned and dipped to my favorite Strauss piece. About three minutes into the dance my right hand moved to the base of my stomach, cradling the baby. Still twirling myself around the room, I moved that hand back and forth between my imagined partner and imagined baby.

As I increasingly felt movement in my womb, I found myself calling it Baby Child, while trying to explain to it what was about to happen. That I chose adoption so it would have caring, attentive parents was something I couldn't envision from me. The more I talked, the weaker the explanation became; and the closer I got to my due date the more I doubted my decision. I began to try to figure out ways to raise Baby Child in New York City while I studied dance by day and worked nights in a restaurant. I imagined Frank's shock at learning he was a father, just as his leaving had shocked me.

I kept this new ambivalence to myself.

Early one morning in April, Aunt Amelia came into my room. She said she had been awakened by a powerful dream. "I will have Uncle Hampton cancel the adoption if you want," she said, speaking as if we were already in a conversation.

I pulled myself up in the bed, grabbed a pillow and squeezed it on top of my stomach.

"What are you talking about?" I knew she knew what I had been thinking. "I'm not canceling anything." Tears spilled from my eyes creating trails down my face.

"You still have a choice, that's all. Don't think you can't change your mind if you ever feel you might want to." I didn't even look up at her. "I'll put on the kettle for some tea." She left me alone with those words.

I didn't dance with Baby Child that day, or the next, or ever again.

In my eighth month in May, as the days warmed and the redbuds and dogwoods bloomed, Aunt Amelia drove me several towns over where no one knew us, to do some window shopping to get my mind off the impending birth.

As we strolled through the streets and shops filled with artisan work of the region, I began to feel intermittent cramps. The fresh air and new scenery was a welcome change, so I ignored my discomfort and kept pushing on. About fifteen minutes later while in The Pitty-Potter Shop, I grabbed Aunt Amelia's arm. She turned and saw my face.

"Something's happening. I think this is it," I said.

"Already? It's early. Let's get going," she said.

We headed for the door of the pottery shop but by the time we got to the street, I was stooped over in misery.

"Stay here. I'll get the car," Aunt Amelia said.

In the car, I started timing the contractions. They were eight minutes apart, each lasting thirty seconds. By the time we got home they were five minutes apart, so Aunt Amelia called the doctor. The nurse said I was probably just not coping with the pain and since this was my first baby, I should walk around and drink some water to get the baby moving. Aunt Amelia didn't like this idea and called Uncle Hamp.

"Hamp, you need to get home right away. Nadine is in labor."

"Already? Oh, goodness. I'll be right there."

After an hour the contractions came every four minutes, so Aunt Amelia called the doctor's office again. "Okay, take her to the birthing clinic. They'll check her out. But if she's not dilated enough, they'll have to send her home." Aunt Amelia repeated the nurse's words to me.

I was in agony; the labor pains came on so suddenly.

When we got to the birthing clinic, a different doctor from the one I saw for my checkups examined me. Stone-faced and abrupt, he wouldn't let Aunt Amelia stay in the room. With narrowed eyes and pursed lips, she glared at the doctor, then said she was going to find Uncle Hamp.

"You're being hysterical," the doctor said dryly with his back to me as he took off his gloves. "It's too early. You're only two centimeters." I didn't know how big that was, but I couldn't believe this baby's head wasn't already showing. After the doctor left the room, another contraction hit, and I screamed again.

"You need to keep your voice down, young lady," the nurse said, bursting through the door. "The doctor told you you're not ready. You're scaring the other patients." She wasn't any friendlier than the doctor.

"It feels like the head is coming out. You need to look at me now!" I yelled to get her attention. She didn't smile or look the least bit sympathetic, but she checked again and this time I was nine centimeters. I wanted to say 'see?' but kept my mouth shut. When the doctor finally agreed this was really happening, the baby was really coming, they admitted me, placed me in a room, and offered gas and air but no other pain medications. I didn't understand why they were so cold to me. Was it because I was giving my baby up? I didn't know, but I didn't have any options. So I pushed through the pain and put up with their lack of concern.

After reporting the clinic's attitude to Uncle Hamp, Aunt Amelia was allowed to come in with me. "I know it's a free clinic," she said, stoking my brow, "and that they see an awful lot of patients every day, but I don't like their attitude. Let's focus on you. I don't have much hope for a resolution before this is over."

After two long hours of reeling from the power of a child trying to get into this world, I still measured nine centimeters, so the nurse told us she had to leave to do other things. Before she left, I sat up suddenly and announced, "I can't give this baby up. I'm going to keep my baby." My words were as much a surprise to me as to Aunt Amelia and the nurse. "Tell them,

Aunt Amelia. Tell them." Saying that exhausted me further and I fell back on the bed.

"Okay," Aunt Amelia said, taking my hand. "You can keep the baby if that's what you want."

The nurse cut her eyes from me to Aunt Amelia and back, grabbed my chart, and stormed out. As soon as she left the room, the heavy contractions began. I felt like my abdomen and back were being squeezed and my body was fighting against the squeezing. The contractions came in waves, starting out mild, getting strong, then getting mild again, then going away until the next one came.

Five hours later on one last push, I screamed out in pain and then felt a giant release. I fell back again, knowing the whole ordeal was over.

The noise of the room had been blocked by my own noise. I heard whispers, a scuffling sound, a door closing and then only silence filled the room.

"I want to see my baby," I said just above a whisper, exhausted and dripping with sweat.

"I'm sorry, miss. You can't," one of the nurses said. "It's for your own good."

"Whose own good? Get me my baby." I tried to yell, but still couldn't find any volume.

No one said anything.

"But I'm keeping my baby," I said. "I told you hours ago."

"It's too late, miss," the nurse said.

I panicked. *Had I waited too long or had Baby Child come too soon? Had I signed my baby away? Was there nothing I could do about it?*

"Is it a boy or a girl?" I called out from the table, unable to raise my body to see anything. "I have to know." Tears blended in with the sweat on my face.

Again, no one answered me.

"A girl," someone finally said behind me.

"I want to hold her. You have to let me hold her." My voice found some power this time but my desperation sounded weak.

"You can't see her. Your baby was stillborn," the voice said in a dry, flat tone, as if it wasn't any of my business.

From that moment on, the pain shifted from my body to my heart. For the next three weeks, the only thing I could do was cry. I didn't know I had so much liquid inside me. I didn't know losing my baby was going to be that hard. Mixed in my sorrow was the fact that the clinic automatically cremated stillborn babies as the funeral expense was just too great for most of the women who came there. And because my baby wasn't mine legally, I didn't even have the option to pay for a private funeral. For secrecy's sake, cremation was the best option in the long run.

Once home, I stayed in my room in bed almost all day and night. Aunt Amelia and Uncle Hamp left me alone except to bring food to me, which I barely touched. There, in my self-imposed prison, I could see out the window to the mountains as the clouds floated in and receded. The pain was buried inside me somewhere; I just didn't know where. Isolated in that room, I wallowed in my grief and wrapped it around my shoulders, my chest, and my heart. I pressed it against my stomach and inhaled each ugly, sad, painful moment.

At the beginning of the fourth week, Aunt Amelia came into my room to pick up my tray.

"Get up and follow me, Nadine. We need to talk," she commanded, marching right back out of the room.

I didn't want to talk and I didn't want to go with her. Talking was the last thing I wanted to do. Wallowing was more comforting, but I knew better than to not listen to Aunt Amelia.

I pushed back the chenille bedspread and got up from my soft womb-like nest. Crumpled tissues were piled high on the nightstand and on the bed. The pink wicker trashcan was filled to overflowing. After I pulled on my robe, I hunted for my slippers and shuffled into the living room, my dancer's posture bent over from grief. I sat down in the armchair across from the couch.

Aunt Amelia walked in with two cups of tea. "It's time to move on, Nadine," she said handing me a cup. "What's done is done. What is meant to be is this moment. It's time to think about your future."

"My future? I can't, Aunt Amelia. I can't. I need to go back to bed." I got up from the chair, pushed against its flowered fabric and headed back to the bedroom.

"No, you're not, and yes, you can. Sit back down." She placed her cup on the coffee table and sat on the couch.

"Are you kicking me out?" I asked, as I obeyed her command.

"No, Nadine, I would never kick you out. I would love to have you stay here forever. You know that. But this is not where you are meant to be. You need to go back home to Beaufort and your daddy's life or go on to New York City and find your own life."

I sipped the steaming tea, following its movement down my throat and into my stomach. Having tea with Aunt Amelia always intensified its effects. "I need more time."

When she sank back into the down-feathered couch, the morning light reflected off her amulet and into my eyes. Startled, I put up one hand to shield the reflection.

"Time will only make your decision more difficult," she said. "If you're scared, why don't you go back to live with your father and try to work things out with him first? Family is important."

I shivered at the suggestion. "No, never. I won't go back." My anger toward Daddy and home took on a new dimension that surprised even me.

"What are you so afraid of, Nadine? He's your father and he loves you even if it's not the way you want him to." The reflection off the amulet made me squint and shift in the chair.

Then without warning, thoughts I didn't know I had formed into words rushed out of me like the force of downstream water breaking through a dam. "I won't end up like my mother. She wanted to be a writer and I want to dance. Daddy took her to that asylum because he thought she was going crazy. She got worse, not better. She didn't even recognize us. Then she died. Daddy didn't have to put her there. She could have stayed home; we could have taken care of her. He doesn't listen to me. He doesn't hear me the way he didn't hear her. She was suffering and he put her away; he didn't try to take care of her. He just put her away. I'm not going to end up like her with some powerful husband thinking I'm crazy because I want to be something different from what he wants."

I fell back into the cocoon-like armchair and realized Aunt Amelia unlocked my grief, the grief that was tied up in my mother, my father, Frank and now, stillborn Baby Child.

Aunt Amelia came over to me, sat at the edge of the armchair and stroked my uncombed hair.

"Then it's settled. You need to go to New York and dance, Nadine Carter Barnwell. Deni has called several times and you haven't called her back."

"I can't talk with Deni about this. If I call her, she'll know something is wrong. She won't let it go until she finds out. That's just Deni."

"She won't let it go as long as you are projecting it. It's time to stop projecting all your loss."

"All my loss. Yes, all my loss."

Aunt Amelia walked over to the coffee table and lit the candle in the center. "Come over here, child."

I got up, walked over to the table and sat cross-legged on the floor opposite her.

"You have a new life waiting for you, one which will lead you to peace in all the areas you are not peaceful now," she said, waving her hands in a circle high above the flame, drawing the air back toward her face.

"But you will deal with them. Give me your hands." We joined hands across the table and encircled the candle.

"There will be many bumps in the road, though. Just remember, obstacles are presented for us to overcome. It's not what happens to us. It's what we do with what happens to us. Life will be entirely different from here on, Nadine. Everything you know, love and trust will not be available to you in the noise-filled, overcrowded, concrete and brownstone universe that is New York City. You will have to find new anchors for your sense of well-being and make new choices all along the way." She closed her eyes and asked me to close mine. "But I do see you dancing, in class and on a stage, living in a comfortable and spacious apartment and in a loving, committed relationship with a man. And one more thing, until you are ready to try for another child, there might even be a pet, something to connect you with home."

We both sat, encircling the candle for a few more moments before letting our hands go. She reached in her pocket, pulled something out and put it in my hand. It was a necklace with a small clear glass box at the end. "This amulet is for you. You will need some extra protection while you're in New York. Don't lose it."

"I won't. Thank you, Aunt Amelia. Thank you for everything." I reached over and held her tightly.

"Now get a shower and clean up your room. And then call Deni."

Deni wasn't home when I first called but I kept trying. Finally, her new roommate answered and I left a message for Deni to call me back. So in the fourth week after the stillbirth when Deni confirmed our plans to go to New York City, my determination to live my own life took over and the self-pitying stopped.

A week later, believing that I was physically and emotionally ready and knowing my secret was safe with Aunt Amelia and Uncle Hamp, I packed up my belongings, met up with Deni and flew away from everything I had ever known—my slow, secure and gentle South Carolina—into the wild unknown of New York City.

CHAPTER 6
Summer 1970

Trust yourself. You know more than you think you do.
—BENJAMIN SPOCK

O NCE AIRBORNE, I WATCHED SOUTH Carolina disappear from sight as we moved northward at an unbelievable speed. From my window seat, the familiar lush green landscape, cut by highways and snaked with ribbons of rivers and spidery creeks, began to fill with tiny rooftops and buildings higher than two stories. To me, New York had to be the most exciting place on the planet. I couldn't wait to touch down at JFK and let my journey with Baby Child recede into the distance. Moving to New York probably seemed a difficult choice for most of the people I knew back home, but my heart told me this was right for me. I convinced myself that life should only get easier after what I just went through.

Deni was as excited as I had ever seen her. Unable to sit still, she turned around to talk to anyone who would listen. The man in the seat across the aisle learned almost everything there was to know about what we were going to do once we touched down.

He knew that Deni and I were going to study modern dance at the Lemire Studio and expected to join a dance company in the not too distant future; and that as soon as we found jobs, we'd get a great apartment in Greenwich Village. Glancing over at them, I saw that he liked her attention and was probably hoping to get a phone number or address. Luckily, she didn't tell him where we were staying. For me, the airplane ride offered some needed quiet time to digest the upheaval of my last ten months.

Even though neither of us had ever been to New York, I'd mapped out a plan for getting us into Manhattan from the airport. I practically memorized the book, *New York On $10 a Day*, which Aunt Amelia found in a bookstore before I left. The content wasn't as reliable as trusted advice from a relative or good friend already living in the city, but it read so true, I chose to believe every jewel I found in it. I accepted wholeheartedly that there was no reason a traveler couldn't get all the way into Manhattan from JFK Airport on public transportation.

Deni and I had agreed on the affordable Hotel Colbert on 10th Street, just off 5th Avenue in the heart of Greenwich Village. The New York guidebook described the hotel as "Picturesque and Quaint; 'a must stay' for those who want the off-beat ambiance of The Village." The description seemed irresistible to both of us, so ready to be in the greatest city in the world.

Confident in our plan and with huge bags on our shoulders and in our hands, Deni and I walked and walked, and then walked some more until we located the local bus which would take us to the subway. According to my guidebook, after the bus, the train would carry us into the city; then all we needed to do was to change subway lines two more times, and we would finally be in Greenwich Village. The directions seemed clear and simple. I had no idea how far our first night's destination was from Kennedy Airport. Back home, we'd be in another state after such a trip.

Standing at the subway stop for the "R" Train, I noticed that the platform began filling up all around us, and I sensed the people knew something we didn't.

"Should we move?" Deni asked.

"No," I whispered adamantly. "We're in a great position to be the first ones on the train when it arrives."

Wrong. As a wind whipped up, pushing aside the stale air, the roar of wheels on metal turned our attention to the approaching train. In less than a minute, the seasoned riders covered every inch of space close to the edge of the platform.

When the train stopped, we found ourselves in between the two doors. Men, women and children poured from the cars on either side of us while the new passengers shoved their way through them. Deni and I saw our miscalculation, picked up our bags and headed toward the door to the left. At the rear of the pack, we realized there wasn't enough room left for us and our bags. We turned and headed for the door on the right. Those doors were about to close in our faces, when I yelled, "No, wait!" A man holding a folded newspaper looked up. With his newspaper hand, he stopped the doors from shutting and we shoved ourselves inside. When the subway started up with a jerk, we tumbled into the people to our left who pushed us back to the right. Someone shouted, "Hey, watch it!"

After we got our footing and claimed a tiny spot holding a pole for balance, I sensed the eyes of some of the other "R" Train riders. Looking around without "looking" was a skill I began to develop right then. It seemed like our backs held a sign saying, "newbies" because soon, two policemen patrolling the train stopped and rode the whole way into the city standing right next to us. I suppose, for them, two girls with more bags and backpacks than they should ever try to carry weren't going to be statistics on their shift; not on that day, anyway.

Four hours after landing in New York, a bus ride and two subway changes and actually eight hours since leaving home, Deni and I climbed the subway stairs with all our baggage, glad to be back to daylight and sidewalks. After figuring out where we were and which direction we needed to go, we walked several blocks across town to The Hotel Colbert. Just as the guide said, this older, ten-story, brownstone building showed the telltale signs dating it as 'postwar' as opposed to 'pre-war,' modernized with high ceilings, elevators and laundry facilities. My education of the city began.

As we entered from the bright outdoors, my eyes took a few seconds to adjust to the dim light of the lobby. Once my sight cleared up, I found myself searching for the quaint part. One stained cocoa-colored, faux-suede couch sat between two ashen Naugahyde armchairs. A wood-laminated coffee table with chipped edges held a few coffee stained tourist guides and newspapers. A giant photo of the Empire State Building hung on the wall opposite the front desk, and on a table near a darkened hallway sat a dust-laden fake flower arrangement.

From the dim hallway I heard elevator doors open. Soon, three black men with oversized afros, kaleidoscopic dashikis and glittering gold necklaces appeared in the doorway to the lobby. Deep in conversation, they glanced at us momentarily and then headed for the couch and chairs, rather than out the main door.

Deni stayed rooted just inside the front door, as if unwilling to commit to taking another step as I made my way to the front desk. Further inside, I realized my nose needed to adjust as well. A pungent odor of age and mildew filled the air. But I was not deterred; at last, 'in Manhattan.'

With the day clerk on the phone, the oily-skinned manager stepped out of the shadows behind the check-in desk and acknowledged our reservation. Our room was on the 4th floor, so he pointed back toward the dark hall to the elevator. After curt instructions, we learned some essentials about the hotel: the location of the laundry and ice machines, the exit doors and at what time they locked the front door each night.

Deni and I dropped our bags and simultaneously sighed as we entered the dreary room which matched the look of the lobby. Deni walked across the room, pulled open a few drawers from the dresser, ran her finger along the edge of the two double beds and moved the heavy brown drapes aside to look at the view. Her shoulders rose and then dropped as she pulled them further back.

"It's just another building," she said, as I came up behind her to see. She walked away, and I closed the curtain.

After unpacking, I made a collect call to Aunt Amelia, as promised, to let her know we were there and safe. I left out the details of the trip into the city with the policemen and the hotel as I found it thus far. It would only concern her. She, in turn, promised to call Deni's mother. The ground rules were set before we left. We were not supposed to waste our money on long distance calls, especially from a hotel.

As I fell asleep that night, butterflies flew around in my stomach. The room rate was more expensive than we'd planned; the entire hotel was dark and tired-looking; I was more exhausted than I thought I would be and I missed Frank terribly. I wondered how long it would be before he'd be able to join me. It was just as well that where he was filming was out of telephone range because I would have begged him to come right away, and no doubt would've told him about our baby. Once we stopped moving, my still recovering body ached from carrying bags and climbing cement stairs. Pushing away the experience of Baby Child was going to be harder than I thought. Just like Aunt Amelia said, choices were before me everywhere and I needed to make each of them as important as the one that took me into the ritual and out of Beaufort. I never looked at my life like that before. But I was never in control of my life until then.

The next morning we got up with a renewed focus. The excitement of being in Greenwich Village made us overlook the minor annoyances of the hotel since we were ready to get on with our new lives. We must have passed some kind of test because we got a second key to our room from a much nicer desk clerk and entered Greenwich Village as residents, at least in our heads. Determined to find jobs in the same restaurant and in The Village, Deni and I got newspapers, bagels with cream cheese and coffee from the nearby *Smilers*. It didn't take long to learn that the returning NYU students already claimed a lot of these jobs, and the rest of the places weren't hiring anyone without experience, putting us at a great disadvantage. I waited tables during college and knew what to say in an interview, but since Deni hadn't, we walked away from several possibilities. I decided to train Deni myself so she could fake her way through an interview.

A few days later after almost every restaurant in the neighborhood turned us down, I was deflated and ready to give up on the notion that we would find work in The Village. On my last sweep of the area before heading uptown for less familiar territory, I decided to try a couple of the smaller establishments I'd passed up before.

On Greenwich Avenue, I remembered a small hole-in-the-wall bar and decided to go in. With only a single dark-tinted window and a wooden front door, it was impossible to know what to expect. I gathered the remainder of my declining perseverance and entered. Inside was dark and smoky, but even in the daytime, several customers were at tables scattered around the room, which was a good sign.

After my eyes adjusted, I marched right up to the bar and with as much enthusiasm as I had left, I asked, "Excuse me, do you have any jobs available?" The burly red-faced woman, wiping off a beer stein, stared at me over her half-glasses. She stood motionless as she scanned me before tipping her head to one side. A grin spread across her somber face like she just got a joke. With a raspy smoker's utterance, she chuckled. I wondered if there was a smudge on my face or pigeon poop on my shoulder. "Yeah, we have an opening, dear–but I–I don't think you would exactly fit in here," she said, looking over my shoulder. From the tables behind me, I heard a chuckle, then another, whispers and a hand slapped a table, followed by a deep belly laugh. Even though I built my rejection tolerance, her reason for not hiring me seemed strange. What did "not fit in" mean? It was a bar with food, not exactly a restaurant, but there were customers in the afternoon after the lunch rush. They needed help and I needed work and it was in The Village. It seemed simple to me. I eased my head around for an explanation. Through the hazy smoke-filled light, I saw the issue as if a fan had blown away the veil: none of the men sitting at the bar, at the tables, playing pool and smoking cigarettes had Adam's apples, razor burn, stubble, moustaches, beards or sideburns. They were–women. The scene before me was not something I would have seen in Beaufort or in any other place that I had ever been. I gulped and turned back to the bartender or maybe she was the manager, smiled slightly, thanked her for her time and silently thanked her for her good judgment. I made a quick retreat out the door. Out on the street just down the block, far enough to be not visible to them, I stopped at a storefront window to regroup. As open-minded as I thought I was after being raised in the most traditional part of the South, I sensed I wouldn't make it there even if she'd offered me a job.

As if that wasn't enough for one day, when I refocused my eyes to see exactly what I stood in front of, I realized the storefront window was filled with baby mannequins dressed in stylish pink and blue baby outfits. Their skins and grins were so flawless and so inviting I had a hard time standing for a moment. After I regained my balance, I had to contain the urge to go in and finger the fabrics and stroke the baby doll faces. Another bell rang, and a young mother, about my age, pushed her baby stroller out the door and onto the sidewalk. The lively infant inside, dressed in a pink jumper and matching hat, looked up, beamed and waved her pacifier at me, then threw it on the ground. I picked it up and handed it back to the glowing mother who thanked me before pushing off down the street. My heart ached for Baby Child again as I watched her disappear into the people coming toward me. I needed to get used to the idea that, contrary to my belief, living in Manhattan didn't stop a whole lot of people from happily raising children amid concrete and clamor.

Back at the hotel, I nodded hello to the dashiki-draped men on the couch as I entered. At the front desk, I stopped to tell the friendly day desk clerk who took an interest in us, particularly our job searches, that once again I struck out. He sympathized with our situation as I'm sure he did with many hotel guests. Then he whispered for me to come closer to the desk. "It would be a good idea to keep to yourself," he said, tipping his head toward the three men who were always in the lobby. I didn't need to follow his head tip. "The professions of our steady clientele have changed over the years, you know, since that travel book you carry was written."

"I see. I suspected they weren't waiting for a callback for a play." I didn't want to judge too soon—a possible fatal flaw for a New Yorker, but by the way they huddled and held watch over the front door most of the day, I inferred their days were filled with more illegal activity than legal. "Thank you," I said, for the second time in about a half hour to a hardened New Yorker. I liked finding the good in people when I least expected it.

Walking toward the elevator, I hoped Deni had better luck than I did. In the room, I found her sprawled on the floor playing solitaire. She looked up long enough to let me know she hadn't found work yet and that I'd received a few calls in the last hour from the same person. She didn't know the caller. I couldn't imagine who it was since no one asked for my phone number in any of the restaurants where I'd applied.

Beat, I sat down on the bed, kicked off my right shoe and began rubbing my calf and the arch of my foot. Before Baby Child, I was in really great shape, but now, walking for hours on the concrete sidewalks of New York made me aware of a completely new set of muscle groups. Hopefully, all this walking would help get me in shape fast.

After I took off my left shoe and continued my foot massage, the phone rang again and Deni answered. She put her hand over the receiver. "It's for you, Nadine. I think it's the same caller."

"You mean they asked for me by name?" I tossed the other shoe across the room.

"Yeah, it's a man, and he said, 'Nadine.' I don't recognize the voice." She stretched the phone toward me.

"Is this Nadine Barnwell?" a man started in.

"Yes, it is."

"A friend gave me your number. I would like to make an appointment with you." The man on the other end did not identify himself.

"You've got the wrong person, I'm afraid," I said. He assured me he didn't and knew I lived at The Hotel Colbert. He heard I was looking for work.

"Well, yes, I am."

He kept referring to this appointment, insisting a friend told him to call.

"What kind of an appointment are you talking about?" I asked.

The other end of the phone went silent for a moment. Then he said, "I must have misunderstood," and hung up.

"He hung up," I said as I held the phone out from my ear and stared at it.

"What in the world was that all about?" Deni asked.

Later, two more phone calls came, wanting "appointments" with me. At first I thought it was a wrong room number. With the second one, I became concerned. On the third one, I hung up. That's when I realized someone was trying to help me start my own business or more realistically, get started in their business—someone who knew my name, where I lived and that I needed money. I wanted to call Daddy but that was not an option. I would never tell him I was uncomfortable. With anxiety forming like a tropical storm in the pit of my stomach, I realized finding jobs, anywhere, was crucial to getting out of the "Picturesque and Quaint" Hotel Colbert.

The next day, frustrated from no work offers again and the mysterious phone calls, I stopped at a small storefront on Sixth Avenue featuring the craft of local artisans. The window display of earth tone plates and mugs reminded me of the stores near Aunt Amelia in Asheville and made me want to go inside. As soon as I entered, a bell attached to the door tinkled and calm enveloped me. Fountains bubbling in the corners were surrounded by verdant green plants creating a backdrop for earth tone pottery, bronze sculpture and handmade beaded jewelry. It was like an oasis. A voice coming from behind a high counter offered to let him know if I needed help.

"Oh, thank you, I'm just looking. Your store is wonderful. It's so soothing in here."

"Ah, a Southerner; my favorite import. Where are you from, Miss Scarlett?" He said, faking a southern accent.

"It's Nadine, Nadine Barnwell from Beaufort, South Carolina. You've probably never heard of it. It's a small town near the coast." I inched along the aisles fingering some items, running my hand over the surface of others.

"I'll bet it's beautiful. Long, tree-lined driveways, white-columned houses and moss draped oaks. Am I close?"

"Closer than you think." For an instant, I ached for the familiarity of home.

After letting me browse for a few minutes, the man asked, "Having a rough time of it?"

"Yes, I guess I am. I can't find basic waitressing work. It's such a huge city but the jobs all seem to be taken."

"So you're not just visiting. You must be new to the city and you must be in the arts," he said, continuing to work at something behind the high counter. "Fine or performing?"

"Performing. I'm a dancer. But how did you know? Is there some kind of a sign on my back?"

"No, not exactly; it's my intuition. Plus, why would you be looking for a job waiting tables unless you needed quick money and a flexible schedule? Around here, restaurant work translates into performing artist–of any kind."

"We, that is, my roommate and I arrived in the city about a week ago. We've come to study modern dance at the Leland Lemire Studios, and we're staying at The Hotel Colbert while we hunt for jobs and an apartment," I said looking up at him.

He stopped what he was doing and lifted his head. A smile spread across his milky face, causing his eyes to twinkle, making him look like that angel in *It's A Wonderful Life*. "Ah, you are an artiste and staying at The Colbert. Many who are now famous used to take this same path."

"Used to?" "Do you know much about the hotel?" His voice sounded fatherly, as if he were talking to a close friend or relative rather than chatting up a customer he might never see again.

"Only what I read in the travel books. They said it was quaint and a 'must see.'" I picked up a blown glass vase displayed in front of the check-out counter.

"Well, I know a good deal about it. It no longer has the best reputation," he said, sounding more serious now.

"In what way?" I was almost afraid to hear what was next.

He moved his glasses down his nose. "I am also the chairman of The Village Citizen Crime and Safety Task Force. Your hotel houses one of the biggest drug dealers in The Village. So please, be watchful."

I gulped. It had to be the dashiki-wearing men in the lobby.

"Other things are going on; it's not quite as picturesque as it appears."

I told him of the mysterious phone calls asking for "appointments."

"They're feeling you out and hoping if you get desperate enough, you will take one of them up on it. They recruit for 'girls' on an ongoing basis. Girls like you and your roommate, new to the city, running out of money and in need of help."

My palms sweated as my stomach storm churned faster. "I don't suppose you need any help?"

"No, I'm a lean operation, I'm afraid. I try to keep it to just me. My niece fills in when I can't be here. She's a painter but she can afford it. She still lives with her mother."

I thanked him for his advice and concern and headed out the door, back to the hotel. I was glad to know someone kind in New York knew where I lived.

We hadn't been in New York long, but already I saw how long it took to get things accomplished. We needed to get settled and get jobs and an apartment before the next session of classes started again at the Lemire Studio in August. Something was going to turn up soon. It had to.

As Deni and I unwillingly began to expand our job search out of The Village, uptown a bit toward midtown, we put our plan for checking out the school and our imagined leisurely strolls through Manhattan on hold. As soon as we did, we were both invited in to interview at the same restaurant.

O'Reilly's Steak and Ale looked almost stately, as those older restaurants in Manhattan always do, with enormous windows in the front, edged by heavy maroon velvet curtains swagged back with twisted gold cords. Right around the corner from Grand Central Station, this restaurant had probably been there for at least fifty years. According to the managers, it was a bustling place, packed for lunch and dinner almost every day of the week. To me, it wasn't as inviting or intriguing as the restaurants in The Village, but my outlook changed when I realized they were hiring.

As usual, experience was necessary. Deni and I agreed I should do all the talking. She sat almost mute in fear of saying something that would show her ignorance, while I swore to the manager that Deni was as experienced as I was. With a little more talking and the promise of the references I made up, the manager said if we got our uniforms together, black skirts and white blouses, we could start the shift between lunch and dinner the next day.

Outside the restaurant and around the corner, I put both hands on the back of Deni's shoulders, jumped and shouted, "Hallelujah!" With this one obstacle down and a couple more to go before we were settled, we headed back downtown together to get our uniforms. After asking the front desk clerk where we should go, we hit 14th Street, the "Mecca of Cheap," for appropriate skirts and blouses on our budget. The out-of-style skirts, while the right price and fit, were much too long. But that was not a problem. After years of making our own dance costumes, I knew Deni could help with this task so I turned the hemming over to her, which she did that night.

Later the next morning, while Deni showered, I re-examined the newly shortened hems and decided the skirts should be pressed. I called the front desk for an iron, was told they were in the supply area of the basement, and if I wanted one to get it myself. Great.

Still in jeans and an oversized shirt, I haphazardly clipped my messy hair on top of my head, grabbed a baseball cap and headed for the elevator to the basement. The basement was dark and a bit spooky. I followed the musty corridors with side doorways to tiny side rooms and passed exposed utility wires and pipes. It took a while but I found the supply area, complete with a surly housekeeper probably not fit for the minimal civility required for general upper floor duties. She acted as if she was posted in charge of a top secret bounty. After a few exchanges, this "supply guard" gave me an iron as if doing me a huge favor. I said, "Thank you," and headed with some speed back to the elevator.

I punched the button for my floor. On the way back up, in my mind, I went over everything we needed to do before leaving for our new jobs. Still calculating as the elevator opened, I crossed the hall to our room. I tapped lightly knowing it would be locked. There was no answer. I knocked louder in case the sound was blocked by Deni blow-drying her hair.

"Hey, open up; it's me."

Then a strange voice shouted back, "Who's me?"

I snapped out of my fog, looked up and realized I wasn't knocking on my door at all. My heart raced and rising blood burned in my face as I turned around and saw a large "3" on the wall next to the elevator door. *Oh man, this is not my floor.* Not only wasn't this my room, I realized, but the door belonged to the main dashiki man from the lobby. Earlier, I overheard the manager and this man talking at the front desk about him being one floor under the "Southern Fried Chickens." They both looked over at me and laughed.

When I didn't answer, the voice again asked, ratcheting up the volume, "I said, 'who's me,' and what the hell do you want?"

I panicked and rushed toward the "Exit" sign over the door to the stairwell beside the elevator and pushed it open. Before that door shut behind me, the door to the wrong room swooshed open over the carpet, pot smoke sucked into the hall and someone began yelling, "Hey, you, stop! What do you think you're doing?"

I sprinted up the stairs, managing to stay a closed door length ahead. Once in my hallway I ran over to my room, praying Deni broke the primary rule of survival and forgot to lock the door behind me. I grabbed the knob and turned. To my relief, it was indeed unlocked. In a split second, I was inside, slamming it shut and securing the multiple locks. I fell back against the door, panting, still holding the iron. The room was empty. I took off the baseball cap and threw it across the room, just as Deni came out of the bathroom in a robe with a towel on her head.

"What in the world is wrong with you?" Deni asked.

Panting hard, I could barely speak. As my normal breath came back, I began to explain what happened. "I must have interrupted a drug deal or something on the floor below." Sudden pounding on the door made me jump.

"Someone better let me in! There is a man in there that was trying to steal from me!" It was the same voice from the floor below. When I didn't answer, the pounding and the voice got louder. "I'm going to knock this damn door down!"

I didn't know what to do. We had to leave for our first day of work in about an hour and we weren't ready even without this interruption. I needed for them to go away so I shouted back, "It wasn't a man, it was me. I just got off on the wrong floor and didn't look. I'm sorry."

"It was too a man and you'd better let me in to find him!" He shouted back.

I summoned my most commanding southern voice, one that sounded more like Daddy than me and told him he was wrong and to go away. But this didn't work. He said he was going to find the manager and get our butts kicked right out of the hotel.

This can't be happening, not now. We've got to leave for our job. Then I quickly explained to Deni what just happened.

She sat motionless, seeming to hold her breath as if this might make her invisible to whatever was coming next.

"Deni, finish getting ready," I commanded. "I'll iron these skirts." I thought action was better than staying frozen in fear.

Within minutes, the man came back with the manager who demanded he be let inside our room. Since I was now positive the manager arranged those phone calls to me, I wasn't too sure I wanted to let either of them in. Deni still offered no suggestions, so I unlocked all the dead bolts and eased the door open.

The "alleged" dealer, a middle-aged black man with an immense afro, a lean angular face, wearing a red and orange dashiki, stood next to the short olive-skinned manager wearing a white shirt, skinny black tie and shiny black polyester pants. The dealer took a quick look, dismissed me and started scanning the room. "Where is the man—the one with the baseball cap?" He asked.

"Where is he?" The manager repeated, directing his question to Deni, who rose from the bed with a blank expression.

The now familiar voice said, "The guy must be hiding here somewhere."

"I told you, it wasn't a man; it was me." Stumbling through the order of events, I went into my story again of tucking my hair up in a baseball cap, getting off on the wrong floor, and that I wasn't stealing anything, I just needed to get an iron.

As they looked at each other and back at the three of us, the dealer's eyes shifted and narrowed and his mouth tightened. The manager looked at the floor and then back at the dealer.

No one said a word.

The dealer ended the silence but not his threatening look. "Don't go knocking on doors that don't belong to you, Fried Chicken."

Then the manager added, "If you ever do that again, you will be out on the street."

The dealer and the manager turned and were gone.

After that incident, every time we passed the front desk, one of the occupants from the room below stood or sat stationed like an exit sentry, monitoring our way in and out. No longer the amusing or naïve new faces on the block; according to them, the "Southern Fried Chickens" couldn't be trusted.

In just a few short weeks, if I were asked to change anything about the trusted travel book's description of the Hotel Colbert, I would change "A must stay" to "A must stay away." My life in New York City was not at all how I pictured it and my nerves were straining. Deni seemed unphased, but I knew if we were going to survive, we needed to get out of there—and fast.

CHAPTER 7
Summer 1970

*The doors we open and close each day decide the
lives we live.*
—FLORA WHITTEMORE

E PUT ON HOLD EVERYTHING we'd said we
wanted to do, like see the dance studio and slowly
walk the streets of The Village. And I wanted to just
talk with Aunt Amelia since I couldn't talk with Frank. After
the encounter with the hotel drug dealers, Deni and I realized
we needed to step up our apartment search efforts. Our biggest obstacle to getting one at all was the first questions asked:
where you work and how long have you been in New York? Both
questions being reasons to not be considered serious tenant
material. Now, in our newly revised stepped-up quest, having
jobs was no longer the issue. Our individual ideas of the perfect
apartment and its location, or better, where each of us didn't want
to live, took its place. The collective "no-way" list included: the
East-east Village, Alphabet City, Stuyvesant, Eastern Fourteenth
Street, West-west Village, Little Italy and a run-down abandoned

area below Houston Street known as SoHo. The West Village remained in play.

We quickly learned that the big newspapers were unreliable sources. Referral agencies collecting tidy fees controlled the better apartments. After repeatedly not finding our Shangri-La through these high priced agencies, I crossed the fingers of both hands when I finally found a small ad in the weekly *Village Voice* for a two-bedroom apartment in the "Heart of The Village."

"Far-out!" I yelled to an empty room. "This is the one." I dialed the number. Before we released any information, the man who answered asked if we had jobs–but nothing else. He told me an apartment on Christopher Street just became vacant.

I put my hand over the receiver and gasped. This was the only street both of us had agreed on.

"If you want it, I'll call the super. You'd better get over there right now," he bellowed.

"Yes sir, call him. I'm on my way."

"You're sure you've got jobs?"

After I told him the name of the restaurant, he warmed up slightly. He and his buddies used to frequent *O'Reilly's Steak and Ale* when he worked closer to Grand Central Station. I wrote down the address and the super's name, Hector.

After changing clothes, I nearly exploded out the door and onto the street.

The building, a seven-story, pre-war walk-up, sandwiched between *Rick's Café Bar* and *The Village Antique Shop*, stood inconspicuously on one of the most famous streets in Greenwich Village. The well-worn granite steps led to an enormous locked wooden and glass front door. To gain entrance, I focused on the panel of apartment buttons to the left, my heart pounding loudly. With a quick scan, I found the super's apartment and pushed the buzzer.

An Hispanic sounding female voice came back, "Yes? Who is it?"

"I'm Nadine Barnwell. I've come to see the apartment for rent."
The speaker clicked off. I waited patiently for a response.

A man's voice came on the speaker. "Miss Barnwell?"

"Yes."

"I'll be right up." He buzzed me in.

Inside, I stood in the barren unlit lobby. Normally, spaces are cramped in pre-war buildings; however, this entrance area was unusually wide and open, giving a much better sense of space than the other ones I'd seen in our price range. It also collected cooking smells. I identified garlic, beef and frying oil. After a few minutes, up the steps from the basement came a neatly dressed man wearing grayish utility-type pants and a matching shirt with his name embroidered over his left chest pocket.

About five-foot-six with a trim medium build and thick dark, slicked-back hair, he looked me over while wiping his mouth and hands with a napkin. The smell of his lunch filled the air.

"Come with me." He smiled and I relaxed a bit.

As he pulled the basement door closed, he shouted back into his apartment, "I go to 2B. Be right back."

My eyes tried to adjust as we headed toward the staircase to the upper floors. Also unusually wide with black wrought iron balusters and mahogany railings, the stairs were even more dimly lit than the lobby. It didn't matter. I followed right behind him like a puppy.

"The apartment is a good apartment but I tell you, not too much light. Windows on this floor, not much to look at," he said, as we climbed to the second floor.

I was beginning to notice a pattern here. But neither of us asked for a sunlit apartment.

He pulled a ring of keys from his back pocket, sorted through them until he found the master, unlocked two locks, turned the handle and gave the door a little kick with his foot. The door swung open revealing, to my surprise, an entrance straight into the kitchen. Strange, I thought.

Once past the kitchen, we entered a small square space he called the living room. Off to the right was one bedroom; straight ahead the other, the bath in between. After I'd walked through the space a couple of times, I stood in the middle of the living room and turned three hundred and sixty degrees one way, and again the other. The place was old and funny looking, but at least it had its own bath, so we wouldn't have to use a tub in the kitchen with a hand-held faucet for our showers, as I often saw on our search. In the more modern buildings, I later learned, the tub in the kitchen eventually joined the same room as the toilet; a sink was added and presto! The bathroom was born.

Even though it was low rent, two splitting the rent instead of three put a lot more economic pressure on us than I budgeted, so I recalculated our expenses once again. With the promise of Frank joining us in a few months, I calculated we could probably just get by if we watched our spending.

Drawing on my highest instincts, as Aunt Amelia taught me, I said, "I'll take it. I just have to get my roommate here to see it."

"Okay, but you better go right away, miss. More people coming this afternoon."

I flew back to the hotel as fast as my feet would carry me to find Deni.

"Oh, man. You really need to see this," I said, hurrying Deni to get dressed.

Deni's first impression wasn't as positive as mine. "I don't know," she whined, pulling open a closet door. "I thought it would look better, have more room." I ignored her. "I think we should keep looking," she whispered, out of Hector's range. I began to sense another pattern with her. She hadn't seen as many apartments as I had and believed she could live like an Upper Eastsider on our miniscule budget. Because time was of the essence, I pulled on Deni's sleeve, directing her toward a corner of the room. Using skills I learned from Daddy, I reminded her why this was the one: on our favorite street, in our price range, and what it would be like to stay at The Hotel Colbert much longer. After she grudgingly agreed, I walked over to Hector, put out my hand, and said, "We'll take it now."

Daddy would have been proud of me. He spent his whole life negotiating with tenants. That's what old money does for a living. They own the land and the buildings, thereby, controlling what businesses can come to town. Daddy counted on me joining him in his world, but I couldn't imagine spending my life worrying people out of their money.

Hector smiled and said, "Okay, it's yours. You go back to the landlord now; bring me lease and I give you keys."

As I turned around one more time, I grasped my distance from the kind of place I grew up in back home. "Tabby Hall," as Mama's family named it, was on the Historic Register, with six bedrooms, four baths and a terracotta tile-floored glass solarium. The dining room held a table for twelve and showcased an enormous green and gold-toned European tapestry hung from crown molding. A pre-civil war round antique breakfast table seated at least six people off the kitchen. But I wanted this darkened two-bedroom apartment on Christopher Street to be my new home, so I silently blessed it as Aunt Amelia would have and promised to embrace it with all the reverence I could muster. I couldn't wait to see Frank's face when I showed it to him.

By four o'clock, it was ours.

"*Mira, Mira,* you pretty redheaded girl. You want to marry me?" a Puerto Rican man called out, pushing a heavy metal garment rack of new clothes down the sidewalk. I recoiled from his words as I searched for the address of the dance school out of the corner of my eye.

Finally, I was starting what I came for. The Leland Lemere Dance Studio was tucked away in the middle of the Garment District in a building on 37th Street between 8th and 9th Avenues, around the corner from the Port Authority Bus Terminal. On 37th Street, I soon learned that every day someone wanted to marry me. A few men came right up to my face to say it. One even kissed me on the ear before fleeing past and into the crowded sidewalk filled with other garment racks moving at breakneck speeds. I chose not to react. I was on my way to something special, something that had been stirring in me nearly my entire life.

Double-parked trucks covered the entire street with raised back doors; racks of clothing in clear plastic bags were lowered on the lifts transporting them to street level. Men rushed from the truck to the building doorways with their cargo, pushing their deliveries into large freight elevators, while others returned with empty racks to get their next load.

The macho workers acted as if they owned the sidewalk with their high and chaotic energy levels. Calling out to young women as they passed was a form of intimidation, so I held myself tight, maneuvering quickly and carefully down the street. I didn't relax my focus until once inside my building and in an elevator built for people only.

On the fourth floor, I found an entirely different world. As I rounded the corner an enormous dance studio, the size of a football field, with one whole wall mirrored with ballet bars, loomed before me. I gasped, raising my hand to cover my mouth as I stared. The ceiling seemed to go up two stories. Probably a sweat shop in the previous century, the offices above overlooked the giant room below; a great layout for management to keep tabs on the efficiency of their workers below. I stood for the longest time just watching the class moving to the instructions of the teacher. The students were already past the floor warm-up, as they stood in line at the side to individually perform an intricate combination across this huge space. Dance classes the world over looked much the same, I imagined. Men and women in leotards and tights, leg warmers, and sweatshirts breathed hard and glistened. The sweat of hard work penetrated the air. It was a familiarity I would learn to appreciate in this unfamiliar new world of mine.

Around the perimeter of the dance studio, dance bags, towels and piled clothing lined the long walls. It almost appeared as if the students were moving in. Upon closer examination of the dancers, I noticed a different "look" to this group from what I was used to in South Carolina. Here, almost everyone was lean and taut, and every woman's hair pulled back and up on top of her head. But what was most apparent to me was the skill level. There weren't just one or two who were exceptional—they were all incredible; lifting, leaping, bending, and turning. Legs, arms and torsos were held in perfect alignment throughout the dance room. It wasn't my college dance class anymore.

I sensed a need to put in many extra hours on my own to work on my technique in order to reach their level. I was even more thankful then for my scholarship. At one time, I would have been able to count on Daddy for this kind of support, freeing me to work out as often as I wanted, but not now. In return for the reduced tuition, I promised to work ten hours a week in the office. The scholarship was important for both the school and for me, since Frank wasn't sharing the burden—yet. Every little bit helped. Unfortunately, Deni did not receive a scholarship; she would have to earn her tuition. I hoped that wouldn't be another potential problem.

After the class ended, I searched for the office. When I couldn't find it, I asked one of the dancers for directions. Following her outstretched arm as she bent over trying to catch her breath, I saw the office in one of the upper-level rooms overlooking the studio. Then she pointed to a set of stairs behind me. I thanked her and headed up.

Inside, a round-faced woman with short cropped graying hair talked on the telephone behind a desk. Another taller woman with a full head of white, slightly longer hair, stood by the filing cabinets with the top drawer opened. In contrast to the orderly classes below, people continuously entered and interrupted, asking for help. The two women handled every request with ease between taking and giving phone messages. They went on like that, talking to students and each other for several minutes before acknowledging me, I suppose since I didn't say anything. Finally, the one behind the desk looked at me and then glanced at her watch. "You'd better speak up, dear; no one can read your mind."

"I'm Nadine Barnwell," I said, before the opportunity passed.

"Ah, the new intern. You're right on time. We've been expecting you. Welcome to *The Leland Lemere Dance Studio*."

The woman on the phone stood up from behind her desk, walked over and stretched out her hand. "I'm Frances."

I already knew who she was by her voice. She'd been my contact all along, encouraging and advising me. On some level, it was her spirit and love of her work with Leland that pulled me through the phone, through the network of telephone wires and deposited me in New York City, right into that studio.

"This is Hilda," Francis said.

Hilda turned from her work and waved. "Did you have any trouble finding us, dear?" Hilda asked.

"Well, no, not exactly. I just had to find my way through all those roadblocks and marriage proposals out on the street."

Both Francis and Hilda laughed. Obviously, they heard that one before.

"I take it you've found yourself an apartment."

"Oh yes, in the Village, right on Christopher Street."

"Oh, grand Christopher Street. A good choice. And some other work? You mentioned you'd be getting a "real" job of some kind."

"Yes, I have," I said, hoping that would remain the truth.

"Okay then, so we need you right away. I'll show you the schedule for your classes and what you'll be doing for us."

"That sounds great." As I looked around, I tingled inside. I was finally right where I wanted to be.

For the next several weeks, Deni and I threw ourselves into taking classes, working at the *O'Reilly's Steak and Ale* and setting up our new home. We managed to outfit our most basic needs: foam mattresses on the floor, linens, cooking pots, dishes and utensils, all acquired at flea market prices on the Lower Eastside. Our home resembled basic "starving artist:" drab and sparse with milk crates, boards and bricks for shelves and unmatched beanbags chairs. I didn't know how Deni felt but I cherished every single purchase because it was ours.

Because we rarely saw anyone else when we entered or left the building, neither of us met any of our neighbors. I knew that affordable apartments on Christopher Street were in high demand, but after a while I began to worry the building was half empty. So every time I saw Hector heading off to fix something, I had to ask who he was going to see. I wanted him to prove to me that more people lived there than I had seen.

"Ha," he said, through a high-pitched laugh as he stopped on the stairs one afternoon. "The building is full, Miss Nadine. I tell you this. Some, I almost never hear from, and some people need me every day." He leaned over and dug through the contents of his oil-stained canvas tool bag, as if searching for a particular item.

Hector and his wife were the only two people I knew for sure lived in the building.

"I would not be so busy with the leaking pipes, sticking doors and clanking radiators if these apartments were empty." From the bottom of his bag, he pulled out a long metal object with a worn wooden handle I didn't recognize. "Ah, here it is." Then he threw the tool back in the bag and hoisted it up on his shoulder.

"Some people never come out of their apartments. I think they're just lonely and want to talk to someone. That's what I'm here for. I don't care if they have real repairs or not. I go anyway."

"You're a good man, Hector," I said, putting a hand on his shoulder. "But I really would like to know more of my neighbors. I guess I'll meet these phantom people someday," I teased, lowering my dance bag to the step.

"Most tenants have lived here for many, many years. They are set in their ways and not necessarily welcoming to the, how you say, "newbies" on the lower floors."

"Why the lower floors?"

"Those apartments turn over more. Oh, yes, that reminds me. The apartment above you is vacant." He lifted his foot to the next step, grabbed the railing and adjusted the bag in his hand.

"It is?" I never even saw the person who lived right above me.

"Yes. I have to fix a few things, and then the new tenant will move in this weekend. He is very friendly. Maybe you will get to know him."

Then a man's voice called out, "Oh, hello, is that you, Hector?"

"I think maybe you will meet this new tenant sooner than later," Hector whispered to me. "Yes, it is Hector," he turned and called to the man below through the opening in the center of the stairwell.

"*Bueno. Como esta usted,* Hector?" I knew it was Spanish, but I hadn't heard anyone else address Hector in that way. I liked the man attached to the voice already.

"*Muy bien, Padre,*" Hector replied.

"*Padre*?" I whispered, peering over the railing to see who was speaking.

"Yes, I'm a priest." I didn't think he could hear me from above, but my voice carried straight down the stairwell as if through a megaphone. "Father Benjamin Vincent Dunlap. Father Benjamin will do."

"Oh, sorry. Hey, Father. I'm Nadine Carter Barnwell, 2D." I couldn't quite see him and turned toward Hector for further explanation. He just laughed.

"Oh, below me. Nice to meet you, Nadine." I saw another head peek up through the opening in the stairwell. "We're coming right up. We've got a few boxes with us if that's all right. We'll take the service elevator."

Feet shuffled on the marble tile floor below; their conversation became muffled; the elevator door rang as it opened.

Since we lived on the second floor, I never took the elevator. It occurred to me that this was how I missed meeting some people.

The elevator door opened above us. There was panting followed by an object with some weight dropping to the floor.

"I told you these apartments aren't empty for long," Hector said, over his shoulder now, as he took the steps two at a time. "These are your new neighbors. You'd better come with me if you want to meet them." With him already at the top of the stairs, I picked up my dance bag and followed right behind him.

By the time I got to the landing, Hector had already unlocked the door and disappeared inside with one of the men. The other pulled several brown cardboard boxes out of the elevator. From what I could see, he was short and wiry. Probably in his thirties he had a look I began to recognize in The Village; close-cropped brunette hair, smooth olive skin and the signature tightfitting black jeans with a black cotton polo shirt. He lifted each box from the elevator, placed it on the hallway floor and shoved it with his foot to get all of them out of the way before the doors shut.

Through the open door, I saw an apartment configured just like mine, the front door opening straight into the kitchen. I entered and found the other man leaning against the counter. Hector banged on a pipe in the next room, babbling in Spanish.

This man's age was harder to determine. He was also slight, about my height with a brown neatly trimmed beard, ear-length dark hair and smooth, pale-pink skin. I felt his kindness before I ever saw any evidence of it.

"Come in, Nadine Barnwell. Please. I'm Father Benjamin and that's Taylor out there, doing all the heavy lifting. He'll be in here in a minute." He smiled at me in a gentle way, a look I rarely saw radiate from anyone in New York since I arrived. Then Taylor squeezed by me carrying a box to the living room. When he came back into the kitchen, I was greeted by a hand shake that turned into an enormous warm hug.

"Did I hear you say, 'hey' just now?" Father Benjamin asked, leaning back against the counter again as if to steady himself.

"Yeah, I guess you did. I mean, I did say, 'hey,' "I'm not from here. I'm from..."

"The South," Father Benjamin said.

"Yes, you guessed it."

"Me, too. I mean, we two." To my delight, I recognized a soft southern drawl.

"Originally from Louisiana," Taylor added as he slipped past again to retrieve more items from the hall.

"How about you?" Father Benjamin asked. Before I answered Taylor held up a box for Father Benjamin to read the writing on the outside. "Office," he called out, and Taylor squeezed by again.

"South Carolina," I continued. "The Lowcountry. Ever heard of it?"

"Yes, I've heard of it, but I don't 'zactly know where it is." He turned and glanced at the growing stack of boxes in the next room.

"It's on the coast between Charleston and Savannah," I explained.

"Ooh, how beautiful that must be." He turned back toward me. "What pulled you away from all that historical grandeur? You have to be doing something special."

"I dance."

"I knew it," Taylor interjected, holding up the next box.

"Bedroom," Father Benjamin said to Taylor, then continued to me. "Yes, he did say that about you already."

"But when, and how in the world did he know?"

"He mouthed it from behind you when he brought in the first box. It didn't hurt that you have excellent posture. You were standing in first position carrying your dance bag like a prop."

"Oh, how silly of me. Or rather, how obvious of me." I looked down at my feet, giggled and lowered my bag to the floor. I wanted to learn more about them before it was too late so I changed the subject from me. "And which church is yours?"

He turned and swept the palm of his hand in a semi-circle across the air. "This is my church, my mission and my parish all rolled into one. Or rather, the office for all of that. I have no physical church."

"No, he doesn't. Not yet, anyway," Taylor said. He brought the last box in and set it on the kitchen floor. "This is marked *kitchen*." He wiped his forehead with the bottom of his polo shirt. I wondered why he was doing all the work and Father Benjamin just gave directions. Then Father Benjamin grabbed an object I hadn't noticed from the corner by the stove. It looked like a metal pole with wide rings attached. He picked up another right behind the first, attached the rings to his arms, gripped a protrusion below and staggered into the living room, reminding me of a drunken John Wayne.

My mouth dropped open like a mailbox lid on a windy day. Taylor came over and put his arm around my shoulder. "You can close it now."

And I did.

"You have just met the first gay priest of the first gay parish in Greenwich Village, New York City. And, as you can see, he's not just the first gay priest; he's a paraplegic with prostheses and forearm crutches—and he's on a mission."

I diverted my staring at Father Benjamin's back and turned toward Taylor.

"Don't feel sorry for him. He's a groundbreaking entrepreneur and unabashed self-promoter. He declared his own title and now offers his services whenever he encounters any of his gay brethren who might be the least bit interested in God."

When I looked back in the living room, I briefly saw daylight streaming through the normally blocked windows surround his body. I was transfixed. This was what I imagined an angel might look like. At that moment, infused with joy I knew he would do many great things.

After I returned to my apartment below, I thought, *Wow.* This wasn't something I would have found in Beaufort, nor could I imagine trying to explain it to my southern Baptist-born-and-raised daddy. But I wasn't around my daddy anymore and I hoped my new neighbors and I would become great friends.

Over the next few weeks, I saw Father Benjamin briefly in the lobby or on the street talking with his flock. We always exchanged "Hey, have a good day," as we went in opposite directions. Finally, someone in the building was on my schedule. Peaceful and easy-going, he immediately made people comfortable I noticed. He represented something I thought New York needed more of.

For Deni, it took a little longer to get used to him. She wasn't comfortable with someone so unable to move freely like a dancer. Some people seem to be afraid of others' disabilities. Maybe she was projecting the question, "What if that happened to me?" But eventually she came under his spell as well.

For me, having Father Benjamin living above us was reassuring, and I prayed for his dream to work out for him. Even though he was calm, slow talking and a giving man, he was also an underdog fighting his way up and out. But looking at him navigate the front steps or the sea of people on the sidewalk, I wasn't sure if his drive was for spiritual advice or if it had anything to do with his own cross to bear.

After a while, at home Deni and I began to hear sounds from above we didn't recognize, something like the opening and closing of an accordion door across a wood floor. It came at odd hours and increasingly late at night, waking us up. We both were curious but didn't know how to ask without sounding nosey or complaining.

One day as I walked by *The Bagel & I*, the daytime Village café hangout for all sorts of "aspiring everythings," I saw Father Benjamin sitting alone inside at a table by the window. Because I wanted to get to know him better and also to find out what the mysterious noise was, I went in.

The heavy glass door swooshed behind me. The wide rectangular room, filled with heavy wooden tables and chairs, invited an assortment of Villagers to linger over breakfast most of the day, drinking end-less free coffee refills while they mostly discussed the perils of being an artist in today's world. Tall, wide windows with hanging philodendrons edged one side of the rectangle and a counter with numerous coffee machines, while bins of bagels and Danish filled the other.

"Father Benjamin, hey." I thrust my hand out with a grin.

"Oh, hey, Nadine. Excuse me if I don't get up."

"No, of course, don't. I saw you in the window and wanted to say hello. Uh, how are you? Are you settling in okay?" I asked, standing beside his table.

"Yes, thank you. It takes me a little longer than most people but it's all getting done."

"Good, I'm glad to hear that." I didn't want the conversation to end but I didn't know much about him, so I grabbed at small talk to fill the silence.

"It sure has gotten cool quickly since Labor Day," I said lamely.

"Yes, it has," he said, as a knowing smile engulfed his face. "Uh, would you like to join me for some coffee?" He pointed toward the empty chair across from him.

Almost before I sat down, the waiter brought me a fresh cup and refilled his. I suddenly began by talking about me; filling him in on Deni's and my new life in New York. Then I explained about Frank and how much I missed him, and how he was supposed to join me after his film wrapped. Father Benjamin listened to every word without any interruption. I meant to ask him more questions about his life, but I found talking to this man incredibly comforting, even if my stories had nothing to do with God.

"I'm so glad you have someone you care about," he offered, when I paused to sip my coffee. "It's important in this city to find some stability, someone you can count on. I certainly understand about the fragile state of the heart. It's taken me a long time to find a lover who would love me just the way I am. Taylor and I have been together for quite a long time now. I wouldn't have made it to Manhattan if not for Taylor."

Although his face reflected a particular underlying handsomeness and strength, in love, I imagined only very special people saw beyond his handicap. Father Benjamin's compassionate personality left the rest of the world feeling they might be a bit handicapped themselves. He never needed anything from anyone from what I could tell. He gave and gave to others all the time and it seemed they always took his gifts.

"How did you get here?" I asked, once he broke my monologue.

"After getting my degree in religious studies at Brandeis and finishing seminary, we moved to The Village to begin my new career. Taylor could work anywhere. He's a registered nurse by day and registered chef by night."

Taylor fell under the charm of Father Benjamin nearly ten years before they began to make their trek to the city together.

Throughout the conversation, we were interrupted by several people who wandered in for a cup of coffee and were compelled to say hello to him, as if this brief interchange was all they needed to absolve their hedonistic sins and take them a step further in getting somewhere with their lives.

"Father Benjamin, I am curious about something," I finally said when there was a break in the greetings. "Deni and I hear a strange noise every night, and I was wondering if you've heard it too." I didn't want to pry into areas that were none of my business, but I was the one hearing it every night.

Father Benjamin set his coffee down, and with a wrinkled brow, pursed his lips and stared into the white mug for a second as if searching for an answer. I hoped I hadn't offended him by asking. Then another grin began to spread across his face.

"I had no idea you heard that. I am truly sorry." He traced the rim of his cup with his index finger as another friend passed by, saying hello. Leaning in across the table he whispered, "It's just that when I get home at night I'm fairly exhausted. I've just about had it with my prostheses. I'm afraid I simply unstrap, unhook and take the darn things off. The only way I can get around without them is to extend my arms, put my hands on the floor and literally drag my torso around."

I swallowed and then hung my head. "Oh, Father Benjamin, I'm so sorry I even asked. Will you please forgive me?"

"Nadine, it's really no big deal. I'll get some rugs to put across those hardwood floors. Once I do, it should keep the noise down considerably. You'll see."

"Do they hurt? I mean, your prostheses—are they new or something?"

"New? Oh my goodness, no. I've had them all my life as far back as I can remember. Most people believe I had some kind of accident. But I didn't. I was born this way; everything from the knees up works just fine. I come from a farm family in Louisiana, with three brothers, and I can do most anything they can do. I may look crippled to you and everyone else, but growing up, "can't" wasn't in my vocabulary. These darn things are annoying sometimes but they are my lifeline to the "normal" world."

"Well, thank you for clearing that up. I'll tell Deni tonight."

"Oh, my, look at the time. I need to get back to the parish, I mean my apartment, now. Are you going to be okay?"

"Yes, I'm fine. Thanks for the coffee."

"I like having another Southerner for a neighbor. Maybe we can do this again sometime," he added, picking up his crutches and fitting them onto his arms before he took his first step.

"I'd like that."

He walked away with ease through the crowded restaurant. Without even looking up the normally abrasive and impatient New Yorkers moved feet, knees, elbows and bags to make his path easier. I could almost see the magic dust sprinkle overhead as he passed them by.

I ordered a refill and finished my coffee slowly to give him plenty of time to get back to his apartment, without having me pass him on the street or the stairs in our building. He was not the kind of person I would have met back in Beaufort and I wanted to know so much more about him. I wondered if I was I going to become one of his groupies. I certainly hope so.

When I got back to my front stoop, a lanky man on roller skates, with a beard and a long brown ponytail, caught my attention. He might have been ordinary except he was wearing a 1950s pink chiffon and net prom dress, and a green army-issued backpack he wore, along with a silver tinfoil wand. Surrounded by a few men, he laughed and talked while the other people walking across the street lost their hard-edged serious faces and called out hellos to "Rollerina." He flicked his wand at anyone who came near him. I suspected many asked for his magic touch as a kind of spiritual ritual, one that would help them transform themselves from their dreary work world into the entrancing street world of the evening. He picked up one side of his gown, pushed off down the street and around the corner, disappearing into the growing twilight, as if hearing other subjects calling for his presence.

Smiling to myself for being in the middle of this wonderful world where anyone could be who or whatever they wanted, I slipped by Rollerina's remaining court and onto the stoop of my building by the row of mailboxes on the outside wall. After I gathered our mail, I lingered a few moments, partly to let Father Benjamin get as far ahead as possible, and partly because I was dying for a letter from Frank—anything. I turned to go up to our second-floor apartment, flipping through the stack as I went, when I suddenly heard loud footsteps beating a quick path down the stairs toward me. I jumped back, dropped my dance bag and the mail and flattened myself against the wall. My first thought was a robber fleeing an apartment. My heart beat straight out of my chest like in a cartoon. When the sound of the feet got to the landing just ahead of me, I saw, to my amazement, a man wearing a black cape over a black Victorian style suit and a top hat. With one hand, the red satin-lined cape swirled over my head and he gave me a nod, touching the brim of his hat with the other as he grandly rushed out the front door and onto the street.

I stood frozen for at least two minutes before regaining my composure. When no one followed, screaming for the police, I guessed he must be another neighbor. After my heart rate had slowed down enough, I bent over and picked up the scattered mail and dance bag before climbing the stairs. Since Deni wasn't home yet to tell all this to, and there was nothing again from Frank, I headed to the bathroom for a long hot shower.

A few days later, I called Hector to fix a stopped-up sink. While he was there, I decided to ask him about the stranger on the stairs.

"That caped man has been in this building for over ten years." Hector laughed, a deep belly laugh. "Don't mind him; he won't hurt you. He works on Wall Street by day and comes home and turns into Count Dracula by night. It's not every night, just a few nights a week."

Since this behavior didn't seem to disturb Hector, I began to look forward to these encounters, nodding back at the Count whenever we passed in the building.

My neighbors were turning out to be anything but normal, and once I embraced this, the colors of my world intensified. My days were full of new adventures around every corner. As hard as it had been to push back all that happened before I left and get settled in this new life, all I wanted now was for Frank to be with me to enjoy it. Long distance phone calls were ingrained in me, as well as everyone I knew, as a frivolous waste of money, and to be avoided unless absolutely necessary. So I impatiently waited for some word from him, once again sensing Aunt Amelia's ritual at work in my life.

CHAPTER 8
Fall 1971

 When it snows, you have two choices: shovel or make
snow angels.
—Unknown

I N MY DAILY VISIT TO our mailbox on the outside of the
building, I learned to check for mail without opening the
box, by putting my face up close and peering through the
cut-out brass covers, as other tenants do. Every day I checked but
didn't see a thing. Then one day I noticed the corner of something
sticking out of the top of the box. I pulled and out came a large
piece of paper. The words, "Come over to the bar. I think we've
got something of yours," were written in neat compact script, and
signed "T & J." At the top, the letterhead read *Rick's Café Bar.*

According to Father Benjamin, the recently opened *Rick's Café
Bar,* taken from the movie "Casablanca," was already renowned
as a more upscale, certainly more visible S & M gay bar. It was
also the street level business right next to our building entrance.

Not familiar with such establishments or their patrons, *Rick's*
scared me a little, while at the same time made me feel safe.

Thankfully, it wasn't *The Anvil*, *The Ramrod*, or *Peter Rabitts*; older, hardcore gay bars, tucked away with dim lights over dark entrances scattered throughout The Village on less frequented streets. I knew the other bars were there but that's all I wanted to know.

Because of Rick's popularity, it was crowded from four p.m. until three or four in the morning. As long as it wasn't raining or snowing, many of the mostly friendly patrons spilled out onto the sidewalk nightly with drinks and cigarettes in their hands. The inside people, seen through giant windows, stood almost shoulder to shoulder, crowding the patrons sitting at the few small round wooden tables sprinkled throughout the main space.

The regulars began to recognize us walking from the subway to our apartment at night after our restaurant shift ended. Soon, some were waving or raising drinks as we detoured into the street to get around them to our front stoop. In a city rampant with safety issues, we always knew that coming home late at night on our block, we had protectors whose names we didn't know. We didn't ever stop to carry on a conversation, only smiled back and waved as we passed.

Having never seen an S & M bar before I came to New York, let alone been in one, the old-fashioned southern girl in me didn't feel quite right walking into this foreign establishment, but I had to. Daddy and his friends would have heart attacks if they learned where I was going. According to them, being gay was crass, unnatural and an enormous sin worthy of sending one straight to hell. But I had to admit, secretly the bar had an air of mystery and glamour to me, I think, because I only saw *Rick's* from the outside, and everyone seemed to be having a great time.

When I opened the door to this forbidden territory, my eyes narrowed to adjust to the lack of light. Even with all the oversized windows, the bar was half underground, keeping it dark in the daytime. Across the room, I heard clanking and whooshing. I cautiously followed the sound. Empty and in the dim light, the place didn't feel ominous or glamorous. When my eyes adjusted, I found two tall slight men washing glasses and wiping down the counter behind an enormous high-glossed mahogany bar. When they heard me clear my throat, they stopped their activities at the same time. As we made silent eye contact, I took in their uniformity: close-cut hair, black leather vests, flannel shirts, tight jeans, belts with silver studs and earrings in their right ears. Perhaps, they were as startled to see a woman in their bar as I was to see them.

"Can I help you?" the taller one asked, while drying a glass.

"I have a note here that says you have something that's mine." I showed them the note.

"Oh, it's you. Are you Nadine Barnwell?"

"Yes."

"Well, hello there, Miss Nadine. I am Tom and this is Jerry. No joke; we're a couple of real cartoon characters."

I laughed as we shook hands and began to relax. They seemed genuinely nice.

"I think we've got a piece of your mail," Tom said, bending down below the bar. After about a minute of shuffling sounds and muffled cursing, he stood with a grin and an envelope in his hand. He handed it to me.

I gasped and laid the envelope on the bar. There it was; finally a letter from Frank. The postmark showed it was forwarded from Aunt Amelia and Uncle Hamp's house in Asheville.

"Sorry, I think it's been here a while. I hope it's not important. At least it's not Ed McMahon anyway. It would have all kinds of scratch-off shit all over the outside," Jerry said.

I didn't respond, just stared at the envelope; then after a moment, up at them. My eyes watered as I smiled at my too obvious reaction and picked it back up.

"By the look on her face," Tom said to Jerry, "it is 'tres impor-tant'. We must have hit the jackpot. Anything you want to share, girlfriend?"

"No, no—just a friend from home," I waved it in the air. "Thanks, I've got to get to work myself." I backed away toward the door. "I appreciate your keeping it for me."

"Let us know if you get anything for us. This postman doesn't always get it right."

After rushing back to our apartment, clutching the letter in my hand, I found Deni in the living room, twirling around in circles like a runway model.

"Hey, Deni, how's it going? I feel like we pass in the night sometimes even though we do most all the same things."

"Yeah, but you have more work than I do," she said.

I then realized why she was twirling. The living room held our only full length mirror and she was trying on new clothes.

"I'm not sure I'm going to have this month's rent for you right away," she added like an afterthought.

"You what?" I asked, dropping my army-issued jacket and dance bag to the floor, but still holding on to the letter.

"I might need an advance. That's all." In front of the mirror she twisted right and left in an ankle length bias cut green skirt. Her perfectly proportioned body was made for long flowing dresses.

"Deni, are those new clothes?"

She turned toward me. "I needed something new to make me feel good. My clothes are the pits."

I couldn't believe what she said.

But before I reacted, she leaned over her purse on the floor, bending from the waist as if at the ballet barre and without picking it up, pulled out a zip lock bag. From the baggie, she pulled out a joint and lit it.

"Deni, you were quitting that stuff." Deni liked her pot and I never thought much about it since at college it was all around us all the time. But for me, it interfered with what I needed to do with my life, so I always passed when the offers of tokes went around the room at parties or privately at our apartments. Moral judgment had nothing to do with my current reaction; it was only the thought of the money she wasted that should be going to the rent.

"I need something to relax. It all goes so fast in this city," she said through inhale. "Hey, what's that in your hand?"

"Nothing, just a piece of mail—delivered to *Rick's* by mistake." I stuffed it in my pocket.

"You went in there? What's it like?" she asked through another inhale before holding her breath.

"It's just a bar, at least by day. Nothing out of the ordinary."

"I hope it's from Frank. It's been way too long since you've heard from him." She offered me the joint.

"No, no thanks." She knew I didn't smoke marijuana but the offer gave me the opportunity to deflect the question. All I wanted was to get into my bedroom, close the door and have a few moments to read this letter in private.

I looked at my watch. "Oh man, I need to hurry. I'm going to be late for work." I rushed to my bedroom. With the door closed, I sat on the edge of my bed. My hands trembled as I carefully opened the beat-up letter. The original postmark read September, two months earlier. "Jesus," I whispered.

Dear Nadine,

I'm sorry I haven't written before, but I didn't have a real address for months. The movie changed locations frequently, and there weren't any post offices like we have in the States. I hope all is going well with you. I imagine you are in New York doing far-out things. And I'm sorry I didn't know your address, so I had to send this to your aunt and uncle like we talked about.

As I told you in one of my last letters or was it our last phone call, the director liked my work and said he had other work for me after the first movie. How about that? But I didn't know then it would be so far away or hard to be in touch.

No, that's not it. Not really. There is no good way to tell you this, so I'll just say it. I've gotten married. It just happened. We met on the set of the first movie and, well, one thing led to another, and now we're married. She's an actress also.

I know, it wasn't supposed to happen like this.

I will always keep you close to my heart, Nadine. You have been so important to me. You'll never know how much.

Always,
Frank

As the taste of wet salt hit my lips, I crumpled the letter in my hand, fell back on the bed and rolled over into a fetal position. I started to cry out from the pain but stopped my voice with my fist, not wanting Deni to hear me.

Then she shouted through the door from the next room, "I'm going ahead, Nadine, I have to pick something up. I'll see you at work."

I could barely catch my breath so I didn't say anything. Just grateful she would leave first.

"Are you all right?" she added.

I pulled myself together enough to say, "I'm fine; I'm just getting dressed. See you there."

"Okay, see you."

When the front door slammed, I let myself fall into heavy sobs, making my body roll across the bed. My mind couldn't comprehend what I just read, but my body seemed to grasp it immediately. What happened? The unthinkable: Frank was now married to someone else. How could this have happened in such a short amount of time? For a moment, my rational mind tried to explain away the irrational circumstances I found myself in. I lost my baby but I never expected to lose Frank too. The day I delivered Baby Child came rushing back to me like a tsunami. I tried to run from it but wasn't fast enough. Sorrow and guilt entwined my whole body, making me unable to move. From my nightstand, I grabbed the glass locket with the silk cloth from the ritual inside and held it to my heart. I carried it with me to New York, always had it nearby, but this was the first time I realized I needed to keep it closer. After a few minutes, I calmed down, at least enough to hear a voice in my head say the loss of my baby was meant to be. I pulled the necklace away and stared at it. Could I truly find comfort in such a thought? Does anyone really know what is meant to be? I let out a soft moan that seemed to have no end.

I wanted to stay in bed but I knew I couldn't. God only knew what Deni was up to. I had to get up and go to work so I could pay for my apartment and my dance classes. Dance was the only part of my life I felt was actually still in my control. I wasn't going to be defeated. After maybe fifteen or twenty minutes, I got up. In the bathroom, a red blotchy face and puffy red-rimmed eyes reflected back. I splashed cold water on my face, squirted in eye drops, combed my hair and headed off to the subway, hoping the trip uptown would be enough time to erase the pain from my face.

I arrived at *O'Reilly's Steak and Ale* a few minutes late, but the staff was so busy just before the dinner rush, they didn't seem to notice. The early shift already set up the thirty tables with white tablecloths, rolled up silverware in matching napkins and placed water glasses and small vases with fresh cut flowers. In the evenings, customers came for large portions of meat cooked almost any way anyone imagined. Their signature dishes were steaks, burgers, chopped meat, meatballs, Swiss steak, Delmonico, t-bones, prime rib, roast chicken, pork chops and spareribs. No part of the animal was left out. The side dishes were equally large, including overflowing breadbaskets plopped down on each table. The meal size was matched by the sizes of hungry men and women who flocked to this restaurant as if in fear of an imminent depression. *O'Reilly's* was a place where customers would definitely not leave hungry.

The kitchen, not anywhere near as appealing as the front of the house, smelled like nowhere I wanted my food to come from. And although the staff scrubbed the room down every night, fifty years of spilled food and grease never completely washed off the floors and walls.

The wait staff consisted of young to middle-aged, chain-smoking, mostly tight-faced Irish immigrant women with strong brogues. Their scowls reflected what appeared to me to be their main aim in life: to keep a secure lock on the hierarchy of the restaurant. They all had variations of red hair, and with my redhead, at first I seemed to fit right in. But I soon learned the difference. They were actually from Ireland, while I hailed from South Carolina. Their block of country allowed them first-hand knowledge of getting the best tables and tips and to have the busboys, chefs and managers wound around their fingers. Deni and I learned right away not to get in their way, knowing they could make our lives unpleasant or impossible. And because Deni was new to this business, she didn't really know the difference, so I watched out for both of us.

The same night I got the letter from Frank, our boss, Mr. G, asked Deni and me to come see him at the end of our shift at his private table. As usual, he was surrounded by three other men who also ran the restaurant: a day manager and two assistants. As the evening customers thinned out, these four men routinely sat together in the corner, eating mounds of food and having many cocktails. The same waitresses were always assigned to them, a privilege for those few. As we approached, my stomach flipped and my palms began to sweat. *Were we going to be fired? That would be the crowning blow.* I shook the idea out of my head and resolved there was nothing else to do but to go over and find out what he wanted.

"Sit down, ladies," one of the assistant managers said, as he pulled out a chair. I sat down first, then Deni.

"Is there something wrong, Mr. G?" I asked. Everyone called him, "Mr. G." I'm not even sure what his full name was or where any of them were from; only that they were not Irish. All four were olive-skinned, maybe Italian, maybe Middle Eastern. The black suits and white shirts with no ties seemed almost a uniform. Mr. G was the oldest, probably in his late forties, short, with the beginnings of a belly, full red lips, oily skin and pudgy fingers displaying several gold rings. The day manager was also around the same age with a receding hairline, bulging eyes and one gold ring. The two assistant managers could have been twins. Trim, and I guessed in their thirties, they both smoked too much and were always eager to please Mr. G.

"No, no, goodness no. You're both doing a great job."

I thought so. I took every double shift he asked me to take since we started.

"I understand you ladies are here to become dancers. Is that not true?" He picked up his amber-colored cocktail and swirled the ice in the glass. We both nodded. "And the road to becoming a "famous" dancer is not necessarily an easy one. Is that not true?"

We nodded again. My mind sped up, trying to calculate where he was going with this conversation.

"And you really work hard now, don't you?" He didn't wait for a nod this time. "You have to balance this job, your classes and maintain your rent and groceries. I'm sure it's a long day by the end of it, isn't it? You're probably both worn out." He took a swallow from his cocktail.

As plates of food were set in front of each of them by two of the "redheaded mafia," we turned toward each other and then back to Mr. G and the managers.

After they were far enough away, he continued, "We have a proposition for you we think will be very interesting." He cut into a thick, juicy t-bone steak and chewed between statements. "We don't like to see our girls struggle so much. Joey here, and Paulie, and me," he pointed to them with a fork full of steak, "would like to help you out. You both seem like nice, reliable girls. You could make some extra money, you know, by doing a little work for us on the side, that is. In fact, you could probably make about a couple hundred dollars a month each. It's really easy and quick." He kept chewing.

I sat upright in my chair in a panic, thinking of the men who called, wanting an appointment with me at the Hotel Colbert.

"No, no, hon. It's not what you are thinking. Joe, look at the look on Nadine's face."

As all eyes went to me, I sat back with a blank expression, waiting for whatever came next.

"All you have to do is open a post office box in your name. It's that simple. We have some goods that come in from the Philippines from time to time and we just want to see that they are received. Now I suppose we should be paying duty on them, but sometimes it's so much paperwork that the customer goes on to someone else."

The Philippines? First Frank goes there, now someone wants me to pick up mysterious packages mailed from it. I couldn't believe a country I never ever thought about before was coming into my life twice in just a few months. "Well, what kind of goods are we talking about, Mr. G?" I really didn't know what he meant at all.

"You know, small stuff; just some trinkets and maybe some small pharmaceuticals; nothing to worry about. It's all quite legal. We just need a few extra box owners to make this work."

It didn't sound legal to me and I wanted out of there before Deni said yes. I looked at my watch and looked at Deni. "Mr. G," I stood up, "it's getting late and I hate to travel on the subway at this time of night. We'll think about this and get back to you." I nudged Deni's arm. "Deni, it's time for us to go."

Deni still sat at the table, looking at the men. "That's all we would have to do for two hundred dollars a month?"

"Yes, Deni, that's it. Now if you don't want to do this, I have some other people lined up who would jump at the chance," Mr. G added.

I needed to come up with something quick before she said yes. "Deni, I forgot, Father Benjamin said he wanted us to come to his apartment after we got off work tonight. We'd really better be going," I lied.

I started to move away from the table. Deni turned to me and back to them. "We'll consider this, Mr. G. It sounds, aah, like a really good deal."

"It is, girls. You go home and think about it and we'll talk again tomorrow."

"Our next shift isn't until Monday," Deni added.

"Well, maybe we can fix that."

Coming back before Monday was the last thing I wanted to hear. "Mr. G, I really need the day off. I've been working round the clock," I stammered.

"Not a problem. Go home and think it over." They turned away from us as a fresh round of drinks arrived. I pulled on Deni's sleeve and pointed toward the door.

Outside the restaurant, we walked around the corner down 42nd Street toward Grand Central Station, taking the doorway to the subway. At the turnstile, we stopped to find our tokens. When I saw the huge smile on her face, an uneasiness bordering on fear entered my body.

"This could be the answer to our problems, Nadine. We could cut back on our hours at the restaurant and take more dance classes and even have some fun. I think this could really work." Deni put the subway token in the turnstile.

"Deni, no, this cannot work," I followed behind her. "We don't know what they're really importing here. You need more money; we both do, but this is not the answer. Please think clearly before you make a big mistake."

"I'm not doing anything. You've been thinking the worst about me for a while. In fact, you don't even talk with me, not like you used to. Why are you doing this?"

She was right. I put her off ever since I became pregnant with Baby Child. In my mind, I needed to keep her at a distance so I wouldn't confess this huge secret I was keeping from everyone.

"I'm sorry. Every step I take seems to be close to being the wrong step. I guess I feel responsible for you and me both. Frank was supposed to be with us, me by now."

"Yeah, where the heck is he?"

"He—he's not coming."

"What do you mean not coming? Wasn't this his idea to start with?"

"The letter. The one I just got from *Rick's Cafe*—it was from Frank."

Deni sped up and moved to the front of me, turned and stopped me with both hands on my shoulders. "What did he say?"

I hung my head down, hands in my pockets. "That he's not coming."

"Wow. Why?" She stepped back and lowered her arms.

"He's married." I started to cry again. I swore I wouldn't but I couldn't help it.

"No! He's not! Son of a bitch! I—I didn't think he was coming, but I never thought that would be the reason." Deni put her arm around me and I let her keep it there. It felt good to have someone else know and to break through the barrier I created.

We rode the subway home in silence, me bouncing between Frank's letter and our bosses' uncomfortable offer; Deni, off somewhere else. Even though we connected over my problem, she wasn't really with me. I knew I'd lost her.

As I fell off to sleep, the words of Frank's letter smashed up against Deni's lure toward the post office box. These two images began whirling around me like Dorothy's house in the *Wizard of Oz*. I felt dizzy and disoriented until my seemingly unending, uniden- tified turmoil was broken when a cooing sound lifted into my dreams. After searching for the origin but seeing only black, what finally emerged from the sound and began drifting toward me was a fully formed baby. As it got closer, the baby floated into my arms and soon clung warmly to my chest. The melding between us was so rich and perfect, I imagined it was like being in heaven, a place where I could lose myself and not think about all my plans or even returning. In a moment in dreamtime, the baby floated back out from my touch and hung in the air at eye level, just beyond my reach, smiling while backing away, then returning once more to my arms and heart before disappearing back into the black. Surprisingly, I wasn't upset. I sensed that the baby came to comfort me and turn my attention from worrying about all the challenges my new life now brought on.

Of course, I knew this was Baby Child, and her image in a dream came to me for the first time, just as Frank left.

The next morning I awoke to exhaustion. "Some dreams have a way of draining the spirit," Aunt Amelia told me more than once. "But don't be fooled, young'un, there is always a reason for what is brought to you." As I left for the studio, I saw Deni still in bed. This told me she was going to skip class again. So off I went by myself, smiling through my tired eyes, reliving the baby dream, rather than Frank's letter and Mr. G's offer, all the way uptown to my class with Gabriela.

"Nadine, come over here before you warm up, please," my favorite teacher, Gabriela, shouted from the far side of the room, as all the other dancers began taking their places on the floor. She sounded serious. Not her too, I thought.

"Yes, I will be right there." I had on my leotards and tights already, so I quickly stripped off my jeans, blouse and jacket, folded them haphazardly in a pile on top of my dance bag, slipped on my leg warmers and threw a sweatshirt across my shoulders.

Hilda, in the office, told me that Gabriela was once Leland's premier dancer. She joined his company when she was eighteen, toured the world with performances and workshops, then settled into teaching after her second child was born.

116

On the walk across the vast floor, I worried she was going to give me bad news, like telling me I would never make it as a dancer. I stood before her, preparing for whatever came next.

"You may know already that I'm searching for a new member for my dance company," Gabriela said, looking me in the eye.

"Yes, I've heard the talk around the studio." I tied the sleeves of my sweatshirt above my chest to mask my unease. I wanted to join her company after my first class with her. We connected right away and she used me as an example for demonstrating what the class was to do next.

"It takes a special kind of person to move beyond good technique on the classroom floor to being able to perform in a company. A member has to arrange their life so that the company and dance come first."

Uh, oh, here it comes. My negativity took over. She's going to offer the position to someone else and wants to ease the blow to me.

"I've been watching you and I'd like to offer you this position in my company."

"You would? You are?" My sorrows dropped to the floor like hot rocks. Feeling as if I could now float like my dream baby, I threw my arms around Gabriela's neck and hugged her.

She hugged me back briefly and then held me at arm's length. "You have to prove you are up to this now. We're not famous like Leland Lemere's company, not yet anyway, and there's no pay, not yet, but I feel I have gathered some of the finest dancers at this school, if not in New York City to work with. Don't make me wrong." She let go of my shoulders and strode to the front of the class to begin teaching.

I felt I might pop from the joy building up inside of me. To be asked to become a member of her company was an honor. But I couldn't share it with anyone there for two reasons: class was about to begin, and many of them had been studying with her far longer than I and hadn't yet been asked to join any company, maybe never would. So I pushed my lips together and packed away my exuberance for the duration.

The only thing I couldn't stop doing was beaming with pride all during class, knowing I was finally going to get to perform again, and right where the ritual took me, in New York City. Surely this would help me take my mind off Frank, Deni and whatever lay ahead next.

For the next week, I put my whole body, heart and soul into my classes and now added rehearsals with Gabriela's company to my schedule. At the same time, I kept one eye out for Deni, hoping she wouldn't take our bosses up on their 'iffy' offer in a moment of weakness when I wasn't around. I stalled on giving an answer to Mr. G, in hopes he would give up and ask someone else. I wanted Deni to get herself back in school and back on schedule. But to not take the post office box offer and not get fired was a balancing act. We needed the jobs. With Deni buying new clothes and not paying her share of the rent, I could see her losing ground quickly. I looked for signs as Aunt Amelia suggested but I still didn't know what to do.

At the end of the week, on my way to the dance studio, Father Benjamin stopped me in the front vestibule of our building.

"Good morning, Nadine. How are you? It looks like another glorious day on Christopher Street."

"Oh, is it?" I said with a "cross to bear" look. "I haven't had a chance to see the light of day yet." I glanced over his shoulder out to the street for signs of "the glory."

"What's with the long face?" he asked.

"Just some things—you know, work, dance, roommates, money."
Nothing seemed right to me at that moment.

"Got time for some coffee at *The Bagel*? I'd love some company," he said.

I was off from work and rehearsals so I said, "Yeah, sure, great."

The Bagel and I was becoming my favorite place in New York
next to the dance studio. Filled morning, noon and night with
writers, actors, singers, dancers, poets, sculptors and painters, I
melded more into this "on their way" creative crowd each time
I went there. Occasionally, a fully achieved renowned Village
person would show up and have coffee like the rest of us, only
over in a corner avoiding eye contact. The refills were free and
that's all anyone needed to know. We all walked around addicted
to caffeine, running on at the mouth, saying profound and silly
things. We were full of ourselves and unsure at the same time.
Occasionally, someone went over the edge, but no one was sure
if the actions were from an acting scene being played out, a sei-
zure, schizophrenia or the coffee. Everyone would look up for
a moment at the commotion and then quickly resume talking
about ourselves. The room teemed with ambition and bullshit.

"How's it all going, Nadine?" Father Benjamin asked, taking
off his brown leather bomber jacket and propping his crutches
against the wall.

"Oh, fine. It's going fine." My red, woolen pea coat dropped
backwards off my shoulders and over the chair.

"'Working pretty hard, aren't you?" He waved at the waiter
who was on his way over already.

"Yeah, that's me; always working hard." I placed my purse under
my feet and the strap under the leg of a chair, like I was taught
by Hilda and Francis from the dance studio.

Our waiter, Felix, a slight, taut, twenty-something man with tight
jeans and a bright pink tucked-in T-shirt, approached us as if he

were Fred Astaire reaching for Ginger Rogers at a nightclub table. He stopped short of pulling either of us up to dance and took our order for two coffees, one black for me and one with milk and a cinnamon stick for Father Benjamin, along with two bagels with cream cheese. The bagels were made fresh each day and I found I loved them far too much. Bread is always the enemy of a dancer.

"So how is this dance company of yours going?" Father Benjamin asked as Felix glided away. He held his head tipped slightly to the left when he asked a question.

"Oh, it's wonderful." I rubbed the table top as if it were a genie bottle. "I can't believe Gabriela wants me to perform with them already. I am so thrilled and lucky." I raised my face to greet gentle brown eyes above hands with crossed fingers resting on the table almost in prayer fashion.

"Well, how did this wonderful thing happen? Did you audition?"

"Oh, no; there really aren't any auditions, not like for Broadway shows if that's what you mean." Two men approached on their way to an empty table behind us, greeting Father Benjamin as they passed. This allowed me to think through what I wanted to say. "For a modern dancer to join a company, it's that the dancer choose a studio, a notable one that is, and keep taking classes there. Many of the teachers are former Lemire dancers and are also choreographers who want to make their mark. They're always watching the students. In essence, it's like you audition every day. But they get to observe your work ethic, which you can't know from an audition. If you have good technique and the right body type, the choreographer will see in advance if you come to class often, if you get to class on time, how you warm up and how you present yourself in general."

"So you must have done it all just right. Congratulations, Nadine. When is this first performance coming up?" Felix returned with our order, placing it quietly on our table without interrupting.

"It's a week from Saturday. Would you like to come?" I inhaled the smell of the warm bagel and hot coffee as if in prayerful meditation before indulging the senses of my mouth.

"I just might do that." We both stopped our conversation to spread the cream cheese on our bagels and took a sip of the steaming coffee.

"And Deni, what's happening with Deni? She doesn't seem to be going to class with you anymore."

"Oh, so you noticed. You notice everything, don't you?"

"It's my job. I notice what other people aren't noticing about themselves. Sometimes the patterns we get in take charge and before we know it, we're in deep doo-doo. Not the most technical of terms, but I like to talk about the patterns." He whispered the last word.

"You're seeing a pattern with Deni?"

"Not just with Deni."

"Oh." I stared into my cup as if trying to read the coffee grounds.

"What's happening with you, Nadine? Who or what has dumped a load on your head?"

"Hah, that's a nice turn of phrase, Father Benjamin."

"You don't have to tell me if you don't want to. Sometimes it's just enough to know that it is obvious to someone else out there in this crazy self-centered world. Maybe a guy?"

"Yeah, maybe a guy." I shifted in my seat then glanced up and around the room, trying to avoid eye contact.

Father Benjamin waited for me to continue.

After more uncomfortable silence, I blurted out all in one breath. "He isn't joining me in New York. He said he was coming. We were supposed to start our lives together, then he got his first movie job on location, and then, damn him, he got another one." I didn't know how to explain something I didn't understand myself.

"Oh, I'm truly sorry to hear that. Maybe it's not his time yet. Maybe he'll still come."

"Yeah, maybe, but not with me."

"Are you that mad at him? Can't he come a little later? Can't he sort things out a bit first?"

"He's not coming at all, Father Benjamin. I just got a letter from him. He's—he's gotten himself married, it seems." I slumped down in my chair.

"Oh, dear Lord. Oops, sorry." He looked upward and re-crossed his fingers in prayer-like mode. "Now that one, I wasn't expecting," he said, turning his attention back to me.

"My fellow partners in adventure, who couldn't wait to get here with me, are now bailing out. Frank is not coming at all and Deni tells me she can't pay her portion of the rent right now," I said, rising from my slump toward my coffee cup, holding it with both hands in a death grip.

Felix swung by for refills but turned in another direction as I crescendoed.

"But Deni may have it all worked out," I continued, unable to stop myself. "Thanks to our bosses at work, she is now considering opening a post office box for a fee to receive pharmaceuticals from the Philippines."

"Ooo, that's not good. She wouldn't do that, would she?" He picked up his napkin and wiped the corner of his mouth.

"I don't know what she will do. But I can't do it all. I can't make everyone hold up their end of the bargain. All I ever wanted to do was dance. That's what made me different from all those "queens" in my family. This was my ticket out to my own kind of sanity."

"You've got queens in your family?" His eyes gleamed.

"Not those kinds of queens—festival queens, a long line of them; my mama, my daddy's two older sisters and two cousins over in

Ridgeland. There's not that much to it. They ride floats and stand next to the mayor for pictures. The town thinks they hung the moon and the stars. I can't go back. I can't go back. What am I going to do?" I fingered the sugar packets in the bowl.

"You and everybody else. We're a great big group of misfits here in the Big Apple. That's the glue that holds us together."

"So, you're saying I'm in the same sinking boat with everyone else?" That wasn't what I wanted to hear.

"Our boats aren't sinking; they're just taking a different course." Someone called a hello to him from across the room and he waved back before he leaned in to the table. "When was the last time you got out of The Village? Have you explored other parts of Manhattan at all?"

"Well, yeah, the garment district area where our classes are; Grand Central Station area around *O'Reilly's* and some of the Lower East Side, while shopping for our furnishings. You know, the usual places."

"I'm not talking about the walk from the subway to your destination. Have you and Deni been to the Upper East Side? Have you strolled down Madison Avenue on a glorious sunny fall afternoon?"

"No, I haven't done that yet. Too busy, I guess." I ran my finger around the rim of the cup.

"Well, whenever I am truly down, a trip to Madison Avenue usually cures me. It's another world up there, a real fantasyland, a little like I imagine Europe to be. You can see how our rich people live without the plantations. Why don't you try it?"

"I—I guess we could." My shoulders dropped slightly from up around my ears.

"But you need a plan. What are you and Deni doing this Saturday?"

"Nothing, other than doing my own workout at the studio. I told my boss I needed more time off. He wants to know about this post office box idea by next week. We may be out of work by then."

"So take the day and go for a walk on the wild side," he said and then laughed at himself. "Well, it's not really the wild side but it is a big change in scenery without having to fly somewhere. You need to do something different to shake up your routine, your patterns."

"This is the advice of a man of the cloth?"

"It just comes through me; they're not my words."

We both laughed. It felt great. I hadn't laughed in quite a while.

CHAPTER 9

1971-1972

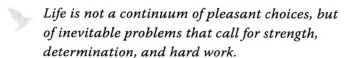

Life is not a continuum of pleasant choices, but of inevitable problems that call for strength, determination, and hard work.
—INDIAN PROVERB

"WHAT ARE YOU LOOKING AT?" Deni asked when she came home that night.

Sitting in my bright green bean bag chair in my powder blue sweat suit with a cup of tea on the floor beside me, I held up the now tattered *New York on $10 a Day*. "We need to go somewhere."

"Go where?" she asked, disappearing into her room to drop her dance bag and change clothes. Whether we were still wearing leotards and tights under our jeans, or our waitressing outfits, both of us had the same habit: put on different clothes as soon as we got home. It was almost like a ritual to us, like declaring the day was over.

"We need to explore other parts of the city..."

"Just a minute, I can't hear you." Drawers opened and closed. Belts and hangers knocked against her closet door.

I raised my voice. "Father Benjamin recommended we take a day and go to the Upper East Side and see something besides The Village, the dance studio and work. Change our focus."

"He did? That's sweet of him," she called back.

I flipped through the pages until I found the section on the Upper East Side. "Listen to this," I said. "*Between 57th Street and 85th Street, Madison Avenue is identified as 'the most fashionable road in New York City.' In this area are where most of the very well-known clothing designers and upper class hair salons can be found. Some of the world's most upscale boutiques are located on Madison Avenue, including Gucci, Prada, Chanel, Oscar de la Renta, Coach, Yves Saint Laurent, Carolina Herrera, Christian Dior, Giorgio Armani and Givenchy.*"

Deni, now in sweatpants and sweatshirt too, leaned against the doorframe. "Wow, that sounds bitchin," she said through a laugh. "Lots of beautiful clothes. I would love to see these shops."

As I scanned the next few pages, I worried about taking her to a place where she might be tempted to spend even more money. Then my eyes landed on *The More Unusual and Affordable Stores*. One place in particular stood out, *Mr. Bertram's Consignment Shoppe*. Consignment sounded intriguing, she agreed, so I made this our goal.

Like our first trip to the city, settling on our destination was simple but actually getting to our destination was more complicated. I laid the red and green-lined subway map on the floor and traced various routes with my finger. If we took the Seventh Avenue Line from Christopher Street at Sheridan Square in the Village, we needed to change trains at Times Square to catch the Flushing Line to Grand Central Station, so we could then hop on the Lexington Line to finally exit somewhere in the vicinity of our destination. Or, we could just exit at Grand Central Station and walk the thirty blocks uptown from there, which should take about an hour at a leisurely pace.

Neither one of us knew what to wear to this new territory we were about to enter, so we knocked on Father Benjamin's door before we left.

"Sorry, but do you have a moment to check out our outfits before we go?" I asked over the phone.

"Of course. I'm always happy to see you two beautiful women whenever."

I pulled Deni away from the mirror and a joint she was about to light. I didn't like the fact that she was using dope more and more.

"Put that down. We're going to let Father Benjamin give us the okay for our outfits." I took the joint and laid it in an ashtray before she got it lit.

"Is this okay to wear?" I asked after Father Benjamin opened the door. Still standing in the hall, I twirled one way and then the other, mimicking a model in black flared slacks, fitted white sweater top and a jean jacket. The long fringe of my suede shoulder bag waved behind me as I twirled. I moved aside and Deni stepped into the spot I vacated, wearing tight bell bottoms, a peasant blouse and a fringed leather vest.

"You look wonderful. I wish I could accompany you just to see all the envious stares you get on the street."

We giggled and struck a pose side by side with one arm over the other's shoulder.

"That's all we wanted to know. We've got to get a move on. The Upper East Side is awaiting us." I leaned in and kissed Father Benjamin on the cheek. Deni gave him a quick wave as we scooted down the stairs and out into the day.

That Saturday morning was a radiant cloudless fall day. Trees, with and without leaves, punctuated the cobalt blue sky on the streets as we walked on Madison Avenue north above Forty-Second Street. Teeming with determined stylish people, most of them in a hurry even on a Saturday, the sidewalks also offered an abundance of saffron and crimson mums and snap-dragons brazenly adorning almost every storefront window box we passed. The strange and wonderful costumes of The Village characters I'd become accustomed to transformed into costumes of another sort. The "high society," Father Benjamin spoke of, was dressed somewhat uniformly in brown, beige and sienna, as if on their way to a polo match or steeple chase. As we strolled for blocks, nudging each other to look at different things as they caught our eyes, we tried not to get tangled in the leashes of dogs so tiny, I had to look twice to be sure they weren't squirrels or river rats. To me, a dog should be as big as your kid sister, or what was the point?

On 73rd Street, we found a placard with the address of *Mr. Bertram's Consignment Shoppe.* However, that was all we found. A store didn't appear to be attached. On further inspection, I found a small black sign with gold letters hanging between two street level shops, pointing up a narrow staircase. Apparently, advertisement wasn't necessary.

Upstairs, we pushed open the door and a light bell rang. Inside, we stopped to get our bearings. A small store, on one side was a long high checkout counter with a cash register and piles of scarves and jewelry. Double-hung racks full of clothes lined the walls on either side, and wooden bins filled with a variety of items located in the center. At the far end from where we stood, two mannequins, adorned in evening clothes, posed in front of a picture window overlooking the avenue.

Three female customers, all old enough to be our mothers, methodically rooted through every hanging rack and bin. A short, over-bleached blonde wearing spiked heels and ornate gold colored jewelry, held a dress on a hanger under her chin in front of a mirror. A heavy-set brunette in a gray suit with a skirt and a black handbag over her arm, flicked the hangers quickly to her left as she scanned the rack for her size. At the far end, a black-haired bony woman in oversized white rimmed glasses and a red pantsuit, bent over a bin. When I looked again, I thought the woman behind the counter could have been a twin to the first one. Skinny, blonde and plastic-haired, wearing too much makeup, her bracelets jangled as she lifted her eyeglasses up to her forehead and back, while she checked paperwork and price tags. I heard a man talking on a phone but didn't see him. The doorway behind the counter was covered by long curtains.

As Deni and I headed in different directions to begin rummaging through the stacks and racks like the other patrons, the old wooden floors creaked beneath our feet. I picked up white silk blouses with ties at the neck, cardigan sweater sets in taupe and pale pink, gold lamé belts and navy double-breasted blazers with gold buttons. I put them all back and continued digging, hoping to find something more suited to my taste or my age.

Deni and I met in the middle, picking through a bin piled with the smaller accessories: scarves, belts, purses and lingerie priced for a quick sale. As I held up two Gucci scarves for a closer look, a man came near us. I glanced at him between the scarves, so as not to be obvious. Tall and slender with salt and pepper hair long enough to be tucked behind his ears, he bent over to pick up items that dropped to the floor after people had dug to the bottom of the box. *He must be the voice I heard behind the curtain.*

"Now, where are you two lovely ladies from?" he asked, as he replaced the items.

We both looked up at him. In a dark navy three-piece suit, burgundy tie and unusually erect posture, I was struck by his elegance. Father Benjamin knew what he was talking about.

"We're from South Carolina," I said, using my finest drawl.

"Oh, are you now? Just visiting?"

"No, not exactly," I said, looking from the scarf to him and back.

"How long have you been in the city?" He smoothed his tie.

"Only a few months," Deni joined in.

"I'll bet you've come here to do something fantastic." He picked through the rack behind us.

There's that sign on our backs again. "We're studying dance... at The Leland Lemere Studio." I shifted my eyes to see if this meant anything to him.

"Oh, one my favorite dance companies," he said, as he swirled around us and over to another part of the store with a pair of pants in one hand and a matching jacket in the other.

Deni and I exchanged glances.

"You've heard of Leland Lemere?" I asked. "I mean, a lot of people don't know much about modern dance."

"Oh, but you are in New York now, my dears. I certainly know about Leland Lemire." In fact," he draped a sleeveless, A-line solid red dress on a dress form, "many of my regular customers were former dancers and patrons of the arts." As he tugged the dress into place, zipped it up the back and smoothed the front to fit over the curves of the headless mannequin, I noticed a large gold and diamond ring and manicured fingernails. "I am Mr. Bertram." He turned, bowed and announced with a pomp fitting the image he presented.

I guess I didn't expect Mr. Bertram, even if he was a real person, to be in the store while we were there.

Deni and I exchanged glances again.

"And you are?" He folded his hands in front of him.

"I'm Nadine Carter Barnwell, and this is Deni Hansen," I replied to his summons. He was the owner of a recognizable store in the very respectable Upper East Side, I rationalized, so being polite was what I was taught. His eyes darted between the two of us as if searching for something more.

"Deni?" he said, after staring at her until she looked up.

"It's short for Denise. My father wanted a boy, I guess." Deni broke the stare and pulled a blue cable knit sweater with pink and yellow flowers on the front from the bin, and held it up to her chest.

"That certainly would have been a shame," he cooed. *I began to not like or trust him.*

Then he turned toward me and put out his hand. When I lifted mine, to my surprise, he grabbed it, turned it over and kissed the back of it. Then he quickly did the same thing with Deni. I was stunned, but I saw that Deni liked it.

"Welcome to the city. It's a pleasure to meet you both," he said.

The woman behind the cash register called his name to come to the phone. He left us.

Deni and I turned our backs to the counter, put hands over our mouths and giggled like twelve-year olds. *What a pompous man.*

After several more minutes of unsuccessful digging, I whispered to Deni that I was ready to leave. As we headed for the door, Mr. Bertram called out with his hand over the phone receiver, "Oh, please don't go yet. I'll be just a minute."

I wanted to explore more of Madison Avenue before it got too late, but Deni gave me a look that said she wanted to stay and see what he was going to do next. Mr. Bertram hung up the phone, poked one arm through the curtain and pulled out two hangers with clothes.

"Now this is perfect for you. Nadine, isn't it?" He held it up in front of my body first, then put it in my hands.

He did the same thing with Deni, only he placed his hand on her shoulder as he held up the blouse in front of her chest with the other. While we stood still, holding blouses up to our chests, he stirred up ancient layers of buried dust from a box, while pulling out accessories to go with them.

I had to stop him. "I'm sorry," I said, "we just don't have the money for all of this but thank you so much anyway." I grabbed the blouse out of Deni's hand, put everything down and headed for the door. *I didn't like this man or his fake generosity.*

"No." he protested. "I won't have you leaving emptyhanded." He picked up the two blouses from where I laid them and flung them across the cash register at the woman ringing up another customer and said, "Bag these for the ladies. They are on me." He turned toward us with a Cheshire cat-like grin and leaned back against the counter.

My eyes rolled. We were trapped. Then I asked to use the bathroom. I needed to take advantage of this situation. New York women have to have strong bladders because no one is allowed to use any store bathrooms unless they make a purchase. Signs were everywhere: For Patrons Only.

When I came out, Mr. Bertram and Deni were huddled by the counter. Deni giggled as he wrote something on a piece of paper.

As I approached I heard, "Good, then it's settled. I will pick a restaurant, and you pick a night." He folded the piece of paper and put it in his suit pocket.

Puzzled, I looked at Deni.

She grinned back at me as if she had solved all of our problems. "Mr. Bertram wants to take us out to dinner, Nadine. Isn't that great?"

I was stunned—again. "Yeah, that's great. We'll let you know." I grabbed Deni's arm again and mumbled something about needing to get going. We were supposed to get away from bad deals—not repeat them. Deni didn't know what I was talking about, but she played along with me once she saw my face. Mr. Bertram handed us our bags, we said our thanks and goodbyes, exited through the tinkling door and down the stairs to the street.

Once outside, I kept us moving with some speed down the block before we stopped at the far corner. "Deni, what have you done? Who is this man? You can't make a date with a complete stranger. What do we know about him?"

"Nadine, stop it. Why are you always so paranoid about everything? He's a nice respectable man and he wants to take us out to dinner. We could, or at least I could use some fine dining. No one else is going to do this."

"We can't take off from work to go out to dinner. We have bills, remember?"

"Fine, I will go out with him and you can stay home or go to work." She turned from me and stepped off the curb.

This was not an option. Crossing the street, I followed a few paces behind her, dodging and weaving through the people all headed right at us. I felt an unidentified discomfort about this man but had no proof to give to Deni.

A few days later as we were getting ready to leave, Deni announced, "I've decided not to take Mr. G's offer."

"You have? I'm glad you came to your senses," I said.

"Mr. Bertram said it wasn't a good idea. He is really kind. Wants to protect us."

I was so relieved I didn't argue. Or ask questions like, "When did you talk to Mr. Bertram again?"

At the end of our shift at work that night, Mr. G summoned us again to his corner table.

"We need an answer, girls. This is a special offer just for you, but believe me, there are others who would gladly do this with no hesitation."

I was more than thrilled, inwardly, of course, to answer him. "Mr. G, this is a generous offer, I—we—know. And we thank you

133

for thinking of us. But we have decided," I looked at Deni for support or confirmation but got none, "not to do it at this time. I hope you understand."

His face reddened and stiffened. "You are making a mistake, girls." He picked up his drink and took a large swallow. That seemed to calm him down. "Okay, not now, I understand. You're too new to the city. We'll talk again when money gets tighter for you. And it will."

We backed away, slipped on our jackets and headed home. We didn't get fired or shot, so we were both happy with this outcome.

Father Benjamin wanted to hear all about our trip to Madison Avenue so when a break in our schedules matched up on Friday, I met him at *The Bagel & I* for coffee. He was already seated with his crutches leaning against the wall beside him when I came from dance class, weighed down with my usual gear, wearing a bright blue tam on my head. We hugged briefly and I pulled out the chair across from him and sat down.

Across the room, a man in a pink sleeveless T-shirt and black skin-tight jeans broke into a soft-shoe, moving toward us between the tables. "Father Benjamin, Nadine, what can I get you?" he asked breathlessly.

"Felix, it's good to see you too. How's it going? How are your tap lessons? Why am I asking? You've just shown me. They must be going fine."

"Aah, so, so SO-SO. I tap and I tap and I tap and I'm still work-ing here. But I'll never give up. You've convinced me that giving up is for sissies. And I would never want to be called a sissy, now would I?" Felix placed the hand holding his order pad on his right hip and raised his other hand in the air, admiring his fingernails.

We both laughed and a few people at tables nearby joined us laughing too.

"I'll have my regular: decaf coffee with milk and a cinnamon stick," Father Benjamin said. Then he added, "And bring one of those lovely muffins I see on the counter. That will do me fine. Anything else for you, Nadine?"

"No, just a refill on the coffee. I've really got to cut back on my caffeine. But I'll start tomorrow."

"So, how was it? Did you find your adventure as charming as I said you might?" Father Benjamin asked.

"Charming. Yes." I swept sugar residue off the table in front of me with my hands. "We walked for blocks, window shopped at the most amazing stores, and gawked and giggled at the people passing us by for almost thirty blocks. That's how long it took us to get to our destination, *Mr. Bertram's Consignment Shoppe.*

Everything was just as you described it—well—almost everything."

"Why? What happened there?"

"The owner was there."

"And?"

Felix came back with our order and was off again in a flourish. We both moved the plates and mugs around for a few seconds, looking for the right arrangement. Another subtle ritual we do every day and don't think about, Aunt Amelia would have reminded me.

"I guess I didn't expect the owner to actually be there. He seemed to really like us; well, Deni more than me. He swooped down on us almost as soon as we entered the store. He introduced himself and tried to give us things. He got our phone number and address from Deni before I got her out of there."

"What is wrong with that?"

"He's sleazy to me. I don't know exactly, but I don't trust him and Deni really liked the attention. It's just that she decided to turn down Mr. G's offer at work after meeting Mr. Bertram. I've got a bad feeling about all of this."

"Pay attention to those feelings. You've got them for a reason and the reason isn't to tune them out or go against them. It's much better to get out of the clutches of Mr. G though. I didn't like the sound of that deal one bit."

"Yeah, I guess it is better. We'll just have to stay tuned to see where this goes."

Soon there was a steady flow of people stopping at the table to greet Father Benjamin. We lost the thread of our conversation but I enjoyed watching his admirers admiring him. Just like all the other people, I always felt better being around him. What a gift.

By spring, Mr. Bertram had become a part of our lives. The more lunches and dinners he suggested, the more I saw Deni's interest in our lives and her dance career wane. I declined most of his offers and tried to keep my distance. He was flamboyant, seemed to know lots of people and liked spending money on us. But I still didn't trust him. To me, he was intriguing and strange at the same time. To Deni, he was just plain intriguing. I think Mr. Bertram knew who to shower his attention on from the start. *Why on earth does he want to spend so much time with two young, naive, starving artists from South Carolina? Surely, the city is full of far more interesting, sophisticated and well-off women.*

There were trips to the Metropolitan Museum of Art, to The Guggenheim and the Museum of Natural History. With all this attention, Deni skipped even more dance classes, and as I took on more hours at work, Deni took on less. Then one afternoon there was yet another offer.

"Please," he pleaded on the phone. "Please come with me tomorrow. I want to take you both to a restaurant I know you will just love. It's in the East Village. Have you ever had real Italian food?"

I didn't know what he meant by "real" Italian food. Food was food, Italian or otherwise, as far as I was concerned. But I had already left Deni alone with him too many times. "Sure, we can make it," I said, as Deni came through the front door. I put my hand over the receiver and mouthed, "It's Mr. Bertram."

Her face brightened.

"When, and where and what time?" I asked.

"I'll pick you up at 7 o'clock—tomorrow. Can you make that?"

"Uh, Deni, is tomorrow at seven okay with you?" I held the phone away from my ear so they both would hear. I didn't want to go but I also didn't want them to make any new plans without me. She mouthed a "yes" from across the room.

"Sure, we'll be ready."

"It's a rather nice restaurant, so look your best. *Ciao!*"

"Ciao?" I said with my hand over the receiver again. He sounded like such a snob. "Yeah, goodbye, Mr. Bertram."

"Please call me Bertram."

"Oh, I forgot. Goodbye—Bertram." If my daddy heard me saying, *ciao* to someone, he'd roll on the floor in laughter for its pretentiousness. And I wasn't sure I would remember to, or even wanted to, call him Bertram.

The next night we were ready by seven. Dressing up wasn't something I did very often so I enjoyed the feeling of it. My red silk blouse suited the ankle-length black straight skirt I already had. I added black boots, a shawl and a small black purse. Deni looked stunning in the black cocktail dress Mr. Bertram gave her. Scooped necked and ending above her knees, it fit her waist and bust like a fifties movie star.

As we waited for Mr. Bertram on the front stoop, the early evening activity had started its transformation of ordinary people into highly costumed and leather-adorned characters. Count Dracula opened the door behind us, stopped to adjust his top hat, tipped the brim with two fingers toward us and rushed out into the evening. Across the street, three men in variations of tight jeans, tight shirts, leather vests and jackets, with silver chains hanging down from their waist below the vest, stopped to light cigarettes. Tom and Jerry whistled and waved at us as they wiped down the tables on *Rick's Café's* patio. By the time we got back, the sidewalks would be filled with crowds of people, talking and laughing too loudly as they moved in and out of the restaurants and bars throughout the streets and avenues. My heart filled with pride as I looked around at this wonderful and wacky life I was in. We were so lucky to have found this apartment. We couldn't lose it.

Shortly, Mr. Bertram arrived in a cab. Looking even more elegant with his gray and white hair slicked back and wearing a black suit, blue shirt and purple tie, he got out and opened the door for us. As he offered his hand to help me, I also noticed gold and jeweled rings on his fingers.

"My, you both look ravishing this evening," he said.

"Thank you, Bertram," Deni said in her sweetest southern accent.

I rolled my eyes.

In the cab, he talked excitedly about what went on in his shop that day. The acquisition of the cast-off clothes of wealthy women already bored me and the evening had only just begun. As we pulled away, Rollerina, twirling in a fifties prom dress and pulling out a magic wand, caught a glimpse of us. He rolled in front of the cab at the stoplight, grinned and lightly tapped our cab with his wand. This made me laugh out loud but it didn't interrupt Mr. Bertram's conversation one bit. And the more he talked, the more Deni focused on him.

At that time of night, it didn't take long to get to the East Village. We pulled up to the cleanest building for blocks around; a stately sand colored structure with massive windows with a small sign reading *Cafe Dellagio.*

As Mr. Bertram entered, the maître d' sprang to attention with such impeccable timing that I imagined he followed Mr. Bertram's every movement across town through a personal crystal ball. Within seconds he escorted us to a table. Mr. Bertram said "hello" to several people seated along the way as he paraded us to our table. Almost at once, chairs were pulled out, our wraps taken from us and the headwaiter asked for our drink orders.

"Let me order for you, ladies," Mr. Bertram said.

"That would be fine," Deni said, while I took in the decor. The elaborate tabletop floral arrangements situated between dining tables caught my eye first; then the stunning dining tables; each with a smaller arrangement on white linen tablecloths; two glasses at each setting and multiple silverware indicating multiple courses. On the walls hung enormous paintings of Italian scenery, and soft Italian arias played through the ceiling speakers.

Ornate was an understatement. I blinked a few times to be sure I wasn't hallucinating.

I turned my attention back to the table as the waiter presented a bottle of wine for Mr. Bertram's approval, opened it and handed him the cork which he sniffed with great drama. We clinked glasses and sipped. It was incredible. Before I took my second sip, an antipasto salad large enough for a whole meal for both Deni and me was brought to the table.

"Please eat, enjoy but leave room for more. You are about to partake in a magnificent seven course meal in the fine old world Italian style," he said.

More waiters swirled around us as the meal progressed, with new plates being brought and old ones taken away in a highly choreographed manner. Mr. Bertram continued his one-sided conversation, occasionally asking only yes or no questions: did we like the restaurant? the cab ride? Did we have enough new clothes? Then the crowning one, "How are the two of you doing—financially, that is?"

"We're doing fine," I broke through his monologue to stop him.

"No, we're not. It's dismal," Deni corrected me in a little girl whine I hadn't heard before.

I stared at Deni in disbelief. The waiter came over and poured more wine and Mr. Bertram ordered another bottle with just a slight nod.

"We pay our bills, Bertram. That is all we need to do right now," I tried again. Quickly, I added, "Wow, this sauce is incredible. What do you think they put in it to give it this flavor?"

"Well, now, I'm not sure. Let me see." He couldn't resist being the hero and try to find an answer to my question. It worked. He took a bite, concentrating on the taste rather than his lecture. "Paulo," he called out to the owner talking to customers at another table, "when you get a moment, please." He made a waving motion for Paulo to come over. "Tell me, what are the ingredients in this wonderful sauce, my friend? My ladies would like to know."

His ladies! Would this night ever end?

"If I tell you, you would try to make it at home and maybe not come here to eat anymore," Paulo said through a thick Italian accent.

"Oh, Paulo, you know that would never happen."

"All I can tell you is it's in the herbs. Would you like a little more on the side, Miss?"

"No, thank you, I am just fine," I said, "It's delicious, though." Mission accomplished.

The owner poured more wine all around before he left us.

Mr. Bertram finally stopped talking to listen to Deni talk about our struggles, like the Hotel Colbert, the drug dealers and finding jobs. I tried to interject our accomplishments as a balance. I spoke of finally being a dancer in New York City and the importance of Leland Lemere's dance school in our lives. I wanted to leave the post office box situation out of the conversation and hoped Deni wouldn't get that far before Mr. Bertram took over again.

"Ladies, I know what we need to do next," he said. "I need to take you on a ride around the city."

"Oh, how lovely." Deni nearly squeaked.

My head was beginning to spin from the wine, and all I wanted to do was go home and sleep off the whole night. "No, I can't do that. Really, it's too late."

"Then I will put you in one cab, and Deni and I will go in another to meet some of my friends."

An even worse idea. I wasn't going to let Deni go off with him alone, so I reluctantly agreed to go.

In the next hour, he introduced us to his friends: Suzette, Mary Louise, Tanya and Valerie, who all lived in separate apartments in the same building off Madison Avenue in the thirties. I hadn't expected these were the friends he meant. After my initial surprise, I realized they were not much older than us and seemed like women I could be friends with. Suzette's apartment was decorated in white and blue French provincial; Mary Louise's, in traditional style with earth tones; and Tanya's in a tiger and leopard animal motif. But when I met the exotic Valerie and entered her apartment, I finally caught a glimpse of what I thought was going on. Her apartment looked nothing like our make-shift setup on Christopher Street. Mr. Bertram pointed out every piece of furniture. With no overhead lighting, it was romantically lit with side table lamps and a floor lamp. The soft dark leather couch had matching arm chairs and ottomans. A metal abstract sculpture sat atop a glass and wrought iron coffee table. Lush Hudson River landscape paintings hung on the walls; imported oriental area rugs covered the mahogany floors and mauve velvety curtains hung over white sheers.

We learned that Valerie came to New York in her early twenties, just like we did. After trying to make it as an actress, she found herself on hard times. Mr. Bertram "befriended" her and set her up in an apartment.

"Something like this could be yours," he said, gesturing around the room with his gaudy gold ring-laden fingers, before placing his arm on Deni's shoulders.

Like hell it could.

For the second time that night, I wanted to get away, get out, get back to my tenement building as quickly as possible and I wanted Deni to come with me. We were trapped for the moment, but I did some more fast talking. "It's really late, Bertram and I'm not feeling well." I feigned distress.

"Nadine, are you all right?" Deni looked genuinely concerned.

"I will be, once I get home."

My excuses were quickly accommodated but not in the way I planned. I was put in a cab for home but Deni didn't come with me.

The next morning I awoke with a pounding head; not just from the wine, but from the late hours and the proposition from Mr. Bertram. Oh, and Deni. I bolted out of bed and headed for her room. "Oh, shit!" I yelled. She wasn't there. But I didn't have much time to try to figure out where she was. It was already late, and I had dance rehearsals in an hour, and then another shift at work.

Rehearsal that day was a disaster. First, I was late, then I couldn't remember the sequences and my muscle control was so poor, I couldn't hold any of the poses.

Gabriella pulled me off the dance floor. "Nadine, you're a mess today. What is going on?"

"I—uh—I don't know." I couldn't give her a quick answer, so I gave no answer at all.

"You've always known what to do and when, always been on time and all that good stuff that most of the other people don't give a hoot about. You're certainly not here today, though."

She didn't have to say anything else. I knew that if I didn't hold up my end of the bargain, if I didn't do it better than anyone else, there was a line of new dancers arriving on the scene every day from all over the country. They would be more than happy to take my place.

I apologized, making a feeble excuse about my health and promised to be back on track the next day. Then I showered, changed and headed off to work.

"Where's Deni?" was the first thing Mr. G asked when he saw me.

"Uh, she's sick. She asked me tell you, and I forgot."

"She's supposed to call in when she can't make it. This is getting to be a real problem now, Nadine."

Since Deni spent less time at our apartment and almost no time at the dance studio, I rarely saw her anymore. She made it clear. She preferred for me to stay out of her private life. When I hesitated or tried to warn her, she told me she could take care of herself. I had no choice but to leave her alone.

That night he and the managers huddled in their corner at the far end of the room. They watched me as I darted around the tables, trying to take care of all my customers. I didn't like the vibrations I got from them. With their heads lowered almost to their plates, and olive oil shining off the rims of their mouths, they talked quietly among themselves.

At the end of the shift, Mr. G called me over again and asked, "So, Nadine, are you and Deni ready to take on the little extra work we discussed a few months ago?"

I wanted to have time to find an excuse rather than give a yes or a no. "Yes" was out of the question, and saying "no" right away might jeopardize our jobs. So I didn't say anything.

"You know business is a bit slow. We are probably going to have to lay off some of the wait staff in the next week or so."

I knew better. Business was anything but slow.

"I'm sorry. I almost forgot. Yes, we're still considering the offer. I will ask Deni again when she feels a little better." Unbelievably, that series of lies worked. He must have really wanted us to do this for him because he easily gave me more time.

As I left work that night, a sinking queasy feeling in my gut told me my new life was already teetering on the edge of collapse. I knew this job was coming to an end. Oh, how exhausting it can be on the way to finding your real life.

CHAPTER 10

1974-1975

It is by chance that we met, by choice that we became friends.
—MILLIE HUANG

O N A SATURDAY AFTERNOON IN September, I eagerly returned to Christopher Street to the smells of home cooking floating through the hallways, enveloping apartments on every floor.

For months, Father Benjamin planned a celebration/thank-you party for all those who supported his Village parish. I had no intention of missing this, no matter what else was going on. I desperately needed to do something fun. With the night off from work and only a short rehearsal scheduled at the studio, I welcomed this party.

Double ovens and ample counter space were not staples in tenement, pre-war buildings, so Father Benjamin asked if he, or rather, Taylor, could use my kitchen to do most of the cooking, leaving his kitchen for mostly cold things and a staging area. I imagined Taylor running up and down the one flight of stairs between our two apartments all day long while he created masterpieces of gastronomic delight.

My apartment door opened as soon as I pushed the key into the lock. I found Taylor standing in the florescent light at the kitchen counter beside the sink, his back to me. From behind, he appeared as neat and pressed as a soldier, only this time he wore black tight fitting slacks, a tapered green checkered cotton shirt and a white apron tied around his waist and neck. As he turned toward the door, his almost black shag-cut hair lifted in the air. A different Taylor faced me, his apron anointed with splotches of flour, drips of oil and tomato sauce. In his hands, he held a wooden cutting board loaded with hunks of cheeses, grapes, pears and apples and small dishes of olives and nuts.

"Ta da," he chirped and held the food out for me to see. As always, he wore a smile on his face; a genuinely happy and focused person, Taylor loved to cook.

"Don't open that oven, under any circumstances, Miss Nadine," he called out. I flattened myself against the cabinets as he sped by.

"No, I would never think of it. Something sure smells good, though." I spied the mess out of the corner of my eye. Every inch of counter space was piled high with bowls, boxes, bottles, canisters, cutting boards and vegetable trimmings. In the sink, pasta drained in a colander.

"It better be or 'Benjie' will kill me." His voice trailed off as he disappeared into the upstairs apartment.

Don't open the oven, I repeated to myself after the door closed. He had no idea how little I understood about cooking.

I called out for Deni. She promised to be back for this party. When I didn't find her, I tried to phone Bertram's shop but got no answer. I didn't have another number for him. Deni wished to be left alone and that's what I had to do, even if it seemed wrong.

Lingering in the shower, I willed the hot water to wash away all my mounting worries. Aunt Amelia's words in her last letter came to me. "Life is a puzzle. As soon as you figure out one section, the other section doesn't look like it will fit. Try to focus on what you are there to do and let everything else work itself out." I knew she was right but it was harder and harder to drop the issues and people around me. *Wouldn't it be wonderful if all the misaligned pieces of my puzzle would somehow remold their shapes and find a perfect fit in my life?*

Looking in my closet through the few choices of clothes to wear, I searched for something a little more feminine than what I wore on a daily basis. To the side behind my jeans and jackets, I found the lavender dress I'd bought when I thought Frank was still coming. *It's time to bring this out of the shadows.*

Ditching my usual ponytail, I lightly blow-dried my hair, guiding my natural waves to fall freely to my shoulders. After adding pale pink eye shadow and mauve lipstick, I stepped into my dress. The rayon, bias-cut ankle length dress lay smoothly over my body. Neither too tight nor too loose and the fabric swayed behind me as I made a slow spin in front of the mirror. Perfect.

The bedside clock said seven o'clock. I was late. Grabbing a bottle of wine left by Mr. Bertram, I headed toward the stairs. As soon as I reached the first step, the sound of the party elevated my mood. I loved going upstairs to visit Father Benjamin. He had real furniture and a sense of design. My apartment was still basic "starving artist's" sparse with milk crates, boards and bricks for shelves and unmatched shiny beanbags chairs. I opened the door and let myself in. Once past the kitchen, his living room transformed into a "garden of delight" and took my breath away.

In the center, a long table stretched across the room with a brightly colored tablecloth from *Pierre Dieux*, angled to show corners of oak beneath. Candelabras, baskets of fruit, wineglasses, beautifully presented food in every dish and bowl imaginable and flowers, many flowers, topped the table.

Back in his kitchen, from the shadows I scanned across the room through all the people. I knew Father Benjamin inspired affection in others but I didn't realize how far his charm reached. Black, white, Asian and Hispanic men and women of all ages, young to middle-aged to white-haired were already grouped, deep in conversations. Their look varied as well: ankle length dresses, crocheted shawls, patched jeans, tailored jackets and leather vests, mixed with afros, pony tails and beards on men and long glistening hair on women.

When Father Benjamin spotted me, he waved for me to come over to where he stood holding court.

I put the wine on the center table and pointed to it so he knew it was from me. He mouthed a "thank you."

"Let me look at you." He stepped away from his group, grabbed his left crutch with his right hand, moved it under his right arm, and with his left hand, he moved me out an arm's length. "You look absolutely magnificent this evening, Nadine. I don't believe I have ever seen you look so lovely." Then he glanced over my shoulder and asked, "Where is Deni?"

"I don't know. She didn't come home again; this time, for two nights. The last I saw her she was with our new friend, the one with the dress shop."

"Oh my, my; Mr. Bertram, isn't that his name? I'm so sorry to hear this. New York can do that to people." He shook his head and escorted me across the room and back to the food table.

Father Benjamin gave me a quick rundown of the offerings. Besides roasted turkey and baked ham, Taylor made a bruschetta with chopped tomatoes and basil, a crostini with a red pepper confit, tiny green beans with fennel and olives still crisp and warm. I was overwhelmed with what came out of my little kitchen and couldn't wait to sample every bit of it. But before I got my first bite, Benjamin introduced me to several people near the table as his "rising star" neighbor. I wasn't comfortable with his description but it worked as an icebreaker. Someone else came in the door and he left me to greet them.

Finally, I inched my way back toward the food and I piled my plate high. I planned to let myself eat whatever I wanted, knowing it was Saturday, a party and Taylor was the chef. Guilt be damned.

At the edge of a larger gathering, I listened to a couple, one a painter, the other a sculptor, explain where they were headed in the next few days. As I eased closer to their conversation, I heard they were moving out of New York the next day. It seemed that after twenty years, they were tired of the grime and crime. Their choice, a new life in New Mexico.

"New Mexico?" someone asked. "What the hell is out there besides cactus and lizards?"

"Santa Fe," they said simultaneously.

"Isn't that just an old cowboy town?"

"Yes, it's a bit rough, but a new artist colony is developing." More people gathered around by now. "We've had enough of the concrete and asphalt and of every part of the city being under construction all the time. We've been mugged three times and our loft broken into twice. We're tired."

As difficult as the challenges of setting up my new life in New York were, I couldn't imagine leaving for any reason. After they finished their story, they said their goodbyes to everyone right there. I felt I was peeking into a time machine: their time machine. *Hadn't they once been just as awestruck and enthusiastic as me? What really happened to them?*

The food was exquisite, my mouth salivated for more, and there were no dance mirrors around the walls reminding me that eating was my enemy, so I unabashedly went back to the table for my second helping. Because I expended so much energy in class and rehearsals, I rationalized I deserved to eat like a stevedore. I thought I was lost in my own world of overindulgence, but while biting into another crostini, I noticed a man watching me from across the room. Then someone started talking to him and he turned away. But I kept looking. Very well put together, he was average height, perhaps five-feet-eight or nine inches tall, wore a charcoal gray mock turtleneck shirt and pleated black trousers with an expensive looking silver-buckled leather belt. With a trimmed beard and the beginning of a receding hairline, at first glimpse, I couldn't tell how old he was. But the warmth of his smile as he talked to others seemed genuine enough.

I could tell he was someone everyone already knew or wanted to know. Once he saw me looking at him, he smiled back. I felt as if I were caught doing something wrong and didn't know what to do. But I didn't have to do anything because once Father Benjamin picked up on this interaction, he pulled the man away from his latest group and led him straight toward me. I quickly tried to swallow the crostini, but it went down the wrong pipe and I began to choke. So I turned my back and took a huge swallow of wine. As the obstruction cleared, I felt their presence behind me. I thought I must have looked like someone who had too much to drink, but it was too late to do anything about it. Father Benjamin called my name and I slowly turned and smiled as if nothing happened.

"Colin Bennett, I would like you to meet Nadine Carter Barnwell." Colin offered his hand and I offered mine. His grip was as strong and confident as he appeared.

"Nadine is my neighbor from South Carolina," Father Benjamin said, pointing to me. "Colin is a theater director and an old friend." Just then, Taylor came in from my apartment with an armload of goodies. Father Benjamin excused himself. With Father Benjamin giving directions, they began refilling the table.

"Excuse me for staring, Nadine," Colin said, "I guess it's the director in me. I noticed you move like a dancer. Have you trained much?"

"Trained much?" I wasn't used to a question like that. Then I got it. "Oh, I'm not an actress if that's what you think. I move like a dancer because I'm a dancer."

"Ah ha. That was too simple. Everyone I know is trying to be something else...usually trying to be an actor." He stroked his neat beard with his free hand as if checking for crumbs or dribbles from his drink. A striking olive-skinned woman in a red satin blouse and a black bolero skirt said hello as she passed behind him. "So where are you dancing? Tell me, what shows have you done?"

"Shows?" I was lost again for a moment, but recovered. "No, no shows. I—I'm not a Broadway dancer; I'm a modern dancer—with a ballet background."

"Oh, excuse me. I see."

I don't know this man but he is a friend of Father Benjamin's, and this isn't going well.

"That's okay. Everyone assumes I'm on Broadway when I say I dance." I took a bite of sliced turkey on a roll, only with more care this time as he sipped his drink and watched me. I thought he would leave after finding out I wasn't Broadway-bound, but he didn't.

"So tell me about modern dance. What makes it modern?"

Is he testing me, trying to see if I know what I'm doing? No one ever asked me that question. It didn't matter; I needed to come up with something. *Now how to explain this?* All I could think of was my History of Dance class.

"Let me see how to explain this. Modern dance is essentially a breakaway from ballet. Think of it as an art form—not unlike the impressionists or the cubists. For me there is a freedom about it unlike any other form of dance."

"Ah, freedom, so is that what draws you to it?" His eyes almost twinkled.

"Not just the freedom." Most people didn't get modern dance and trying to explain it was difficult. I looked down at my feet to gather my next words. "Essentially, it was the development of an entirely new visual language. The dancer uses the body on the stage like the artist uses paint on a canvas for visual communication."

He stared at me for a moment. "You put that very well. Thank you. So where do you do your modern dance?"

"Oh, I study at the Leland Lemire Studio. That's where I "do" this modern dance." I didn't know if he was playing with me.

"Let's sit." He pointed to an antique velvet sofa in the corner. "That is, if you've had enough to eat." His eyes fell to my newly empty plate. "Get yourself something else; I'll be over there."

We sat on the couch, he, with his drink and I, with my third plate of food. Suddenly it got easier, and I was surprised at how much we had in common. We talked about theater and dance and why we were both in New York. Colin was from Rhinebeck, a small town north of Manhattan. I didn't know much about the smaller communities that fed into the city. But one thing for sure; I liked being in a conversation about theater with a man again. At first it reminded me of how much I missed Frank, but as we talked, I realized I didn't miss Frank at all. And unlike Mr. Bertram, Colin seemed like a fascinating man. He talked about his early success with plays that led him to his current production at Joe Papp's Theater in the East Village. In between, he travels outside of New York where he directs regional theater or industrial films and commercials to help pay the bills.

"You do commercials?" That surprised me. In college, Frank let me know what he thought of "legitimate" versus "commercial" in anything relating to theater. According to Frank, doing commercials was beneath good actors.

"One thing you should know about me," Colin grinned, "whatever job is available, I believe in taking it. 'Work begets work' is my proverb."

"Sounds like a good philosophy."

"So, how did you ever get involved with modern dance to begin with?" he segued back to me with skill.

Being with someone who wanted to know about me was extremely appealing in a city full of people who only talked about themselves. With all his accomplishments, he appeared to be mesmerized by my devotion to a low paying, under-acknowledged art form.

"I didn't mean to get so involved. At home in between hunting and fishing trips with my daddy, Mama used to pull me away so I could study ballet—like every other young southern girl. Daddy wasn't wild about how much time I spent in classes. And don't get me wrong, I loved the hunting and fishing. But he didn't realize how much I took to dance and how I yearned to get my hands on my first pair of toe shoes. Then one day I was finally on pointe. I felt absolutely beautiful: tall, elegant and powerful in pink tights and chiffon. The feeling stayed with me until I watched a modern dance class in college. From the doorway, bare feet dancers in only black leotards and feet-less tights moved freely across the room, leaping, jumping, turning and seemingly flying all over the room. I took one class and then another and before I knew it, I was hooked. With the training of a ballerina and the freedom now to move as I wanted, I was in my element. My daddy wasn't pleased at all. Festival queens should be studying ballet to be teachers, not taking classes in this modern dance stuff."

"You mean beauty queens?"

"No, we called them festival queens. I come from a long line of them. Festivals are big in the South and they always need a queen. There weren't any contests, at least not on a stage. My family would never put up with the bathing suit aspect. Usually a committee of town leaders picked the queens."

"Festival or beauty, looking at you, I'm not surprised."

"Thank you, but I'm no beauty queen. You have to work at pageantry, too, you know and I'm not interested. I could have taken it easy, gotten myself on a float like my mother, her sister and my cousins did. I could have floated regally into adulthood with the rest of them but I needed something else. I had too much energy. I needed to move."

"Was that where you felt most in control?"

"That's exactly it. In control, yet out of control." I was surprised he understood me so quickly. "Anyway, there I was giving dance my all, all the time and now I'm in New York City, trying to give it my all, but not knowing what that really means anymore. I go to class, rehearsal, work and then to sleep. Somewhere in between, I eat and then I do it all over again the next day. And now I may lose my roommate."

"You may? I'm sorry."

"God, I finally made it to New York, have a place to study, have a dance company to perform with, a great apartment and a job but I can't afford this town by myself." I suddenly realized how much I opened up to a man I hardly knew. "Oh, I'm sorry, I'm telling you too much. It must be the wine. Really, I'm sorry."

"Don't worry. I'm a good listener." He leaned over and hugged me. At that same moment, three people walked over and stood next to us. He broke away, smiled and introduced me. "This is Nadine Barnwell, everyone. She is a dancer from South Carolina. And these are my oldest dearest friends: Paul, Jessica and Adrian." He pointed to each person as he said their name. "Paul is a gifted actor who works in my shows whenever he is free from his many obligations with other adoring directors and producers." He grabbed him by the shoulders with one arm. "I just hope I don't lose him to Hollywood." Paul smiled and said it was nice to meet me. Their deep friendship was obvious to me.

"Jessica is married to Paul," Colin continued. A striking, petite woman in her middle thirties with curly brown hair and a wide toothy smile, I learned that she was an actress turned-set designer who also worked with Colin whenever possible, leaving the world of acting to her husband.

"This is the funny, quirky Adrian," he explained. She was gorgeous and didn't wear or need any makeup, I noticed. "She began her career as a model and eventually switched to acting where she really belonged. She sings, dances, acts and holds comedic court with the best of them. But don't let the joking fool you. She plays strong, capable women." He put his arm around her shoulder. "We've known each other since summer stock in the Berkshires when we first came to the city. We've been friends ever since."

"I'm sure that was more than Nadine needed to know," Adrian said while eyeing the food table. All three said they were happy to meet me and left us alone again.

Almost as soon as they were gone, another woman, tall and pencil-thin with perfectly straight blonde hair, porcelain skin and a skintight dress approached. She asked Colin if he would take just a moment to speak with some other people across the room. She put her hand under his arm as if to be sure he didn't slip away. He apologized to me and asked if he could excuse himself for just a moment.

"Of course," I said.

"Please stay here. I'll be right back." He put his hand on my arm as if to root me in place.

He didn't know it, but a pause was what I needed. Talking about my whole life made me tired.

I sat back on the couch and watched as admirers soon engulfed him across the room. I added up what just happened in a short amount of time. Colin was smart, good-looking, fascinating to talk to and definitely appealing. And I wanted to get away before I lost my focus and myself again in another man.

In the kitchen, I whispered my excuses in Taylor's ear. He said he understood and that since most everything was out of my kitchen, he would wait until the next day to clean up. I thanked him and made my way toward the door, back into my bean bag apartment and fell off to sleep on my foam mattress on the floor.

Sleep was fitful, the kind where I fell in and out of sleep all night long. Images of the party and Deni flashed in my mind. Just before it was time to get up, I fell into a deep sleep and into another dream. In this one, a beautiful laughing two-year old child with curly crimson hair sat playing with a bucket and a pail, like in a sandbox or at the beach. I turned to watch a bird nearby and when I looked back, she switched to playing with a doll and a tea set. It was then that she looked up at me with a smile and my heart filled with unimaginable joy. I moved forward to pick her up. But as in most dreams, I moved as though through molasses. Each time I got close to her a noise distracted me. I thought I heard someone call my name, but I didn't see anyone or recognize the voice. I turned to see who it was but found only haze behind me. When I turned again, the smiling child floated backwards away until she vanished from sight. Then I heard the voice again and turned toward it, but the buzzer on my alarm clock blared, jarring me out of the dream. I rolled over, staring at the time, feeling exhausted and wanting to fall back to sleep more than anything in the world. "Pay attention," I heard Aunt Amelia's voice say in my head. "Every dream tells us something important." But I didn't have time to try to figure what this meant; I needed to get to work. While dressing, the wonderful conversation with Colin slipped back into my mind, but I looked in the mirror and told myself to drop that too. My focus needed to be on me and where I was going next.

It was a couple of days later before I saw Father Benjamin again and could thank him for the party. We met in the lobby as we often did, my leaving the building and his coming in. He asked if I was all right. "Colin was disappointed and I think a bit confused when he came back and you were gone. I thought you two were getting on."

"I can't really explain why I left. He stirred something in me. Whatever it was scared me. Maybe another time without so many people around would be better."

"I'm afraid Colin left the city yesterday. He's directing a series of regional plays. He did say to tell you how much he enjoyed meeting you though."

"Oh, I see. Well, when he gets back then."

"Yes, when he gets back. It could be a while." The elevator bell rang.

"Oh, I better go. I'm due for a counseling session. Bye." He kissed my cheek and then held the side of my face in his palm for a second, just like Daddy used to do when he needed to leave me for some other much more important meeting.

"Bye. And thank you, really; I loved every minute of the party."

The elevator door closed and I stood staring at the doors engulfed with thoughts of Colin again.

The next night when I got home from work, all of Deni's things were gone. I found a note saying that she was sorry, Mr. Bertram offered her a wonderful apartment she couldn't refuse. It didn't say where. Also inside the envelope was some cash; enough for her share of the rent for a couple of months. Then what? Exasperation and recrimination popped through me like a fireworks display. Torn between Deni's terrible lack of judgment and my looming financial predicament, I charged around the apartment like a bull in a rodeo, slamming my hands into the walls and cursing out loud. Then I fell back into my bean bag chair and leaned my head against the wall. *What could I have done to stop this? What the hell am I going to do now? Maybe Daddy was right. Maybe I can't survive without his support. How can this be? He is wrong about one thing: my talent. Most people struggle for years to get where I am in dance.*

Early the next morning the sound of a phone ringing awakened me. Whenever I'm awakened by that sound, it always put me on high alert, as if an emergency somewhere needed my attention. After the fifth ring, I realized it was real and jumped out of bed and into the living room to answer it. My jumbled mind flashed on Deni and then on Frank; but it wasn't either of them.

"Oh Aunt Amelia, it's so good to hear your voice." I struggled to sound awake.

"I'm awfully sorry, dear. Have I called too early? Did you work late last night?"

"No, I mean, yes, I was asleep; no, it's not too early to talk to you."

"Good. I've tried calling many times, but never seem to get you at home. Our schedules are so different. Letters aren't the same as hearing your voice. I get these premonitions about you. Has something happened?"

"Oh, my God, you always know, don't you? So much has happened. Where do I start?" I leaned back on the icy green beanbag chair and pulled a blanket from the couch around my body to cut the chill. I couldn't see the sky from any window but heard garbage trucks backing up, trash cans slamming to the sidewalk, and the knock and clang of radiator pipes in the early morning stillness.

"Since Frank's letter to you about his marriage, your letters always sound like things are just fine. I do read between the lines, though."

She knew more about me most of the time than I did. "I know, I'm sorry, I don't want to worry you, and I certainly don't want anyone to come and get me. Daddy hasn't called, but you know he's just waiting for me to fail so that I will come back and keep the good Barnwell name alive. And keep the Barnwell women on their pedestals and on their parade floats."

"Yes, I know. It's not just your mother; it was your grandmother, too. We were given a lot of instruction about this kind of thing. The women in our family have always been strong, but within limits, if you know what I mean. Think of families being like tribes. The tribe believes it offers the members everything they need, and doesn't look favorably when one member believes they are different. They try to hold on tight. You are different, Nadine, and don't you forget that. No matter what happens—and what is happening exactly? How is your dancing? Are you eating?"

"You've always believed in me. Thank you for that. Yes, I am dancing and it is wonderful. It's fantastic. But, you know me; I want more. I have to be patient, though. But the bad news is my life around dance is crumbling. Deni moved out." I chose to not tell her that my work hours were cut so low; that I needed to find a new job. I vowed to do this without her financial help and knew she would send money if I asked her.

"Deni moved out? Did she give up and move back home? I haven't heard about her moving back."

"No, she didn't. She took up with an eccentric older man and moved out and into one of his."

"One of his apartments? What does that mean? Is he a landlord? How many does he have?"

"No, not exactly a landlord and I'm not sure Deni really knows what it is he does. I know what I suspect he does, and it's not what we came here for. But there is no talking to Deni anymore. She wants to live the high life, and that's exactly what she thinks she is doing. I'm afraid she is going to have a rude awakening."

"What does the school and her job say?"

"The job doesn't like it when employees just don't show up. But there's always someone else waiting to take the job, so they don't care. The school is concerned, but they are also used to people dropping out. According to Hilda and Francis, dancers come to their studio with great enthusiasm and determination and then find they aren't cut out for this life. They understand that they are not always going to find out what happened to everyone who enrolled at the school. It's a kind of self-elimination system."

"Oh, my, this doesn't sound good, for her or for you. I know that you love her, but you can't live her life for her. She will have to work this out on her own. We each have to go forward on our own path. You know that, don't you, dear?"

"Yeah, I guess I do. But I can't help worrying about her."

"What about your social life, Nadine?"

"You know I don't have time for that. I can't let a relationship get in the way, if that's what you mean. It got in the way once before, and I won't let that happen again."

"I'm sorry about what Frank did. He never was the one for you, Nadine. I just couldn't tell you that at the time. I had to help you get through your pregnancy."

"I try not to think about that anymore. There's nothing I can do to change what happened. I wish I had your radar. I should never have gotten involved with him in the first place."

"This may sound tough, but you need to let go, Nadine. We can't always control the way we work out the bigger picture. You're where you want to be, doing what you want to do. You need to live your life, the one you were meant to live."

"Oh, that's what I want to do. It's just so hard." I didn't exactly know why, but I chose not to tell Aunt Amelia about the baby dreams. I rationalized that if I didn't talk about them, maybe they would go away. It was easier over the phone than in person where she would see it in my eyes or posture or even my aura and call it out.

If she thought there was something else, she let it go because the next question was just as telling about her sensing abilities. "Now tell me, haven't you met anyone yet you would consider going out with?" Her persistence made me feel like she had a hidden wire somewhere on me, tuned into my every move.

"I did meet this one man, through Father Benjamin. His name is Colin."

"Oh, I like the name, and he's a friend of your Father Benjamin. What's wrong with him?"

"I don't know. I want a relationship, but I don't want one. I want to dance, and I'm afraid. I just don't know—it doesn't matter. He's not here anyway, and he's probably met someone else by now."

"My premonition, if it means anything to you, is to not throw this one away. I haven't met him, but this is my gut feeling."

That was my gut feeling also, but I was afraid to say it out loud, as if it would put a jinx on whatever might be. So I changed the subject.

For the next half hour, I asked about everyone from home. Nothing changed. She told me Daddy listened when she gave him updates on the generalities of my life, but he always shook his head at the end of their conversation, wondering where he'd gone wrong with me.

I could hear his voice in my mind. "She'll be back. She just has to get this out of her system and when she fails, she'll be back, begging for my forgiveness."

Ha. I'm not calling him. He'll have to call me to see how I am.

Aunt Amelia didn't hear any of this, but she knew what I was thinking. She always did. Listening to her talk was comforting. She made me realize that even with all the mess around me, I felt reinforced about my decision to come to New York.

"I do have something else to tell you, dear. I've been putting it off—I went to the doctor for some tests recently and the results came back."

"What tests? What's wrong with you?"

"I never told you, but seven years ago, the doctor found a small tumor in my kidneys he said could grow into something more serious. You know me, I didn't accept that as the truth. Not for one minute. With my own medicines, I've been able to keep it from growing all this time. I'm afraid it's not responding to my treatments anymore. I have a good doctor here. You know, one who understands me also. He was amazed it didn't progress all these years. Now I have to accept what they are telling me as true. I start on their medications next week."

"Oh, Aunt Amelia, no. Will these medications make it go away?"

"I don't know, sweetheart. The doctor is highly optimistic. Of course, he is supposed to be." There was silence. "Hampton and I are being positive, and we only want to believe this is the case. I'll tell you more, as I find out."

I let the phone drop away. I didn't want her to hear my gasp. Selfishly, I only thought of myself. I didn't have a mother, and Lord knows I didn't have a father any more. *How could I live without Aunt Amelia?*

"We won't dwell on this right now. I couldn't keep this from you."

"No, you couldn't. I'm—I'm glad you told me. I just wish there was something I could do." I wanted to sound strong for her even though I was anything but strong.

"I've got to run. Hampton is waiting to go to the store. He doesn't want to do anything without me right now. He's going to drive me crazy."

More silence.

"But he could never really drive me crazy. He has been a good husband and a good friend," she added.

"Oh, don't talk like that. You're going to be fine." The silence strung out between us also held us together. "I love you, Aunt Amelia," I blurted out with quiet force.

"I know you do, dear. I love you too. Things always get worse before they get better. It's part of life. Things are going to get better for both of us. I promise. I'll call again later. Bye, bye."

"Bye." Suddenly, I couldn't move. Aunt Amelia wouldn't have brought the subject up if it wasn't serious. But, it didn't matter what she said. I lost my mama, my daddy, my home, Frank and Deni. I wasn't ready to lose her too.

Once again, Aunt Amelia was more concerned with me than she was with her own problems. My thoughts bounced between my daddy and Aunt Amelia. They once were the two most important people in my life. I lost one and was possibly going to lose the other. I must have sat in the beanbag chair for an hour, doing nothing. Even though I felt like I was trying to walk through pluff mud, I realized I had to pull myself together and get to the studio. I rolled over on my side, cheeks stinging from crying. In the bathroom, I splashed cold water on my face, but it didn't do any good. My face still looked puffy and red. I threw on my dance clothes, then my jeans and crocheted poncho, grabbed my dance bag and headed out the door, hoping the stress and weeping would not show in my face when I got to the studio.

On the train ride uptown, I pulled myself together. Finding a new roommate was the best option. People in New York changed roommates all the time, so how hard could this be? And that was the next part of the problem. What if, after they moved in, I hated my new roommate? Luckily, Francis and Hilda came through for me again by suggesting I offer a trial arrangement for at least a month. I started asking around the dance school. At least I would get a recommendation of some sort. But when nothing turned up, I resorted to advertising in *The Village Voice.*

I didn't need to worry because I interviewed three different roommates over the next two weeks. They were an odd assortment of artists, all looking for their "place" in the world, just like me. But I didn't get a sense that any of them was capable of settling in. From listening to their stories, they seemed to have a nervous energy which kept them moving around like a dog turning in place, looking for a comfortable spot, only to get up moments later and move to another spot. Maybe, like animals, they were following the path of sunlight as it moved through the day. Ultimately, I remained living alone.

By then, I was tempted to take the post office box offer myself. I even rationalized how it wouldn't really hurt anyone and would get me through for a while. But luckily for me, with Deni gone from the deal, Mr. G didn't seem as interested in convincing me to do it. I imagined I didn't have the same vulnerable, needy qualities others saw in Deni. Bending the law wasn't for capable people. And to prove that I wasn't the right person for their extracurricular activities, when I looked at my upcoming schedule, it only had one shift on it. I had no choice but to start looking for a new job.

CHAPTER 11

1976

*You meet people who forget you. You forget people you
meet. But sometimes you meet those people you can't
forget. Those are your 'friends.'*
—UNKNOWN

FEW DAYS AFTER MY CONVERSATIONS with Aunt
Amelia and Father Benjamin about my dancing and my
roommate situation, I picked up the "Classified" and
found exactly what I was looking for. I couldn't believe my eyes.
Steiger's, a long-time, very popular steak house located right where
I wanted to be in The Village, advertised for young "college-type"
waiters. I applied and was hired immediately.

I did ask myself, though, was this a coincidence or somehow
Aunt Amelia's intervention? I liked to think the latter, that as
my guardian angel at home, her powers ranged all the way to
New York City.

There was one small problem though. Because the ownership
recently changed hands, making it now part of a restaurant chain,
the new hires weren't the only ones waiting tables in this eatery.

A separate staff, employed for over twenty years, was protected by a union contract, guaranteeing that their jobs were safe even if the restaurant sold. With twice as many waiters as needed, we became an odd mixture of employees: the new hires were young, white and mostly female, and the original staff was not so young, black and entirely male. For the men, it was a career, as opposed to the rest of us who used our profession to support our creative habits.

I didn't care. I needed a job, preferably one nearer my apartment and as far away from those post office box con-artists as I could get.

For a while, it looked like a stand-off between the old guard and the new. Corporate's bottom line couldn't afford to keep all of us, so eventually, some were let go. Luckily, not me.

At first, most of us were uncomfortable with the union men; we found no way to engage them in conversation. The only thing we had in common were the tips in the old restaurant from the regular loyal customers who were really good. I jumped to the conclusion that as career waiters, these men didn't have much in the way of other marketable skills, so this was probably as far as they would get in life. I didn't know much about the circumstances of other people's lives, but I did finally realize that they certainly had far more to lose than we did.

As it turned out, the standoff continued, and more and more of the fresh young faces were let go. The older professionals hung in with calm determination, knowing the law was on their side. I managed, somehow, to hold on to my job through all the cutbacks, and after several months, we began to know a little bit more about each other.

Marvin Jenkins, who studied to be a concert pianist before life, family and other circumstances intervened, was the friendliest of the group and helped me whenever I needed anything. Mitch

Brown had been a successful low-wage schoolteacher for a long time before giving it up for the lure of the tips earned in a place like *Steiger's*. Then there was Arthur Samuels, from whom I kept my distance for quite a while once I learned he served time for murdering his wife. He didn't seem like the type to me. I was sure there was more to this story but no one talked about it.

"Dealing the Dozens" was one of the first phrases I learned, slang for "taking care of business." And there was always some kind of business going on around there. If they had anything in common besides their profession and their race, it was their love of the "horses," the effects of which may have been what kept them together for all those years. The pay phone, halfway up the stairs between the kitchen and the first floor, was in constant use. Occasionally, I needed it too but rarely got the opportunity. All night, endless calls were made to and from bookies.

So, shortly, I learned two things: one was they were quite adept at controlling the pay phone, the other that they were exceptional waiters. The talk, though, was that management intended to keep the union men, in accordance with the law but slowly wear them down. They assumed the older men would fall by the wayside one by one because they wouldn't be able to keep up with the young white college types. They were wrong. The men knew their clientele, and their clientele asked for them by name.

Then there was the actual manager. Miss Renee, as she liked to be called, was short, model skinny with country western-styled bleached blonde hair. She wore ridiculously high heels, only designer dresses and didn't seem to know where to stop when applying her makeup, making her look more like a wax museum piece than a real person. Rounding out her comical look, her ornate gold jewelry clanked and jangled as she sashayed through the restaurant, checking up on each of us, looking for any reason to let the next waiter go. For someone who was on her feet all night, I didn't get why she wore those stilettos. Perhaps she found more power higher in the atmosphere.

Tough and controlling, she pushed everyone around like a drill sergeant. Behind her back she was nicknamed "Miss Thing" by the staff. With her combination of glamour and iron fist, people joked about whether she stood up or sat down when she went to the toilet. This was The Village, after all, where disguise was the norm. I assumed she was a she, but I didn't actually know or care.

For me, this new job seemed to be working out, despite my roommate situation. Over the months, a number of roommates moved in and then moved out. Some left by choice and some by my recommendation. I used the "Hilda and Francis Rule" to not commit to anyone too soon as my basic tenet. There's nothing worse than ending up with someone you really can't tolerate in a small space.

By working as many shifts as allowed, I was able to make enough money to get by. Maybe it wasn't the totally exhilarating New York life I imagined, but considering how close I was to not being there at all, I reflected on the ritual and Aunt Amelia's words: a grateful attitude is far more necessary to overall success than a sorry one. Each night, I thanked the universe for my new job in The Village, for learning to love all my co-workers, for still relishing going to my dance classes and company rehearsals, and for being able to perform whenever Gabriela's company got a booking. I endeavored to keep my beats up, but my thoughts about home never went away even though I never heard anything from Daddy.

After about nine months, *Steiger's* popularity started to dwindle. Newer restaurants with trendy decor and cuisine opened up along Bleecker Street and Greenwich Avenue, and the crowds who used to come to this one exclusively began experimenting around. Ultimately, the battle of union verses non-union, young versus old, and black versus white became moot points. None of us knew how much longer the place would stay open. But we all had our bills to pay, our dreams to fulfill or reminisce about, and so we bonded in the knowledge that we weren't going anywhere unless we were fired.

Near my one-year anniversary at *Steiger's*, I took a final trip to the bar for my last customers before closing time. The funny, frizzy-haired bartender, Summertime, saw me, held a hand up to the man she was talking to at the far end of the counter and strolled back toward me. Every bit The Village hippie, her long gauze skirt swished above a pair of beat-up brown cowboy boots as she walked. Her gold bangle earrings pointed to a full bosom rising from a tight-fitting, low-cut white top.

Out of the corner of my eye, I noticed a single man across the u-shaped mahogany bar. I felt his stare before I saw it. To my surprise, there sat Colin Bennett. When Father Benjamin told me how in-demand he was and that his work took him out of town for long periods, I thought I would never see him again.

He lifted his glass in a mock toast and smiled a warm hello. His thick, shaggy-cut hair bounced as he raised his arm. To my surprise again, it felt like liquid sunshine on a frosted day.

He looked better than I remembered. I couldn't help but smile back and noted some relief at seeing him. I gave my order to Summertime and walked over to where he was seated.

"When do you get off?" he asked, as if it was just yesterday we first met. A crisp new looking, red plaid shirt peeked out of a black V-neck sweater. A tan suede jacket draped over the back of his chair.

"In just a little while," I answered in the same nonplussed manner, and then looked at my watch. "In about a half an hour." I tried to act indifferent, but cordial. A sensual, oaky after-shave scent surrounded his body. I recognized it from other customers in the restaurant but didn't know the name.

"If you don't have any plans, will you join me for a drink?"

"No, no plans and yes, I suppose I could," I said as I walked back to the drink station. I realized I hadn't hesitated at all.

Summertime laughed as she set the drinks on my tray. She adjusted an exposed bra strap, then hoisted an immense container of clean glasses on one shoulder and carried them to the other side of the bar.

As I walked back into the dining room, the heat from his eyes penetrated my shoulders and the back of my head. A flush of happiness washed over me, and this time, I just let it be.

The other waiters were all winding down also. Mitch and Marvin had the only two tables left, while the rest of us were finished for the night.

As soon as my last customers left, I went to the back room to change. I pulled off my apron, order pad, skirt and blouse and changed into the clothes I wore to work. After I splashed water on my face, brushed my hair and added a quick swipe of pale pink lipstick, I stood back and shook my head at what I saw. In faded jeans and an old maroon and pink zigzagged patterned knit top, I thought I looked sad. My forced frugality kept me from spending money on new clothes, and now I regretted it. I hated seeing Colin for the first time in a year looking like this, but I couldn't stop myself. He was at the bar, waiting for me, so I rationalized if he wanted to see me that much, he would have to take me as I am.

As I walked back toward the bar, I took further note of this man I met only once, a year earlier. His face, strong featured with an engaging wry smile, was still appealing and full of life. This time, I saw something else, something extremely powerful; it was a face that wanted to talk to me rather than order food or drinks. I looked forward to just having a change of focus for a while.

"So, how are you?" he asked as I approached.

"Great, how are you?"

"Great, too, now that I've found you," he said, as he gave his drink a stir.

"I wasn't lost." I leaned across the bar and ordered a gin and tonic from Summertime. But I was surprised when I felt a zing of attraction, a wave of excitement and it flustered me. My body, which hadn't felt much desire in a long time, suddenly sprang to life just looking at him.

"I know that; I'm sorry. I mean, now that I see you—you left me high and dry at a party a while ago—I asked you to stay—said I was coming back." With his arms over his chest, he leaned back in his bar stool. The corners of his mouth took on an exaggerated droop, reminding me of a lonely puppy. I thought immediately of my dog from home and imagined what Bear felt like when I suddenly left with no explanation. At that moment, I missed Bear more than I could ever imagine.

"I knew you were," I stammered. "I just—I guess, I got exhausted—I don't know. I just had to leave."

"I wish you hadn't."

Just thinking about letting another man into my life forced anxiety to overtake desire. I may have jumped way too far ahead, but something told me this was exactly what could happen. Thoughts zoomed around in my head. At one time I loved Frank with every particle of my being. He awakened and fed my desire to take my creative soul to another level, to be a professional performer and be part of New York Theater. I also counted on him to be there for me during all this crazy time, but in the end I lost Daddy, our baby and him.

I twisted in my seat. "So what have you been up to?"

He laughed at my obvious move. "I've been in London, directing *Twelfth Night* at the Royal Shakespeare Theater." He looked away.

My jaw must have dropped because when he did look at me, he started to laugh.

"No, actually, my last job was in Texas, directing a series of summer stock plays at The Long Dog Theater."

I shrugged, not knowing what he was talking about.

"Sorry, I always think everyone knows about regional theater. It's a fairly well-known summer stock theater. The last one of the group was a swift little version of Albee's *A Delicate Balance*."

"Summer Stock Theater in Texas, not London? Okay, how did that go?"

He lowered his forearms on the bar, hands on both sides of his drink. "Oh, fine. It was sold out every night for six weeks, a twelve-hundred seat theater. I just would have liked to recast most of the parts and change all the sets and costumes. But other than that I think it went pretty well, under the circumstances." He pushed his drink back and forth on the wooden bar, making trails of wetness, then wiped it up with his cocktail napkin.

"You directed *A Delicate Balance*? I love that show. They did a production of it at my college." Frank starred in that too. I shook off the thought. "But if it was sold out then, what was the problem?"

"Albert Bartlett," he said into the glass.

"Albert Bartlett? The TV star?"

"Yes, that one."

"I've never seen his show because I'm always working, but I hear it's really great."

"Yeah, he's really great. Can you imagine? He hadn't done a stage play since college. And what did he pick, but the one play where the lead character has to be on stage ninety percent of the time. That's a lot of dialogue for one character in any play. That would be a lot for Richard Burton."

I laughed so hard I almost spit and had to clamp my hand over my mouth; I immediately regretted my reaction. It was an amusing story but probably not hilarious. I heard my name called behind me, and I turned to say good night to Marvin and Mitch. With this distraction, I was able to shut off my laughter and pull myself together. But I knew only wishing wouldn't make the redness retreat from my cheeks.

Colin didn't respond to my outburst. He politely paused and smiled. I liked that.

"Basically," he continued, "I never knew what Bartlett was going to do or say next...his fellow actors also didn't know what he was going to do or say next either. Thank God they are all seasoned pros. Summer stock can be grueling enough on its own. But having to jump through hoops for rich celebrities who have forgotten what it takes to genuinely create a believable character and make it fresh and captivating each night is doubly hard."

"Really, he was hard to deal with?" I didn't know much about this life that Colin was immersed in, but like everyone else, I was fascinated.

"Well, not really hard—okay—yes, hard to deal with. He thinks he's God's gift to...Colin looked around the empty bar. "Now if you ever tell anyone I said this, I'll deny it, because all my actors are wonderful. They work hard for me, and I appreciate them. But ultimately, they make or break a show. Los Angeles really has made a mess out of some of these people. Sometimes, they think more about the power of their money than their talent—or is it they have more money than talent?"

I was confused. I put all famous people up on a pedestal. His words were hard to absorb.

"Let me tell you, he had them lined up outside the theater though." Colin lifted his hand and pointed to his empty drink. Summertime slid his drink across the bar, picked up the empty glass and disappeared into the kitchen. It was quitting time and I knew she was done babysitting the clientele. Most likely, she was happy to see that I was the one having my ear bent and not her. By her wink, I guessed she thought that listening to someone who looked like Colin was not such disagreeable duty.

"On top of that..." he picked right back up as if this story had been waiting to find the proper escape route, "instead of resting his voice between shows on a matinee day, he went outside to the loading dock of the theater, where all his fans were gathered in the parking lot, and began a sort of lecture. You want to know what his topic was?"

Of course, I nodded.

"He ranted about people illegally selling T-shirts with his picture and TV show logo on them. He claimed that because those items were not endorsed by his company, they were not true fans; that they were ripping him off. And this speech was more important to him than resting or going over the lines in the show he couldn't seem to get straight. Then in his final show on the circuit, he went into the dressing room of the seasoned character actors and delivered yet another piece of his mind. He ranted at them about everything they had done wrong in the play from day one, followed by a speech about what real professionalism is all about. He was the furthest thing from an example of professionalism I ever ran across. He should have thanked each of them for covering all his blunders." He stirred his drink a couple of times, leaned back with his arms folded across his chest, and added, "And his money just keeps on rolling in."

For a moment, I wasn't sure if that was the end of the story. When it looked like it was, all I could think to say was, "Wow."

"I'm sorry. I didn't mean to bend both of your ears with this. I love my job and my actors, but not all of them. That's not how I wanted to start this conversation—let's start over. What about you?"

"Whoa. Wait a minute. Let me catch up here. So why do you do it?"

"Well, regional theater pays my bills in between doing the work that I really want to do. I guess it's not unlike what you are doing, making your living at one thing, in order to be able to do the thing you really want to do."

"Yeah, only waiting tables isn't exactly another form of dancing. You're still directing. You're directing famous people at a famous theater. I'm supposed to feel sorry for you?"

"No, not sorry, never sorry for me." He turned in his seat toward me and put his hand on my arm. A surge passed through me again. "I guess whatever level you get to, you just want to be at the next level as soon as possible. It's part of the ladder we're all climbing."

I must have looked scared rather than excited, because he took his hand away. "So what is happening with your roommate situation? Did Deni, is that her name, come back?"

"Oh, Deni. I'm sorry to say she is still gone. I don't really know what's happened to her. She came back and got all her things while I was out. Before that, when I asked her questions about her and Mr. Bertram, she told me I needed to stay out of her business. I tried to do that but it isn't easy. I'm hoping she'll come to her senses and just come back." I didn't want to talk about her. It made me uncomfortable, as if I was responsible for her not having the life she wanted. I knew I wasn't but there was still nothing I could do about it, I kept telling myself. "On a happier note, my dance company is starting to get more bookings, which is thrilling."

"That's great. You are really on your way now." He raised his glass to mine.

Back from the kitchen, Summertime was watching us as she continued to wipe more bar glasses. She seemed wistful like she was moved by what she heard, too.

"Well, almost. Like for most other modern dancers, it's not paying anything right now. But if I want to be around when the checks start appearing, I have to be around when there are no checks. The work is great though. I like the director's style and think I'm suited for it, even if I say so myself."

"I want to come see your performance sometime."

I hesitated, not expecting that. "Uh—yeah—uh—sure."

"When?"

"Umm, there's a performance next weekend. But I'm sure you already have other plans."

"No, I don't. Tell me where and when, and I'll be there. Do I need to get a ticket in advance?" He was clearly excited.

What was I saying? Did I truly want to invite him? But it was too late for that question. There was no turning back.

No one I knew, outside of teachers and classmates, had seen me dance—in New York, anyway. Everything in New York was about measuring up—or not. I didn't know how I measured up against anyone else. Now this successful theater director wanted to see for himself. As we set the date and time, a different quiver vibrated in the pit of my stomach.

After Colin got the check, he asked, "May I walk you home?"

"Sure, if you like," I said, without any hesitation.

From the restaurant, we made our way to Greenwich Avenue, over to Fourth and around the corner to Christopher Street. I loved walking by the elegant brownstones with immense wooden doors adorned with brass kick plates, ornate knockers and wreaths for each season of the year. They all seemed full of life. The inhabitants lived in a whole house, not just a tiny apartment like I did. These brownstones had multiple bedrooms and baths, living rooms with fireplaces, giant kitchens with pantries and dishwashers and best of all, outdoor gardens in the back. There, I imagined the owners grew ivy and petunias around elegant stone fountains, tried to get a tan during the few minutes the sun made an appearance between the buildings, and sat outside on warm summer evenings, gazing at the sky while grilling steaks. Like my lost home in Beaufort, the brownstones seemed incredible to me, something to wish for. I wondered, though, even if I had all the success and all the money, would I truly be able to make New York City my home? Sometimes I thought *yes* and other times I yearned for the magnificent oaks draped in silvery green moss, the hushed narrow streets, stately tabby houses and the swift flowing creeks. While rooting myself more deeply into my new life, I also yearned for my old life. I wondered if I was the only one being haunted with such mixed messages. Probably not. Then I would remember the main reason I came to the city. If I still lived in Beaufort, I wouldn't have the opportunity to perform in a company like Gabriela's and be part of the most creative theater in the world.

As we turned onto Christopher Street, I saw one of my favorite places in The Village. Bon Temps Ice Cream Shoppe glowed from dimly lit lamps behind lace curtains, showing the outlines of customers at tables, eating and talking even at one o'clock in the morning.

"Do you like ice cream?" I asked.

"I love it," he grinned.

Like a French café, the shop was long and narrow with small, round wrought iron tables and chairs on black and white checkered ceramic tile floors. Cascading deep green plants and hanging beveled glass ceiling lamps offset richly colored impressionist paintings in ornate gold frames on the walls, as piano jazz played softly in the background. Ice cream at Bon Temps seemed to invite quiet conversations, unlike the loud banter in bars created through the haze of alcohol.

We looked over the long menu and both of us ordered hot fudge sundaes with vanilla ice-cream.

"So summer stock at The Long Dog Theater, what is it you really like about it?" I asked after the waiter left.

"You know, the shows are not all exactly alike, but for the most part they put on ten shows in ten weeks. You know, mostly popular hits that have already "made it," at some point, on Broadway. It's kind of like assembly-line work. The shows are mounted, rehearsed and played at the original theater all in one week. Then they get sent off on a short tour. The stars are the draw. It's a great package. Circle in the Square or Joe Papp, it's not. There's not a lot of innovation going on."

"Who owns these theaters?"

"Now that's an interesting story. The Long Dog Theater was founded by a creative and highly eccentric entrepreneur named Joe Penny. He's crafty and a genius at what he does. He finds Hollywood actors whose stars have faded over time, or ones in need of a stage instead of a camera for a while. He matches the right vehicle to their talent, and voila. The regional audiences can't wait to pay good money to go to see them. He's got the over-sixty-five crowd locked up. They're not going to travel to New York City to see anything, so he brings the second best thing to them...and with the stars they remember from years back." He tilted his head, brought his hands across his heart, in a mock swoon.

"Wow. Is that what they call a real win-win situation?"

"Yeah, he's a winner. No grass grows under his feet. He was once a vaudeville hoofer. Now he could be an attraction all on his own, but he prefers to command that ship rather than be commanded by it and nobody messes with him."

"What do you mean...an attraction on his own?"

"Well, he's what you call a hermaphrodite."

"A what?"

"He has the body parts of both sexes: breasts and a penis."

"You're making this up."

"In the summer, in Texas, he lives as a man in a shirt and tie, and in the winter, in Florida, as a woman dressed in furs and pearls."

"Holy cow. A hermaphrodite. I thought I knew it all, living on Christopher Street. That would be wild to be around." Our ice cream sundaes arrived with long silver spoons, and we both dug in immediately.

"Okay, who were the other actors?" I asked, catching the whipped cream with my spoon as it slid off the opposite side of the sundae.

"Well, do you remember Vincent Price, Ann Miller and Jane Powell?" He did the same when his whipped cream fell.

I nodded.

"They all had a show this last summer. But Albert Bartlett was probably the biggest draw Joe Penny ever had."

"And you got to direct him. That's something, isn't it?"

"Yeah, I guess so." His voice dropped for the first time. "But I don't plan to do this for long. I have my sights set on directing a Broadway show within the next year or two. I'm one of hundreds who want to do this. The only difference is, I am going to do it."

"And I think you will." The amount of positive energy pouring out of every part of his body electrified the air, and for a moment I needed to look away. I genuinely liked this man, even more this time than the last, even though the last time I ran away.

When we were finished, he walked me to my front stoop, which was only a few buildings away. I put the key into the lock and held the massive door open with my foot. The moment was awkward. I didn't know what to say or do. But he did. He simply leaned forward, hugged me gently and placed a soft kiss on my cheek. "I look forward to seeing you next weekend, Nadine Carter Barnwell." Then he backed down the steps and into the still full Saturday night crowd on Christopher Street.

As I let the front door close, I could hear him call out in the distance, "And don't forget to put aside a ticket for me."

I did put the ticket aside, and he came. Since I was in three of the four dances on the program, it turned out to be the perfect performance for him to attend.

In black leotard and tights in a pool of light downstage left, the first piece opened with me on one knee, my other leg extended behind, my head and arms folded in close to my chest. As the music began my arms lifted, bringing my body to standing on one leg while extending the other forward at waist height. Once upright, I began to turn while still within the circle of light. Slowly, I moved out from the spot around the stage, with the light now following me. I didn't know if it was because I was well rehearsed or because Colin was there, but I felt unusually good about my performance. It was the best I gave since I started with Gabriella's company. From the moment the light faded up, I felt powerful and centered. Not every performance was perfect, but I had enough confidence that even if I missed a step, I would be able to cover elegantly. That night the entire company was nearly flawless, and the audience sprang to their feet in applause at the end. We took three curtain calls, which, for a small, unknown dance company, was exhilarating.

Colin waited in the front of the house for me to clean up and change. He looked every inch a successful theater director, all in black: black shirt, black pants and a black sports coat.

"It's been a long time since I've been to a dance concert," he said after I came out. "I think I saw a few at college, but nothing compared to what I saw tonight. Your dance company is wonderful."

"Oh, thank you. That means a lot to me. I...I was really nervous with you coming."

"It didn't show. You must be starved. I know this great restaurant in Chelsea. It's small, quaint, hidden."

"Yeah, that would be great." I hoped he would ask me to dinner.

He hailed a cab and on the way downtown had a thousand questions.

"So tell me about Gabriela as a choreographer and how you got to work with her."

"Actually, it all started before I left home. In my last year of college, I was offered a scholarship to attend The Lemire Studio... I think I mentioned it when we first met." His mouth smiled, but his eyes indicated he was searching his memory for that piece of information.

"I'm not sure I would have had the courage to come here without it. It's not just the help with the money, but the affirmation beyond my peers of some talent." As the cab wove in and out of traffic, it alternately sped up and then slammed on the brakes. I grabbed the bar above the door handle. When we swung back to the right, I fell into Colin and he took the opportunity to put his arm around my shoulders to steady me. Strength emanated from him even through my coat.

"I thought I wanted to become a part of Leland's company," I said, trying to sit back up, "but really, Gabriela is the next generation. In her choreography, her years of training with Leland really shine through, but so does a growing style of her own. And so after watching me in class for a few weeks, she said I fit her image of the kind of dancer she wanted performing her work."

"So she came to you—you didn't audition?"

"Yes, she did. No, I didn't—audition formally. I didn't even know she was watching. It's funny; in two of the pieces tonight, I had solo parts. But this wasn't true in the beginning. I'm glad that by the time someone I knew outside of dance came to see me, I would feel good about my work."

Just then, our cab pulled over. As Colin paid the driver, I got out and looked around. All the businesses on the block seemed closed.

But Colin assured me we were in the right place. He pointed to the store right where we stopped and walked past me. It didn't look like a restaurant to me. It was an ordinary storefront with angled window displays on each side of the tiled walkway leading to a recessed front door. The windows were filled with Victorian oak furniture, so I assumed it was an antique store.

Colin pulled the handle of the front door which opened to a small reception area as old and dark as the outside of the building. A woman standing behind a high desk seemed to know Colin. She said they were expecting us, smiled as she checked his name off a long list and turned toward a dark drab door behind her. So far, I was underwhelmed with his restaurant choice.

But once through the second door down a corridor filled with a rolltop desk, an ornate mahogany armoire, a Tiffany-style lead glass floor lamp with a pull chain and a fringed paper lampshade, we stepped into a completely different world. The spacious room beyond the next door was transformed into a Parisian parlor I imagined from the *La Belle Époque*. The room glowed with fountains, skylights, draping ferns, and graceful indoor palms and ficus trees filled with twinkle lights. White linen covered tables were sprinkled throughout the main area and in the smaller rooms which jutted off from the center. Chamber music played softly, and at every table people were either deep into eating or conversation, giving off a warm lively atmosphere.

A man in a black suit came over, then led us to a quiet corner table near one of the fountains. Herbs de province, sautéed butter, fresh baked bread, basil and brie filled the air.

After listening to the specials for the night, we spent a few minutes looking over the menu. I was overwhelmed with the choices. Colin asked if I would like him to order for the both of us.

"That's fine." He then took the wine list and did the same. The waiter concurred with all of Colin's choices, then turned on his heels and disappeared. In a flash, he was back with our wine, going through the ceremony of the opening of the bottle with considerable fanfare. Colin made the obligatory sniff of the cork, swirled the tasting pour around in his glass and took a sip to confirm. I laughed inside, thinking of dinner with the pompous Mr. Bertram; only this time, I knew my date and the surroundings were much more suitable to me.

After he poured the wine, the waiter disappeared again. I couldn't quit turning around in my seat to see what I missed. Then Colin drew my attention back to him when he raised his glass and said, "To Nadine, a dancer with extraordinary grace and immensurable stage presence."

"Thank you, Colin. It's nice to have someone come to see just me." I sipped what may have been the best wine I ever tasted.

"Your theater presentation is quite different from mine; simple, uncluttered. You don't have props and sets to worry about and certainly not any dialogue or songs."

"No, we just have our bodies, and not much in the way of costumes; usually it's plain leotards and tights."

"But you do have incredible lighting, which almost acts like sets and powerful music. It's like art in motion. Space, lines, curves, stillness, staccato; it's really beautiful."

I couldn't believe how this affected him. "Well, if you would like to see more, you may have the opportunity soon. Gabriela said there were people at the concert tonight who were deciding which of the smaller companies around the city they would invite to perform as part of a festival at The Joyce Theater." I couldn't believe I just invited him to my next performance, but I did. "In fact," I added with my newfound confidence, "I believe the theater is just around the corner from here."

I hoped he would be in town. Even I had to admit that the attention and compliments were quite appealing and I welcomed another round of them, especially from someone as smart, sophisticated and successful as Colin.

"Count on me. I have nothing but free time for the next couple of months. My next play doesn't start rehearsing for a while. After that, my days and nights won't be my own again." He took my hand and raised his glass. "To the beginning of a beautiful friendship." Smiling over that well-worn toast, we clinked glasses.

"Assuming you don't run out on me again, that is," he added, as though looking straight into my heart. Then I caught myself. *Was I beginning to desire this man for other reasons?*

Remembering why I left Father Benjamin's party that night made my insides get all tied up. After Frank, I didn't want to lose my focus in another relationship. And I didn't want to end up desperate like Deni. The ritual was still my driving force, and I wasn't anywhere near where I thought I needed to be. I simply had too much to do. I sipped my wine to cover my feelings while Colin searched my face. Then, from across the room, our waiter rolled a cart up to us. The theater of preparing a salad at the table changed both of our focuses. I was relieved to break the moment.

After we were served and ate our salads without talking, Colin's face lost its brightness. "What is it, Nadine? Is something bothering you? Is it me? Have I said or done something—again?"

"Oh, gosh, no." I didn't realize my silent evasion tactic made him so uncomfortable, but then after my previous behavior, why wouldn't it? "No, you've been—are wonderful."

"But?"

"But–I don't know. I don't know. You do scare me a bit."

"Why is that?" At that moment, two waiters arrived, one to clear the salad plates and the other to serve our main courses: Coc au vin for me and Boeuf Bourguignon for Colin. The aromas mixed in the air between us, creating a moment where inhaling was almost as good as tasting. This also bought me more time from having to go further than "but." The food was incredible, the wine was incredible but the conversation lacked its former sparkle.

After a while, Colin's eyes crinkled at the outside edges as he put his fork down and poured more wine. "I think we were talking about your being scared."

"Oh yes, well, it's just that..." The right words still didn't come to me.

"It's just that what? Help me understand you, and if I can, let me help you. Maybe it's too obvious, but I really want to be around you, in a big way."

"It's just that I want to dance and I want to live my life on my own. But everything keeps getting in the way." The worries in my life were mounting rather than subsiding, and I felt sometimes as if they clung to me like the Spanish moss on the giant live oak trees back home. I didn't want to tell him about my terrible financial and roommate situation or Frank and especially not ever about my lost baby. What I wanted was to be transported from them...not dwell on them. "I need to stay focused on my goals."

Colin must have gotten something out of the little I said, because he smiled warmly again and gracefully changed the subject. I almost hated that he did that. His charm was becoming more and more apparent with everything he said and did.

I declined desert after such a huge meal, and we decided to walk back to The Village instead of taking another cab. From Ninth Avenue, we strolled across 23rd Street and headed for Seventh Avenue. We moved down the brightly lit streets with residents entering and exiting the various quaint apartment buildings they called home. The contrast of those buildings to the landscape I grew up in shot through me like an arrow. A yearning for my own streets, rivers and creeks rose from within again.

"Transitions are never easy," Aunt Amelia told me as I anxiously left her to meet Deni after losing my baby. "But time will tell you everything. Don't push it; just ride things out."

"So are you ready to talk yet?" Colin asked. He took my hand and I let him. "I know we haven't known each other that long, but I can tell you that I am crazy about you. I want to know you better, and I think something is really bothering you."

I was stunned. *What is wrong with me? He is telling me how much he likes me and I can't think of anything to say.*

We walked a few more steps in silence before he asked, "Is there someone else?"

"No—no one else. I mean, there was, but there isn't anymore." My emotions were clearly ahead of any rational explanation. I grasped for the words to take over and deliver me from a near panic attack. "I've wanted to come to New York to dance since I was about twelve. It was a just a dream. I never imagined it would happen and now I'm here. The dream, though, hasn't exactly worked out the way I planned. Everything is so hard." I could feel that I wanted to spill out all my worries, let him lift them from me, clean them up, and hand them back in a calm tidy package. "Oh, I don't know what I am saying. Things are fine, really."

"No, they're not. That's quite clear to me. As long as it's not another man I can take it. Just tell me."

"Mostly, it's my aunt—Aunt Amelia," I blurted out before I knew it.

"The one you went to stay with after graduation?" He almost sounded relieved.

"Yes, she just told me she's sick. She has a tumor that is grow-ing." Tears began to spill down my face. "She's not supposed to be sick. She's the one who heals everyone else, who takes care of everyone else. She's the one who takes care of me." My dam broke.

Colin put his arms around me, and I sobbed into his shoulder. "I'm sorry to hear this. She's important to you, isn't she?"

"Uh huh," I eked out with my face against his jacket.

"I'm so sorry." He stroked the back of my head. "But I'll bet she's getting the best care available. If your uncle is worthy of this woman you so admire, then he won't let anything bad happen to her. The good guys do that. You'll just have to trust what I'm saying. But the other thing," he took my shoulders in his hands and stretched away from me, "you just said something about everything being so hard. That's true. It's hard work being here. That's part of the deal. No one gets their dream without a struggle. It's a law of some kind. What you've accomplished is not that easy. I don't know everything about you, yet look at what you've survived already just to be standing here in New York City, with me, right here, right now. You've gotten to this point all on your own. That means you can get anywhere you put your mind to. Give yourself some credit; no, give yourself a big hand." Then he let me go, stepped back again and started clapping, loudly. Between my high drama tearful scene and his out-of-place applause, even the blasé New Yorkers on the sidewalk slowed down or turned around to see why he was clapping.

I reached out, tried to grab his hands. "Stop that, Colin. You're embarrassing me."

"There, see—now you've stopped crying." I realized he knew exactly what he was doing. My tears stopped and I almost started laughing. He put his arm around my shoulder again, and we walked on down the street toward my apartment building.

By the time we reached my stoop, I was exhausted from the performances, both on the stage and on the street; and to his credit, we parted once again with only a hug and a kiss on the cheek.

Getting ready for bed, I couldn't help being amazed at Colin. There was something truly loving about what he did. Over the course of the evening with considerable patience and skill, he got me to open up, release my built-up tension and return to a calmer reality. It was nothing short of a miracle. How many men know they don't have to try to fix it or run away when a woman cries but are centered enough just to help get the problem out in the air and then move on? *Not many*, I heard Aunt Amelia say in my head.

CHAPTER 12
1976-1977

What lies behind us, and what lies before us are tiny matters compared to what lies within us.
—RALPH WALDO EMERSON

FTER THAT NIGHT, MY BARRIERS collapsed, and Colin stepped across the threshold and into my life. He convinced me to take some time off from work, so he could show me the city as he saw it, in ways starving artists rarely get to. In a few short months, we attended productions on Broadway, as well as at the Met, City Center, The Public Theater and Circle in the Square. We ate at Sardis and Joe Allen's, Cafe Carlyle, Cafe Des Artistes and The Russian Tea Room. We rode the Staten Island Ferry, climbed the Statue of Liberty, took the elevator to the top of the Empire State Building and walked slowly through Central Park and around the Boat Basin. We ice-skated in Rockefeller Center, visited the New York Public Library and the Metropolitan and Guggenheim Museums. We wandered through Bloomingdales, Henri Bendel, Bonwit Teller, Bergdorf Goodman and Zabar's. In return, I took him to the dance concerts of Merce Cunningham,

Paul Taylor, Alvin Ailey, Jose Limon and Martha Graham. He opened me to his New York, and I opened him to mine.

When I asked if he should be spending so much money, he waved off the question. His string of out-of-town jobs over the last year paid him more than enough to show me the town. Working those productions also meant he could now take the more important, but lesser paying projects in Manhattan. For directors, being seen in New York by producers was just as important as actors being seen by casting directors. Here, he could direct the workshops, Off-Off Broadway plays and staged readings that might or might not be the next big hit.

Our stories were different but our passions the same. We learned everything about each other—as much as I was willing to tell, anyway. I talked about Deni and how we got to New York, about Frank, and how he didn't. He learned about my mother's illness and death, my estrangement from Daddy, my deep love for Aunt Amelia and Uncle Hamp, the breathtaking landscape I grew up in and my contradictory need to get away from it. My story was as mixed up in my telling as in my mind. One thing I was clear about: I told him nothing about my baby.

"I'm the offspring of a pair of energetic, theater-loving parents, Marjorie and Brent Bennett, who met each other fresh out of college in an Uta Hagan acting class," he told me over wine at Joe Allen's.

"They were both theater people. That's so cool Off-Broadway. What a perfect match, both emotionally and career-wise." My daddy knew almost nothing about theater.

"Almost cool. After giving the New York Theater their youngest and most carefree days, they found themselves pregnant." He smiled and pointed to himself.

"Oh, I'm sorry. I mean, not for you being born. I mean..."

"It's okay," he laughed. "Marriage for them was not questioned for a second. They were each other's soul mate. With a child on the way, my father accepted a position as a drama teacher at a high school in Rhinebeck. Mother became a local celebrity, performing in all the community theater productions with Dad as the director. During that time, Brent also wrote plays. Marjorie always had the starring role."

"Yeah, I guess they worked it out pretty well."

"They were—are—great parents. I lucked out. They tried hard to give me as much as possible, which to them meant an education in the arts. As soon as I could sit still in a theater seat, I went with them to On- and Off- Broadway shows. Rhinebeck was small town living close enough to The Big Apple for me to benefit easily from their enthusiasm."

I didn't expect to feel envious. My background was nowhere close to his. I wanted to get away from those with whom I felt little connection, and here he could go home and talk with his parents about Joe Papp's latest Shakespeare production at *The Public*. I didn't even want to go home. But listening to him, I thought, maybe I just found "my home."

At the mailbox, Father Benjamin was all smiles when I explained what was happening with Colin and me.

"I knew you two were a match from the minute you and I met. I have a good sense for such things." He pulled a wad of white envelopes from his box and began sorting through them.

Tom and Jerry whistled and then waved to us as they wiped off the outside tables at *Rick's Café*. Rolerina whizzed by, made a 180 degree turn in front of the stoop, dipped his wand toward us, then Tom and Jerry and skated the rest of the block backwards observing the people's faces he just passed.

"You and Aunt Amelia. She told me right after your party when Colin and I met that she had a good feeling about him and not to throw this one away just because of what Frank did. I'm really kind of glad Colin was gone for a year. I needed that time to get over Frank's letter."

My box only had one letter in it, and it was from Aunt Amelia. She often jotted off notes and clipped articles she found enlightening and would send them to me in between our weekly phone calls. Sometimes I longed for a letter from Daddy. Today was one of those days, but, of course, nothing was there.

All this talk made me aware that the one place I still needed to visit was where Colin now called home. Then one night, he invited me to his apartment for dinner. Apartment was not the right terminology though. Where he called home turned out to be an incredibly enormous space called a loft, housed in an old factory building to the south of Greenwich Village in an area called SoHo. This bleak neighborhood looked the same for many years, like something from a war-torn era. But Colin recognized great potential; along with a few other brave adventurers, he took possession of one of these loft spaces before the tide of popularity took hold.

The first time I went there it seemed a little scary. By day, I found only run-down abandoned buildings, trash-littered sidewalks, broken street lamps and the smell of urine and garbage mixed in the air. At night, lights glowed through half-covered windows on the upper floors of a few buildings, music emanated through open windows, and flavorful cooking smells masked everything else. These inhabitants, all artists of one form or another, were real ground-breakers, the brave Avant-guard of housing, Colin called them.

And although the buildings seemed like nothing on the outside, inside was like stepping into another world. In the same way, the brownstone captured my heart in The Village, the loft captured my heart in SoHo. These remarkable places were open, spacious and called out for creative minds to arrange their interiors to match the talents of their owners.

"How did you find this place?" I asked, after being there for only a few minutes. I wasn't sure what to wear for the first evening at his home, but by process of elimination of what I didn't want to wear, I chose my white gauze, scooped neck peasant blouse which showed off my neck and shoulders, a long wine-colored skirt, and black leather boots. Colin greeted me in charcoal corduroys and matching cotton turtleneck.

"Well, it's kind of interesting," Colin said, while scanning the countertops for something. The open kitchen was only a few feet away from the front door, allowing for a small entrance space with a coat rack. The vast living and dining areas lay beyond a butcher block counter with bar stools which created its own boundary. Behind the kitchen, Colin pointed toward the only bedroom, a bathroom, a large storage closet and an office.

"When we ground-breakers first saw the space..." He paused, leaning in the refrigerator. "Oh, here it is." He stood back up with a bottle of wine in his hand. "I think you will like this one." With a small knife, he removed the foil from the bottle. "The lofts were in terrible shape. We needed to spend a great deal of money to make them livable. That was the big risk. The landlord wouldn't put anything in writing about our improvements to his building." He inserted an opener in the cork. "We soon learned the landlord was about to lose the building to the city because he owed so much in back property taxes. We didn't want that to happen, so I got the potential tenants together to discuss our options. By the end of the meeting, we'd come up with a plan." He took two wine glasses off an open shelf and placed them on the counter and began to pour.

"A plan? What kind of plan? I can't imagine telling a landlord anything," I said, slowly glancing around the room, taking in the size.

"We proposed to pay his back taxes, if, in return, he would agree to give us a long master lease at a low rent, permission to fix up our own spaces any way we wanted, and retain the right to sell the improvements if we vacated. To keep his building, the landlord jumped at the idea; we struck a bargain and this particular building began to have life again."

He walked over and handed me a glass. "You look wonderful tonight, well, every night. To us," he said.

Goose bumps formed on my arms at hearing the word "us."

"Soon, floors were stripped and varnished, light fixtures repaired and replaced, kitchens installed where there had been none, bathrooms remodeled and expanded, closets built and furniture moved in. After I cleaned the windows, for the first time in many years, curtains went up, bamboo shades attached, and trailing green plants hung from hooks in the brick walls and by the windows. Voilà, a neighborhood began."

As I looked at the "before" pictures of this space, then at the space now, my admiration for his pioneering nature grew. I thought the story of how he made this ragged, dirty broken-down space a home was totally out-of-sight, but when he served dinner, my amazement level grew to new heights. We started with a green salad with red peppers, scallions, blue cheese and red grapes in a homemade vinaigrette; poached salmon followed with fresh asparagus in a dill sauce and wild rice pilaf. While we ate, we sipped a dry white Chardonnay and listened to Bill Evans piano jazz in the background; I sensed everything was perfect.

After dinner, he didn't let me help him clean up. Banished to the living room with another refill of wine, I heard the click and drop of a new record. As the sound of Herbie Hancock filled the air, I began to sway to the gentle rhythms, while trying to imagine the people who worked in this building when it served as factory space. I thought about the clothes of the employees over time: women in long skirts with bustles and high-necked blouses, men in starched shirts and suspenders. What would they think of how things changed; how we were using where they used to work?

I put my glass on the coffee table and began to turn my hips and torso, lifting my arms to the beat of the music. All my worries seemed to vanish that night and in their place a real knowing, that I was in the right place with the right man, took over.

"Hey, that doesn't look like modern dance," Colin called out from the open kitchen.

"Oh, modern dance isn't all I do." Almost automatically, my feet tapped in place along with the beat. Then my toes pointed in towards each other and back out as I let my feet carry me away from the stereo toward the opposite wall, not unlike James Brown moving across the stage. When I paused, my arms swayed over my head while my hips moved in the opposite direction from my torso. I turned and lifted my right leg, then snapped my foot back in toward my left leg. Holding that pose for the next several beats, I then snapped back into the groove of the music, twisting and gliding in one direction, then quickly turning in another direction back across the floor.

While I paused with my back toward the kitchen, I felt a hand around my waist. Colin pressed his body up against me. Without turning around, we swayed to the music. Then he moved his hands up my sides from my thighs past my waist to my armpits.

His hands stayed up under my arms, and I leaned back into his chest. After a slight hesitation, his hands moved forward and rested under my breasts. Then he began moving his fingers over my nipples in slow circles. Although not discussed, both of us knew this kind of touching was way overdue. Then gently touching my shoulders, he turned me around to face him, took my wrists and pulled my arms around his neck. With no space between our faces, we kissed—a long slow kiss. It was so long, that at one point, I had to pull away to get air. When he kissed me once again, he pushed the edges of my scooped necked top off both shoulders. In a second, my blouse fell to my waist, and he began softly kissing my breasts. My back arched as I lost myself completely, that is, until I realized the shades were still raised on all the windows.

"Colin, your neighbors...they can see in." I pointed toward the uncovered windows.

He looked up at the enormous windows that were never covered and laughed before he carried me into his bedroom.

"I like watching you dance, but I like dancing with you just as much," he said as he lowered me to his bed.

By the end of 1974, Colin and I were almost always together. Partly because we were enamored with each other, and partly because of the continuing saga of the circumstances of my life, we spent most of our time at his loft. My last roommate stayed longer than anyone else since Deni, but I needed to be alone in my apartment. Or maybe I needed to be away from her. An aspiring concert violinist, her Asian mother envisioned no other life for her daughter than to be molded to her violin. The pitch of her vibrato, drone of scales and the intense pounding out of Brahms, Sibelius Concerto, 3rd movement, Paganini: Caprices

Bach Chaconne Mendelssohn E minor, St. Saens Concerto No. 2, Carmen Fantasy Paganini: Tchaikovsky, Liszt, and Schumann all day and night, burned my ears and blocked my ability to think. I welcomed the invitation to stay away more often.

But the magic didn't completely stay with me. Soon *Steiger's* closed, followed by my roommate telling me she was moving to a bigger apartment on the Upper West Side at the beginning of the New Year. With these two things happening at once, I began to wonder about my ability to ever get settled in New York, to not have life always be a struggle. I didn't want to spoil Colin's and my New Year's Eve celebration, so I kept the news of both events to myself.

As Aunt Amelia taught, for those who are watching, when one door closes, usually another one opens. And open it did. On New Year's Eve, unaware of my new financial complications, Colin asked me to move in with him. By then, we were so close the idea seemed perfectly natural. Not wanting to appear too anxious, I asked if I could think it over, overnight. So on New Year's Day, 1975, after a call from Aunt Amelia and Uncle Hamp, and a brief talk with Father Benjamin and Taylor, all encouraging me not to do anything except follow my heart, I accepted.

"Nadine, I want you to feel like this is your home too," Colin said a week later, as we carried lamps, bean bag chairs, and boxes from my apartment through the door to his loft. When I looked around for a place to set them down, I realized loft spaces were deceiving. The space was enormous, yet there wasn't any place to put my things. Colin's clothes filled the only closet in the loft. Some clothes were on hangers and some piled on the floor or tossed over chairs. Extra shelves, built-ins, hutches and cabinets were non-existent.

He put down what he was carrying and took the boxes out of my hands. Panic crept into the pit of my stomach. I hoped my discomfort didn't show. I never set up house with a man before. It wasn't marriage but was quite similar. I was leaving the remaining control I had of my world and joining Colin's, and he didn't seem ready for me to merge my things with his.

When he realized he hadn't cleared any space for me, he fell all over himself making room. He moved piles off countertops, emptied drawers, stumbled over chairs, backed into doors and threw clothes from the floor into the laundry basket. This was not his usual pulled together on-top-of-it-all image. To me, this kind of reception was incredibly sexy.

"I want you to be happy, Nadine. I really do. Things are a bit of a mess right now. I promise they'll be better. You stay here; I'll get the rest." He kissed me lightly and sprinted out the door for another load from the borrowed double-parked van.

With that, I began to relax. I realized the working out of the space wasn't what actually bothered me. I was afraid my freedom would be taken away, as so many things had been taken away from me. I kept silent; I didn't want to break the spell. This unique living space, on a not-so-lovely run-down street, was almost as alluring as Colin. I had no idea that within two years of being in Manhattan, I would be in such a place. I pressed the button on the stereo. Soft, acoustical rhythms began to lure my worry away from me. I began to move. I turned, then lifted my right leg and left arm high in the air as the loft again became my stage and my escape.

After a couple of minutes, I glimpsed Colin standing with a box at the propped-open doorway. When he put down his armload and leaned against the brick wall, I quit. "Oh, sorry, I'm doing it again. I thought I was alone."

"No, don't stop. This is great. I want you to do whatever you want, whenever you want. I love watching you dance."

I allowed the music to take possession of me and once again began swaying and turning.

At the end of a turn, he caught me by the waist with both arms and pulled me into him. "I don't want this feeling to end. I don't want to lose you, Nadine."

As he twirled me around, improvising his own version of Nureyev and Fontaine, I held a *relevé* and let him take the lead. The turn ended with me right in front of him. I lowered down from my toes and met him eye to eye, his arm still tightly wrapped around my waist, holding my chest to his. He leaned in and kissed me softly at first and then harder, until I nearly fell backwards from the pressure.

"Easy there now, boy," I said. "Don't break me; you just got me."

This broke us up, and we fell down on the rug, rolling around, tickling, wrestling, and squealing like a couple of kids.

Two weeks after I moved in, Colin came home with a new set of shelves and a chest of drawers for me. He left the shelves in the hallway, and I held the door for him as he toted the chest of drawers into the foyer of the loft. Once he got to the bedroom door, he needed help, so I propped the door open with a brick and went over to help him.

Just as we got it through the doorway, I heard the sound of a throat clearing. We both stepped back so we could see the front door. In the shadow of the dim hallway, a woman stood just outside the still open loft door. When she stepped toward us and into the light, I sat up erect as if I touched an electrical socket.

"Where did you come from?" I blurted out. "I mean, how did you know I was here?" I jumped up, ran over, and threw my arms around her. "Are you all right?" I stepped back. "No, wait a minute. I'm mad at you." She didn't say a word; her large round eyes now looked sad and hollow.

I then remembered Colin on the floor and turned toward him.

"Oh, Colin, I'm sorry—this is Deni Hansen."

Colin jumped up, bounded over to where we were standing and put out his hand. When she didn't raise hers, Colin lowered his. As she stared in at the loft between the two of us, I stared at her full-length, mahogany-colored mink coat. *Geez Louise, where in the hell did she get this?* My eyes widened like they were popping from my skull.

"I'm sorry. I don't know why I came over here. I've got to go," she said in a monotone.

"No, wait. You can't go. You just got here," I said, trying to cover my uncomfortable staring.

"Come on in, have a seat. I'll make some coffee," Colin said, pointing her toward the living room. From behind her, his eyes seemed to ask what was going on.

"Yes, a good idea." I lightly touched her arm as I walked her toward the couch, shaking my head almost imperceptibly toward Colin. "Let me take your coat," I said, not knowing where this was going.

From the kitchen, I saw Colin watching us as he made the coffee.

Deni didn't stop me as I eased it off her shoulders and draped it over my arm. I placed her coat, reeking of perfume, over the back of a chair across the room.

Colin and I exchanged another quick glance when we glimpsed what she wore underneath. A tight, skimpy black knit dress and high heeled boots accentuated her long legs. Her simple, long straight dancer hair was replaced with hair-sprayed loopy curls framing an overly made-up face. I bit my lip to keep from looking shocked. Deni never wore makeup; she was beautiful without it. Someone must have convinced her otherwise.

As she sat at one end of the couch, I sat in a chair directly across from her. From there, I could see Deni and Colin at the same time. "So, Deni, how are you?" I began lamely.

She looked past my left shoulder, expressionless. Finally, in a robotic-sounding way, she answered, "I'm fine. How are you?"

"Good, good." I searched for some kind of conversation starter. "So really, how did you know I was here? How did you find me?"

As she turned back toward me, a bit more presence came into her eyes. "I went to our apartment, and you weren't there. Then I saw Father Benjamin. He told me you were probably over here."

Colin brought over a tray with a pot of coffee, mugs, cream and sugar. I moved magazines and old newspapers aside as he placed the tray on the coffee table. Thankfully, he was adept at this. In his early years of being a go-fer for producers and directors, he learned about making the "big cheeses" comfortable.

Colin poured for all of us. "Cream or sugar, Deni?" he asked.

"Uh, yeah," she said, turning again and looking around the loft now.

"Here, I'll let you do it," he said, offering her both.

She leaned over and added two teaspoons of sugar and poured cream in her mug, then sat back, stirring as steam rose.

"Where are you living now?" I asked, afraid of the answer.

"On the Upper East Side. I have an apartment."

"Oh, really? That's nice." Her non-communication began to annoy me. "I have everything I need, you know."

"That's good. So you are doing okay, I take it," I said, trying to coax more out of her. Part of me was so glad to see her, and another part wanted to let her have it for leaving me like that, but she seemed too fragile. "You know," I said, "your mother called a few times. I told her I would leave you a message. I didn't tell her I didn't know where you were. Did you ever call her?" No answer. "I guess you did. Your mother finally quit calling the apartment."

"My mother? Yes, I've talked to my mother. She thinks I'm living with a boyfriend."

"Well, you sort of do, don't you? I mean Mr. Bertram. That's who you're living with, aren't you?"

"Not exactly. I live in one of his apartments."

Colin and I exchanged another look. I wasn't surprised, but I wanted her to tell me in her own words.

"Wow. That must be nice. He pays for your apartment."

"Yeah, he does." Her tone changed, adding an edge. "Colin pays for your apartment, doesn't he?"

"Well, we haven't quite worked all that out yet." I didn't like her insinuation or comparison at all. "So what brings you here?" I wanted to get off that subject, for the moment, anyway.

"I don't know. I was in the neighborhood."

"Oh, in the neighborhood. Good, that's great. I'm glad you decided to come for a visit." My annoyance with her grew. I hoped she didn't sense my frustration, but as soon as I finished refilling her cup, she stood up and slipped back into her mink coat.

"It looks as if everything is going good with you. I've got to go now. Thanks for the coffee."

"Oh, don't go yet. You just got here." I turned to Colin. Deni moved toward the door.

Colin stood up. "Deni, how about staying for dinner? I'm a damn good cook, and there's plenty." He must have seen the desperation in my face.

"Some other time. I've got to get back now."

"But how can I reach you? Give me your phone number and address at least." I looked around for a pen and something to write on.

"Uh, I'll contact you. That would be easiest. I know where you are now."

With that, she was gone. I slowly closed the industrial size front door and leaned against it. Then I ran over to the windows overlooking the street and caught a glimpse as she got into a taxi which must have been waiting for her the whole time. The cab disappeared after turning right onto Houston Street.

I fell back onto the couch. "What just happened here?"

"I don't exactly know. I hoped you could enlighten me," Colin said.

"I don't have a good feeling about whatever is going on with her."

"That was kind of obvious." He sat next to me. "You can't worry about her. She's an adult, and she's..."

"She's what? She's doing what she wants to do? I don't think she is. I think she's got herself caught up in something she can't get out of. I've been worried for a whole year, and I am more worried now."

Colin leaned over and pulled me into him. "I'm sorry. You're worried. All we can do is be here for her if she comes back again." He sat up straight and knocked his forehead with his hand. "Oh man, I'd better finish unloading that van and get it back to the theater." He headed down to the street for the last load from my apartment.

When I spoke with Aunt Amelia that week, I told her that even though Deni's visit disturbed me enormously, I tried to push the image of her to the back of my mind for a while.

"You're doing the right thing, child. You can't do anything about her choices, only your own. You have a new life with a man you adore and who seems to be totally wrapped up in you. You don't want anything to disturb that feeling."

Thank the Lord for Aunt Amelia. I don't know what I'd do without her.

Over the coming months, Colin and I tried to make adjustments to his living space. He quickly realized that we needed to make this space "ours" and took me shopping for new furniture. The first item we found was an oak dresser for me at the newly opened antique shop around the corner on Spring Street and Sixth Avenue. The second item was a large round mahogany table and chairs set that seated eight people easily and ten if we needed. This replaced the teak dining set that Colin's parents gave him when they were redecorating their Rhinebeck home.

We didn't go overboard, but I loved having money again to buy these things. And a few new pieces of "our" furniture made a significant difference. As sad as I felt about leaving Father Benjamin and Taylor on Christopher Street, I loved my new home, and I was more than happy to be sharing it with this generous loving man.

Months later, after we got into bed and I turned toward the lamp to read, Colin slid up behind me, put his right arm around my shoulders and fitted his body close to mine like a matching jigsaw puzzle piece. "Are you happy, Nadine?" he asked.

"Happy? Oh yes, I'm very happy, Colin."

"Good. Me too." He squeezed me hard, almost too hard, and I flinched.

Out the window, the nearly full moon hovered above the buildings across the street. An airplane emerged from the black sky, crossed in front of the moon as if by magic, and then disappeared into the darkness.

"Then when are you going to tell your father about us?" he asked.

"Daddy?" I rolled away from him, sat up and reached for the covers.

"You have to tell him sometime, is all I'm saying." He kissed my shoulder. He rolled me over on to my back and touched my face with his fingers, circling from my forehead to my chin and back up the other side.

"Family is important. And I want to meet your "daddy."

I didn't say anything. I slid down under the covers and rested my head on the pillow. His hand caressing my face felt so soothing and caring.

"Don't you think family is important?" he asked. His questions interrupted my enjoyment.

"Of course it's important, but Daddy, he doesn't want to hear from me. And...and I don't want to talk about this right now." Colin took his finger away from my face.

"What is it, Nadine? How can this have happened with your father? No one stays mad forever. He will come around. Don't you think he'll like me?"

Who wouldn't like Colin? What would Daddy say to my finding another man in theater? "Acting is for ne'er-do-wells!" How many times had I heard that?

"Hasn't he ever come to New York to visit you?"

Everything that happened in the year before I left for New York flooded my mind and raced through my body. I didn't want to feel those emotions again. I couldn't tell Colin, who came from such loving parents, how hard it would be to love my daddy again.

"He cut me off. He gave up on me," I said, when I pulled myself together.

"But he still loves you."

"My daddy used to love me. He once gave me anything and everything I ever wanted, but he changed. After Mamma died, he changed into someone I didn't know and eventually, I didn't like one bit."

"He was devastated, too, Nadine. He may not have handled his wife's death right, but everyone acts like a jerk sometimes.

I'll bet he misses you more than you know. How about if we go down to Beaufort and visit him?"

"No!" I shouted, surprising myself. I didn't want to talk about my daddy. Aunt Amelia was my only family, as far as I was concerned. Then more softly, I added, "I mean, I can't. Not right now. I've got too many rehearsals. And you've got rehearsals too. I'm... we're, too busy."

"Okay, I'm sorry. You don't have to tell me anything else right now."

Colin didn't ask about Daddy again.

Our lives and careers moved forward with more successes than interferences over the next year. I reveled in rehearsals and performances without worrying about having to leave early to get to a job. Colin's directing plate filled even more than before; he had so many job offers, turning down work became his norm. After all my mis-starts since I'd come to New York to dance, I couldn't believe how smoothly everything was going, and, most importantly, how happy I was. Then I would remember the ritual and know I was moving forward on some plan that I couldn't really put my finger on. I'd always known the plan was beneath me at all times, but when each day was a struggle for survival, I never rested comfortably. Finally, I was seeing my path heading upward as Aunt Amelia predicted I would.

Then boom! In 1976 right after the next New Year, all my joy began to collapse. First, Gabriella gathered the entire dance company together and announced, "We should be rehearsing for our next performance season which is still six months away, but I have something I need to tell you. I'm so very sorry, but we're going to have to go on hiatus for a while or shut the dance company down entirely. Additional funding, i.e. grants from the National Endowment for the Arts and the state-wide grants, which we all know are vital to our art form, have gotten extremely tight with this new administration. It appears that they don't want any money funneled to the arts. So, as much as I hate to say this, we're all going to have to find our other work. It's not going to be easy to get another dance job since this will affect everyone in the arts, and even if you did, we all know the pay is not exactly a living wage. But I know you will all find something to keep you here and keep you taking classes. Don't forget; classes are our lifeline. It is the only way to keep your instrument tuned. Please don't lose this."

The silence and the sadness were palpable; our postures bent like wilted sunflowers. For some, the news was so hard to take that they dropped to sitting on the floor. Others touched the shoulder next to them, or grabbed a hand and leaned into that person.

"Now, as for me, since I knew this was coming, I've been able to be proactive. I didn't want to tell you until I knew for sure, but I've been offered my old job at Sarah Lawrence, teaching dance classes. There's something out there for everyone, so don't let yourself fall into panic, and don't go home unless you just have to. All I can do now is to let you know if things change."

While riding the subway downtown, I couldn't stop thinking about what to do. I understood there were funding problems in the arts all around; and worse, Aunt Amelia having cancer. I didn't think it would get this bad. This news was hard to believe. Everything else in my life had been nearly perfect, and I was feeling a comfort and completeness I hadn't known in such a long time. I suppose I could always take classes, but going on without performing was unthinkable. According to the ritual, performing was what I was sent here to do. What was I going to do?

Then in January 1977, as I began to go over my plans for Colin's birthday, my first dinner party solely prepared by me, Deni appeared at the loft again. At first, I took her re-appearance as a sign that she wanted to give up her life with Mr. Bertram and come back to dance and to me. Her eyes and cautious demeanor, though, were as distant and unlike herself as before. She claimed her life was going great, but sadness tinged with fear showed in her inability to hold eye contact with me. With any questions I asked, I could feel her unease. When the phone rang, she jumped at the sound as if she'd been poked in the back or shocked by electricity. I walked over to pick up the phone, but when I turned around she was gone.

"Damn," I said to the empty loft, putting my hand over the receiver. I hoped to keep her with me; find out what was actually going on. But she wasn't about to let me. Her look and actions felt like she was a runaway, like the sad children around the Port Authority Bus Terminal. I wondered at what age parents gave up on those children, decided they were beyond saving, or that it was too late and they had already adjusted to their new life. And who made these decisions? I wouldn't want that job.

I remembered the phone in my hand. "Oh, Aunt Amelia. I'm sorry. Deni was right behind me, and now she's gone." I told her about Deni and how haunted I was by my disappearing friend. She expressed her concern but warned me again, "You have to let Deni go. You feel partially responsible since she followed you and your enthusiasm, but you can't make her stay. You can't fix her. She's got to want to come back on her own." After I settled down, she wished me a Happy New Year and filled me in on everyone at home, including Daddy.

"There isn't much to say about Sam. He's still working, managing all his properties. One of your Varnville cousins is helping him. Your daddy doesn't trust him with anything too complicated. You know your father; he's extremely private about his business. You were the only one he trusted after your mama died." I listened, but when I didn't hear that he ever asked about me, I didn't say anything back.

"I tell him about you, too, you know." It was like she read my mind. "When I tell him, he does the same thing you are doing. Nothing. I know you both are listening, though." Then she hit me with her news. "I'm starting chemotherapy at the end of the week." She paused, and I sucked in my breath. "I detest chemicals. I have only trusted treatments that come from the earth, but they say many women never have a problem again after the chemo." She paused again. "We all have to make hard decisions that go against our principles sometimes. Everything will be fine, dear. I just wanted you to know."

Chemo did not sound fine to me. I had no choice but to believe her. I guess I still expected her to make a full miraculous recovery from this nasty disease. She acts as if she had never been acquainted with a cancer cell in her life. She was still invincible to me. I didn't want her to hear me crying. That would seem as if I didn't have faith in her choices or abilities. So we offered our love to each other and then our goodbyes.

I raced home right after our meeting, with my head throbbing. All I thought of was why were bad things happening again when my path was opening up and clearly heading in the right direction? I needed to talk with Colin, but he wasn't there. With his career still sailing upward, like on the wings of Pegasus, we saw less and less of each other. Our busy lives seemed natural as long as I was as engaged as he was. So, when the phone rang and Father Benjamin asked me if I had time for coffee, I dropped my dance bag and loneliness and hurried off to join him at *The Bagel & I.*

CHAPTER 13

1977

 Passion is the trigger of success.
—Anonymous

"**Y**OU KNOW YOU'RE NOT IN Kansas anymore, don't you, Nadine?" Father Benjamin propped his crutches against the wall and pulled out a chair to sit down. "But it's really great that you could stop your busy life and join me. I can't believe how long it's been."

"I'm so happy you called when you did. I hate that I don't see you as much since I'm living in SoHo with Colin. But I wouldn't change it for anything."

Father Benjamin lifted an arm to signal Felix.

Felix whooshed in with our standard order and then whooshed back out to tend to his other customers. Unless one of us had an urge for something different, our order was two black coffees, his with a cinnamon stick and two plain bagels with cream cheese each for us.

I sensed Father Benjamin watching me as I spread the cream cheese on the warm fresh bagel.

"You look absolutely wonderful, my friend; your hair, your clothes. Is this the same girl who fell off the turnip truck by way of Kennedy Airport, how long ago? The same girl who had everybody's problems stuck to her like beggars' lice? No, no, it isn't. I would say you have changed, grown, blossomed. Definitely conquered Manhattan. And Colin—I have never seen him this happy. This whole thing brings me such joy."

"Yes, I guess it is something." I felt my face redden. I hated that about myself, never being able to keep a poker face. "I am truly happy. You know that."

"Then, what's wrong? Something seems to be slightly off center here. Is it something you can tell me about?"

I didn't realize my worries showed. I was trapped among Deni showing up again, Aunt Amelia's deepening illness, and my fear of never performing again because Gabriella's company was on indefinite hiatus. I hoped meeting and moving in with Colin meant I was headed in exactly the right direction and that the ritual's effects were in full force. Maybe they were, but sometimes it just didn't feel like it.

"Deni reappeared recently." I began with the easiest for me at the moment. My worry- based priority list shifted daily, if not hourly.

"Oh my. What happened this time? Is she okay?"

I explained briefly about her visit. "I don't know what she thinks she's doing. I want to grab her and drag her back with me. But I can't."

"Tell me about it. I want to grab every young boy I find who gets off that same turnip truck and give them my "facts of life" speech. They think because they escaped the persecution from family and friends and gave up their home, they have found Shangri-La. They act as if they are somehow free and safe, now that they are in The Village. "Father Benjamin's face darkened for the first time since I had known him. "It can be just as dangerous out there with their own brothers as it was back home in isolation. Some gay men try to beat up on other gay men because it was done to them. These new kids have no jobs or money. Many of them end up "tricking" to make a living. The police are particularly brutal to those they find doing it. And of course, there are the angry straight men with violent streaks who think their problems will ease by bashing in the face of a homosexual."

I sat back, placed my hands in my lap as if praying, taking in his words. "I hadn't thought of it that way. I guess there are some similarities with Deni, except she wasn't persecuted. But maybe she felt she was."

"Maybe," he said. For a moment, we acknowledged the hard reality for those who make the wrong choices early on. "They come here with ambition, just like you or I or anyone else."

"What can you do for these young boys?" I asked. "I mean, will they listen to you? What do you say to them?"

"It's a slow process at best. I remind them that they are all children of God, and God loves all his children. It works best for me if I think of it as playing the odds. For every twenty newbies I try to talk with about God, about safety, about their future, one seems to hear at least part of what I have to say. The rest become victims or statistics and the cycle repeats itself."

Wow, my three main problems pale next to his. He has a whole village to worry about. I slid the salt and pepper shakers back and forth like chess pieces, looking for my next move.

He laughed. "Now this story isn't the case with everyone, as you can see." He turned and gestured with his eyes and his outstretched arm. "There are plenty of gay men who have worked hard to put the ugliness behind them in their early years and strive to make something of their lives. But even they go through

213

hard times; I try to talk with them too. The more men I can reach and show how to feel the power of a bigger love, the more a trust in God gets passed on."

Anyone in the room who knew anything about The Village had a spot in his heart for Father Benjamin. These men might not believe Father Benjamin would accomplish all he said, but they rooted for him to succeed. My own situation wasn't so different. I was rejected too. My daddy made it abundantly clear he didn't want anything to do with me if I left with Frank, crossed the Mason-Dixon Line and worked in theater in New York City.

"Everyone out there has a story," he continued after a pause, "and they're all telling them to me. It takes a good bit of time to be a man of God around here." He laughed at himself.

That's when I first realized he was the "Aunt Amelia" of Greenwich Village.

Felix whirled up to us again offering refills. In order to avoid being hit by the swift moving hot pot, we both sat up straight and leaned back in our chairs. This snapped me out of my own worried thoughts before they showed up on my face again. But when Felix tapped his way back across the room to the kitchen, I found it easy to change to a smile.

"Oh, now, before I forget, you and Taylor are still planning to come to Colin's birthday party in two weeks, aren't you?" I asked.

"Yes, of course. We wouldn't miss it for the world. What can we bring? Or rather, what can Taylor bring? You know I'm not a cook."

"The cake, please. He does such fantastic cakes, and I don't." His whole face brightened as I explained my excitement and nervousness about the upcoming birthday party for Colin I was throwing. I hadn't hosted a party since—I couldn't remember when. Maybe college. First, I never knew when Colin would have a free night, as was the problem with a successful career in theater; and second, I was a bit intimidated at the hosting skills of his friends after being invited to their apartments for dinner. They never minded our last-minute acceptance when Colin found he was off in time for someone else to cook. Seeing my discomfort on the subject, Father Benjamin skillfully re-routed the discussion.

"So, how are the other things going with you?" he asked.

"Things are great." I gave the robotic answer I heard my daddy and mama say for years when things were clearly not great. "Okay, almost everything is great. Aunt Amelia's tumor began growing, and she says she needs to have chemotherapy." My body slumped back into the chair like a deflated balloon.

"I'm really sorry to hear that. But chemo is a good thing, not a bad thing, for two reasons. One, because your aunt is watching its effects closely; she can stop this before it gets out of control; and two, this is life, Nadine. You can't make it better for your aunt or Deni. You can only be a sounding board, send them your love, and be there when they need you. You'd be surprised at how important just doing that is. It's the same for me. I can't fix these boys I am so concerned about, but I can be an anchor when they are ready to look in a new direction."

"Thank you. You always help me too. But there is one more thing. It's not Colin—Colin and I are definitely great. I just wish I could get a chance to show that I am a choreographer as well as a performer like Gabriella. That's what I trained for in college, not just as a performer. I choreographed my own work in almost every class, not only for my Senior Recital. I didn't really know how much I would miss it. It took not being able to perform for me to realize this.

But modern dance work is not as abundant as roles in plays and musicals. There is much more demand for his "legitimate" theater. Sometimes it makes me angry. I work hard and—I wasn't going to tell you yet, but the truth is, Gabriella's company has to go on hiatus for a while; it's problems with funding, which translates into 'I don't even get to perform anymore.' Other than that, everything else is, you know, fantastic. More than I could have imagined. But this news makes me sad. Really sad."

"Oh no, not for you too. I know all about the funding issues facing artists right now. I can't understand how our leaders can cut the NEA budget and think we'll continue to be an advanced society. I'm so sorry to hear this is affecting you. Does Colin know about this change you're wanting in your dance career? Does he know you want to choreograph, too? He can be your best asset in your search, you know."

"No, he doesn't know. I like to do things myself, but I guess this is an area I need some help in. Maybe there's a show looking for a choreographer. You know I'd take anything; off, off, Off-Broadway, something in a public school, I don't care; I'll start anywhere. When I was performing regularly, I wouldn't have considered it. But now it looks as if my performing days are numbered."

"See there? You're on your way already. Can you feel it?"

Before I could answer, I happened to look up. Colin stood at the front door scanning the room. He saw me and waved as he wove his way through the tables and chairs blocking the path to where we were seated.

"Oh, there you are." Colin reached over and kissed me squarely on the mouth, holding his lips to mine far longer than I expected. "Mmmm," he uttered. Blood rose in my cheeks from the intensity and the public display.

"Hey, Father Benjamin. How are you?" he said after I pulled back long enough for him to get the hint.

"I'm fine, and I'd ask how you are, but that seems fairly obvious."

"Yes, yes, I am pretty darn fine. I am actually the best I have ever been." He grabbed an empty chair from the next table, grinning wide. "Well, do you want to know why?"

We both looked blankly at him.

"I'll tell you why," he answered. "I got the job."

I didn't know what he was talking about. He was working on a show already. Neither one of us said anything. Then Father Benjamin asked. "What job is that?"

"The job I have been waiting for my whole life."

"You don't mean–a–a," I stuttered.

"I am going to direct a Broadway show."

"Oh, my God. You are?" I leaned in and grabbed his hand.

Father Benjamin put out his hand to shake Colin's. "What is the name of the show?"

"*Dreamwatchers.*"

"*Dreamwatchers*? I've heard of that. Let me think. Someone I know is working on it. One of my parishioners. Oh yes, I remember; Rick Borders. But, isn't that already in production?"

"Yes and no. It started rehearsals here in town but hasn't left yet. The director quit for health reasons, and they want me to take his place."

After a moment of no response from either of us, he leaned into the table, energy vibrating from every muscle in his arms and neck. "Well, don't just sit there; tell me what you think!" Colin said.

"Oh, Colin, this is so totally cool." I leaned over and threw my arms around him. I pulled away to see his whole face and asked, "When do you start?"

"Tomorrow."

"Tomorrow? My God, that's fast." Joy and disappointment intertwined in my stomach. My arms, released from his shoulders, hit my mug and splashed coffee onto the table and plates. I grabbed some napkins to wipe up the spill, realizing I was excited about his new job, but immediately scared that with the size of this show, he would be taken away from me.

"I start working here," he leaned in to help clean up, "but then it goes to Boston for out-of-town tryouts in a month," he added.

"In a month? Boston? What do you mean, Boston?" I stopped wiping. "How long will it be there?"

"I don't know for sure. It's scheduled to be there for three months."

As my stomach knotted, my smile melted off my face. "Three months, Colin? That's forever."

"Nadine, I know it is. But I have a plan." He took both of my hands, and with eyes full of glee, looked into my vacant eyes. "I want you to work on it with me."

"Work with you?" I pulled my hands away. "Doing what?"

"I'd like to say dancing in the chorus, but the show is already cast. What I do need is one more assistant stage manager, and I know you would do a great job. We could be together."

I felt Father Benjamin and Colin's eyes boring into me, waiting for my response.

I guess when Colin felt it was too long a pause, he added, "Well, honey, now what do you think?" Colin was clearly excited with his solution.

"I–I don't know. This is all so sudden." A thousand thoughts raced through my head. First was his upcoming birthday party. Then, more importantly, I didn't want him to leave, and I didn't want to go with him. He had no idea how much I now needed work, more dance work, not stage manager work. But it didn't seem to be the right time to tell him about Gabriella's company. How could I explain all this to him?

"Yes, but we can be together. That's the important part." He stood up. "I've got to run now. They've scheduled a meeting. This is a fantastic opportunity—for both of us. Think it over, sweetheart." He kissed me, shook Father Benjamin's hand and disappeared out into the street.

I sat back, trying to absorb what just happened.

"So, are you going to do this, Nadine?"

"I don't know. I have to get my bearings here." Neither one of us said anything. Then it all came out at once. "My performing career has come to a screeching halt just as my love life is soaring. I'm torn between wanting to spend every moment with Colin and every moment involved in dance."

"You know, it could be exciting, working in the trenches of a Broadway show. It's not dancing and choreographing, but it could be extremely interesting. I'm not trying to persuade you one way or the other. I just remember what you told me about your old boyfriend; what was his name, Frank?"

Frank? Why did he bring him up at a time like this?

"As I recall, he went off on his dream job without you and never came back. Now I'm not saying Colin would ever do that. Gosh, no. He's just not the type, and he loves you deeply. I'm just suggesting you think about it. Relationships are hard even without long separations, especially in this business. You can find your choreography job after you get back. There, I've said enough. I've probably talked too much. I'm sorry. Okay, now, I'm going to be late. Forget what I just said. You will know what to do. You will do the right thing."

He got up, steadied himself on his crutches and kissed me on the forehead. Before he left, I grabbed his hand. "Wait, I need to move this birthday party up a week. He'll be too involved in the production in two weeks to care about a party. It has to be this Saturday."

"You're probably right. I'll tell Taylor right away." He touched my cheek. "You don't need to panic. We'll help any way we can to pull it off this weekend. Do you need me to tell the others?"

"That would be a big help. It's the usual group: Jessica, Paul and Adrian."

"Consider it done."

"Thank you so much—for everything."

I watched and silently laughed as he made his way out through the obstacle course of tables, chairs, tote bags left on the floor, and waiters moving too fast. He always had to stop to chat with his parishioners, so it took him quite a few minutes to get out the door.

Because Colin's new show was already cast and in rehearsal, he began running in a hundred different directions at once from that moment on. We barely had time to say goodbye in the morning, weren't even able to celebrate until Friday, and the party was on Saturday. I could have combined our celebration with the birthday party, but that little voice inside told me to do this one on one. Colin wanted to go to a restaurant, but I knew going out would most likely involve running into lots of people, and we'd never be able to finish a sentence, much less a meal. I convinced him to stay home so we could spend some needed alone time together.

My cooking confidence wasn't strong, but I thought it should improve with practice and around someone I wanted to please. So I planned to serve him one of his favorite menus.

Over a dinner of Steak au Poivre with nutmeg and pepper, roasted red potatoes and a green salad with pears and blue cheese, he raved about my cooking between a steady reporting of the latest developments on his newest and best job ever. I loved watching his face as he spoke. His eyes gleamed with enthusiasm and joy as he alternately waved a fork or knife in the air for emphasis. He still didn't know about the fate of my dance company or my desire to choreograph, but I didn't want to interrupt what had to be one the most thrilling moments in his life. I let him talk and talk, hoping he would eventually wear out from the topic altogether. I didn't want to discuss my going with him and taking a job on the show. I wasn't ready to give him an answer, and I think he knew better than to push too hard.

After dinner and before we left the table, he came over to my chair, pulled me toward him and kissed me. I slid off the chair and onto him, and we rolled onto the floor. Right there on the wood floor, we made love; slow sweet love. I imagined that Colin didn't need to bring up the job; he'd found a better way to let me know what it would be like without him. He held my face in both of his hands, a gesture that always made me feel as if I was taffy coming out of a machine at the fair. His hand moved to my waist, then up under my blouse to my ribs, and slid around to my sides before rubbing my back, making me arch. With one hand, he unhooked my bra and pulled my blouse off over my head. By then, I was as ready as I would ever be.

When the floor got too hard to lie on comfortably, he pulled me up and carried me to the bedroom, where we did it all over again. After, I was exhausted, but wide awake. Like a dance workout too late in the day, sex always stimulated me, kept me from falling asleep for far longer than I wanted. With Colin snoring lightly, I glanced over at him and glimpsed a peaceful grin on his face. I so envied him. I had a dinner party to get started first thing the next morning. Finally, I, too, drifted off, falling in that other world almost immediately.

Dreams come to each of us in different ways at different times, Aunt Amelia said. Some people don't remember theirs at all; some only get flashes of disjointed information, and some get a whole story complete with dialogue.

In flashes, I found myself dreaming of Frank. Not welcoming him, I tried to shake it away, even in my sleep. Why was this happening? I had the man I loved lying next to me in my bed, lived with him in a wonderful loft and enjoyed an exciting, though unpredictable, life in theater together. If I could control where

221

my dreams go, I would know my life, just as the Full-Life ritual promised, would be moving in a direction beyond my expectations. But as Aunt Amelia often told me, unfinished business doesn't just let go because we tell it to. The pain and betrayal of Frank and his sudden marriage, still poked holes through my confidence and joy, especially now that Colin was about to leave for this job. That night my dream played out in a totally different way from my short bursting baby dreams. This one was almost like a movie or a scene from an Off-Broadway play.

The Prologue:

In my sleep, through a fog-like setting, I saw a tall woman, around five-foot-eight, with smooth tanned skin and glossy, thick, dark hair past her shoulders. Her evocative round eyes focused straight ahead. I wasn't sure where she was at first. Then my view panned out like a camera shot to reveal her perfectly proportioned body as she purposely walked toward something I couldn't see, hair floating off her shoulders in ripples.

As the dream ether lifted lightly, I saw what her focus was on. It was Frank. He sat in a room or a tent, a shelter of some kind, one leg crossed over the other, ankle to knee as most men do, his left hand gesturing in the air, a magazine or book in the other, lips moving, but no sound came out. I recognized the image immediately. He was studying a script.

For whatever reason, I knew the woman with the floating hair worked on the film also and offered to help Frank learn his lines. I sensed or was given the information that the director was impressed with him because of his rugged good looks, calm demeanor, and ability to take direction. Because of her close connection with this director, this woman, this slick package, alluded to Frank that she knew what actors should do, what to expect, and how to get noticed to get ahead. She pretended to be helpful to a newcomer, but I sensed something else: her visceral attraction to him. Frank was eager to make an impression. And even though he was a natural, within a short amount of time, this woman convinced him she was the reason.

I felt all of it, knew it in my bones, but he saw only what he saw. I wanted to warn Frank to stay away, but he was too excited about his role. When I tried to speak, nothing came out of my mouth.

The Story:

Fast forward to after several days of coaching him on the set. Evocative woman invited Frank over for dinner at her apartment. Oh, brother. Everything was ready when he arrived: a simple meal of pasta, bread, salad and wine. I used to cook him that dinner. But wait, something is unusual, not quite right. As they talked in the kitchen while she finished cooking, she added more herbs to the sauce. It looked just like oregano, tasted like oregano, but it wasn't oregano. Frank, watch out!

He couldn't hear me. After they finished their second helping, Frank and the woman began laughing for no reason as she cleared the dishes. Leaving them on the kitchen counter, she led Frank into the dimly lit living room where Marvin Gaye sang *Let's Get it On* in the background. Frank was a terrific dancer and always loved Motown. He began showing off, dancing with hips swiveling, shoulders punching each beat, arms circling in the air, just like he used to do with me, until his coordination failed and he tripped over an ottoman. Evocative Woman leaned in to help him, thrusting her chest into his chest. When he lowered his arms to steady himself, his hands landed right on top of her breasts. As if in slow motion or a freeze-frame from the movies dailies, he stopped dancing. With his hands not moving away, a child-like "oops" popped out of his mouth, but she didn't budge. In fact, she took his hands in hers and began rubbing them in a soft, circular fashion all around her chest. I could see Frank's eyes following her hands on top of his. Yikes. Stop, Frank, you're stoned. *Stop now*, I called out into a vacuum.

Evocative Woman's face filled with pleasure as her eyes closed and her head tilted back. Frank looked beyond wasted to me. Seeing no resistance from Frank, she took his hands down to her waist and up under her blouse. She moaned softly as Frank rubbed and squeezed to the music. Oh man, what is this? Get me out of here. My head thrashed on my pillow, but I couldn't make myself come back to earth. It was as if I was forced to watch something I should have only suspected, something too painful to see. The end of my relationship played out in my dream as if I was actually in the room.

When she crossed both arms, lifted her blouse up over her head, and threw it across the room, Frank froze. Immediately, I knew all other images, including me, were wiped from his mind as they fell onto the couch in a frenzy of arms, legs, and glistening bodies. Luckily, I was able to squint my eyes and ears shut for the duration. When I opened them, I found them both asleep from exhaustion.

I was exhausted also, wanted to get out, but the dream wasn't over. Frank woke up disoriented. I could tell that his first thought was that he was lying next to me back in South Carolina. When he realized it wasn't me and they were both naked, his face contorted. Panic struck him like a bullet. Oh, man, Frank. He eased off the couch, trying not to wake her. But she woke up and turned her naked body to Frank. She wriggled and stretched as if feigning waking up.

"What happened? I don't remember falling asleep on this couch. We're both naked. Did we...?"

"Yes, we certainly did. And you were amazing." She sat up and leaned in toward Frank, attempting to kiss him, her chest brushing across his.

"Wait, I can't do this." He tried to sit up. "I have a girlfriend."

Now you remember. Too late, Frank. Way too late.

"Had a girlfriend, you mean. You have me now."

"But I'm going to New York to be with Nadine. I thought I made that clear."

Frank was truly confused, and I almost felt sorry for him.

"You seem to have forgotten last night, Frank." She pulled a quilt from the back of the couch over her body and tossed her hair back from her face.

Frank started to get up and then stopped. He looked all around, picked up pillows and put them back.

I felt myself begin to recede from the dream.

She leaned over, dropped the blanket, grabbed Frank's shirt off the floor, and put it on as she walked toward the kitchen.

"Hey, I need that. Where are you going?"

She stopped and leaned against the door frame with the shirt wide open. "I am going to make us coffee, darling. I have a whole breakfast planned."

Then it was over. The dream probably only lasted a few minutes, but it seemed as if it went on for hours. Disoriented and not sure which world I was still in, I slipped out of bed and walked to the bathroom, where I hung my head over the basin and splashed cold water on my face.

In the mirror tired eyes looked back. But on closer examination, I saw, or maybe felt, relief. I wasn't sure why my dream showed me so much detail, but I realized it put Frank's abandonment of me in a perspective I hadn't understood before. This perspective was important. To be fair to Colin and our relationship, I needed to come out of limbo. I needed to know, or at least, believe, I understood what happened with Frank. It also became clear as I looked in the mirror, if I wanted to keep looking in this mirror, in this loft, I would have to decide how to handle this next critical decision.

I padded back to bed, and once under the covers, rolled over to Colin's back and molded my body up next to his until daylight.

CHAPTER 14

1978

We must make the choices that enable us to fulfill the deepest capacities of our real selves.
—Thomas Merton

THERE WASN'T TIME TO DWELL on or try to analyze this dream. The next day was Colin's birthday, and I knew I had to pull a party together and do it quickly. Aunt Amelia taught me to believe in the messages of the night, so I accepted this dramatic—bordering on comical—version of what happened to Frank as truth and vowed to put it all behind me.

I planned a menu for seven people. Besides Father Benjamin and Taylor, Colin wanted me to invite Jessica and Paul, and the high spirited Adrian. Everyone made it a habit always to get together for one another's birthdays. They had all been friends for several years; I was the newcomer and was welcomed with no hesitation. I later learned they all finally approved of one of Colin's girlfriends. I didn't want to disappoint anyone with my party planning skills, so before making a decision about going to Boston, I proceeded to plan the best celebration for Colin that I could.

Father Benjamin and Taylor were the first to arrive that evening. I knew Taylor would come to my rescue if I needed him. He would even make the food and let everyone think it was mine if I let him. But I didn't need to have Taylor do much of anything. By the time they rang the buzzer, the food was cooking, bar set up, appetizers out and the table was set.

Jessica, Paul, and Adrian arrived next. The only one left was the guest of honor. Colin was still on the phone in the bedroom. His parents called to wish him a happy birthday just before Father Benjamin and Taylor got there. Luckily, everyone made themselves at home, and I scurried around the loft, making small talk with my guests.

There was just one question I needed to ask: how long do I let the roast sit before carving, and I needed Taylor for the answer. I saw my mother do this many times but had no idea of the length of time. Balancing the outcome of all the dishes was my most pressing concern.

"Has anybody seen Taylor?" I asked after scouring the loft.

"He went to the car, I think," Father Benjamin said, easing himself onto the leather recliner. Because it was easier for Father Benjamin, he and Taylor were the only ones who kept a car in Manhattan out of this group.

"What for?" I asked bringing out more wine glasses. "Did he forget something?"

"I think he said he wanted a sweater." Father Benjamin laid his crutches on the floor beside the chair.

"A sweater? It's seventy-eight degrees out. What does he want with a sweater?" I handed Father Benjamin his usual glass of red wine.

"Oh, I'm sorry. I really want white tonight," he said. "Here, I'll get it." He started to get up, but I promptly stopped him.

Jessica, Paul, and Adrian headed for the small balcony on the north side of the loft. On a clear night, everyone usually wanted to see the view as soon as they arrived. Sometimes the city just popped out of the darkness like a 3-D movie. From this vantage point, Manhattan looked like a fairyland, the place Dorothy and her friends were searching for, a place with all the answers to those big questions about life.

Back inside, the small questions were still being asked. "What do you want to drink, Adrian?" She re-entered the loft. "Jessica, Paul, how about you?" They followed right behind her.

"Wine for me," Jessica said.

"I'll have wine too," Adrian said, turning her head back toward the view. "I can't have any more vodka for a while. You all nearly killed me on my birthday with those non-stop frozen daiquiris."

"Now let me see," Paul pondered. "What is the proper drink this year for celebrating the birthday of such an esteemed member of our merry group of misfits?"

"'Merry' I can accept, Paul, but 'misfits?'" Jessica said, as she reached in her purse, pulled out a small bottle and dabbed perfume behind her ears.

"I can go with misfits," Adrian said. "That's a compliment to me."

"Hey," I jumped in. "I don't have a problem with misfits. I think we've been called much worse. I rather aspire to misfits." I hoped to sound like one of the group but still felt like a newbie myself.

"Speak for yourself, Jessica," Father Benjamin said, still in the recliner. "I've never been anything but a misfit. But I think that now I'd rather be referred to as royalty." We all laughed.

"And speaking of royalty," Taylor interrupted, coming in on the end of this conversation with a sweater over his shoulders. "Where's the Ringmaster, the newest Broadway director? Have we gathered before his arrival, or is he out of town and we're pretending he's here in order to once more overeat and drink and laugh?"

"That settles it," Paul decided. "I need a gin and tonic right away. I almost forgot what I am really here for."

"Ah, my friends," Colin called out as he entered the living room, and the party began.

After the second round of cocktails, I sent everyone to the rooftop deck where I set up the dining table. Taylor helped me bring up the plates, platters and pots from the kitchen. Under the glow of a string of white twinkle lights and the New York skyline, we dined on prime rib; a sour cream and scalloped potato casserole; green beans with shallots, walnuts, and bacon; crusty French bread; and a radicchio salad with goat cheese, red onion and orange slices.

To my delight, everyone raved about the meal and my much improved culinary skills. Once Taylor brought out his famous coconut cake stacked with birthday candles, my part in making the evening a success was behind me, and I finally relaxed from the stress of cooking. It was then that I tuned into the underlying stress I couldn't shake.

All during and after dinner the conversation focused on Colin's upcoming Broadway show. His friends had a thousand questions and almost as much advice. Jessica was the only one who wanted to know what I was going to do while he was away. Of course, he jumped in and told them he had a job for me.

As I began clearing the plates, the discussion turned to whether or not they thought I should go. Thankfully, no one asked me since I still hadn't made up my mind. With a lively dinner table and lots of wine, Jessica got up and followed me with an armload of dirty plates; the subject moved on to an analysis of the merits of the cast, and my decision was once again left with me.

Just as we finished putting the last dish in the dishwasher, Taylor burst into the kitchen, grabbed my arm and whisked me back up to the rooftop. As we ascended the stairs, I asked what he was doing, but he just kept going forward, pulling my hand as he went.

Back on the deck, everything was changed. The table was moved aside, the chairs arranged in two rows, and the deep maroon Oriental rug from our bedroom lay before me, covered with several large green and blue pillows. In the background, a string quartet played softly on the stereo; and when I turned again, a bottle of champagne and glasses were set out on the table, now covered with a fresh white tablecloth. Across from that, I saw an arch formed from trellises I recognized from Colin's last play. Sheer white fabric draped over the top and cascaded down the sides onto the surrounding rooftop floor. White candles dotted the night on the table, edges of the rooftop wall, around the area rug and in the hands of our guests.

Astonished and perplexed, I asked, "What the heck is going on? Why did you..."

Colin walked up to me, stopped me mid-sentence, took my right hand in his, and guided me toward the pillows on the carpet. Right there, before all our friends, he got down on one knee and said, "Nadine, I am so grateful you came into my life. Everything is so much better now that you are here. I can't imagine being without you." He pulled out a small navy blue box and opened it. Inside, a silver filigree antique ring with a single diamond in the center sparkled up at me.

I gasped and covered my mouth with my hands like a surprised child. I looked from it to Colin and to each of our friends who moved in around us in a semi-circle, all holding candles.

"This is only the beginning of what I want to give to you. Will you be my wife?" He slipped the ring on my finger without waiting for an answer, then stared up at me with eyes shining with love. As I took in the scene unfolding before me, my eyes grew as large as the moon overhead. Our friends stood still, seemingly holding their breaths. Just behind them, the moon was golden against the smooth black sky and candles flickered all around. I blinked to hold back a tear and my nose began to run. When I could no longer stand it, I sniffled, wiped my nose on one sleeve and brushed the side of my eye with my other hand.

"Yes. Most definitely, yes." Applause and whistles filled the air. Colin stood up and we fell into a long deep kiss in front of God and this merry band of misfits. The next thing I knew, Taylor removed the apron from around my neck and handed me a bouquet of flowers, all white: roses, mums, daisies, hyacinths and baby's breath. Jessica placed a delicate, tiny white pearled veil with white flowers on my head. And Adrian began singing Ave Maria acappella. My head spun. It was all happening fast, but I didn't have one moment of hesitation. I felt totally surrounded by love and peace.

Father Benjamin stepped forward, now dressed in his official Priesthood robe, purple with orange trim. This must have been what Taylor really went back to the car to get. Colin stood up, kissed me again and then turned me toward everyone.

"Since time is of the essence," he said, "I thought we might do things just a little bit backwards. If you would do me the honor, I asked Father Benjamin to perform a ceremony in the presence of our friends on this glorious summer evening, with the Empire State Building looking over us in the background. What do you say?"

"Right here, right now?" I asked. In my bewilderment, my head turned to each of my guests, to the skyline, to the moon and stopped on Colin's face.

"I'll take that as a yes."

Before I could say anything else, Colin turned me back around and Father Benjamin began, "Dearly beloved, we are gathered here tonight to honor the union of these two wonderful people in marriage. I have known Colin for twelve years now and have had the pleasure of getting to know Nadine separately in the last six years. Even though I take credit for introducing them, they did find their way to each other as any perfect match made in heaven should. We are grateful when love finds its own path; Colin, the creative genius that he is, and Nadine, the beautiful essence of grace, warmth and love herself. We step back this night from all of our celebrations of any other kind and honor the joining, in the eyes of God, these two people down here on earth. May their light always shine bright and strong through all adversity. May their light be a beacon to others. And without further ado:

Do you, Nadine Carter Barnwell, take Colin Hamilton Bennett to be your husband, to have and to hold from this day forward, for better or for worse, for richer, for poorer, in sickness and in health, to love and to cherish; from this day forward until death do you part?"

"Yes, yes, I do."

Do you, Colin Hamilton Bennett, take Nadine Carter Barnwell to be your wife, to have and to hold from this day forward, for better or for worse, for richer, for poorer, in sickness and in health, to love and to cherish; from this day forward until death do you part?"

"Yes, I do."

"Since there are no wedding rings yet, I now pronounce you man and wife. Please kiss the bride—again."

I couldn't believe what just happened. Within the span of a few minutes, I went from having a boyfriend, to being engaged, to being married. And Father Benjamin got to perform a ceremony he was not entirely used to: a marriage ceremony.

Afterward, our guests toasted us with champagne as the moon and the Empire State Building projected their delicate glow down upon us. To me, it seemed as if there was a direct line from this rooftop to that remarkable historic building forty blocks away. From a city usually known for its driving ambition, chaos, and crime, I felt a beam of love, strength and safety.

"I guess this means you'll be going to Boston with Colin now," Adrian said, with a smile and another glass of champagne in her hand.

"I-I don't know. I haven't gotten that far." I was thrilled with the event that just happened and didn't want to think about taking Colin's job offer right then. As far as I was concerned, the only thing we needed to do in the next few weeks was to go to city hall or some other place to make it legal in the eyes of New York State. But Colin thought of everything; a date was already arranged.

As Colin and our dear friends began carrying the dishes and all pieces of the set and props back down to the loft, I curled up on the stack of pillows and stared at the Empire State Building. Alone, I was able to come down from my cloud long enough to give this next huge decision more thought. Walking away from dance was risky. I hadn't worked this hard to give up so easily. But letting Colin go alone to Boston, with all those leggy chorines and attention-seeking actresses was even riskier. Maybe Gabriella's decision about shutting down the company was a gift after all. It was the first time I realized that to have what the ritual promised, a Full-hearted life, my own career might have to wait.

I thought I would take more time to decide, for sure by the end of the night. But with these wonderful exciting friends surrounding us and celebrating us, I found myself totally caught up in Colin's view of the world. Before I knew it I heard myself accept the job with *Dreamwatchers* and promised to be ready to leave with him for Boston in three weeks.

On Monday afternoon, Colin and I went off in search of wedding rings and applied for a marriage license.

That night, I dreamed of dance. In an open space with a wooden floor and undefined walls, I extended one leg forward as I bent back from my waist and raised my arms over my head. Gentle music played in the background, and I felt free, alive and powerful. Then at the edge of the dance floor, as if coming through a fog or a scrim, I heard the laughter of a baby. The baby crawled forward from the mist toward me. It was the same baby girl from my previous dream. I walked over and began to lift her up. Light as cotton balls, she came easily to her feet although she was wobbly. We danced around in a circle and laughter spilled from her throat. I began to laugh, too. Then someone called my name behind me, and I turned for just one second. That's all it took to break the connection. When I turned back, my arms were still outstretched, but there was no child at the other end. I heard the music again and continued to dance alone.

CHAPTER 15

1978

There are two mistakes one can make along the road to truth...not going all the way, and not starting.
—BUDDHA

W HEN I CALLED AUNT AMELIA to tell her of my rooftop wedding and plans to go to City Hall in a few days to make it legal before leaving for Colin's new Broadway show, she was silent on the phone. *Oh no, she can't think I've made a mistake.* "I hate that you and Uncle Hamp can't be with us," I said trying to cover over her imagined disapproval, "but it's all too last minute for you to get to New York. And then Daddy would probably find out and maybe even try to come. I don't want his anger at me to spoil Colin's and my happiness."

Her next words were succinct. "I can't say that I'm not disappointed, but," and there was another long pause, "you're doing the right thing. He's good for you, Nadine. Go ahead and get married to your Colin. I've not met him, but this much I know to be true. I told you two years ago not to ignore this man. And I'll keep it from your father if that is what you want."

"Yes, please don't tell him. When I see him again I will have a whole new life, be a whole new person. He will see that he was wrong."

"There's no right or wrong here, only the contrast between how each of you sees the world. I hope upon hope that you two find your way to each other again. But I can't make that happen. Only the two of you can do this."

"Thank you, Aunt Amelia. I'll send pictures. I love you."

"Good bye dear. I love you, too."

By the following Friday, life had become exhilarating and confusing at the same time. Colin and I were officially married in the eyes of the State of New York at City Hall. The Friday after that, we would be on our way to Boston for the out-of-town tryouts of his Broadway directorial debut.

As the assistant to the stage manager's assistant, I was hired to step in when the main stage manager had to follow behind the director. I'm not sure this position had a real name. It didn't matter. I was married to the director and whatever my director husband wanted, he got.

After the first few days, to my dismay, Colin and I found little or almost no private time to be together. Once we settled into the hotel, we never stopped moving. I stayed somewhat near him at the theater and in meetings until the number of requests coming in from his actors diverted my attention altogether. Actors' perceived and real problems became my area of expertise. Once I proved successful at handling a few issues, I was off and running, literally running.

Oh, God, what was I getting myself into?

I shouldn't have been surprised. Jessica, Paul, Adrian and Father Benjamin sat me down for a little 'prep' talk before we left New York. "Joining the production stage of a Broadway show is a bit like taking the bus to Beaufort headed for Boot Camp at Parris

Island Marine Corps Recruit Depot. The journey seems like a pleasant ride in the country-until you get there." Paul delivered this advice like a Shakespearean actor.

Father Benjamin added, "Creating a masterpiece is hard work, but once you have your first success, you will walk tall. And then an unbelievable high will come over you, knowing you helped make this newly sought after-production a reality." Jessica and Adrian nodded in agreement.

"Got it." I sat back, not truly understanding what he was saying, but grateful they took the time to try to help me.

We all hugged as if I was going off to climb Mount Everest or to cross the Sahara Desert. It wasn't world peacemaking, but to them and to most New Yorkers, it had the implication of something almost as big. I was already falling in step, and I hadn't yet gotten on the bus to boot camp.

In Boston, the theater, located at the edge of the Boston Commons, was also the edge of a part of town called "No Man's Land," considered to be the most dangerous part of the city. The stage door, practically hidden at the end of a dirty, dumpster-filled, narrow alley way, was smelly and depressing. I learned right away to leave the theater at night with the rest of the cast and crew or call a cab rather than to walk to the hotel in any group fewer than four.

Because everything was unionized, there were rules about what I was allowed to touch. I couldn't help carry the set pieces or props. Those were under the jurisdiction of the local crew members. I couldn't help carry the costumes from the trucks on which they arrived either. Yet I still found plenty to do that did not involve stepping into someone else's territory.

The "load-in" of all the constructed pieces and parts from New York moved along fairly smoothly until the actors descended upon the theater. Once everyone and everything was in the building, the activity level rose dramatically, and energies spilled out like rising floodwaters. Just as Paul, Jessica and Adrian also warned, as the size of the company and crew grew each day, the number of needs to be satisfied grew exponentially.

"The actors always need something," one seasoned crew member tried to explain to me. It's their way of coping with the mounting pressure to excel."

Those actors also know about the line of equally talented people waiting in the wings to take their place. But the chosen few were people full of life. Their personalities were grand, effervescent, confident, and appealing; I soon found that being around theater people energized me too. My world of dance was different, mostly silent, except for the music; the expression was more subtle, perhaps delicate and abstract.

As the word on the street about the show grew more positive each day, I noticed more and more famous people coming back stage to talk with Colin. One night we went to dinner with Paul Newman and Joanne Woodward. Later, Woody Allen, Hal Price, and Stephen Sondheim came by to say hello and offer support. Then came the songwriting team of Fred Ebb and John Kander, followed by Michael Bennett and Neil Simon. But the downside of this much too early positive feedback and attention meant some of the actors got a little too cocky. They started to do what Colin referred to as "believing their own press."

"Believing you can do no wrong before opening night is a serious danger in a fickle business like this," he said one afternoon. We were eating sandwiches in the auditorium and going over the latest changes made just that morning. Like the phrase, "from your lips to God's ear," only in reverse, the stage manager approached us and told Colin his female lead was complaining about her costumes with considerable vehemence. Apparently, she threatened to "not go on" until the problem was solved.

The ingénue lead was no newcomer to theater, having multiple professional credits on her resume in a relatively short time in New York City. But she never carried the weight, or burden, of the lead role in a Broadway show before.

Colin laughed. "I've seen this before. She is good, but not great—yet." He came down on her pretty hard since they arrived in Boston, trying to move her to a higher level. "What this really means is she is frustrated with her performance and blames everything on her costumes."

The stage manager explained about the tension which developed before the show left New York for Boston. The conflict between the costume designer and the actress grew to such a degree that Jeanette said she wouldn't go onstage with those "awful clothes." The show's Tony Award winning costume designer, Veronica Newsome, was not only supremely skilled at her craft, but she was also a long time veteran in the business with scars to prove her right to command. According to the gossip of the other costumers, Ms. Newsome would never cave in to the whims of Jeanette Damien, no matter how good the word-of-mouth.

Normally, only Colin dealt with "his" stars, but this time, he asked me to step in for him to help resolve this situation. There were much bigger problems for him to deal with. Primarily, *Dreamwatchers* was scheduled to open in The Schubert Theater on 43rd Street, a highly sought-after venue, in a month. But the company manager and the producer were just informed of a huge change by the theater owner. This change was not just an inconvenience, it was possibly a make or break concern. The theater in which a production opens has a great deal to do with the long playability of the show. All of a sudden, the theater owner shifted things around on his Ouija board and *Dreamwatchers* was re-slotted to The Lunt Fontaine Theater on 46th Street. An ornate gorgeous historical theater, it was not on the prized 43rd Street and did not have the same draw as The Schubert. I couldn't understand what difference a theater made. To me, if the show got favorable reviews, the public would line up at any theater, or at least that's what I thought.

Knowing Colin's plate overflowed, I didn't see any reason not to try to deal with the leading lady's issue and made a plan which seemed logical to me. I wanted first to meet with the actress, find out which costume or costumes were being blamed, then call the costume designer and see what she could do to help. If the phone call didn't settle the issue, my next plan included setting up a meeting between the actress and the designer. It sounded easy enough to me.

On the way to Jeanette's dressing room, I found her dresser, Gertrude, in the hall taking a break. A stocky red-faced, middle-aged woman with salt and pepper hair and a dry sense of humor, she was always ready with something to say about the mini dramas going on backstage, especially when it came to insecure actors, a redundancy to her.

"It's because of that actress friend of hers," Gertrude said, dragging on her cigarette. "The friend is highly opinionated and critical, primarily of plays she's not in, I would guess," she added in her gravelly, chain-smoking voice. "The night she came to the show—I think it was last Friday—Jeanette stumbled through some of her lines. After, she made excuses for her stumble. She said it wasn't her fault and that the daily script changes were getting worse instead of better. That's when the know-it-all friend suggested to Jeanette the problem wasn't the script; the problem was her costume. The other actress then said Jeanette didn't look very good in it." Gertrude took another drag and then flicked her ashes in the paper cup she held. "Ooo, not looking good is not a healthy thing to say to this one." Then she added a warning for me, "Just so you know before you go in there, hon, Veronica Newsome isn't going to change this costume—for her, for you, or for anyone else.

"My plan began to fall apart already. At least she offered something new to help me re-calculate my approach. Gertrude pulled out another cigarette. I thanked her for the information and headed up the stairs to the dressing room, thinking more deeply about each of the two powerful women I would have to deal with.

About five-foot-eight and built like a forties pin-up model, Jeanette Damien was a natural beauty who looked stunning in and out of makeup. But that's where it stopped. Her aggressiveness bordered on just being plain angry. I heard she was a child beauty queen, Little Miss Pageantry, being how her single, pushy stage mother made extra money or maybe no money. Raised to seek people's attention, Jeanette knew exactly who was and wasn't looking at her at all times.

Veronica Newsome, on the other hand, was Latin, sleek and carried herself like royalty. Pencil thin, her artistic queenly attitude turned on and off as she discovered what was needed in each situation. Combined with being unusually creative and able to deliver whatever was needed, she was a highly sought after asset to any new Broadway production resume.

"No one quite understands the power of the clothes on an actor," she told me when we first met. "Costumes are integral to the building of the character. They support and define the actors. With good costuming, the actor becomes what they wear."

I knocked on Jeanette's dressing room door.

A chair scraped across the floor, footsteps and the turn of the lock followed. Jeanette stood between the wall and the half-opened door with her hair wrapped in toilet paper and cream on her face. Like the star she was or wanted to be, she wore a gold and green ornately embroidered oriental robe and jeweled slippers with curled toes, right out of *The King and I*.

Her stern look changed to a smile once she recognized me. I presumed because I was married to the director, she widened the door opening and stepped aside to let me enter the room.

With pleasantries already over, Jeanette didn't waste any time. "I take it you're here about these damned costumes I'm expected to wear. You can tell that so-called costume designer I have no intention of wearing that God awful dress in Act II or any other Act, for that matter. And she'd better come up with a suitable replacement ASAP!" She flopped down on the ottoman at her makeup table, dipped her hands into a jar of cream and applied even more to her face.

I inconspicuously winced at the action. "I'm sorry you're having a problem with one of your costumes. I'm here to see if I can help." I looked around for the item in question. Hanging by one sleeve on a wall hook, the dress looked sad, almost doomed.

"A problem is an understatement. I can't wear that thing." She lifted her long arm and pointed without looking at the dress. "It's clearly not right for me. I mean, for my character."

"What kind of dress do you see yourself in?" I asked, looking closely at the spectacular black taffeta dress. I imagined most any other actress would be thrilled to wear it.

"To begin with, something flattering to my figure would be helpful," Jeanette said, filing her nails.

I didn't follow her lead.

I presumed by now the cast and crew all heard the rumor about the change in the New York theater. Even though the Boston audiences seemed enamored with the show as it was, the venue change could be interpreted as the show needing more work before coming to Broadway. Following that thread, the show needing more work might also be interpreted as Jeanette's performance being the weak link. She was riding high, and all of a sudden, she sensed the fate of the production resting on her finding missing nuances and making the needed changes to her performance. Still, I didn't understand this childlike attitude. To me, flowing with change and making improvements was her job.

"Something more flattering, Jeanette?" Start with sugar, not vinegar, Aunt Amelia used to tell me when I would get put out by Daddy's demands. "This is a wonderful dress and you look stunning in it."

"I do not. It looks like hell on me and it's throwing me off. I can't act in that rag."

"Is it the color, the length, the fabric?" I wanted to bring the discussion back to the reported problem, not her blame game.

"I don't know!" she shouted.

Her vehemence made me jump. I moved in front of the dress, almost unconsciously, blocking it from her view.

She glanced up at me and then lowered her tone, but sharpened her words. "I am not the designer. You tell that Veronica Newsome I wouldn't wear this dress, even if it was the last piece of clothing in the world. I would go naked first. You tell her that."

I stepped back. *Whoa. I can't pass on words like that. What have I gotten myself into?* I knew Veronica was still operating out of the New York costume shop as she wound down the work on this production. She was also starting work on at least two others shows. According to Gertrude, Jeanette already called Veronica and expressed some version of these sentiments to her. The world famous designer dismissed them or Jeanette. She wasn't sure which, in a wave of the hand, her assistant said.

In my naive desire to be helpful, I realized I was caught in the middle. Could Colin's first Broadway show fail because I didn't convince this actress to wear the black taffeta dress? That's absurd.

But once the thought entered my mind, I couldn't take the chance. I needed to come up with a new plan to fix this situation.

I really wanted to slap her and tell her to be grateful she had such a fantastic job. But that wasn't an option. I dug deep and started again. "No one wants you to be unhappy, Jeanette." I leaned back against the door, the only open space I could find. "Unfortunately, Veronica won't be available for a while, but if you really don't want to wear it, I would be only too happy to take it off your hands. It won't be a problem. I need something to wear on opening night, and if I look half as good in it as the stage hands all think you do, then I'll be getting a pretty good bargain. And if the producers won't let me have it, I happen to know your understudy really likes this dress, especially how it fits the bust line. She would love to wear it...that is, only if the occasion ever arose where she needed to go on for you. I know, I can give you the understudy's costume, a simple black dress off the rack from Macy's until someone can come up with something else."

Jeanette's smooth forehead crinkled and cracked like the top of fresh baked cornbread, and her eyes narrowed to slits. "The stagehands like this dress on me? That's not much of a recommendation."

"Well, I assume they are all stagehands. I see them gather in the wings during this particular scene," I pointed toward the dress, "just to watch you. But it's dark, and there's lots of people backstage. I only know they are all men." I walked over to the dress, lifted it off the hook and placed it on a hanger. I walked toward the door with the hanger over my shoulder. When I looked back, I could almost see the calculations in Jeanette's head; to be catered to by the designer or adored by men. Jeanette grabbed the hanger from me and placed the dress back on the hook. "I guess I can live with it until something else is done."

"Great. I'll tell Colin you're okay with the costume." Her mouth pursed and shifted sideways as if she was going to say something else. I quickly added, "For now." I slipped out the door before she had a chance to restart her complaints.

On my walk back to the auditorium to find Colin, I felt pretty pleased with myself. At the same time, I couldn't help but wonder what I was doing in Boston, other than being with Colin. Even though we were newlyweds, we didn't see much of each other alone except to fall into bed late at night and then get up early and back to the theater by 8 a.m. Where was all the expected glitter and glamour? This was Broadway, after all. Calming the jittery nerves of anxious actresses wasn't making the best use of my talents. But I made this commitment, and I would see it through.

Once the Boston tryouts were over, and we headed back to New York City, my life changed again. The theater venue issue was worked out, and Colin got his way. *Dreamwatchers* opened in The Shubert Theater to rave reviews. With such a renewed, brilliant performance from Jeanette Damien, even reviewer Clive Barnes at *The New York Times* couldn't find much to complain about. Adrian, Paul and Jessica made sure I understood if *The Times* doesn't like a Broadway show, nobody else will come.

Because it was an enormous success, I thought it meant Colin and I could both relax, get back into the groove he created on the rooftop the night he proposed and then married me under the skyline and the stars. But that notion was short-lived. A successful Broadway show not only brought pride and money, it also brought Colin more work offers than he could take on. A good dilemma, for sure, but I worried about what I would do now that this experiment for me was over. I didn't have to wait long because almost immediately, the jobs started showing up for me as well. I got calls to work as a production assistant or some other kind of assistant on Broadway shows, commercials, movies and even on a TV show.

I didn't know if I simply felt flattered at the offers or afraid to be left behind as Colin's career rocketed forward at warp speed, but I accepted almost all the work offered to me as long as the dates didn't conflict. Soon, my head began to spin as I ran from one job to the next, one actor star to the next. There was no time to think, let alone question what I was doing. Being sought after in employment and love can be addictive, so before I knew it, I was immersed in a new career.

CHAPTER 16

1978-1980

Don't you ever wonder maybe if you took a left turn
instead of a right you could be someone different?
—UNKNOWN

A LONG WITH MY WONDERFUL MARRIAGE and my stampeding new career, the baby dreams kept coming. After my dream about Frank, and then *Dreamwatchers* opened, I promised Aunt Amelia, now in remission, that I would try to analyze their meanings. Question one: Would having a child of our own make our lives feel more settled? No, I heard myself say emphatically. Question number two: What other message is coming at me? I haven't a clue, I replied. So with the analysis giving me more of a headache than answers, I decided to gently push the necessity of their meaning from my mind. The baby dreams evaporated slowly like smoke. I still sensed something about dreaming but was no longer able to put my finger on any exact images. What I really yearned for, with both of us now working continuous projects, was to simply spend time with Colin, in conversations and in his arms. The dreams knew more than I did.

When Colin finally came back from Minneapolis after the production phase of another play ended, I literally jumped on him the second he walked through the door. With my arms around his neck, and legs around his waist, his travel bags thudded on the floor. Apparently, he wanted this too, as we stayed embraced and stuck together stiff like a statue for a couple of minutes. He shifted slightly to the right, kicked the door shut with his left foot, and began walking us both toward the couch where we fell into long, wet kisses.

When I learned Colin had a whole week off while the New York producers considered the commercial viability of the Minneapolis play, I made sure I was free also. We filled the days and nights with going out to dinner and plays, strolling through The Village in the evenings, sleeping late and making love, and, of course, he told me the details about his work. I missed Colin, and he missed me, but by the end of the week, something told me his love of directing was catching up with his love for me.

"Are you still happy, Nadine?" Colin asked, while pouring the last of the wine at the Chelsea antique store restaurant, the place where it all started for me, anyway.

"What a thing to ask." I pushed my last piece of veal picatta around my plate with my fork, his question uncharacteristic to me. Always the picture of self-assurance, after this long absence, he seemed even more confident about his work, but less confident about us for some reason.

"I just want to make sure," he said, tilting his head, looking me in the eye.

I reached across the table and took his hand. He squeezed mine back, like something else was going on in him. I wanted to know what, but decided to let him tell me in his own time. I started to pull my hand out of his, but he stopped me.

"I want to talk about our future, Nadine." His focus was clearly on me this time.

"Our future? What about our future? Aren't we living our future?" I shifted in my chair slightly.

"I want to talk about us having a child."

I jerked back as if I touched a hot stove. My hand began to shake as a cold chill ran down my spine. *Did a rabbit run across your grave?* popped into my head, a phrase my grandfather always said about cold chills. My whole experience with Baby Child raced through my mind in a flash. My body shuddered when I got to the delivery room in the clinic. I couldn't save Baby Child then, how could I risk not saving a second one? I didn't know it, but part of me still needed to honor her empty space in this world. I wasn't ready to replace her with another.

"A child? You want a child—now?" I felt the color drain from my face. Colin saw it too. I needed to say more. My first impulse was, *No, hell no!* But he wouldn't understand such a strong reaction. I kept my secret and never told him anything about Baby Child. To try to gather my thoughts, I picked up my glass and sipped. I attempted an explanation. "I-I'm not ready for a baby yet. I have a wonderful husband whom I love deeply. We live in a gorgeous loft in SoHo instead of a cramped, tenement walk-up in The Village. I'm in an unbelievably creative world with more work than I can handle. Many people want to be where I am right now. I-I love my life the way it is. A child right now changes everything."

His eyes lost their brightness. Leaning back in his chair, he folded his hands in his lap and stared down at them, looking deflated. My answer wasn't what he wanted to hear, but I hoped he understood. I felt awful. Part of me wanted to shout, "No, I'm sorry. Please don't look like that. I was wrong. I will have your baby." But I couldn't.

"Okay," he said, after a short silence which felt more like an hour. He lifted his head, his face lightened before me. His eyes regained their alluring sparkle, and he seemed to transform himself back into his usual positive heightened state of awareness. "Okay," he repeated. "You didn't say yes, but you didn't say never. I'm going to take that as a not-right-now, wait-until-later response." His eyes brightened and his smile shone with love.

Before Colin was to leave again for another out of town play, he told me he needed to spend his last day in New York doing business. The week was too short and I missed him already.

Late in the afternoon, he called to say he'd be home soon. Like the sweet man he was, he wanted to be sure I was already home. Of course I was; I was busy preparing a memorable dinner for our last night together.

Almost as soon as we hung up, the lobby door buzzer rang. *Now who could that be?* I stuck a paper towel in my cookbook for a bookmark and raced over to the intercom, wiping my hands on my apron on the way. "Yes?" I said, annoyed at being taken away from my cooking.

"Hi, Nadine. It's me."

"Colin? I thought you were uptown on business. Why are you ringing the buzzer? Don't you have your key?"

"Yes, I do, I wanted to be sure you're still here. I have a surprise for you. I'll be right up."

"Okay." I pressed the buzzer anyway; a force of habit, I guess, and returned to the kitchen.

In the middle of slicing squash and onions, I didn't turn when I heard a key inserted and the lock turned; that is, one of the locks. That sound was followed by the sound of weather stripping sliding across the tiled entrance floor. Knowing it was Colin, I continued to concentrate on my task at hand.

The heavy steel door sucked shut.

"Hi there, honey," I said. "Just a second." I wiped the corners of my eyes with the back of my sleeve. Onions always made my eyes water, and I wanted to finish the vegetable slicing and get everything into the skillet before I turned around.

Then I heard something like a tapping or a clicking sound on the hardwood floor.

"What is that?" I asked, my eyes still blurred. I moved from the butcher block cutting board to the stove, carrying a hand full of zucchini, carrots and onions.

As I dumped the veggies into the pan, I felt something cold and wet on my ankles.

"Yikes! What the heck?" I jumped back. When I wiped my eyes again, I looked down. A blonde tail lightly beat against me and a cold nose sniffed my feet and calves. "A puppy!" I put the towel down to greet my guest. "Colin, whose is this?" The curly blonde dog lay down and rolled over to expose his belly, offering it up to me for a good scratch, as a reward for finding him, I suppose. Almost as quickly, he jumped back up on all fours and began licking and gnawing on my vegetable laced fingers. In the next instant, he ran out of the kitchen and into the living room, sniffing his way around every piece of furniture.

"This is our new puppy," Colin said, grinning.

"Our new puppy? What do you mean?"

"I called about an ad for blonde labs in *The Village Voice* and got a puppy from the newest litter. Since I'm leaving again tomorrow, I couldn't leave you alone."

The puppy ran back to me and quietly lay across the top of my shoe. With his warm belly on my foot and his heart beating directly into my instep, he appeared to fall asleep. He had my love in an instant. Across the kitchen, Colin beamed as if he directed the dog to do this very thing.

Immediately, the reservations surfaced. With Colin gone and new work of my own, I didn't know how to handle the needs of a puppy alone. Young animals require lots of attention. I took one look at Colin's face and knew not to say that. After what I told him about not having a baby yet, I could see he felt he did just the right thing and was so proud of himself.

Reservations or not, before the night was over, I named the puppy Houston, spelled like the city, but pronounced like the major two-way street across Manhattan from the West Side Highway to the Brooklyn Bridge: HOW-STON. I spent the next few days totally wrapped around this puppy's paws. I had to admit, once Colin was gone, the empty loft didn't seem quite so lonely anymore.

After raising dogs outside, crate training was new to me. Thankfully, Houston was smart and quickly learned to hold his bladder until I got home. It eased my worries about leaving him for long periods of time. As soon as I walked in the front door, though, his whole cage rattled as he began to prance up and down like a go-go dancer, waiting for me to come to him with a leash.

In the beginning, it was hard to convey the concept that he was to hold it until we got out the door, down the elevator and onto the street. He was a puppy, after all. I carried paper towels and a spray cleaner for any accidents in the building along the way. It didn't take him long to get it right. Even though this was a lot more work than I was used to with a pet, my love for him grew each day. Still, I looked forward to Colin coming home so there would be two of us to take on this task.

Watching Houston chew on a rawhide bone, I realized I missed my dogs immensely, far more than I missed my daddy. Maybe their attention substituted for the loss of love from my mother.

Houston reminded me of home where we owned, at any given time, at least four dogs, all of which were outside pets. When I was young, they followed Daddy around everywhere. They must have sensed a change in him, too, because they started to follow only me. They loved me no matter what I did or where I went, and so in my more sad and lonely times, I leaned on their affection. Sometimes I sneaked my dog, Bear, into my bedroom when no one was around. He curled up on the floor near me while I read a book or did dance exercises. Dogs were forbidden in the house at all the times, so if I heard a car, I quickly led him down the back stairs to the kitchen, and out the door before anyone knew he was there. Bear seemed to understand everything about me, like Aunt Amelia.

Houston loved to play and he had two thousand square feet of loft space to do this in. When Father Benjamin and Taylor came over, the puppy entertained us all for hours. A dog was not something Father Benjamin ever owned. With all his prostheses and crutches, a pet was likely to trip him and send him flat on his face. But he got to enjoy Houston whenever he wanted.

He was an enthusiastic audience for me, too, whenever I put music on the stereo and begin to glide around the room until the rhythm connected to a place deep inside of me. A world I loved and missed came back to me as my body moved and began a duet with myself, creating an experience most people found only in church.

Three months after Houston came into our lives, Colin and I sat in the living room after dinner. I was thrilled to have my husband home again with me and only me. Colin's success with *Dreamwatchers* became more and more evident. His career kept growing, like kudzu in the south. Success brings more success, I always heard in New York. You get offered more work as an actor when you already have a job, just like getting more attention from someone else when you're already in a relationship. So it wasn't surprising that all his conversations continued to be consumed with stories of what he was doing. As I relaxed in my chair to listen to my husband, I found I envied his creative focus; the yearning to get back to dance consumed me. But the time still wasn't right. Colin hadn't brought up having a baby again, and I wanted to keep it that way. I was afraid if I complained about not being able to dance in a company, he might say now was the perfect time to have a child. So I kept my longings to myself and said goodnight. After that night, the baby dreams returned.

A few months later as I watched through the loft window, the sun lowered itself between the buildings into the cobalt blue Hudson River. The sunset reminded me of the wonderful nights Colin and I sat and watched the day end together on the roof or from the living room sofa. I missed him terribly. Our routine about phone calls was set. He called most evenings around dinner time, since he knew his cast was on a break then and he could get away. There were plenty of times he couldn't call and I understood completely.

While Houston chewed his rawhide bone at my feet, I reached over and picked up the newspaper from the coffee table. The section on top was the "Classifieds." Hmm, why not at least look? I turned to the "Help Wanted" pages and began checking for anything to do with dance. I scanned the ads, skipping the exotic dancer ones, hoping I might find a teaching position or a position as a choreographer in a school or a community theater. I planned to travel out of Manhattan if I needed to. A high came over me, just looking for a dance job. My eyes landed on a real ad: Choreographer for a Children's Dance Theater Company in

Poughkeepsie. Wow. It read like it was written for me. I circled the ad with red ink and went to bed.

Early the next morning, I dialed the number. "Hello. I'm calling about the choreography position in *The New York Times.* Is it still available?"

"Oh, yes, it is. But the application deadline is actually today and we're cutting the applications off early. There have been quite a large number of applicants."

"Oh, am I too late?"

"Umm—let me see."

"I really think I am the right person for this job." I crossed my fingers and legs and squeezed my eyes shut.

"I guess since you called before the end of the day, I can mail you an application. First tell me a little about yourself, so I know if you're qualified."

I explained my dance background: training of ballet began at age five with recitals once or twice a year; falling in love with modern dance in college; adding frequent performing and choreography to my skills; being offered a scholarship to Leland Lemire's Dance Studio in New York City; and earning a spot in Gabriela's professional dance company. I finished by emphasizing how much I choreographed in college and wanted to pursue this opportunity.

"You've been in a dance company in New York. This is good. I guess you do have more background than most of the people who've called or applied. But let me tell you a little about the position. This job is part of a New York State Arts Commission project," she began, as I wrote it all down. "The commission plans to fund the development of a new dance company whose mission is to bring modern dance performances into the community and the schools. The job starts locally here in Poughkeepsie, and if the new company gets the response expected, the plan is to move beyond New York and into the tri-state area."

There was silence as I scribbled the rest of it down.

"Are you there?"

"Yes, sorry, I was writing it all down."

"Then do you feel this description still meets your criteria?"

Without hesitation, I said, "Yes, it does."

"I'll send you an application. In the meantime I'll set up a meeting with you and the board of directors. The start dates are still up in the air, but whoever they hire needs to be ready to start within a month or two at the latest. Can you do all of this?"

"Yes, yes, I can." After I hung up the phone, I realized this was the most excited I felt since my wedding. I began to draft my resumé on a legal pad right then. At the bottom of the page, I stopped my pen dead still, looked up and out the window. What was I going to say to Colin if this worked out? It was my fault he knew nothing about my yearning to get back into dance. And why? Because I didn't tell him. It was like I was protecting him in some way, like I used to protect Daddy. Oh, my God. "I'll always be here for you," was what my actions said even while my heart moved in an entirely different direction.

Two days later the application arrived in the mail. It was ten pages long. I couldn't imagine what they were asking for, so I laid all the parts of it out on the kitchen counter, leaned over and scanned it for the information they wanted. On a piece of paper I began a list of what I needed to gather.

The intercom to the lobby door buzzed; Houston barked and I jumped. It was early in the day and I couldn't imagine who it could be; maybe Father Benjamin or Adrian. I hadn't even taken my shower yet. I planned to do my dance workout in the loft first, since getting to class on a regular basis was nearly impossible with my new erratic daytime work schedule. I pressed the intercom button. "Who is it?"

"Nadine, it's me, Deni." Even through a whisper, I recognized the voice right away. I wasn't able to get the next words out before she added a little louder, "Can I come up?"

"Deni, yeah, sure, I'm on the sixth floor, oh, but you know that. Yes, come up, please come up."

I turned to the mirror by the front door. My hair stuck out in one place and was flat to my head in another. I smoothed it and adjusted my black dance pants and Capezio T-shirt as I set my coffee cup in the kitchen sink. Houston ran to the door and sat still.

When I opened the door, Deni stood still and solemn. I kept my hand on the door knob and took her in from her head to her feet. The first thing I noticed was widely smudged mascara and eyeliner making the circles under her eyes even more prominent. A black tailored pantsuit, low-cut red satin blouse showed cleavage and black high heeled sling-backs made her tower over me. Her hair, piled on top of her head, reminded me of the dancers on *Laugh-In* or *Hootenanny*; only the neatly placed curls, which must have once been bobby-pinned in place, straggled down around her face. Altogether, she looked as if she had a bad night's sleep, then rushed out the door before cleaning up. Houston sniffed her various parts. "Sorry, this is Houston. He's a bit friendly." I pulled him away and told him to go to his mat in the living room, as I taught him when new people came into the house. Some of the time it worked.

"Oh, Nadine," was all she said before she threw both arms around my neck, almost knocking me off my feet. She began to sob into my shoulder. When I put my arms around her, I felt her body heaving, as she inhaled several times in a row without an exhale, like a tiny baby. Houston came back over to either get in on the hug or protect me. I sent him back again.

"Deni, come inside," I now whispered too, pushing her back from me long enough to close the door. She stood, head down, shoulders rounded, still crying, but softer now. I guided her across to the living room and sat her down on the couch. Now that we were in his vicinity, Houston stayed put on his mat.

"What has happened to you?" I moved my hand across the top of her head, lifting the fallen curls from the front of her face.

"I-I left. I can't stay there anymore." Fear showed in her eyes.

"Okay, you're not there; you're here with me," I said gently, then reached over to the tissue box on the end table and pulled out several for her, giving us both a little time. "But you have to tell me what happened."

She blew her nose and wiped her tears.

"He wanted me to do something with my date last night."

"What date?"

"I go out with some of Bertram's business clients in exchange for the apartment and clothes and stuff."

"You do?" I wanted more, but was afraid I'd scare her off if I asked too many questions.

"Yeah, I do." Her eyes looked off to the side of my shoulder; they wouldn't focus on mine. "Anyway, I told him I wouldn't do it. But my date didn't get the message...I guess, and when I told him no, he kept coming at me and grabbing at me, and then he..." Deni stopped and blew her nose again.

"And what? What did this man do?"

"He forced me. First, he took my jacket off, then he started rubbing my breasts, and then himself up against my body. He pulled my blouse off, and then...he was stronger than I was."

"Oh, my God."

"And he was in the room the whole time, watching."

"He? He who? You mean Mr. Bertram? He was in the room, too?"

"Yes."

"That son of a bitch." My cheeks burned like a fever. I grabbed a corner of the sofa pillow and twisted it as if it was his face. My mouth tightened and my eyes narrowed as I took in the scope of what she just told me. I didn't want my anger to get in the way of her talking to me.

I put my arms around her and held her tight. Her body went limp against mine. We stayed like that for several minutes, rocking lightly. I had a hundred questions, and when I sensed she was ready, I asked the first one.

"How did this whole thing get started? How long has this been going on?"

"It wasn't supposed to be like this. He wanted me to work at his shop and sometimes go out with him when his business clients were in town. In exchange, he promised me an apartment, clothes and an allowance. I immediately agreed."

"Wow, he was giving you all that? But what about what we came here for? I thought we came to dance."

"I didn't want to struggle with dance anymore. It comes easy for you. It comes easy for all those other people at the school. They're all the best dancers from wherever they came from. I was never the best. I was never going to be as good as you. I have the body but not the art, and it turns out, not the heart. You saw how those friends of Bertram's live. They weren't in tenements with cockroaches and views of an airshaft."

"But didn't you suspect he wanted something more?"

She pulled away from me and moved down the couch. *Oh, why did I say that? Don't confront her, don't accuse her or tell her she's wrong.* "I'm sorry. Tell me what else went on with Mr. Sleazebag, Bertram."

"My life was wonderful for a long time. He really treated me like a queen. I loved it. But this last year, things started changing. It started about the time I came over here. I thought I could handle it. But I couldn't. We played drinking games. He sometimes asked me to take my top off in front of his clients, but no one was allowed to touch me. As long as no one touched me, I didn't think it was any big deal. No one ever tried anything else...until last night. He knew what that man was going to do the whole time."

"Oh, Deni, I'm sorry. I'm really sorry." I leaned back on the couch and stretched my arm across to her shoulder. Houston came over again and placed his chin on Deni's thigh. I couldn't make him leave this time.

"I'm the one who should be sorry. I know I treated you wrong, but can I stay with you for a while? I've got nowhere to go. Please, please, please."

"Of course you can. Colin is away working on a show. You can stay until you get...restarted."

We both laughed.

"But I'm calling the police."

"No, no, don't do that. I don't want him to know where I am. Please don't call the police." She shook and then stiffened her body. Her fear of him stood out like a shield.

"Okay. I think you're making a mistake, but okay. Let's get you a hot bath."

"That sounds good."

"What about your things?"

"I have a suitcase in the hall. I didn't want to bring it in, in case you kicked me out."

While Deni took her bath, I made up the bed in the guest room/office space. She slept all that day and the next night. It was good for me in a way. I got a chance to get used to the idea of her being back, living with me and could think about all my decisions before Colin called again.

In the evening after I checked on her again, fed Houston and ate my supper, I picked up my resumé, the stack of mail and a glass of wine from the kitchen counter and took everything to the living room. Houston followed with his rawhide in his mouth. I turned on the stereo and sat down on the couch. The next record dropped, and *It's Raining Men* filled the airwaves. Stopping to listen, less to the words than the beat, made my whole body smile. Normally, I danced around the room for a few minutes to any lighthearted disco tunes. But I couldn't muster any pull this time. On the coffee table, the newspaper was still open to the "Classifieds," the dance job circled in red. I picked up my resumé and read it over. It looked sad to me. I began questioning whether to go through with the application. My committing to this upstate choreography job, if they even offered it, seemed risky. The job was a great idea; the timing wasn't. I didn't know how much I wanted Deni to come back until she did. She begged me to take her with me and somehow I felt responsible for her. I hated thinking she was slipping down into a darker side of New York City and there was nothing I could do about it. Maybe if I had paid more attention to her when we started—but I didn't. As much as I wanted this dance job, I couldn't lose her to the lure of all the "Mr. Bertrams" out there again. This choreography job would not only take up all my time and energy, but also being ready to travel was a requirement. Deni needed someone nearby who loved and cared about her if she was going to change back into the girl I knew from home.

"Life is change, my dear," Aunt Amelia always said.

Houston lay at my feet, chewing and slobbering.

I put the resumé down and sorted through the stack of mail. The first three pieces were for Colin, and I noted the return addresses from the times he called. Then the phone rang. It was Colin. I jumped in before he got started. All in one breath I told him Deni was in the guest bedroom, the story she told me and my offer to let her to stay with us for a while, at least until she got a real job and back on her feet.

"Wow," he said. "I completely understand. And you know she is welcome to stay as long as you think she needs to." I expected his support, but was glad to hear him say it.

"This is amazing," he added. "What do you call it—seren... something?"

"Serendipity, is that what you're looking for?"

"Yes, serendipity. That's the word."

Usually it was defined as good luck in discovering unexpected things, as in luck, fortune, coincidence or chance. Aunt Amelia believed strongly in serendipity. As she explained it, when there is a coming together of unrelated events for the highest good of all involved, serendipity happens.

"I just happen to have some really great news for you, maybe for all of us."

"You do? What is it?"

"You'll be getting a call from Veronica Newsome."

"Why would she call me?"

"She's going to offer you a job, a really good costume job. And you know what, you can probably eventually hire Deni to work with you too."

He sounded happy, even pleased with himself. It reminded me of when he brought Houston home. But I wasn't as thrilled this time. If I was going to take a new big job, I'd rather apply for the dance job in the paper. "Are you sure? I don't know what I will say if she does." I squirmed on the couch and spread out all the envelopes. I stared at them, hoping to find a sign to tell me what to do.

"You'll say yes."

"I will?"

"She's probably the most sought after costume designer on Broadway. She not only designed *Dreamwatchers*, but she has designed more shows and won more Tony Awards than anyone else, ever."

"Yes, I know." What I remembered was she carried herself as a queen and everyone else as her subjects. In fact, I thought I heard she actually did descend from royalty.

"Sweetheart, this means we can work together more often. If she offers you a union position, then you're in for life, and I can get you hired on any show I am working on. If it's out of town, we can get an apartment and take Houston with us. That's what we want, after all, isn't it? "

His vision of our future didn't match mine, but that wasn't the time to go into it. I didn't want any conflict between us with Deni being so fragile so I didn't say anything rather than risk saying the wrong thing. One thing my mama used to say was you have to pick your fights.

"You still love me, don't you? You still want to be with me?"

"You know I still love you. What a question." I complained of him being away too much, but I wanted him to work in New York, not bring me along with him on every show of his.

"I'm just checking. I miss you like crazy."

"Before or after directing?" *Oh, why did I say that? I didn't want to sound like I was complaining. I now needed to take care of Deni and didn't want Colin to come home the next week to any tension between us.* "I'm sorry. I know how important this is to you."

"I always put you before my plays." He laughed at himself, then proceeded to deliver everything he'd been through on the show since our last conversation. I wondered if he really knew how single-minded he was becoming. I understood it was partly because we weren't together and didn't have shared experiences like on *Dreamwatchers*. And it was partly because he truly wanted to talk to me. I didn't have the heart to break in to his long monologues. Figuring this would all go away once he got home, I listened with half an ear as I flipped through the mail. About halfway through the stack, I found a hand-written envelope addressed to me but didn't recognize the writing. Then Houston came over and brought me a ball to throw. I held the phone between my left ear and shoulder and threw the ball with my right. The envelope addressed to me was still in my hand and it went flying at the same time. Houston was more interested in the mail than the ball and tried to pick it up. When I realized he might rip it up, I asked Colin to hold on while I retrieved it. I took the letter out of the envelope and picked up the phone. Colin jumped right back into his story. But after reading the short letter, I didn't hear anything he said.

August 16, 1980

Dear Ms. Barnwell,

I know you had a baby on June 5, 1970. That's my birthday, too. I just found out I'm adopted and I think you are my birth mother. I want to meet you so I can know if this is true. I will come to your house or meet you somewhere else. Please write me back soon.

It was signed A. Smith, with a New York post office box below the name.

"Hey. What do you think?" Colin asked, when I didn't respond to a question I never heard. "Are you still there?"

"Yeah, I mean yes, I'm still here," I lied. I wasn't really with him at all.

To my relief, he needed to go to meet a producer for drinks and promised to call again the next night. After we hung up, I must have re-read the letter twenty times. How can she think I am her mother? My baby died. More than that, how did she find me? She must have known I'd been pregnant. But how? If she knew who I was and where I was, she might tell Colin or Daddy or even Frank. A panic raced through my body, as if I'd touched a live electrical wire.

I didn't sleep that night myself. The problem of this child now became my problem. I hated that. The next day Deni got up for some cereal and coffee and then went back to bed. I was just as happy. I needed to think about this letter some more and what I planned to do about it.

The next night I jumped when the phone rang a second time.

"Is this Nadine Barnwell?" The woman's voice on the other end with an unidentifiable accent conveyed confidence and poise. It sounded familiar but I couldn't place it.

"Yes, it is." Houston sat at my feet, leaning into me almost on my lap, begging for me to throw the ball again.

"Ah, Nadine, good. I hoped to find you home."

There was an uncomfortable pause; I expected further information from the caller.

"Do you know who this is?"

"I'm afraid I'm not really sure."

"Veronica Newsome."

"Oh my goodness, yes, Veronica, I'm sorry I didn't realize...hello, how are you?" I completely forgot Colin said to expect her call. I stumbled all over myself as if caught doing something wrong.

"I want to talk with you about a little project I am doing."

"A project? Oh, what kind of project?" This got my attention.

"I have a new Broadway show coming up, darling, I think you are just right for."

Work on? Veronica wouldn't be calling me directly just to join her crew.

"Sorry, darling. I mean be the production supervisor."

"Supervisor?" This sounded more ridiculous as the conversation went on. Is she asking me to manage all the costumes and crew on a whole Broadway musical? Yikes, there are hundreds of costumes and twenty to thirty crew members on these kinds of shows.

"I need you right away. We start on Monday."

Literally, my jaw dropped, but she couldn't see it. "I, I—I certainly would like to hear more about it," I hedged.

Her silence translated to exasperation to me. It was obvious she was used to people saying yes. "It's another large extravagant musical, darling, probably four hundred costumes."

"Are you sure you want me to do this? I haven't the experience of so many others." It usually took years of backstage work in any given department before being offered the job of assistant, let alone production supervisor.

Before I answered, she started in on her sales pitch. "Of course you can. We, that is the producer, director and I feel this particular project needs someone special overseeing the costuming throughout the run. And I need someone organized and reliable; someone who can manage the thirty or more staff needed just for this department; and most importantly, someone who has the taste and discernment necessary to make sure the show remains true to my designs at each performance. I believe that person is you." She said she remembered how I'd handled Jeanette Damien in *Dreamwatchers* and appreciated my tenacity and follow-through. But I knew this was also Colin's doing.

"But four hundred costumes? I—I don't know what to say."

"And it pays quite well."

"Yes, I imagine it does." I glanced at the open "Classifieds," at my resume lying next to it and the letter from the girl. A quick re-check of the situation made me realize that although the woman from the dance job sounded interested in me, it was a really long shot. Here was an amazing opportunity. Jumping into a costume supervisor's job with someone like Veronica Newsome, before climbing the ranks of the many jobs below, was unprecedented.

My eyes darted throughout the loft, searching for a sign as Aunt Amelia taught me to do whenever I needed to make a big, but quick decision. What came to me was Colin's continued absence, not being sure when he would be home for good, Deni's return to my life or just "life," and my wanting any excuse to put off answering this young girl's request to meet with me. Although I still had huge reservations about my ability to do this job, I found myself saying "Yes" to Veronica.

After we hung up, I closed the "Classifieds" and straightened up the magazines and mail on the coffee table. Not wanting Colin or Deni to ever see the girl's letter, I carefully re-folded it and placed it back in the envelope as if I never opened it. Then I buried it at the bottom of my purse and went to bed.

CHAPTER 17

1981

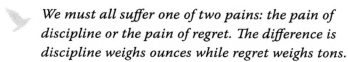

We must all suffer one of two pains: the pain of discipline or the pain of regret. The difference is discipline weighs ounces while regret weighs tons.
—JIM ROHN

TWO DAYS LATER, I PULLED out the application again. I started to put it away, then to fill it out, then I put it away again. I picked it up and put it down so many times I completely forgot where it ended up. The next time I looked, I couldn't find it. *Did I throw it out with the stack of newspapers on the coffee table? I guess I did.* To me, that was a sign in my heart to let the job go. I turned my focus to help Deni get back on her feet and prepare her for working on Veronica's new Victorian era musical with me.

Aunt Amelia and Father Benjamin were both interested in this turn of events in my life when I talked with them. They never met each other, but it seemed to me they were a piece of each other. When I asked what they thought of my supervising the costume department on a Broadway show, they both said the same words, "why not?" Could Aunt Amelia have arranged her clone to come into my New York City life? Of course not, but it was an interesting idea.

Sadie Burnside was a large whimsical musical about a Mary Poppin's kind of character who dukes it out with a Peter Pan-type character for the love and sway over four siblings in an orphanage, near the turn of the century. It seemed to have a little something for everyone in the family.

In the week before the actors moved from their rehearsal space downtown into the Lunt Fontaine Theater on West 46th Street, I decided to break away from all the fittings with Veronica at Adami's Costume Shop and check out my own costume shop in the theater. I hadn't yet met all of my new crew and needed to get acclimated to the theater environment.

Drama happened on and off stage, day and night. It was never ending, like the heat and humidity that set in back home and didn't lift until fall. Singing emanated from every corner of the theater; orchestra members tuned their instruments; stage managers rocked forward and back calling out cues and changes over headsets; and actors shouted out lines onstage and complaints off stage. People moved at a rapid pace, carrying set pieces, props or costumes, calling out "Clear," "get out of the way," "move, you idiot," as the speaker system bellowed out everything that was happening on stage. Once I got to the place where I could hire Deni and she could actually start working with me, she would have to get used to this, but making it gradual was my aim.

The backstage doorman directed me to the stairs at the end of the corridor. Underneath the stage itself was the largest open space in any Broadway theater, other than the actual stage, and it is used for a multitude of purposes. For actors and crew members, it was the route to invisibly cross from one side of the stage to the other without being detected, while the show was in progress above. For the entire orchestra, it acted as a staging area for the times they weren't in the pit.

That's where most all costume rooms were set up too. As I descended the stairs, I noticed a dank musty smell permeating the air. I stopped after the last step to get my bearings. What I finally saw was an enormous dark space with low ceilings, hanging work lights, and dust laden overhead pipes. Eerie looking hallways resembling tunnels were almost hidden from the main open area, leading to unglamorous places like electrical and furnace rooms.

My skilled crew had worked in the theater for a couple of weeks already, setting up the costume room while I helped Veronica. The lights from inside the wire caged room illuminated the space enough to see four people: two men and two women sitting quietly at tables, engrossed in work.

"Hi everyone, I'm Nadine Barnwell," I said, standing at the entrance, leaning into the side of the cage.

All four looked up at me. They were surrounded by costumes hanging on racks behind them, off the openings above their heads and laying across the surfaces, spilling over onto their laps. Clear plastic boxes with small drawers, often used for fishing supplies or nails and screws, were stacked around the edges of the tables. These were filled with the necessary sewing supplies to run a big Broadway musical: spools of colored thread, boxes of straight pins, sewing needles and small red pin cushions in the shape of tomatoes. Scattered around the table tops were other small boxes filled with a variety of sizes of safety pins and hooks and eyes. Opened bags of shiny sequins in red, magenta, purple and blue sat on table tops throughout the area. On other parts of the tables, scissors, tape measures, beads, zippers and buttons were spread out like a Saturday morning flea market.

"You the new boss?" A middle-aged bearded man in khaki pants and shirt, almost like a janitor uniform, broke the silence.

I nodded.

"Rafe Barstow, here." He half stood up, reached across the table, offered his hand and sat back down.

"Welcome to the funny farm. I'm Alicia." A plump young woman with porcelain skin, black and red streaked hair adorned with a royal blue ribbon, long dangling silver and beaded earrings, stood up and shook my hand too. Rows of thin metal bracelets clinked and chimed up and down her arm. From the bottom of her orange, ankle-length skirt, silver-tipped, indigo blue cowboy boots peeked out.

The other two, a man and a woman, fortyish, wearing jeans, T-shirts and aprons holding their personal tools, just tipped their heads toward me and returned, expressionless, to their work.

That's Helene and that's Bobo," Alicia said, pointing with her bangled adorned arm. "They can talk when they want to, but it doesn't look as if they want to right now."

"Hey," I said and gave them a small wave.

"Your desk is around the corner," Alicia added. I liked her already for knowing that.

"Let us know if you need anything," Rafe said.

The other two didn't look up.

Good, there are at least two I can count on to give me a chance and help me out. With the mixed reception from these four, I hoped they didn't think I got the job because of my successful husband's connections. I wanted them to feel like I fit in, even though I was the boss, as Rafe said. Cooperation was central to my success. *One thing at a time.*

As I started toward the space Alicia pointed to, I stopped short and jumped back as a man swirled around the corner, arms lifted high over his head, carrying two voluminous gowns on hangers. I flattened myself against the wire cage wall surrounding the room to let him by. His hips swiveled in his tight black jeans as he ducked his bald head through the doorway and into the costume room.

"Honey, do I need to bow and scrape when I walk by you?" he asked loudly, turning toward me as he lifted the gown to hang it on the wire cage. Bruce Patton was a loud sarcastic, though at times, funny, crew member. I recognized him from the crew of *Dreamwatchers.* As a costumer on the Broadway scene for at least ten years, he acted like he knew more about everything than anyone else. It was telling that he was still doing the same job.

I looked around to see if he was talking to someone behind me.

"I thought you looked different the moment I first saw you," he continued without taking a breath, "but I just couldn't put my finger on it." His attitude rose with his volume. "Well, you do have it all now, don't you, Little Miss Thing?" he asked sarcastically. "You have a husband, a loft and a dog, I hear."

Then I remembered someone mentioning that Bruce couldn't enter a room without commanding everyone's attention, usually by digging into whomever he felt like at the moment. This particular day it appeared it was going to be me. I carefully considered how to respond to his statement that was clearly designed to make me uncomfortable, and not feel like a member of the crew.

He lifted the outer skirt of the first gown, exposing several layers of petticoats beneath, and began scouring the costume for missing buttons, hooks, bad zippers, rips, tears and underarm aromas. The other crew members kept their heads down, focused on their own work.

"Those are wonderful things now," he continued since no one else spoke, "but they are not things I imagine I will ever have. Not in this lifetime, I assure you." He lifted his chin, cocked his head to the left and picked up the ragged hem of the gown. "The best I can hope for is for my Phil to just get his sexy little ass back here from that damn Army base. Then who knows...maybe, just maybe, we can talk about how we can get a place together ourselves." He shook his head at the dress as if talking to it and not to me. "But a loft and a dog, and in Manhattan on our measly salaries? No, no, I don't think so. Not everyone can have it all, I suppose, now, can they?" He looked back at me and rolled his eyes.

A husband, a loft and a dog? His tone made it seem like I was just presented into high society while he was relegated to sweeping the floors. *What is he doing?* I wanted him to shut up but also didn't want to start a fight on my first day with one of my crew.

Before I thought of the right thing to say back, he carried the dresses further into the recesses of the costume room to take his place at a lighted table to begin the repairs.

"Don't mind him," Alicia interjected. "He's got to make someone uncomfortable or he's not happy. And Bruce not happy is something we don't encourage."

I chose to let the scene end there.

A few weeks later, everything started to settle in. Even though deadlines loomed for each backstage department, Bruce backed off, my crew began to listen to me and Deni was with me as a part-time staff, stitching, pressing and smiling like she found God. This made me extremely happy.

Once everyone moved into the theater, set up their own spaces or found a place for their charge, sets, props, lighting, sound and hair and makeup, we jumped into high gear. By this time, I'd joined my crew in getting the long list of costume alteration work done on time: hemming with delicate stitches; changing out tiny buttons for large snaps and Velcro; waxing zippers for fast changes; and gluing the rubber back on to the bottom of dance shoes. When I wasn't called by the director to take costume notes during a rehearsal,

I was busy doing something else: ordering supplies and equipment on the phone; redoing my budget so the company manager would give me more petty cash for all the requests; or meeting Veronica and her staff for further fittings on actors at the costume shop downtown. When I was finished I, too, found a bright lamp, grabbed the next item on the list and worked alongside my crew. If they knew nothing else about me, they knew I worked as hard as they did and supported them one hundred percent. This went a long way in countering the "Bruce Pattons" of the theater world.

A few days later I had a lull so I picked up the next costume in the queue. A manila tag on a large safety pin hung from the hanger of an enormous gown. On it was a list of what needed to be altered. Since there was no space left at the tables, I lifted it over my head so it wouldn't touch the floor and headed for another room. Longer than my height, the dress obscured my vision as I traversed the darkened path to the stairs. On the stage level, I navigated the heavy velour curtains hanging on chains and ball bearings, then I remembered that the prop table was already in place for the rehearsal. But when I swerved to the right to avoid it, I ran smack into a body. My foot caught on the hem of the dress and the giant hoop skirt popped up, hit me in the face and I lost my balance. As I began to tumble, I felt two sets of hands try to catch me, but they weren't fast enough. Buried beneath the purple and lavender layers of tulle and satin, I felt out of control, like Alice going down the rabbit hole.

"Oh, excuse me. You okay?" one male voice said as the dress began to move above me.

"Couldn't you see me with this huge gown?" I focused on making sure I wasn't sitting on any part of the costume as it was lifted off me.

"I'm sorry. I just took a step backwards. It's kinda dark." A hand reached out to try to pull me up.

"I'm sorry too," I grabbed the hand and rose to my feet. "I guess I should have called out or something. I really didn't think anyone was over here."

"Nadine, you need to slow down," another male voice said, as he grabbed the dress by the hanger. When he stepped forward into a little more light, I saw it was Luke Bosco. Head carpenter and about my father's age, Luke took a guardian angel kind of interest in me when we first met on *Dreamwatchers*. He was the go-to person on the crew. Everyone either looked up to him or deferred to him. He claimed it was only because he'd been around the theater since Vaudeville, but we all knew better. Nothing happened backstage without Luke's okay. I was happy to know he was working on this show.

"Yes, I guess I do. But this dress has to get fixed ASAP or there will not be an entrance by Delia in ACT II." The tiny buttons, carefully attached to the dress before it left the costume shop, just weren't made for the Broadway stage. Authentic would go only so far during quick changes in the wings. At six-foot-three, Luke easily held the dress up high off the floor. At least here was one stagehand with some appreciation for the costumes and the beating they took every time they were worn. *How was this dress overlooked?*

"Thanks, Luke," I said, brushing off my clothes and my slightly embarrassed ego.

"Not a problem, honey. You know I'm always here for you."

"I've got to get back to work." The other stagehand looked at Luke like he needed permission to leave. "Sorry again," he said, slightly nodded his head and hurried away.

Luke started to hand me the dress and I opened my arms to receive it.

"Just a second; I almost forgot." Luke placed the dress in my arms like a limp body. "There's a fella upstairs who needs some help. I didn't know what to tell him. He's looking for his dressing room. I don't know anything about dressing room assignments and the stage managers aren't here."

"Well, the actors aren't due to really move in until tomorrow, and I don't think that the dressing rooms are ready anyway." I tried to see if any further damage was inflicted on the $5,000 gown.

"Are you sure you can't help me out here, Nadine?" A voice coming from the darkened corridor behind Luke, said. I hadn't looked up yet, but it sounded familiar. Then a chill rushed through from my feet to the top of my head like a hag just passed through me.

I dropped the dress again, and Luke caught it just before it hit the floor.

From the shadows, a man stepped forward and I froze.

"Frank?" I asked in utter amazement. "What in the world are you doing here?"

My college boyfriend, Frank, who was supposed to come to New York with me ten years ago, so we could start our new lives together, and whom I never saw wear anything but jeans and a faded blue work shirt, stood before me in pressed khakis. With it he was wearing a red and green plaid shirt and an expensive-looking beige suede jacket he held with two fingers over one shoulder. His wavy strawberry blonde hair fell over his forehead just above his eyes. He looked the same, but different; more sophisticated than I ever saw him.

As excitement and fear flooded me the walls appeared to move in; I lost my equilibrium and again stumbled toward Luke.

"Whoa, Nadine, are you all right?" Luke asked, grabbing my arm before I ended up on the floor.

"Yeah, I'm all right. I'm sorry," I said, trying to regain some poise.

"You know this fella? Is he a problem?" Luke asked, as I returned to vertical. With his full frame standing erect and away from the wall, Luke's posture took on a stance meant to be intimidating.

"Yeah, I know him." I lifted the gown back up off the floor.

When I glanced back, Frank's eyes were filled with light and warmth. He reached out to give me a hug and I reflexively backed away. He settled for touching my arm. Luke watched the whole thing.

"I'm in this show. I'm replacing the Eddie Parsons character."

What am I hearing? "You—you're going to be in this show?" I stared at the script under his arm and almost toppled again. Luke took the gown from me this time. Then, like I'd been struck by lightning, all the rage and regret for what happened long ago entered my body, filling me like liquid nitrogen, ready to explode. Overwhelmed with conflicting emotions and feeling like I might throw up or stab Frank with my sewing scissors, I yanked the dress from Luke's hands and sped away.

Back at the costume room, I entered an open area slightly walled off by some old metal fencing and high shelves. I threw the dress at the nearest crew member and shouted some quick instructions. Then I ran down a dark corridor I'd never been in and had no idea where it led. At the end of the passage I found a table, with cards, dice and ashtrays, obviously used for poker games by the stage hands.

I took the farthest seat in the poker area where my shoulders touched the enclosure of the two walls in the corner. The ceiling hung low above me. I lowered my head down to my folded arms onto the card table. My breath caught and I raised my face to inhale more air. Leaning over again, I tapped the table with my forehead, hoping it would knock these feeling out or some sense into me, but it didn't. I sat up and rocked in the chair, like a child. "Why does this hurt this much after all these years?" I asked aloud. As I bent back over the table again and sobbed, I thought of our baby, the one in my dreams, the one we never had, the one he never even knew about.

I bent over my arms on the table and let the tears roll. In a few minutes in the distance, I heard someone call my name.

What in the hell is wrong with me? I didn't have time for this drama right now. But Aunt Amelia always said, "Buried pain never waits for the right moment." Still, I tried to stuff the rising anger in an effort to get some control over myself. I breathed in and out, counting to ten, willing my psyche to end this nonsense and get back to my work, my duties, my crutch.

For a moment, the pain seemed to slip back into its hiding place, like a fish back in its hole. Then without warning it started up again. *Please don't find me,* I prayed as the voice continued to call my name. The sound of footsteps made me move far back into the corner shadows, Luke eased into the space. Once he saw my face in the dim light, he backed out without a sound, and in a moment I heard him tell someone he saw me leave the theater to buy some supplies. He told them I said I'd be back soon. Following that conversation, I heard Luke redirect a few stagehands who wanted to disappear into this very sanctuary too.

I let my shoulders fall from up around my ears and sat back in the chair again. Seeing Frank again felt as if someone took the cap off a can of rising dough. I needed to find a way to stuff the dough back down until later. Who was I kidding? What later? Working fourteen hours a day, seven days a week until the show opened, I didn't know how I would be able to face him again and again.

Stop! I screamed in my head. I wanted to go home and be alone.

I wanted Colin home to help me deal with this. Oh no, that would not be good. When I saw Frank, a flood of desire pushed magnets to the surface of my body. But my head wouldn't activate them because of what he had done. I began gasping for breath again. I wouldn't allow myself to think about the baby. But the image of the baby from my dreams filled my mind's eye, and I couldn't seem to do anything about it. Seeing Frank again made it all come up back, ending my steadiness.

Then a tiny door began to open inside me, letting some of the air back in. I began to shake. Cold and hot alternated control of my bloodstream until I could no longer hold myself upright. I lay my head back down again on the make-shift card table.

Slowly, I began to regain my composure. I knew my face would be red for some time. I couldn't hide a good cry from anyone. If I stayed a bit longer and breathed deeply, I hoped the redness would subside and the dark cloud hovering over my brain would float away into nothing.

I got up to walk around the cramped space to get my circulation going again. An overwhelming urge to disappear came over me. If I got out of the theater and into the crowd-filled streets, I could walk briskly and anonymously. I stared at the passage with a door at the end behind the card table. I hoped it was what I thought it was, the way the stagehands got to Rusty's Tavern during a show without going out the stage door and being caught. I needed to tell Luke first so he wouldn't send out the hounds looking for me. I poked my head around the doorway back to the stage where Luke stood guard.

"Luke," I whispered, not wanting to alert any of my crew nearby. He didn't hear me. "Luke," I said again, moving closer to him. He turned around this time and moved toward me. "I have to get out of here. Is that the door to Rusty's?" I asked, pointing to the back.

"Yeah, that's it. Do you want me to throw that guy out of here?"

"No, you can't do that. He's in the show now."

"I don't know what he did to you, but if he tries to do anything again...ah, it can be taken care of. Don't you worry about that guy."

"Thanks, Luke, but, hopefully, that won't be necessary. I've got to get out of here now. You'll cover for me for a little bit longer?"

"You know I will. This is not life or death here in the theater. They just act as if it is. Life goes on whether the show is a hit or not. Then there's always another one around the corner. Get going now. I'll see you later."

I turned and exited from the secret room through the secret tunnel and into the light of day.

I wasn't sure where to go. I moved to the end of the alley and looked both ways before stepping into the sea of people walking briskly in both directions. I knew that if I went to the left and then the left again, when I hit the corner I would at least be walking toward Central Park. If I couldn't get home and bury myself under mounds of comforters and blankets, I needed to be in nature.

Since I had to go by the stage door in order to do this and didn't want to run into Frank again, I moved to the outside of the sidewalk stepping off the curb and into the street. There were just enough bodies outside the stage door at that moment for me not to be noticed.

Several blocks ahead I saw Columbus Circle, the entrance to Central Park. I kept my head down, not wanting to encounter anyone I knew. *Just get to the park! Just get to the park!* Finally, I crossed the street at Columbus Circle, not an easy thing to do. As I entered the park a car sped by, splashing yesterday's rain on my side of the street. *Of course.*

I had a strong love for Central Park, partly because it reminded me of home. The park architects also designed one of the most beautiful plantations in South Carolina, right near where I grew up.

The more I walked, the more my heart fractured into tiny pieces. Now every step reminded me of all I left behind. A pang grabbed in my stomach like hunger.

Almost as soon as I took my first step into the park's natural beauty and inhaled its long history, a new pain began to flood me. I missed my home and longed for the simplicity and open space, the winding brackish rivers and creeks, the moss-draped trees, the unpolluted air and the kindness of the people. And for the first time I realized I missed Daddy too. At least the man I revered as a child. Daddy so proudly introduced me to all the plantations surrounding Beaufort, wanting me to understand what his family stood and fought for, the splendor and grandeur that was considered the hallmark of the South. He told me his ancestors once lived in one, but gone now, burned by Sherman on his march to the sea during the Civil War. He always bowed his head when he spoke of the war even though he was several generations removed from the actual struggle. His pride for these remaining plantations was equal only to his love of the natural surroundings.

Now, as I stepped into pockets of sunlight pooling between giant oaks and poplars, I let myself be carried back to the same sun and air from home as it bathed my body. I let my thoughts of being outdoors with Daddy consume me; those lovely carefree days before Mama's illness was too much for either of us. That's when I began to settle down inside.

After wandering the park paths for about twenty minutes, I checked my watch and sighed. As much as I hated to go back, this was not a good time to have a breakdown. The list of work yet to be done before the rest of the cast arrived for their first run-through that evening was long. *Crisis time is over.* I stamped my foot into the grass. Even though I didn't know how I would handle Frank being in this show, my strength began to return as I retraced my steps back to the theater on Forty-Sixth Street.

Near the backstage entrance, Luke stood outside talking with a couple of other stagehands. He opened the door for me. "That fella's gone now. But he'll be back with the rest of the cast in a few hours. Just thought you might want to know."

"Thanks, Luke. That "fella" is Frank Prescott, someone I knew a long time ago. I guess he just surprised me. He's in the show now and therefore has a right to be anywhere in the theater he wants to be. And besides, you have your hands full with your job, too. So you know, though; I really appreciate it." I slipped by him, touching his arm as a symbol of thanks and went back in to my designer, director, duties and crew.

Two hours later, the theater brimmed with activity. As the cast arrived and began to search for their dressing room assignments, the backstage filled with a new energy as the bigger-than-life personalities took over. Alicia and Rafe said they always looked forward to the actors' arrival even though the list of demands and complaints began almost immediately. Following the actors were the director and his staff, the designers (lighting, sound, sets and costumes) and their staff, Adami's costume shop staff, the orchestra, the conductor and the makeup and hair people.

Once graced by America's foremost husband and wife acting couple, Alfred Lunt and Lynne Fontanne, the historic stage door to this theater opened and closed hundreds of times, making the already tight space nearly fill to capacity. With their arrival, I dropped my worries like a heavy stone.

I managed to steer clear of Frank for the next few hours as I focused on directing my crew to step up their speed and join in the new energy and air of emergency all around us. After I told Deni, which of course I had to, she wanted to find him and give him a piece of her mind or the end of her boot. I pleaded with her to stay out of it. She calmed down and said she would do whatever I wanted.

After finishing a conversation with one of Veronica's assistants about new changes to the costumes in Act One, I flopped down on a musty, upholstered armchair outside the costume room left there just for that purpose, to look over my newest notes list and the schedule for the evening run.

A voice close behind me startled me. "Are you really working backstage?" Frank stepped up beside the chair. I didn't panic or react in any way, just ran my eyes over him before I spoke.

"Yes, yes, I am. I'm the costume supervisor for this show."

"You mean wardrobe supervisor?" He stepped wide and put his hands in his pockets.

"These are expensive, intricate costumes and that's what I call them, my position, and my workspace." I tried not to sound defensive but I wasn't sure I succeeded. I never liked the term wardrobe. I never thought it fit the regality of the clothes or the job.

"Costumes, yes, I can see that. A supervisor, wow. That's quite a big job."

It sounded like he was trying to recover from correcting me. I now saw the elite actor in him.

"Yes, it is. In fact, I am going over my crew assignments right now, making sure all the quick changes are covered with enough people and in the right spots." I pointed to the folder and papers in my lap, shoving the newest change list to the bottom.

"But what happened, if I may ask, to dance? That's what you lived for."

"This is only temporary." I felt myself bristle at his words. "I've been in a dance company for a few years but, unfortunately, the financial end for the other less commercially supported arts like dance isn't good right now." *Talking too much. Why do I think I owe him any explanation?*

"Yeah, I've heard." He leaned into the wall next to the chair. *Oh great, he's staying, not leaving.*

"So, where do you live?" he asked next.

"In SoHo." His face scrunched as if he questioned my neighborhood choice. "In a loft," I gloated.

"Cool." He smiled and moved his body toward me slightly. His face, now out of the basement shadows all around us, showed he wanted more than to just talk. I shifted my papers and torso to the opposite arm of the chair, feeling the need to set my armor on straight and block everything about him.

"I live there with my husband." My first block.

"Uh, no, I didn't know. But I guess I'm not surprised." He didn't seem fazed by this announcement.

"Colin Bennett. He's a director." I threw this out as my second block.

"Yes, yes, of course. I know of his work. He directed *Dreamwatchers*, didn't he?"

I sensed a slight discomfort in him and liked the effect.

"Is that how you got started back stage?" he asked, recovering quickly.

"Sort of," I lied. "After Colin and I got married, and my dance company went on hiatus, I asked to join him. That turned into a job, and now I have more work than I know what to do with."

"I can see that. So where is he?"

"He's in DC with a new play. It should have been back here and running already, but they've decided to take it to one more city for a tryout. They're going to Philadelphia next."

Awkward silence.

"I'm sorry. This doesn't seem like you. Is this what you really want?"

Why in God's name is he back to that? "You don't know anything about what I want." Fire burned my cheeks. "You gave up that right a long time ago," I said, with more anger than I wanted to show.

"Yes, I guess I did. I just remember how much you didn't want to stay in your daddy's life in Beaufort, how much you wanted to be a dancer. But here you are in New York and doing something else entirely."

Ouch. Who the hell does he think he is?

"I am not. This is temporary. I've got other things in the works right now. What the hell do you think you know about my life anyway?" I couldn't hold back.

"I'm sorry, I shouldn't have said anything. It's none of my business."

"You've got that right." I gathered the papers in my hands, ready to bolt.

"I didn't mean to make you upset, really I didn't. That's the last thing I wanted to do." He still had that same way of dropping his chin and eyes like a little boy when he wanted me to feel sorry for him.

"Nothing about me is your business," I said, throwing out my last block before getting up to leave.

"I want you to meet my daughter," he blurted out.

"Daughter?" My fingers curled into fists under the papers I now held to my chest. "I didn't know, I never thought of you with—you told me you didn't want children."

"Yeah, things happen fast sometimes. This one did. And I want to explain." He reached out to touch my arm, and I pulled away.

"You want to explain? Now?" I couldn't believe what I heard. Being left like that devastated me; then receiving no real explanation after what we'd meant to each other. That kind of rejection was humiliating. No, it was torture.

"Yes, yes, I do." His eyes sharpened, and his whole body seemed to plead for me to listen. "Very much."

"No, you don't have to explain anything, Frank. It's your life and it's been a really long time."

"Yes, I do. It's been too long. I guess I just didn't know what to say...I got into a situation."

"Situation? Is that what you call it?"

"Let me try to say this, please, Nadine. On the movie set, they wanted to offer me a better role, an upgrade. The assistant director said it was mine if I could memorize the lines overnight and the director approved."

"This is not the time or the place." I looked around to see if anyone was overhearing us.

"There will never be a good time. Just hear me out." He touched my arms, as if to hold me in place and I shrugged him away. "That was my first film and I was so excited to be there. I wanted to do anything to stand out. So anyway, this woman came over to help me with the lines. She turned out to be the director's cousin, and coaching actors with their lines was part of her job. Anyway, she was extremely helpful and I got the upgraded role, thanks to her."

I crossed my arms tightly around the papers and my chest, keeping my eyes up and to the right of him. "Then after, she invited me over to her apartment for dinner to celebrate my success. I thought we'd be there with a lot of people but it turned out to just be the two of us."

"And you married her after one dinner, because she could help you with your career?"

"That wasn't my intention. But one thing led to another, and I guess I had too much wine and whatever. The truth is, I passed out."

Oh my God. What he is saying is just like in my dream. But unlike my dream, I now want to slap him.

"Isn't that wonderful to hear, Frank? I'm really happy for you. I've got to get back to work now."

"No, please. I've got to get this out. I'm in this show and we're going to see each other a lot."

Actors and crew members hurried by in opposite directions. We flattened our bodies to the wall to let them by.

"Can we move somewhere else?" he asked.

Reluctantly, I led him to a space in the middle of the basement up against another wall directly under the center of the stage, out of the path of everyone else.

"Melinda and I are separated and getting a divorce, but my daughter, she is the greatest part of my life."

"You got the kid? How did that happen?" I hoped the darkness of the corridor kept him from seeing the shock on my face.

"First, I want to tell you how I "got the kid," as you said."

"Frank, I know where babies come from. What is your point?" I'd had enough of this conversation but I couldn't leave.

He continued telling me the story of how Melinda seduced him, and then told him she was pregnant. Again, it played out so closely to my dream that a chill went down my spine. In his dramatic telling, I had to stop myself from feeling a little sorry for him.

"That's quite a story, Frank. You left me for another woman, and cut me off as if I didn't exist." I contained my rage only because of the circumstances. I didn't spit out that while I was pregnant with his baby, he married another woman; that our child died at birth, while he became a father with her. *Goddamn!* I wanted to tell him everything back and hurt him the way he hurt me. But I didn't.

"It's not a story, Nadine. It's the truth. I've wanted to tell you for such a long time. I know what I did was wrong. I'll have to live with that the rest of my life. Giving you up was the hardest thing I ever had to do. But now, well, if things had turned out differently, I wouldn't have Ariel. And more than likely, I wouldn't be where I am in my career today. You probably wouldn't be where you are today either. The two of us might still be living in a five-story walk-up, scraping together the rent each month, waiting tables at night."

I fell back against the wall this time. A long night of work was ahead and I was already exhausted.

"But look, I've got a daughter and I get paid to act. And you, you're a production supervisor on Broadway married to a famous director; you live in New York City like you planned, and in a damn loft. How many people live in lofts in Manhattan? I've got to hand it to you, you've really done it; you've got it all."

I turned my back and shook my head as the noise of the theater filling with actors and orchestra rose. I didn't have it all. If he only knew that my husband was away more than he stayed home; we didn't have a child and I lost the love of my daddy and the Lowcountry. I felt a twinge of envy for a connection to family, a connection I'd lost. In moments like this, all I felt was the weight of estrangement.

I looked around the darkened theater full of creativity and chaos. My hearing sharpened, cutting out the competing noises until the pounding of the dancers' feet on the stage overhead filled my ears. One more thing I wanted but didn't have. A jagged pain grabbed me in my stomach. At that moment it seemed so massive I wanted to run away from everything and everyone.

When I turned back to Frank, the light from the hall caught glistening rivulets on his cheeks. He took my hands in his. "I miss you, Nadine; I'm sorry. I had to say this too. I really miss you."

CHAPTER 18
1981

 When you come to the end of your rope, tie a knot and hang on.
—FRANKLIN D. ROOSEVELT

TWO NIGHTS LATER THERE WAS a second letter in my mailbox from the young girl when I got home. The gist of this letter was she really needed me to meet her. Now there were two things I hadn't told Colin.

Already feeling exhausted from the work load on the show, I so wished I could get away from everything at the theater, especially Frank, to get this new turn of events in perspective. He made it quite clear he was ready to talk further with me whenever I was ready. Every time I looked at him it hurt so much, I wanted to scream. But I didn't show it.

Deni didn't say much to me about seeing Frank. If she had an opinion, thankfully, she kept it to herself. I suspected she didn't want to upset me any further and possibly jeopardize the beginning of her new life.

The show, although still in preview for one more week, had many sold out audiences already. If theater critic, Frank Rich, contained his golden and acerbic pen and saw it as the rest of the world did, triumph was ours. This was terrific on many levels. Deni would have secure employment; Colin would love the success of my new career; and I could finally take a break and figure out what to do about this young girl and Frank.

To my surprise, Colin called me backstage at the theater.

"I'm proud of you, Nadine. We hear nothing but raves down here about your show. Isn't this great? We are both working on hits. I'm so happy I could bust."

"You sound like something out of a corny musical."

"What do you expect? I live for corny musicals. This is my life."

Yes, his life. He forgot it wasn't my life. But I loved knowing his world intimately. I wondered if he would do the same for me: be involved in my dancing career if and when I ever got a chance to get back to it.

"I'll be home next Sunday. And you know what I am going to do? I'm going to ravage your body."

"Shush, Colin." I turned around to see who was near enough to hear Colin's booming voice through the telephone on the wall. "You're embarrassing me. I'm right here in the middle of the whole production."

"You don't want me to ravage you?" he laughed.

"Ravage sounds good to me. And the sooner the better." He had no idea how soon I needed this.

When the show came down that night or in the theater lingo, "it ended," my crew hustled to put the room in order. After the last person left, Deni and I grabbed our purses and jackets, turned out the lights and locked the door to the costume room.

As veterans of late night subway riding, Deni and I had our tokens out and in our hands as we walked slowly across 53rd Street from 8th Avenue toward the subway entrance on 6th Avenue. Normally, 11:15 pm wasn't too late go home on the "B" Line. It was a much cleaner subway than the 7th Avenue Line.

The crisp air felt liberating like a veil was removed at the close of summer. With the inversion layer lifted, the farther we got from Broadway, the fainter the smells of the night became. I noticed only the occasional odor of urine emanating from a dark corner.

The block between 7th and 6th Avenues was deserted, as usual, until three men emerged from the darkness, moving toward us. Deni and I kept walking and talking, acting assured and casual. But as soon as we passed them, Deni began to walk fast and I fell into pace with her. At the subway entrance, we both instinctively raced down the cement stairs leading to the token machines.

At the entrance, technically, we were trapped between a floor-to-ceiling iron turnstile at one end and the narrow stairway back to the street at the other end. I put my token in first and waited to hear the clink of connection before pushing.

Then, as I was about to make my way into the revolving gate, I heard steps behind us. We both turned, saw the three men coming down the stairs and in a reversal of roles, Deni said in a calm, but firm voice, "GO—NOW."

I pushed the metal bars as hard as I could and the turnstile began to inch around. It felt heavier or stiffer that night than ever before, as if I were pushing a car through mud. Then, like the handing off the baton at a relay race, Deni stood poised to drop in her token as soon as I was all through. Once I was around to the platform side of the gate, Deni inserted her token. Then, at the same time one of the men neared the bottom of the steps, Adidas sneakers and red nylon athletic pants showing first. Deni swung her enormous shoulder bag around to the front of her chest so she couldn't be grabbed by it and began to move into the narrow slot. I prayed the turnstile wouldn't jam. By then all three were at the bottom of the steps and there wasn't a soul on the platform. The first man down the stairs got close enough to almost catch the bottom of her jacket. The second man grabbed the other side of the turnstile trying to pull Deni back toward him.

"Pull, Nadine! Pull!" Deni shouted. I grabbed the section of the turnstile closest to me and pulled on it with all my might as Deni pushed from her side. Then the gleam from a knife caught my eye as the third man approached. By some miracle, we managed to push and pull hard enough, and Deni got all the way around and on the platform side before any of them got to her. Relief lasted only a few seconds as I looked around and realized there was nowhere else for us to go if they put in tokens and came through too. Deni and I looked at each other, simultaneously backed against the side wall of the platform out of their sight range. I'm not sure what Deni did but I stiffened like a statue, hoping the contraction of my muscles would carry me into an invisible dimension. Wind whipped up around us from down in the tunnel and the smell of diesel fuel got stronger and stronger before we ever heard the sound of the approaching train. We sighed with relief while the three men placed their hands up against the heavy metal bars, rattled them and laughed eerily while spewing out warnings and expletives. Then slapping footsteps receded back up the stairs.

I slowly released my muscles, leaned over with my hands on my knees and as I looked up at Deni she was shaking. We were both out of breath.

"Shit. That was way too close. Are you all right, Nadine?"

I nodded at her and then turned toward the darkness of the tunnel. The approaching train sounded like the flapping of a thousand angel wings. A rush of rote spiritual prayers swirled through my mind as the subway slowed to a screeching stop. The doors opened, we got on and both flopped down onto the nearest empty seats. Panting like prize fighters after the eighth round, we rode in silence.

I finally broke the stillness. "Damn it, damn it!" I shouted. "What is going to happen to me next? We were nearly robbed and maybe killed just now. What the hell am I doing? How did I get here?" The few late night riders looked up briefly, then dropped their gaze back to newspapers, books or off into space. I imagined it was an annoying outburst to their otherwise quiet ride, but I'm sure I looked harmless.

Deni stood up as the train pulled into the 14th Street station, took my hand and said, "Why don't we get out and find a taxi from here?"

"Yeah, that's probably a good idea."

We stopped at my mailbox before taking the elevator up to the loft. Inside, Houston greeted me, wagging his tail, tapping his paws up and down on the tile entrance floor and licking the back of my hands. I dropped my bag, leaned over and grabbed his face. I tossed his head around, flopped his ears and hugged him as if I hadn't seen him in months. Just seeing him actually calmed me down almost instantly. *I'm home*, I thought as I rechecked and rechecked all the locks on the front door.

While Deni poured two glasses of wine, I threw the ball for Houston until he kept it. Still shaky, I flipped through the stack of junk mail and bills. In between some flyers, I found a manila envelope with the return address of the Arts Council in Poughkeepsie that I'd called just before Deni came back. I wondered what it was since I never mailed the application. Picking up the letter opener, I slowly slit the envelope open, pulled out the folded piece of paper and began to read:

Dear Miss Barnwell,

We would like to inform you that you have been selected to formally interview for the position of Director/Choreographer for The Upstate Dance Theater Project through the New York State Arts Commission. As a requirement of the position, you must be available to begin work by October 15th in Poughkeepsie, N.Y. and be available for traveling with the company. Please fill out the enclosed paperwork and return in the addressed envelope. All documents must be signed and returned within two weeks.

There was a hand-written note at the bottom.

You are clearly the most accomplished of all who have applied. And after interviewing Gabriella and The Lemire Dance Studio staff by phone, we decided not to hold any other interviews. You will still need to meet with the Board of Directors. Please make me proud of my choice.

I sat down and read it twice, not believing what was written. I stood up and read it again. "You won't believe this. I've been offered the job."

"Another job? Aren't you kinda busy now?"

"It's a dance job—to direct and choreograph a dance company. I can't believe it."

"You have? That's wonderful," Deni said.

I looked down at the letter again. "But how did they get my application? I started to fill it out but after I got the job with Veronica, I never sent it in."

"Uh, maybe somehow, someone found it and mailed it. You know, by accident."

"You mailed it?"

"It was sitting on the counter in the kitchen and looked as if you forgot to mail it. I saw the address so I looked it over, filled in a few more blanks, sealed it up and took it to the post office. I guess I just forgot to tell you. I thought I was doing you a favor."

"Oh man. I decided not to apply after you came back. I can't believe it." I walked over to Deni and threw my arms around her shoulders. "This is for mailing the application and for surviving the near-miss mugging with me." We held each other tight.

"When does the job start?" she asked as we pulled apart.

"Let's see." I held the letter up again "Oh, yeah, it says I start in October," I said, walking back to the couch.

"But aren't you under contract at the theater?" She handed me my wine.

"Yes, I am but I'm going to get out of it." I smiled at the letter as if it was a check from *The Millionaire*.

"Get out of it? How are you going to do that?" Deni sat across from me.

"I don't know yet but I can't go on like this." Houston snuggled on top of my feet as if to keep me from flying off the sofa.

"I know this incident tonight was upsetting, Nadine, but maybe you need to step back a little before you do something you'll regret."

"I hear what you are saying, Deni." I had to acknowledge the wisdom now coming from my previously lost friend. "But things happen for a reason, Aunt Amelia says. As scary as this was tonight it was a yet another sign." I clasped my amulet necklace with the fabric square from the ritual still inside. Then I rubbed my hand over the pages of the letter. With each pass I felt safer and more sure of my decision. "Colin is going to help me."

"What will he say?"

"He won't like it. He's gotten used to me working in his world. He's gotten used to knowing I can be found in a Broadway theater with the same people he knows, doing work he understands and is in charge of."

"But what will you do if he won't help you?"

"I guess I'll deal with that when it happens. But truthfully, after tonight I don't care. He can have the crazy drama queens, the extraordinarily long days and nights, the continuous complaints and the addictive applause. I'm doing this with or without him."

"You mean you might walk away from everything if he doesn't want to help you get out of your contract?" She looked around the loft taking in my everything. "But how can you leave all this? And for what? A starving artist dance company? Living in a tenement on Christopher Street, and it wouldn't be on Christopher Street anymore. It would be the East Village—Alphabet City is more like it. That's where affordable is now but it's also pretty dangerous."

"Look, I've finally realized tonight, after getting this close to being mugged or worse, that I'm killing myself trying to fit into Colin's image of what our life should be. It's not my life. I guess I wanted it to be my life. I wanted to do anything to keep me distracted from myself."

"Distracted from yourself? You're not making any sense. Why in the heck did you do this in the first place?"

"Because I needed to do something more...because I'm not a mother. I should have been one." I fell back onto the soft mohair couch.

"A mother? I don't understand. I always thought you didn't want children." She came over to me. As we sat there with her arms around me, I let myself cry a deep animal sound into her shoulder.

"It's okay," Deni stroked the top of my head. My wail became so deep at one point she said, "Breathe, Nadine, breathe. I know it's been a rough night but try to hold on to yourself."

"It's not the night. Deni. It's not the night." I sat up, my face swollen and red.

"It's me. It's what I've done. You don't know what I've done."

"Okay, why don't you tell me? I'm a good listener. You know I am or I used to be." Trying to calm me down, she began lightly rubbing my back.

"It's just that—I've never told anyone else this, here in New York—not you, not Colin, not Father Benjamin—not even Frank."

"We all have secrets, Nadine. You have to get yours out or I think you might die. Let's hear it."

"I lost my only chance to be a real mother and I'm never going to get it back."

"What do you mean?"

"I was pregnant. That is, Frank and I were pregnant, only he never knew it. I didn't tell him."

"You were pregnant? When was this? Wouldn't I have known? Oh my God, Nadine." She sat back from me, put her hands on her knees and shook her head.

"It was in my last semester at school—you know—when Frank and I were planning our trip to New York. After, he told me he was taking the movie job first so we would have to postpone our going. We had one too many spontaneous moments, I'm afraid. One of us could have stopped and I should have made him get a condom, but we didn't. The next month when I missed my period, I didn't think anything of it. Then Frank left to make that film. It was such a great beginning for him. I couldn't tell him. I couldn't tell Daddy either. He would have stopped everything and made us get married. I—I didn't know what else to do."

"Geez Louise. How did you hide this from me, your daddy, and everyone else?"

"I guess because I was thin anyway. I called Aunt Amelia and Uncle Hamp and they offered to let me stay with them to think everything through. At first, they tried to talk me out of keeping my pregnancy from everyone. When they understood the whole picture, they wanted to help me quietly have the baby and give it up for adoption, without anyone else knowing, without hurting anyone."

"Man, oh man, Nadine. This is the last thing I ever thought would come from your mouth. I guess I considered you the saint and me the sinner. Not that you are a sinner exactly, but I can see I'm not the only one who has messed up. And frankly, I feel as if I might let myself off the hook just a little."

I knew I deserved her reaction. We both reached for our wine glasses to let my revelation sink in further.

"A boy or a girl?" she asked, after a few moments.

"A girl," I said sadly.

"And that's why you disappeared up in the mountains to Aunt Amelia's right after your graduation."

"Yes. Yes, it was. I'm a damn mess."

"You're not a mess, Nadine. You're holding everything together."

"I know and I can't do it anymore. I'm going to take this dance job and become the choreographer I always wanted to be. Colin is just going to have to live with it or not."

"What about your child? Have you ever tried to find her? How old would she be right now?"

"Uh, how long have we been in New York?" I counted on my fingers. "She would be ten. But, what I haven't told you is that actually I don't have a child out there. In the final two months, I realized I couldn't give my baby up and changed my mind.

When my water broke early, Aunt Amelia rushed me to the clinic and—and—she was stillborn."

"Oh, my God, Nadine. I had no idea. I am so sorry. Why didn't you tell me?"

"Don't you see? I couldn't tell anyone except Aunt Amelia and Uncle Hamp. I couldn't raise a child on my own and I couldn't go back to Beaufort. I guess this sounds kind of selfish, but I couldn't take a chance on Daddy forcing us to get married and ruin three lives."

"Yeah, selfish, I understand a thing or two about that word. You did what you had to do."

"Look, Deni, I think I need to go to sleep now. I'm exhausted." I wasn't ready to tell her about the letter from the girl looking for her birth mother. I was handling all I could at that moment.

"You sure you're going to be all right?"

"Yes. I just need some sleep right now."

"When are you going to tell Colin? You know you have to tell him."

"I don't know. I just know that I have to tell him. He wants us to have a baby but I said no. He won't understand this."

"And what exactly are you going to say? That you're the director of a new dance company in Poughkeepsie, and, by the way, you had a child with the boyfriend who just returned and got a part in your show? What is it you really want? Can you tell me that?"

"What I want? I don't know exactly. I used to know. I used to know what I wanted. In college whenever I complained I wasn't able to achieve what I wanted, Frank would laugh and say I was the most focused determined person he knew."

"He was right. You take on a project as though it's life or death. You've done that for as long as I've known you. Now you're doing it again, leaving the theater job for the dance job. If you do, use your determination in the right way."

"What is the right way?"

"Only go from your heart, Nadine. Not everything is going to work out perfectly, but at least it will seem perfect if you approach it from the right direction."

"How did you get this enlightened all of a sudden?"

"I'm not that enlightened. It's always easier to see through someone else's problems than your own. It's like it's always easier to interpret someone else's dream than your own."

By the time Deni went to bed, I rationalized it was too late to reach Colin. Truth is, I was wiped out from the near mugging and from confessing my long-held secret to Deni. I did re-read the letter from the young girl who was sure I was her birth mother. I knew I couldn't be and was sad for her certainty, which again triggered the loss of my daughter. I didn't fold up or hide the letter this time. With the paper in my hand, the girl's words and I slept next to each other through the night.

The next morning I sent Deni on ahead to the theater with some instructions to get my crew started, so I could call Colin in private before we were both too far into our day. As I leaned in to pick up the receiver, the phone rang and I jumped.

"Hi, Nadine, this is your Uncle Hamp." He didn't need to tell me his name; no one else sounded like Hamp. This concerned me right away. He never made the calls. Aunt Amelia always did and then would sometimes put him on to say hello. He tried to sound cheerful. Another reason to worry.

"Uncle Hamp, is anything wrong?" I stood erect as if bracing myself.

"Your aunt, she isn't doing too good. She's asking for you."

"Well, put her on the phone."

"No, she doesn't want to talk with you on the phone. She wants to talk with you in person."

"In person? Oh, I see."

"She needs you right now, Nadine. I would never call and ask if she didn't need you. I know how busy you are up there in that big city doing all those important things. The cancer, it's gotten worse. She wants you to come to see her."

Leave before opening night? If there was one thing to know about Broadway, it was if you were the boss, you better be there every day and night before a show opened, or you would likely never work in the business again. Actually at the moment with my new job offer, not working there again suited me just fine. But right then I needed to be wherever Aunt Amelia needed me to be.

"Tell her I'm coming. I'll get there as soon as I can, Uncle Hamp. It will depend on when I can get a flight." *What am I going to do about the show?*

"Of course. Just let me know when you're coming in and I'll pick you up. It will be really good to see you, sweetheart. Really good." A weariness I never heard before entered his voice.

"I'll book a flight right away."

"Colin, when are you coming home?" I asked on the phone after I hung up with Uncle Hamp.

"It shouldn't be much longer. The play is about to open, and we're still working on some small details to make it all run more smoothly. Why? What's up?"

"I need you here, with me." From trying to choke back tears, my voice quavered and cracked.

"I'm here on the phone. Talk to me, sweetheart." It was the second time I'd been called sweetheart in the last hour.

"You're not here; you're there. I—I almost got mugged last night."

"Mugged? What happened? Are you okay? Were you alone?"

"Deni was with me. I'm all right. I guess I am. I don't know. I mean, no, I'm not."

"Did you get hurt?"

"I didn't get hurt, but only by a split second. I did get shaken up. Really shaken up."

"Do Father Benjamin and Taylor know?"

"Not yet. It happened late last night."

"Why didn't you call me then?"

"After we got back to the loft, drank some wine and decompressed, I just fell asleep." I stretched the truth ever so slightly. "Anyway, I'll tell them but not right this minute. I need you first."

"But I can't leave yet. I have to meet with the producers and some potential backers. They want to bring this one in to Broadway too. The reviews are fantastic but we still don't have the money we need to make this happen. They think I can convince these people to invest in the show better than they can. I don't want to do it but I have to. I don't see me getting home before, say, Saturday."

I held the phone out from my ear and looked at the receiver. This was not what I wanted to hear. With his increased production schedule out of town and mine in town, we were getting more and more out of touch. The more he worked, the less time we spent together and the more distant we became. *This is getting just like it was with Daddy and me after Mama died.*

"Colin, you're not listening. Saturday will be too late. Uncle Hamp called and said Aunt Amelia is asking for me. I'm leaving for Asheville as soon as I get a flight. Hopefully by Tuesday."

"But your show is about to open. How can you leave?"

"The hell with the show. Aunt Amelia needs me." *Oh, why did I say it like that?* But that's exactly how I felt. I didn't tell him about Frank coming back. I didn't tell him about the letter from the girl who thought I was her mother. I didn't tell him about the dance job. I might have told him but he wasn't listening, not truly listening to me anymore.

"I'm sorry. Do what you've got to do. You know what is best." He didn't sound convincing to me. He sounded as if he needed to get off the phone and back to his money people. *Is the pressure of this business at the top getting to him? Is this the price of success?*

"What would be best would be if you were here right now, so we could talk. You're always away and you don't even know what's going on with me."

"That's not fair. I'm working. I'm working damn hard, too. And your job keeps you busy too. But this kind of life takes up a lot of time. We have a great life and we are going in the same direction. And the best part is we're going together."

"That's just it. You are working hard at what you love—and I'm not."

"You mean you're not dancing? Hey, your company folded. Most of those dancers are working at the Danskin store or are back waiting tables. You have a pretty damn big job on Broadway. That's not exactly small stuff, you know. It's not that easy to get into these positions."

"Frank is here."

"Frank? Frank who?"

I remained silent.

"You mean that Frank? Your old boyfriend, Frank?"

"Yeah, that one."

"What's he doing in New York? I thought the last you heard of him, he was living in LA."

"That's what I thought too. I mean that's what I heard through Aunt Amelia, through some of her friends. It's not only that he's in New York; he's in my show. He's replacing the actor who was in a bad accident. It's just a coincidence. He didn't know I was even working on Broadway."

"That's some coincidence."

"And there's something else. I've been offered another job..." I paused. He was silent. "...as the director of a new dance company. And I'm going to take it."

"Yeah, yeah, just a minute. Tell them I'll be there in a minute, will you?" I sensed a change in the sound of the phone as if he had put his hand loosely over the mouthpiece. He left me hanging for several minutes. I hated it when he did that. I hated being cut off in mid-sentence, mid-discussion mid-anything.

"Nadine, are you still there? I'm coming home. I'll be there Friday."

"That's three more days. I won't be here. You can finish your other conversation now. I've got to get to the theater. Goodbye, Colin."

I put the receiver back, counted to ten and yelled loud and long. When I finished, I calmly dialed our travel agent. I told him I needed the first flight out to Asheville the next day, and no, I didn't know my return date. Then I called the stage manager, the company manager and Deni at the theater. I told each of them all that Deni would cover for me while I was gone. She agreed without hesitation. Both the company manager and the stage manager said they understood, but in a colder tone than I ever heard from either of them before. The unspoken rule was no one left a show before opening night unless he or she was on their own deathbed.

It was time to break some rules.

CHAPTER 19

1981

 Life is the sum of all your choices.
—ALBERT CAMUS

AT THE THEATER THE NEXT morning, Deni and I met to go over my list of the most crucial items needing attention in the week leading up to opening night.

"Here's a list of alterations, repairs, shopping for missing items, rubber bottoms for the new dance shoes, jewelry alterations for quick changes, dry cleaning to send out and get back on time and supply ordering; like plenty of men's dance belts and women's dress shields and hose." The list seemed endless but everyone was aware of how much work was yet to be done.

"Not a problem. You don't need to worry. We'll get it all done," Deni said with the confidence of a seasoned pro. I counted on Deni being up to this job. Ready for a new life she was eager to please and got along with all of my crew. I had no doubt she would become a fantastic supervisor when her opportunity came. When I looked over her shoulder, Rafe and the other crew members were standing behind her giving her a thumbs up.

That afternoon I flew to Asheville with all my worries outside of the show traveling with me: Aunt Amelia's health, Frank being back, Colin being away too much, my dance contract, and, most importantly, the letters from the young girl.

Though the image of my lost baby continued to visit me in my dreams, I tried not to think about her in my waking life. But something about a change of focus and environment, like traveling, brought it straight to the front of my worry list. The child in this letter hopes I am her mother. I knew I couldn't be. But to ignore her and not meet with her also seemed wrong. But to meet her meant to admit I was pregnant and gave birth at one time. The repercussions also seemed enormous.

I wondered if bringing all my problems with me might needlessly burden Aunt Amelia, but not filling her in on my life was not an option for either of us. Even if her body was weak her spiritual connection was as strong, if not stronger than ever. I couldn't not talk to her at all. Aunt Amelia would understand the importance of the letters.

Before I was lured by the dance position in Poughkeepsie, before the letters from the girl, before Frank showed up again in my life, I thought I was so close to living my Full-Hearted life according to the long ago ritual. My life was once so simple, but not anymore.

Uncle Hamp met me at the airport. Looking at him I hurt even more. The khaki work shirt he always wore looked slept in. His face appeared drawn, eyes turned down like a frown or a wilted plant. Deep lines I'd never seen before stood out like grease smears.

At the house, we found Aunt Amelia in the living room rather than in her bedroom. Thankfully, Uncle Hamp had already prepared me for how she looked.

"Aunt Amelia!" I dropped my purse and ran toward her. She was seated in her favorite arm chair with her feet on an ottoman and a soft butter cream-colored throw across her lap and legs. The thinness of her face emphasized translucent skin, not the rosy complexion of someone who'd spent her life outdoors tending healing herbs. Once gray, now almost white hair seemed sparse with scalp showing through. It was hard for me to take in but I didn't let on my surprise.

"I'll carry these to your old room, Nadine," Uncle Hamp said behind me, referring to my luggage. "Then I'll start supper. You must be hungry."

"Thanks, Uncle Hamp." "Yes, thanks, dear," Aunt Amelia said to her husband, taking my hand in hers. "Now don't be upset. I really feel much better than I look. I promise you. The inner me needs more work than the outer me so I have to let the outside go for now."

Clearly still tuned into her own rhythms, Aunt Amelia's wisdom, I hope, might extend to me some day. But with all going on in my life right now, I sensed it was a long journey yet for me to be like her.

"You know, just because someone is a healer doesn't mean they have nothing to overcome themselves. This is life. We take what we are given and try to be the best stewards of our path. Like me, those who loved and followed her advice now understand we can't actually control everything that happens to us while on earth." Aunt Amelia understood the conflict created between her work and her current health situation. Would I ever have her strength?

"I'm beginning to understand that. Nothing seems in my control right now. Everything I have might be gone in an instant." I snapped my fingers and sat down.

"In an instant? Is it as bad as that?"

"Yes, I'm afraid it is. But I want to know how you are first."

"I don't want to be the subject of our conversation. Helping you helps me more than anything I can think of. I'm always tuned in to you even if we don't see each other or talk all the time. For instance, I sensed strongly that you needed to get away from New York. I'm not well but I'm am not dying today, so tell me what's going on."

I moved to the edge of the couch, leaned in and began to tell her everything. I jumped from Colin's long absences with his new work, to my growing hunger to get back to dance after my company folded, to the new dance company offer, to Deni's return, to Frank's return, to the theater job with Veronica Newsome, to realizing I missed Daddy, and the most worrisome of all, to the young girl's letters. After I'd finished, I fell back on the couch and splayed my arms out wide. Releasing my list of stressful events and decisions to Aunt Amelia made me sleepy. If released, bottled up energy can do that.

"My, my, dear. You do have a lot going on. But we're going to try to sort this out." She coughed then sat up in her chair to take a sip of water.

How in the world does my pile of problems even begin to compare with what is going on with her?

"I'm fine, dear. Don't look so forlorn. I'm right here with you. I promise. I've still got time left on this earth. Now bring me my box from over there." She pointed across the room to the bookcase next to the fireplace. Following her finger, I first saw a smiling moss-colored Buddha, a serene-faced chestnut robed Jesus, and an ivory-gowned angel. On the shelf below were two small white votive candles and several gray polished river rocks in a tray of sand. Then in the corner shadows sat a cerulean blue rectangular container about the size of a shoe box dotted with broken pieces of mirror tiles. I gasped at its beauty.

"I will need the candle, too," she said, her voice more frail than I ever heard.

I picked up the box from its position in the altar-like display and carried it and the candle to a table next to her chair.

"We will do another ceremony," she said. "Hamp—Hamp dear, can you come in here and bring the ashes bowl with you."

"Yes, I'll be right there," he called.

From the kitchen, we heard cabinet doors open and close and pans or bowls clank before Uncle Hamp came in with the clear glass bowl. Aunt Amelia opened the box and pulled out sheets of blue lined paper, several pens and a jeweled brass container of matches. Already, I knew this ritual wasn't going to be like the first one back at Camp Pinckney, the one which gave me the courage I needed to leave home and begin the crazy journey I have been on ever since.

"The first thing I want each of us to do, and I say 'each' because we all have a new path in front of us, is to take a sheet of paper and begin to write down our most pressing concerns of all the problems before us. Then when you have done that, under each concern, write how this unease, this perceived negativity, can be seen as a blessing."

She waited a few moments, I presumed, to see if we understood. She added, "Hamp, this is not just for Nadine; it is important for you to do it, too. You and I have a large hurdle to get over so it's also for the two of us."

Uncle Hamp closed his eyes. I read this gesture as trying to envision his life without his devoted wife of forty years or maybe to stop the vision from overwhelming him.

"Nadine not only has herself to be concerned with," she continued after Uncle Hamp opened his eyes, "but also the lives of at least five others, from what she has told me. These lives are connected to her, dependent on her on many levels and she, likewise, depends on them. The choices she makes after leaving here will have a profound ripple effect, and we want them to be the right choices—for everyone."

Uncle Hamp took my hand and squeezed it.

Aunt Amelia then spread out the supplies, and we each took sheets of paper and a pen. Since I'd just recited them all, I knew exactly what I wanted to put down and began to write with fury. I left enough space after each issue to come back and add more although I didn't know what. I stopped after I filled up the pages and glanced over at Aunt Amelia. She sat with her pen still in her hand, and her head back against the top of the chair, looking as though she'd fallen asleep.

"You're not finished, Nadine. Write down your solutions," she said, without raising her head. How did she know I stopped? "At least the solutions that immediately come to you, no matter how far-fetched or ridiculous they may seem. Everything you are going through is interrelated."

Listing my complaints and problems was much easier than figuring out a positive outcome. Even if I came up with solutions for most of them, there was nothing I could do about, or for, my beautiful aunt.

"Get it out of your head and onto the paper." Her voice sounded stronger this time, like the old Aunt Amelia and I obeyed.

Below all the names, I wrote how I felt about each one. I loved Colin deeply even though his work increasingly pulled him further away from me. I was thankful Deni came back even though I continued to worry about her and feel responsible for her. I was furious with Frank, again, for walking out on me as he did and for suddenly showing up after ten years. I admitted that I was equally afraid to talk with this young girl as I was with Daddy. Then for me, I added that I really needed to get back to my original motivator, dance.

"Now, finish up with what would make each problem a blessing," she said.

I read my entries again, looking for the answers to pop off of the page. Suddenly, I realized that most of it boiled down to communication and trust. I still wanted Colin to be successful, but needed for him to find a way to be with me at home more often like we used to be. I wanted Deni to be able to care for herself and find work, love and peace. I needed Frank to accept that we were through and to leave me alone. I also realized how much I needed to find a way to make up with Daddy. I lowered my pen one more time and ended by writing this question below the others: Is now the time to tell everyone about my stillborn baby?

"Now write one thing at the bottom which would sum up everything you want."

"Only one thing? But there are many, many things," I said. My own desperation for clarity rang in my voice.

"One thing," she emphasized.

As Uncle Hamp finished his writing, the kettle whistled. "I'll be back with our tea in a minute." As he put his papers and pen down, his face looked smoother, more relaxed in some way as if he'd been watered. I was amazed and wanted that feeling for myself.

I searched the room for my answers. Out the back window, Aunt Amelia's magnificent garden appeared to still be tended, no doubt with loving care now by Uncle Hamp. I studied the furniture, the Buddha, the angel and the statue of Jesus. When I turned to the pictures on the mantel and walls, I saw myself at all ages. The faces looking back were full of joy, uncluttered with the problems of the world. I saw photos of Daddy and Mama, Aunt Amelia and Uncle Hamp in separate pairs, and with all four together, looking as if they had the world all figured out and nothing except happiness was in front of them.

When I turned back to Aunt Amelia, I knew what I needed to write next. I placed one word in bold letters on the page: CLARITY. To possess this gift fully would mean pushing away all the noise around me in my head and in my heart. To get to the bottom of what I wanted, I knew I needed clarity to come from within me, not from the wisdom of anyone else. I didn't need any other rules or commandments or tenets thrown at me. I didn't want to hear from the Christians, the Jews, the Buddhists or the Muslims. I didn't care about the genius of Jung or Freud, or of Plato or Aristotle or even Shakespeare. I only cared about what was right for me, even if it meant losing and/or leaving everything important in my life.

Uncle Hamp brought the tea to us into the living room and then went right back to the kitchen. After a few more expletives, the sound of the faucet running, he returned with a large copper tray, a pitcher and a pair of tongs and placed them in the center of the coffee table.

"Now read what you have written one more time, fold the paper in half and come over to me." Aunt Amelia held out the jeweled box, and I took out one wooden match. Hamp filled the bowl with the water from the pitcher.

"Now strike the match and using one corner, hold the paper with the tongs and light the paper over the water. When only a small corner remains, drop it into the water. This will make the request a reality and set it forth in the universe."

After we each stepped forward and did as she asked, she finished with, "And so it is."

Uncle Hamp poured from the tea pot and handed out the cups. As we sipped in silence for the next few minutes I felt more relaxed and supported than I had in many months.

Over the next four days, I stayed in Asheville, taking care of Aunt Amelia, allowing Uncle Hamp to take care of many things he couldn't get to before. I was caring for the caretaker. Perhaps he wrote those words on his square or maybe she did.

On the fifth day, I packed to leave for the airport. No concrete solutions came to me yet and I began to feel uneasiness creep back into my psyche. Deni called several times to ask how to handle some issues on the show. Colin checked in too. Unable to talk for long, he repeated how his latest project wasn't coming together the way he wanted, I suppose, so he hoped I would understand. I heard the stress in his voice. He couldn't hear it in mine. To be fair, I hadn't told him.

"Don't let the noise overtake you again, Nadine," Aunt Amelia said as I came into the living room ready to leave for the airport. She looked much better than when I'd first arrived. I found it hard to believe she wouldn't make a full recovery. "It's an easy thing to do. You needed to get away from everything to find everything. That's the most important part of why I insisted you come here now."

"What would I do without you?" I desperately wanted her to live forever and still watch over me. Who else would ever be this tuned into me? No one.

"You, you will be your own guardian, dear. Don't you see? This is what I have been leading you toward your whole life. Soon you will have to test your own wings and I know they will be strong. Then it will be time for you to be the guardian for someone else. That's the way it works."

I leaned in and we embraced. I didn't want to let go, ever. Uncle Hamp called from the front porch.

"I still don't know what to do about the letter and the girl," I said, after kissing her cheek.

"You will know. By the time you land in New York you will know what to do. I love you, sweetheart. All will be fine. You'll see. Now don't keep Hamp waiting." She gently pulled her hands from mine.

CHAPTER 20
1981

Once you make a decision, the universe conspires to make it happen.

—RALPH WALDO EMERSON

T THE AIRPORT THE FOG rolled in, abruptly creating a giant pause in the momentum of the day. Unless it lifted at the same rate, I was either going to fall asleep or become best friends with my seatmate. Normally, I wasn't much of a talker on airplanes except for take-offs and landings. Talking through the scary part seemed to work better than anything else I tried. Ironically, this trip back to the city felt like one long take-off for me, given what waited for me at the other end.

After we taxied a short distance from the gate, I looked back and couldn't see the terminal and yet we were still close to it. Who knew when we would get airborne? Maybe it was okay. Everything was already moving too fast. As I loosened my seatbelt, adjusted the pillow and positioned my head comfortably to at least pretend to sleep, I suddenly missed the Lowcountry and longed to see it again.

I thought of how Memorial Day always invited in the humidity, bidding it to stay until long after Labor Day. How the pleasantly warm spring air became hot and laden with moisture, making sunsets seem to procrastinate as they settled across the river. Salt breezes encircling the landscape carried scents of ancient oaks, adolescent pines and born-again moss as the muted gray-green smell of the Lowcountry merged with the rising flood tides, filling creeks and sloughs along with my heart.

I glanced over at my seatmate, a pretty young girl who couldn't have been more than fifteen or sixteen. Dressed in baggie jeans and a tight white T-shirt with illegible writing on it, she wore headphones to a Walkman that had her complete attention. While singing the words to a song I didn't recognize, she ripped the wrapper off a giant chocolate candy bar. Thankfully, she didn't seem interested in having a conversation. I turned back to the blank window and leaned my head against it. My overactive thoughts switched to why I moved to New York City in the first place.

I remembered that for years I felt nothing but awe for what Manhattan represented for me. When I first arrived, I saw something new around every corner. The buildings, the history, the people and the energy all fascinated me.

The weight of this sank me further into the seat of the airplane. I felt glued, unable to move, as in a dream where I was running, but not through air, through molasses. I was now on my way back to New York to face something unimaginable, at least to me. If I did the right thing, I was going to meet a child who thought she was my stillborn baby, a child no one except my aunt and uncle knew anything about; not my Daddy; not my husband Colin; not even the father, Frank.

A voice brought me out of my reverie. "When do you think we're going to get going?" my seatmate asked, taking off her headphones.

Oh damn...she talks. I didn't look at her, hoping not to engage in anything more than a quick exchange. "Well, by looking out the window, it's not going to be anytime soon."

She tried to adjust the air vent overhead but couldn't make it work.

Before I knew it, the polite southerner in me offered, "Oh here, let me. They make these out of reach for most women. Even I have to unbuckle my seat belt to adjust them." She thanked me and went back under.

I didn't know if having more time to think about what lay ahead was good or bad. But this time I wasn't even sure I wanted to get off the plane at the other end. There was too much waiting for me.

The silence broke again. "Are you from New York?" She must have come to the end of her tape.

"No, not exactly from there but I have lived there for quite a long time."

"Yeah? That's so cool. I wish I could live there for a while. What part of New York do you live in?"

"Manhattan."

"Manhattan! Yes! That's where I am going to live someday. I'm going to be an actress . . . on Broadway," she said, with certainty.

The words caused me to turn away. I moved closer to the window. "Oh yeah? That's great. Good luck," I said, with as much grace as possible. What I thought, though, was *Oh brother, here we go again.* The last thing I wanted to talk about was my theater career. I picked up my book and tried to look engrossed.

An announcement came over the speaker. "We apologize for the delay, but the fog is still a little too thick at this time. We are third for takeoff as soon as it lifts." The pilot's voice was clear and confident. Waiting and being cooped up with this wannabe actress was better than taking off into the density of the fog.

321

The stewardess came by and offered us a beverage. I hoped my seatmate would drop the conversation now and listen to her music so I could go back to sorting through my swirling feelings.

No such luck. "Where about in Manhattan do you live?" she asked as she set her Coke on the tray table.

"I live near The Village, below Houston Street."

Her face scrunched up in puzzlement. She waited for further explanation, I assumed, as to why I would live there.

"I live in a loft," I offered.

"Oh, a loft—way cool. I have to stay with my aunt on Park Avenue when I come to New York. She doesn't much like that area of the city. But I do. I'll bet your place is really cool."

"It's pretty "way cool" now. It took quite a while to get there, though."

After we sat back with our drinks, the girl continued, "What do you do in New York? I mean, do you work there, too?"

I knew I couldn't avoid this question. I should have stuck to my book or napped. I was a New Yorker after all, transplanted or not, making me able to shut out the world while on a crowded street or subway with the best of them. This was just one little girl, but the two seats with high backs on this airplane created a false intimacy that was difficult to avoid.

I took a sip of my water and suppressed a cringe. "I work in theater," I said, and then, of course, her eyes lit up like the Empire State Building on a clear winter night. I feigned a grin, knowing I was trapped. This brief exchange was about to turn into a real conversation.

"You do? No way. What do you do? Are you an actress? You look like an actress."

"No, sorry, I'm not an actress." I always cringe a bit when people who aren't in theater but wished they were somehow connected to it, asked me that question. When I would tell them 'no' I work in costumes, disappointment filled their faces. Celebrity sightings seem so important to most people.

"Oh." As if on cue her eyes dimmed slightly. Then she recovered. "I'll bet you know lots of famous people?" The next question most people asked.

"Yes, some." I said in my most blasé tone.

"So who do you know? Do you know Barbra Streisand?"

"No."

"Do you know Mary Tyler Moore or Bonnie Franklin?"

"No, not either of them." I then listed a few names of people I thought she might know, some other well-known Broadway actors and movie directors and with that she was ecstatic.

"That's so cool. I would give anything to be able to work with famous actors and actresses."

Be careful what you wish for, I thought.

Her questions started me talking far more than I wanted to, but there was something about this young girl that reminded me of myself so I kept on with my list of celebrities. What else was there to do?

When the names became unrecognizable to her, she lost interest and turned back to her tape player. I picked up my book.

A few minutes later the intercom came on. "This is your Captain again." The girl lifted one earpiece and I lay my book in my lap. "Sorry to have to tell you this, but the fog isn't clearing up as quickly as we had hoped. We'll let you know when it's safe to take off." The stewardess came by again and offered pillows and blankets.

"I know I'm still young but I can't wait to get my own place and start living in Manhattan," the girl started up again. "My parents tell me that if I go on my own, I won't be living like I do with my grandmother, though. Thank goodness. They think I won't want to live like the rest of the theater people.

But I know I will." She pushed the buttons on her tape player again, searching for a particular song I presumed, put it down and turned toward me. "So, what was it like when you first went to Manhattan?"

This seemed rather astute to me. Maybe there was something to talk about with this girl. "Well, first, have you got a name, Miss Wannabe Actress?"

"Oh, yeah, my name is Sabrina."

"That's a perfect name for an actress. I hope your last name is something just as dramatic."

"No, it's just Jones."

"Oh, your agent will take care of that. But you might consider a new last name before anyone gets to know you. Oh, no, please don't tell your parents I said that. They won't like the idea one bit. Forget I even said it. Sabrina Jones sounds great."

"So what is your name?"

"Nadine, Nadine Carter Barnwell. Pleased to meet you, Sabrina." We shook hands. "Are you sure you want to hear all of this?"

She tucked her tape player and headphones in the seat pocket in front of her. "Yeah, I do, I really do. But I've got to go to the bathroom first."

As Sabrina got up, her possessions tumbled through the air. The tape player, back pack, and candy wrappers landed everywhere. I pictured what her bedroom at home must look like.

In keeping with her energy field, after she left my empty cup dropped to the floor. I bent down to retrieve it and when I looked up, I saw Sabrina up ahead in line talking to a young man about her age. After five or ten minutes, I didn't see either of them standing there anymore. I sat up tall, staying on the edge of my seat. I didn't want to look as though I was trying to find her. Peering through the seats in front of me, I glimpsed the back of her head. Her hands lifted and waved through the air, indicating she was deep into a conversation with someone. I assumed it was the young man from the bathroom line.

I picked up my pillow, placed it against the window and within moments drifted off to sleep.

A dream woke me up. For a second, I didn't know where I was. Then I looked at the empty seat beside me and realized I was on the plane, and my new friend Sabrina still wasn't back from her trip to the bathroom. I rubbed my face to try to get more fully awake. I wasn't sure what I dreamed, only that I did. It was a vague feeling that stayed with me, kept me slightly in the other world, but without a clear image attached. Aunt Amelia used to say, "We dream about things we still need to work out in our awake life. When you know you've dreamed, and you can't remember the dream, it means you've broken through and have begun to work something out."

When I tried to find Sabrina again I saw her with the same young man, only now they were standing and talking and she had her arm raised toward me. Sabrina smiled and pointed toward me. I had a good idea about what she was saying; how excited she was to talk with someone about Broadway theater. She would be surprised to learn I was contemplating leaving what she yearned for. I had no doubt she would ask how I could consider walking away from all I had. That's when I saw my life with clarity. Yes, clarity was what I had asked for in the ritual with Aunt Amelia. This clarity showed me that the more rungs up the ladder of someone else's image of success I went, the more underground I ended up, both physically and emotionally.

Wake up Nadine. If I have any chance of having this Full-hearted life I've been led to believe is waiting for me, I first need to put my concerns in order. Before I can begin to straighten out my perfect life, I must meet the young girl from the letter and begin to do just that.

CHAPTER 21

1981

Promise me you'll always remember: You're braver than you believe, and stronger than you seem, and smarter than you think. Christopher Robin to Pooh
—A. A. MILNE

A S SOON AS I GOT home from the airport, I sat down at the desk to write a letter to the girl. It took me four or five attempts, but in the end I simply said I would be at *The Bagel & I* at 10 a.m. on Monday and included the names of the cross streets, just in case. Then I thought, how will we know each other? I added a P.S. at the bottom. I would hang my red dance bag with a black infinity sign on it over the back of a chair. Done. All I had to do was not change my mind.

I tried to keep a low profile and not return to the theater. Deni was doing a great job and I figured no one needed to know I was back. After months of long hours on the show with no days off; having Frank reappear in my life; being with my failing Aunt Amelia in Asheville; sorting through the dance contract and receiving this young girl's request; all I wanted to do was sleep.

Colin never did come back to New York, as I guessed he probably wouldn't. He stayed to work even harder on his messy play. Even though we talked, with his focus elsewhere he hardly knew I was back in Manhattan. But two nights before the meeting with the girl, when I got my "check-in" call he took me by surprise.

"I'm coming home," he said with glee.

"When should I expect you this time?" I wasn't counting on seeing him for a while yet.

"What's the matter? You don't believe me?" He laughed.

"Well, you have said this before because your show hasn't been working out the way you wanted. And I know you. You'll not let it go til it's perfect. That's why they all want you as their director." I blathered on, trying to think of what to do if he came back too soon, before I met with this girl.

"But things are working out now. There's been a major break-through in the script and a few actors' performances. Both the writers and the actors are taking credit, and it looks like the word on the show is turning around. You're not back to work yet and we need some time together. I'll be home tomorrow evening. I should be there in time for supper with you. I'll take you anywhere you want to go. How does that sound? You make the reservation."

"Tomorrow?" I couldn't believe what I was hearing and I'm sure I didn't have the right degree of happiness in my voice. "You don't want to see me?"

"Of course, I want to see you. It's been way too long. This is great. Sounds wonderful." I attempted to ramp up the enthusi-asm this time.

"I hate being away this much and I can't wait to see you, sweetheart."

"Me too." He was called away, again. "Can't wait to see you tomorrow," I slipped in before I lost him altogether.

The next day one more emergency arose for Colin. "I'm sorry," he said when he called. "Don't say anything. There's nothing I can do. I have to stay one more night. I'm booking myself on an early morning flight the day after before any of my actors or writers wake up."

"Okay. I understand," I lied. *Now he's arriving the same day the girl and I are to meet. Oh, Lord.*

Early the next morning, the eastern sky awakened me by reflected light from the loft windows across the street; then the silence of the dawn was pierced by barking dogs, walked by their owners, no doubt vying with other dogs for territory. Before I left for *The Bagel & I*, I composed a note for Colin.

> *Hi, sweetheart. Since it will take a while to get in from LaGuardia at this time of the morning, and I'm not sure when you'll actually get home, I'm keeping a breakfast date with Father Benjamin. I know you need some rest so please take a nap. I'll see you back here when we're done. I'm so glad you're back.*
>
> *I love you. N*

Father Benjamin had already planned to meet me for breakfast. That part was not a lie. I hoped Colin would be grateful for my thoughtfulness to let him take a nap.

Inside the restaurant, the stronger smells of bacon, sausage, pancakes and omelets trumped the softer peaceful smell of roasted coffee. The low drone of surrounding conversations interrupted with louder laughter, competed for attention as patrons shifted from one table to the other, saying "hello" or "hey, man." Although on the streets each man or woman was an island, friends and strangers seemed to get to know each other easily within these four walls.

Father Benjamin was already at a table. I waved and made my way over to him. Before I sat down, I carefully hung the red dance bag on the back of a chair. After Felix took our order, I dropped my whole story on Father Benjamin, recapping the parts he'd already heard. I went over falling for Frank in college and planning our new lives in New York; being cut off by Daddy; and ended with the big one—my pregnancy and stillbirth. Then before he could react, I handed Father Benjamin the girl's letter.

"This is what came to me in the mail a couple of months ago." *Now someone else knows.* I flopped back in my chair like a deflated ball, relieved not to be carrying this secret by myself anymore.

While he read it, Felix brought our order.

"Well, are you her mother?"

"How can I be? My baby died at birth."

"Yes, I guess that would be a problem for this to be true." Father Benjamin folded the letter and handed it back to me. "So this is what has been underneath your fast lane drive all these years. I sensed there was more but wouldn't ask and couldn't figure it out. I didn't think it was only your broken relationship with your daddy." He didn't seem terribly surprised. But then he never was, with all the complicated tales he had already heard from his flock.

"I thought if it didn't hurt anyone else, then why talk about it? Eventually, it would dissipate and not be an issue, even to me. But I guess that was foolish. My burden showed to you anyway." I glanced over at the entrance, looking for the young girl.

"When are you supposed to meet her?"

"Today. This morning." I checked my watch. "Oh, man, in about fifteen minutes now. Where did the time go?" I fingered the edge of a folder I brought with me.

"And what's in the folder?"

"The contracts for the dance company job. They came before I left to be with Aunt Amelia. They want them signed and back by the weekend. And I haven't told Colin that I'm taking this job or about my pregnancy or about the girl."

"Talking about the dance company can wait, but you haven't told Colin about your baby and the letter from this girl?"

I placed my head in my hands and spoke to my omelet and home fries. "No...no, I haven't."

"Okay, this is getting complicated." He checked his watch too. "Your secrets from Colin will have to be dealt with later. What do you want me to do when the girl gets here?"

"I hoped you'd stay and be my backup. And if things get dicey, I'll need your help to get away. Say, we have somewhere we have to be. Help me end it if she won't let go or something like that. I don't know what she is going to say."

"I'm not sure my sitting at the table with you is a good idea. I'll move to a seat nearby, like over there." He pointed to a table not far away next to a wall.

When my eyes followed his arm, I realized the restaurant was nearly full. As I scanned the room, checking for the girl, Deni came through the front door. When she saw us, she waved as she walked over to our table, moved my dance bag to an empty chair halfway between our table and the next one and sat down. I started to protest about moving the dance bag since it was what the young girl was told to look for, then thought better of it. Even though I told Deni about losing my baby, now was not the time to try to explain about this girl who thought I was her mother. I didn't have the time or the patience.

"Deni, I thought you were working at the theater today." I sounded almost accusatorial, even to me.

"I am but I don't have to be there until noon, so I'm treating myself to a real breakfast. And look who I find here. This is great."

Deni waved at Felix as he whooshed by delivering coffee and bagels at lightning speed. "I'll have my usual," she called to him.

"Coming right up, Miss Deni," he said. After Felix served everyone, he winked at Deni and did a pirouette, holding the tray to his chest as he turned before racing back to the kitchen.

"You look like you're still tired, Nadine. Have you been able to get some rest since you've been back?" Deni brushed some sugar residue off the table.

I nodded, but with my nervousness escalating by the minute, I thought better of saying anything that might be taken the wrong way.

"Nadine is meeting a friend here and I joined her for only a moment," Father Benjamin jumped in. "I was about to move over to another table." His voice trailed off as he glanced toward the door. With unusual speed, he bent over and picked up his crutches. "Deni, why don't you join me over there?" He fitted them onto his arms and stood up.

"Who're you meeting?" she asked.

"Can you bring my coffee?" Father Benjamin asked Deni and then moved faster than I ever saw, before breaking Deni's train of thought.

"Yeah, sure, no problem," she said, scooting back to let him pass. Picking up his cup, she followed him as he asked, and I put the dance bag back on the chair near me.

Then I saw what Father Benjamin saw. A young girl wearing jeans and a navy blue sweatshirt with the hood up over her head walked through the front door. The suction from the Canadian air front slammed the heavy door closed as soon as she let it go. For a few moments, she stood inside near the entrance, with her hands in her front pockets, turning her gaze from one end of the room to the other. When she spotted the dance bag, she began to walk toward it. From across the room, I saw red hair poking out from under the hood and a face that looked somewhat familiar. *But how can this be? A coincidence? My imagination?* She looked like me at her age.

"Is this bag yours?" she asked as she got to my table.

"Uh, yes, it is."

"Then you're Nadine Barnwell?"

"Yes. I am. Are you A. Smith?" I pointed to the letter on the table in front of me.

"Ariel. My name is Ariel."

"Ariel Smith," I repeated.

"Smith is not my real last name," she said matter-of-factly as she reached into her front pocket, pulled something out and placed it on top of the letter.

I jumped in my chair. A photo of me, pregnant, stared back up at me. I looked at it in disbelief. There was no mistaking it; it was me standing with Aunt Amelia and Uncle Hamp. I definitely looked pregnant. "Where did you get this?" My voice raised even though I tried to whisper.

"You're my mother," she stated calmly as she sat down in the chair across from me, staring. Her maturity struck me even in the few words we exchanged. She carried herself like someone much older—or was it wiser?

"No, I'm not your mother. I'm not anyone's mother," I said, holding on to what I knew to be the truth. "I know you think I'm your mother and believe me, I would like to have a daughter like you—I'm sure . . ."

"Is this you?" She cut me off mid-sentence and pointed to the photo.

"That's me, of course, but I don't have a child. I mean, I did have a child but I'm very sorry to say my baby died at birth." I strained for her to understand.

"What if she didn't? What if they just told you that?" she pushed.

"Just told me my baby died?" I couldn't comprehend what she was saying. I studied the photo again, then her face. "You mean the clinic? Who would do such a thing? The plans were already set for the baby to be adopted but I changed my mind. No, it couldn't be. My uncle arranged everything. He would never get involved with anything like that." I looked at her as if she were an apparition trying to come to life.

From her pocket, she pulled something out that looked like a newspaper clipping and laid it on the table too. The headline read, *Babies Taken From Mothers, Illegal Adoption Ring Uncovered.* I read down the first column. *"An attorney and a doctor planned and executed an adoption scheme using young frightened, rural unwed mothers looking for a way out of their dilemma. The doctor set up a clinic in the mountains for poor people who couldn't afford hospitals. And because he delivered lots of babies legitimately, no one ever knew. Girls who came to the clinic for their delivery, through the advice of a particular attorney, were told that their babies didn't live. Then they sold the newborns to couples wanting to adopt quickly with no hassle. They operated in North and South Carolina and in Georgia."*

Speechless, I stared at this child with new eyes, at least what I could see of her with her hood still up on her head. She stared back. At least for me, my reality began a slight altering. For a few seconds, a strange kind of peace settled in. Then my left brain took over and dismissed the whole idea as wishful thinking on her part.

While reading the article I hadn't noticed someone standing a few feet back from our table behind Ariel. At first it was his back and then he turned around. I jumped. *Oh, no. What is he doing here?* It was Frank. My peace evaporated. I tried to cover the photo of me with the article. I wasn't ready to tell Frank we once had a baby, and if I did, I wasn't ready to explain to this child that the man standing right behind her was the father of my stillborn baby. Since she was sure I was wrong about the stillbirth, she would turn him into being her father. I couldn't believe my mind was working this fast.

"Hey, Nadine, I'm sorry to interrupt," he said, before I thought of some way to get rid of him.

Ariel sat still with her back to him, pulling down on the edges of her hood.

"I'm looking for my daughter. She left a note saying she was meeting someone here." He scanned the room while he talked.

After he spoke, the girl picked up the picture and turned around.

"Ariel? Is that you?" Clearly astonished that she was sitting right below him and with me, he pushed back the edge of her hood. "What are you doing?"

"Dad, are you following me?"

His face relaxed at having found her. "I thought you came here to meet someone who might be your..."

"This is your daughter?" Now I was equally astonished.

Before he could answer, Ariel asked, pointing at me, "Do you know her?"

"Nadine is—an old friend of mine."

"Old friend?"

"Nadine and I used to know each other in college."

She held up the picture of me and he took it.

The tension in his face returned as the corners of his mouth twitched slightly, like they used to back then. He focused on the picture and his eyes narrowed. "This is you, Nadine?"

"Yes, it's me." I sat up straight, ready to shake off my armor.

"What the heck? Nadine, you look very pregnant here. You have a child?" He turned the photo over. Someone had written *Nadine, Amelia, Hamp 1971* on the back.

"She's my birth mother," Ariel broke in.

I wanted to run away as fast as I could. But I couldn't. This was a huge misunderstanding. I didn't care what she thought; there was no way this child was my daughter—the laughing baby in my dreams. But now I couldn't run away, not under any circumstances.

"No, no, I'm not," I said emphatically to Ariel. As the unbelievable revelations swirled around all of us, I found myself reverting to my original story, not ready to deal with anything else. "I was just telling her, I guess...I mean your daughter, that my baby, sadly, was stillborn." I lowered my head and flicked at the edge of the manila folder holding the dance contract as my secret was brought, unceremoniously, out into the light of day.

When I looked up again, Frank's eyebrows lifted and narrowed before his lips pursed. "It says 1971.That's when I left for that movie." I could see the computations in his head. "So, who's the father?" His voice rose with each sentence, each revelation.

"Who's the father?" I stalled for time, counted to five. "You were, Frank. You were," I whispered.

"What do you mean? You didn't tell me you were pregnant." He grabbed the chair with the dance bag to steady himself.

"I couldn't. You were off working in your first movie already. We were supposed to get out of South Carolina and start exciting new lives together. I had my scholarship to study dance in New York City and Daddy told me not to come home if I left." The same pain flooded back again, causing me to shudder. "I planned to not hurt anyone by giving my baby up for adoption. But—the baby was stillborn." He didn't deserve to know about "our" daughter but here he was right in the middle of this drama.

When Frank came around to the other side of the chair and slumped down into it, his face contorted in confusion. I grabbed the opportunity to change the conversation's focus. "Of everything you told me the other day about your experience on that movie set, you conveniently forgot to mention that the child who got you to marry Melinda was, in fact, adopted. I thought you said she got pregnant."

"Nadine, I swear I didn't know about the adoption until recently. Hell, Ariel knew before I did. Then she ran away from home right after she found out."

"How could you not know?" My patience fell thin. *Good grief, what else is he going to he say?*

"I wasn't there for the birth." His hands went up in the air on either side of his face. "I was working on the next film."

Oh, God, how much more complicated could this morning become?

Frank turned toward his daughter. "You may as well hear it all, Ariel."

Thankfully, Felix came by with a refill for me and to take an order for Ariel and Frank.

"Coffee and plain bagel for me. What do you want, Ariel?"

"Hot chocolate and a cinnamon bagel."

Father Benjamin and I exchanged glances. He wouldn't believe what was happening at this table. Deni just looked puzzled.

By the look on Felix's face, he knew something was up, and rather than saying something glib and performing a soft shoe he turned on his heels while saying, "Coming right up."

After Felix left, Frank lowered his head for a moment before starting to spill his story. "Okay, this is what I've pieced together in the last few months. And Ariel, you may not like all of it. I'm just warning you."

"It's okay, Dad, I can take it."

"My *twenty-five year old* ten-year old." Frank put his hand on her shoulder, and a brief moment of love zinged between them. "Between fights with my wife and her mother, I think I understand what all happened. Or better, why all this happened. Melinda and her mother arranged everything." He pulled his hand away. "After the movie wrapped, the director asked me to work in his other two films, only they were shooting out of the country, in the Philippines. You can find similar landscape there for these movies and much cheaper production costs. Of course, I jumped at the offer. I knew it was partially because of Melinda's close relationship to the director but chose to think it was because I am a pretty good actor. It wasn't long before she told me she was pregnant. I'm sorry to say, I couldn't deny the possibility because there was this one night at her apartment. I didn't mean for it to happen, I swear. But it did." He looked at me when he said that last part. I looked away. "Anyway, she said she wasn't going to have her child born in the Philippines and went home to her mother in Winston-Salem for the birth. I couldn't leave and she didn't expect me to. When I got back, there was this perfect baby girl, and I never questioned anything." He picked up Ariel's water glass and drained it. I sat frozen in my chair like I was paralyzed or unable to stop holding my breath.

"She wasn't pregnant," he continued, "she just assumed telling me she was would get me to marry her, which it did. She and her mother knew my heart was somewhere else and were afraid I would leave if I found out the truth." He looked at the floor this time, avoiding Ariel's and my eyes. "So Melinda's mother arranged a private adoption of a baby exactly the same age ours should have been. Within six months of my coming back to the states, to Winston-Salem we all moved to California. After my film career started, L.A. was where the work was for me. All these years I never questioned it."

He grabbed Ariel's hand and kissed it. "But then a few months ago, Ariel overheard her mother and grandmother talking, or rather arguing about the truth of her birth and she came running to me for an explanation." He still had her hand in his. "I couldn't believe what she was saying; so I just dismissed her, said she must have misunderstood, or that it was her imagination. That's when she first ran away." Ariel pulled her hand out from his and Frank gently but firmly put his hand on her arm, as if he was afraid she would bolt again.

"I got into a screaming fight with Melinda about what she did and then about what we were going to do about Ariel knowing. Ariel must have heard that one too because once we settled down and went to look for her, she was gone. Melinda got hysterical with worry while I paced, trying to come up with the likely possibilities for where she could have gone." He grabbed my water and downed it as well.

"Then the phone rang and the mother of one of Ariel's best friends called to tell us she was at her house so we wouldn't worry. But she also warned us that Ariel told her she would run away again if we came to get her. We trusted the mother and left our daughter alone to cool off and for us to come up with some kind of plan. The next day the phone rang again and I jumped, but it wasn't Ariel or the friend's mother; it was my agent. He told me I'd been offered a replacement part in a Broadway show that I had auditioned for months ago." He looked straight at me.

"I didn't know. I swear I didn't know you were working on it, Nadine. To tell you the truth I forgot about it after I learned it was cast and in production. But it turned out to be exactly what we—Melinda, Ariel and I needed. When Ariel finally came home, I told Melinda we were over, and I was taking my daughter with me to work in New York. Ariel started packing her suitcase as soon as I finished telling her mother. Melinda backed off for the first time in her life." Frank's forehead glistened. He lifted his hand to rub the perspiration. Ariel didn't move and I finally exhaled allowing my shoulders to drop a little from their position up around my ears.

But he wasn't done. "On the way here, Ariel told me she wanted to find her birth mother. Once I got over the shock and anger—no, once I thought my feelings were under control I tried to reason with Ariel about looking for her. Ariel has the right to find her birth mother but then she said she'd already found her and that the woman was in New York City. I refused to believe it, hoping she'd drop the whole idea once we were both away from Melinda for a while."

He looked at Ariel but she did not return the gaze this time. "I didn't know until this morning that a meeting was set—for breakfast. When she told me what she was doing, it was all a surprise to me and I guess I didn't handle the news the right way. First, I wasn't going to let her go anywhere on her own in Manhattan; and second, I told her I was coming with her to meet with this "alleged" birth mother. I worried she might run away again if this meeting didn't work out. But it turned into a fight this morning and while I showered, she left. That's why I followed her. We're staying only a few blocks away and there are only a couple of places within walking distance for this breakfast meeting. I went to three of them before this one."

Ariel sat back with her arms crossed, not smiling, looking stubborn and determined. I recognized the willfulness.

He stopped, giving us a few moments to absorb his story. The silence at our table emphasized the pinging and scraping of utensils on plates and coffee mugs and the rising din of conversation around us.

"Are you her mother?" Frank finally asked.

"No, no. My baby, our baby, died at birth. Stillborn." I raised my voice. I felt as if I was in a dream; no, a nightmare and didn't want to believe any of this.

Ariel interrupted again. "No, it didn't. It...I mean I...was taken away." She picked up the article and handed it to Frank.

"An adoption ring?" he asked, after reading the headline.

Nobody said anything again as he read the article.

"Then we, you and me," he waved his finger between us, "could actually be Ariel's parents?"

"No, Frank. I'm sorry, we're not. I know what the article says, but there is no proof those people's scheme had anything to do with my clinic or me." This was more than my brain could absorb. I lived with the fact that I'd lost a baby at birth for ten years. No one was going to turn this around in twenty minutes, especially into such an outlandish story.

"Oh, my gosh; yes, you both are," Ariel said with calm conviction and turned toward Frank. "I found out everything from Grandma the night before I ran away the first time."

My focus turned to Ariel as she began to explain what she knew.

"My grandmother was mad at my mother because Mama wanted to go to a marriage counselor with Daddy. I heard it. Mama said Daddy was really unhappy. He wanted them to go see someone or he was leaving. Grandma told Mama not to go because she was sure the truth about me being adopted would come out. I couldn't believe what I heard. Grandma didn't want anyone else to know, said what she did wasn't legal. When Mama didn't back down, Grandma threatened to find you." She pointed toward me, "and tell you everything. Grandma told Mama you would come and claim me and Daddy would find out the truth. Then Daddy and I would leave Mama all alone. I didn't understand what that meant. First, I learned I was adopted and then my parents were going to get divorced over it." Pain settled on her face like a hard deep wound.

"If this is all true," I asked, "how in the world did you end up with them in the first place? How would they have known I was pregnant with your father's child?" This couldn't be true so I tried to find the holes in her story.

"Yeah, that's the reason I ran away—to find out the real story. I couldn't believe my grandmother or my mama anymore. I knew this kid at school and his father is a private detective. I told him what I found out about me and my family."

Felix arrived with the orders, quietly placed them on the table and scooted away like a cat rather than a circus animal. The arrival of the food and drinks was a welcome moment to put a pause to this drama as this child and her story continued to stupefy me.

I cut my eyes toward Frank again. He shrugged and lifted his hands to either side of his body.

"Don't look at him. He doesn't know any of this," Ariel said, following my eyes and his gesture. "My friend's dad didn't want me to do something crazy like run the streets—like I would do that—so he promised he would help me find out anything he could. First, he wanted to take me back home; I told him I was staying with my cousins and that I would show up at his house each day to see what he found out. Actually, I went to another friend's house I stayed with a lot. Mama and Daddy were seriously mad at me but I'm the one who should have been the angriest."

She focused her words on Frank. A smile of recognition from him lightened the moment. I felt their enormous love, the kind of defiant love I used to have with my daddy when I was about her age. Then she turned her face toward me. "But they didn't see it that way."

"Anyway," she sat up and fingered the sugar packets in the container, "every day, her dad gave me some information. He thought I could handle it better if I heard the story in pieces, over time, instead of all at once. He needed to know who handled my adoption. I didn't know. He said there had to be a file somewhere in the house with my birth certificate and the attorney's name. So that's when I decided to go back home. And it was easier to find than I thought it would be. I was born near Asheville and the guy's name was on a contract. That's how my friend's dad found out about the baby ring." She lifted the newspaper article again and I took it from her to try to understand this better.

"Between what I heard at home and what he found out on his own, he kinda put it all together. He said Mama met Daddy on the movie set and she told her mother and her girlfriend she planned to marry him. But Daddy was going to that other country and then to New York City to meet you." She pointed to me. "That's when Mama told Daddy she was pregnant. But she wasn't—ever."

"How in the world do you know all this is true?" I asked, unable to stop my rising voice.

Frank sat still with a stunned look, unable to utter a word.

"My friend's dad gave me this report." She reached behind her and pulled something out of the waist of her pants. She held up a document with a cover and opened to the first page. "Grandma called all these attorneys in North Carolina looking for babies to adopt," she said, pointing to a list of names. Only two were circled, one in Raleigh and one in Asheville.

"But how did she know to come to Asheville where I was?" I asked, rubbing my right temple, feeling a headache begin to form.

Frank leaned into Ariel and in a near whisper, said, "Your mama knew about Nadine and that she was living in Asheville with her aunt and uncle til I came back. That part wasn't a secret." He glared at me. "They both must have had their eyes on Nadine's whereabouts. Then when Grandma canvassed the few lawyers who handled this kind of transaction, she found out that Nadine, of all people, was pregnant. It doesn't take a genius to figure out that your grandmother," he pointed to Ariel, "didn't want you," he pointed to me, "showing up with a baby and causing a problem. That's when Grandma went to Asheville to find the lawyer and you." He pointed at me again. I wanted to slap his hand away but girded the impulse in front of Ariel.

When the room began to spin, I grabbed the papers from her for some focus; like putting your finger in front of your eye to stop dizziness, and began to read for myself.

"Once in Asheville," I read aloud to drown out my confusion, "Ariel's grandmother found the attorney in question and told him her daughter and supposed husband were looking to adopt a baby privately. He happened to know of a pregnant woman in his area who fit the general coloring and body types of Melinda and Frank, who wanted to give her baby up for adoption. She even gave the woman's name and address." Frank was right. I looked up. "That was meal right." I turned back to the report. "Because this kind of adoption wasn't legal, and to keep the two sets of parents from finding each other, the doctor and his nurse who were in on these deals invented a story that the pregnant woman's baby died. They took baby Ariel from the clinic and gave her to Melinda and your grandmother."

"Yeah, and nobody ever told Daddy or me," Ariel added, as she slammed back in her chair, putting her hands in the pouch of her hooded sweatshirt.

Both of my temples began to throb and my stomach felt queasy. "This is quite a story. I don't know if I can believe it all or not. Surely I wasn't the only one having a baby that day. But I do have to ask one more question. How could you get mail to me or from me without your father knowing?"

"The detective." Ariel sprang up in her seat again. She clearly liked this man and for a ten year old, what came of knowing such a person.

"I thought he was in California."

"He was, is. He has contacts here, well, all over the place. We used someone's post office box and the telephone here. When Daddy left for the theater, I was alone in the hotel room. The man in California wrote the first letter and the man in New York wrote the second one. I just told this man what to write. He called as soon as he got your letter and told me how to find this place."

Ariel then reached under her sweatshirt and pulled out another paper. When she laid it on the table, I glanced at the top. The first thing I saw was the clinic name and logo. Just under that was my name and the date of birth of my child. But where the box should have been checked "Baby Died" it said "Adopted".

I looked at Ariel and then at Frank. Frank's face was white; Ariel's amazingly calm. *No, no, no. I couldn't have let this happen to Baby Child. I couldn't have missed my own child's life all these years.* The room closed in around me and the sound of the restaurant fell away. The tables and plates seemed to rise and float. *Had I turned my back on her as Daddy had turned his back on me after Mamma died?* I felt nauseated as the truth pushed through my resistance. As my eyes filled I tried desperately to hold the tears back.

Wanting, but not wanting to look either of them in the eye, I lifted my gaze over and beyond them toward the entrance and saw Colin come in through the front door.

CHAPTER 22
1981

Forgiveness is the fragrance that the violet sheds on the heel that has crushed it.
—MARK TWAIN

THE SOUND OF CUPS HITTING plates, muffled conversations on top of intermittent laughter, and chairs scraping along the floor all drifted out of earshot as Colin walked toward me, hair mussed either by the wind or his pace. Even though he looked tired and hurried, his concern for my well-being showed through, at least to me. I was glad to see it back in his face. I feared I might lose him to the power of success. Over the last few years, it happened to more than one person I knew in the business. But then I caught a new worry like a Charley horse. Would Colin be able to hold on to this level of concern for me once he met everyone at my table? Aunt Amelia's gentle face appeared in my mind, and I made a silent prayer hoping that would get us through the next few minutes with ease.

"Nadine, I got in earlier than I thought I would. The cabbie knew some great shortcuts and, somehow, we beat the rush hour traffic.

I found your note and came as quickly as I could. I didn't want to sleep." He leaned in and gave me a strong kiss. "You know what it's like in production on a show." He addressed Frank and Ariel as if he already knew them. "Every day is like the first seven days of creation. You can't stop." He laughed. I understood what he was talking about. "Hi, I'm Colin Bennett." He stuck out his hand to Frank.

I started to explain as I thought I should, when Frank spoke up.

"Hi, I'm Frank Prescott."

Colin stopped mid-shake, dropped his smile and then his hand.

"This is my daughter, Ariel," Frank said, as he turned his palm up and toward her.

"And this is my husband," I jumped in a little louder than I planned, trying to gain some control of the situation.

The two men nodded at each other. I could almost see flashes of thoughts racing through Colin's mind as he tried to place Frank's name.

"Frank from South Carolina? Nadine's college boyfriend?" he asked Frank. His face showed that he already knew the answer.

Frank continued nodding.

Ariel broke the nodding when she stuck out her hand to Colin. He took it automatically, a puzzled look still on his face.

"And I'm her daughter too." She gestured with her free hand toward me.

I wanted to crawl straight under the table, between everyone's legs and slither out the door. Or better, I wanted to become invisible; yes, invisible would be much easier and quicker.

"You're her what?" Colin chuckled as he used to when he didn't understand what was being said. Then he gently pulled his hand from Ariel's.

"She's my birth mother." Ariel smiled for the first time since our meeting began, and again I saw myself in her. I couldn't help being fascinated with a replica of myself sitting across from me.

Then she thrust the birth certificate at Colin.

Oh, my God. This is happening way too fast.

Colin read for a few moments and looked over at me. "Your daughter? Is this some kind of joke? How could you have a daughter and I don't know about it?"

Ariel picked up the *Baby Ring* article and handed it to Colin. He scanned it and put it back on the table.

We all waited while he digested what just happened, possibly because we were all still digesting it, too.

"If he's your father," he said, pointing at Frank, "and she's your real mother, then you," he turned and pointed to me, "and Frank had a child you never told me about?" The concern and love he came in with dropped from his face, replaced with disbelief.

Yes, he has the facts straight now. My big secret, the one I'd always thought I could keep to myself and handle on my own, was truly no longer a secret. In the short space of a few minutes, everyone knew about it.

"I would like to hear this explanation, too." Frank sat back, arms folded across his chest.

"I—I didn't tell anyone about her, Colin," I addressed only my husband, "not even Frank."

Colin took a step back from the table and away from all of us, his face plastered with hurt.

"It's complicated. Sit down. Please sit down, and let me explain."

Colin was the consummate communicator; he needed to be, in his line of work. Conflict in theater was dealt with on a daily, hourly, sometimes minute by minute basis. I knew he would at least hear me out, and when I finished he would understand.

He rubbed his forehead with one hand, covering part of his eyes. "This is why you didn't want to have a baby with me. It wasn't because of dance. You lied to me. What else are you lying about?"

Then he did something I never thought I would ever see him do. He turned and walked back through the tables of customers and out of the restaurant.

We all watched him leave.

I wanted to run after Colin but I couldn't leave Ariel and Frank either. I owed them my full attention too. There was so much to talk about, to try to sort out, if, in fact, this was all true. I didn't know any way it wasn't, at this point with all the evidence this ten-year old had gathered and brought with her.

"I'm sorry," Ariel said, looking genuinely sad. "He was kinda surprised too."

"Well, this has been some morning," Frank said to Ariel. "You've got three adults . . . no, five, counting your mother and grandmother in quite a tailspin, young lady."

"Yeah, I can feel my tail spinning round and round." Ariel kept her head down, not looking at him. She didn't seem as confident as she did when this meeting started.

"I didn't know; I swear I didn't know," I blurted out. "I would never have left you, Ariel. You have to know that. I had already changed my mind about the adoption. I wanted to keep you. But you came early and they told me you were stillborn." Knots in my stomach punched through like out of a spring.

"Would you have told me then?" Frank asked.

"Frank, you married someone else." My anger at him butted up against my overwhelm.

"But at least I told you."

"I didn't think it mattered after that." Anger took the lead. "I would have told you when you got to New York like you were supposed to, after the movie. But you never came, did you? You lost your right to know."

We all started fidgeting with whatever was in front of us, not looking at one another. But once I realized we were a family of some odd sort I broke the silence. "What have I done to everyone?" I said, barely audible.

I looked over at Frank and Ariel, then across the room to the front door. I had a husband and I wanted to keep him, so continuing the conversation would need to wait. "I'm sorry;" I turned toward Ariel. "I've got to go talk with my husband right now. We'll have to continue this later. I'm sorry."

I got up from the table, grabbed my red dance bag and my purse. Father Benjamin and Deni, who turned around to watch the unfolding drama, stared with questioning faces. I shrugged back to them before walking through the maze of tables, chairs and bags on the floor to the front door and back to the loft, to Colin.

Once inside the loft, only Houston greeted me. I called out Colin's name, went from room to room with Houston at my side, tail wagging, ball in his mouth. But Colin wasn't there. On the kitchen counter, I found a note.

> *You need some time with your daughter to figure this out...and I need some time, too. I don't know when I'll be back.*

He signed it with a big C at the bottom; no "love," no "later," just "C."

All I could do was wait.

A few minutes later, the buzzer rang. I jumped up and flew to the door, thinking Colin was back and forgot his key.

"Hey, it's me," Father Benjamin said through the tinny tunnel-like speaker. "Deni and I came to see if you're okay."

"Come up." I buzzed them in.

Once they were inside, I told them Colin was gone and showed them the note. Then I spilled the rest of the story to Deni and then a synopsis to both of them about what happened at the table with Frank, Ariel and Colin.

"Your stillborn baby is alive and Frank has been her 'adopted' father all this time? What a mess!" Deni said.

"You can say that again," I said.

"I'm not one who should judge what anybody decides to do with their life, though. How can I help?"

"Yes, that's what I want to know as well," Father Benjamin said. "I can talk with Colin. Do you have any idea where he went?"

"No, no idea at all. But I'm sure he'll show up after he's cooled off," I said, but didn't feel it was true. "I'd really like to be alone right now, if you don't mind."

"Sure. Deni, you can come over to the Parish with me."

"Oh, no. With all this happening, I forgot; I've got to be at the theater, well, right now. I'm late. But you can call me there if you need me."

"Okay, I guess we'd better go. I hate to leave you like this."

"Too much has happened in a very short amount of time. I need to be alone with myself."

After they left I tried to lie down but sleep was not an option. Neither was any kind of rest. All I did was stare at the ceiling and replay the scene in *The Bagel & I* in my head. A couple of hours later, the phone rang and I jumped like I touched electricity. It had to be Colin saying he wanted to talk, to listen to my side of the story. But no, it was Frank.

"How's Colin taking this?" he asked.

"I have no idea. He wasn't here when I got back." I let my exasperation show. I didn't tell him I didn't know when Colin would be back.

"Nadine, I'm sorry about everything. You have no idea how sorry I am. I know I had a lot to do with your original decision to give the baby up. But now, now everything is different. I am thrilled to know that Ariel is our child."

"I'm still trying to understand this, Frank. I lost a child and for ten years, struggled with how and why this happened to me." I needed to get this out and getting it out over the phone seemed easier than in person.

"If I could do this over, Nadine..."

"No, let me finish." I cut him off. "We can't do this over. I thought I put it behind me but I found myself dreaming about babies, or this baby. It was as if she was trying to get my attention through my dreams. Even though it wasn't my fault, I couldn't face her death, and all these years I tried to push it further down. And now I find out I do have a child. She's beautiful and smart and everything a daughter should be, except maybe a little too smart for her age."

"She's been a small adult most of her life. She always sensed the tension between Melinda and me and kept coming up with ideas to try to get us to work it out. I don't know where she got this wisdom but she's got some kind of gift."

I thought of Aunt Amelia. *Did Ariel have her gifts?* But before I could follow that train of thought further, I got another shock.

"Look, I know this is all sudden to you and you know it is to me too, but we can still work this out, Nadine," Frank began. "I've missed you for a long, long time. I didn't know you were Ariel's mother but I wanted to tell you at the theater. I want you, us, back."

I held the phone away from my ear and stared at the receiver. *No, no, this can't be happening too.*

"Hello, are you there?" Frank said, when I didn't say anything.

"Yes, I'm here. I don't believe what you just said, though. Frank, our time has come and gone. We will have to see each other because of the play and because of Ariel, but get back with you? No, no; that is not happening."

"Well, think about it; please think about it. That's all I'm saying. If Colin can't handle it or whatever, I'm right here. I wasn't there for you before, but I am now."

I had no idea if Colin would be able to deal with this or not. I never saw him walk away from any situation. In my mind I thought he could handle anything. But he already walked away.

"I don't know what to say. I'm in love with my husband and I've hurt him. I've got to go. He might call and I have to keep the line open."

Frank had the grace to say he understood.

The next day Colin still hadn't come home or called. But Ariel did.

"Can I come over?" she asked on the phone.

"Yes, yes, of course you can." In the twenty-four hours since we met, I wanted to see her again as much as I wanted Colin to walk through the door. "Do you know where I live?"

"Well, I have your address. I mean, that's how you got my letters."

"Oh, right. How could I forget?"

"But Daddy will have to bring me. He won't let me go that far without him. But he won't stay. I told him this was a visit just for us."

"I would like that. I would really like that."

"Okay. Is now good?"

"Oh, sure. I guess now is perfect."

I fixed a quick lunch: tuna salad sandwiches and potato chips. We sat at the kitchen island and Houston lay still at Ariel's feet, as if he had known her forever. In between bites, she began to fill me in on her life from her birth up to this point. She was brought up in L.A. but never much liked it. Then she added, "I've only been in Manhattan for a little while but I know I love it already." I understood that connection. It was exactly how I'd felt when I first saw the city right after she was born.

354

"But what about where you grew up? About your family in South Carolina?" she asked, after we exhausted talking about her last ten years.

"My family, hmm, where do I start?" I picked up the plates and carried them to the kitchen sink. Then leaning over the island across from where Ariel sat on the other side, I started to tell her about my home.

"The Lowcountry of South Carolina is where I was born and raised. It is filled with swift flowing and winding rivers and creeks, verdant green marshes, playful dolphins, elegant live oak trees draped in sliver green moss, and people saying 'hey' for hello, 'ya'll come see us sometime' for goodbye. In the afternoon, my family would sit on wide front porches fanning themselves, sipping sweet tea and never thinking not to speak whenever someone passed by." As I rinsed our dishes, I felt myself drifting back into the ease of the life I left behind.

"Wow, that sounds beautiful. L.A. is nothing like that. It's a lot of white stucco, red tile roofs and traffic jams. I used to ask Daddy about South Carolina but he didn't say too much. He didn't like to talk about it. I guess because of you." She sipped her Coke, slid off her stool and began walking around, picking up framed photos of Colin and me on table tops, finding more on the walls. In her hands or before her eyes were pieces of my life frozen in time, looking as happy as anyone ever looked. Photographs can be deceiving. I watched her for a reaction.

"Why the heck did you want to leave?" she asked, after Houston came up to her with his ball, tamping his paws up and down and wagging his tail for emphasis.

"My mother died when I was fifteen."

"She did? Oh, that's terrible."

"Yes, yes, it was. But her sister, Aunt Amelia and Amelia's husband, Uncle Hamp, lived next door. Daddy kind of changed and they took care of me a lot. Aunt Amelia was like my second mother. I tried to take care of Daddy as best I could, but it wasn't always easy." Ariel came back over to the counter by me. "It was a hard decision for me to think of leaving in the first place, and with your father. I don't know how much he told you. We were going to start our lives together, in theater in New York, but that wasn't what my daddy wanted. He was furious with me and said if I left, not to come back."

"Never come back?" Ariel's face changed. Maybe I read more into her than I should have but I sensed her envy change into surprise, then pity.

"He needed me to be just like him, I guess. But I couldn't be. That's when I knew I needed to have my own life and leave everything behind. Maybe he meant it; maybe it was only a threat. But once I left and didn't tell him, well—we haven't spoken since."

"You haven't talked to your daddy in ten years?" She looked distressed at the idea.

"No, I haven't." I felt ashamed to say it. "But I still kept up with him through my aunt and uncle. Now they live in Beaufort, part-time and in Asheville, part-time where you were born. Oh, I want you to meet my aunt. She is a special woman. You two would like each other a lot."

We talked for the next several hours. She learned about me and how her birth in Asheville came about. I learned about her love for her mother and her wariness at the same time. I sensed she was an "old soul," as Aunt Amelia said about certain people.

Then, as we sat on the sofa watching daylight turn tangerine and gold behind the buildings out the window, and the street lights begin to beam, the phone rang.

"Hello," I said eagerly, hoping again it would be Colin.

"Hey Nadine, this is your Uncle Hamp," he said in his warm southern drawl, as if I wouldn't recognize his voice. Listening to his voice made me wish I was sitting next to him with a cold glass of tea while he regaled whoever was there with one of his charming stories.

"Hey, Uncle Hamp." I wanted to tell him about Ariel and everything that happened in the last twenty-four hours, but by his voice, I knew this wasn't the time.

"Your Aunt Amelia has passed."

I gasped and put my hand over my mouth. It shouldn't have been a surprise, but it was. Immediately, her absence hurt like a hot poker, like I was kicked in the stomach.

"Was it bad, Uncle Hamp? Did she suffer, I mean?" Ariel moved over closer to me on the couch and pressed her shoulder up into mine.

"She went in her sleep, sweetheart, without any pain." He sniffed as if he had been crying. I figured that saying it to me made him want to cry all over again. "She had her healing herbs, her rituals and her enormous spirit. All in all she controlled her pain, you know, as best she could."

I began to cry. Ariel reached over and handed me the box of tissues from the end table.

"I'll get a flight right away," I said when I felt a little calmer.

"Good. But not to Asheville. We came back to Beaufort a few days ago."

"Beaufort?" I sat up and Ariel moved over a few inches. I didn't know which was more surprising: not telling me they were back in Beaufort or that I would have to go there myself.

"She wanted to go home, sweetheart, and be laid to rest in her hometown. As much as she loved our home in Asheville it wasn't her real love. It was mine. She wanted me to have my choice the last ten years of her life."

"No, I didn't know. She never let on that she wanted to go back to Beaufort. I knew you visited a lot, but—why didn't she tell me this when I was there?"

"She didn't want to tell you because she knew she was close to the end. If she told you she was moving back then you would know, too. She was afraid you wouldn't go through with meeting the young girl. The one who thinks you are her mother. Did you meet her yet?"

"Uh, yes. Yes, I did meet her." I pulled up a clean tissue from the box to wipe my eyes then placed my hand on Ariel's knee. "I'll get there as soon as I can but I'm not coming alone." I looked over at Ariel.

"Oh, I expected Colin would be coming."

"No, Colin isn't coming. I'm bringing my daughter."

"You really think she is your daughter? I just don't know how that could be."

"Yes, Uncle Hamp, she really is; and I'll tell you when I get there."

"Okay," he said in a low tone as if he couldn't take another piece of bad news. Then he asked, "But where's Colin?"

"I don't know. He came in at the end of my meeting with my daughter and only heard a part of the story before he walked out. When I got home, I found a note but it didn't say where he was going or when he would be back."

"I'm sorry. That must have been quite a shock. Give him some time. I think your aunt would agree with me."

"There's more but I'll tell you when I see you. I love you, Uncle Hamp."

"I love you too, sweetheart. Call me after you arrange you ticket. I'll pick you both up in Savannah."

The next day I left another note for Colin, explaining what happened and where I would be. I didn't know when or even if he would see it. Frank brought Ariel back to me with a packed suitcase and we got in a cab and headed to LaGuardia Airport.

In a few hours, Uncle Hamp picked us up at the Savannah airport. I introduced him to Ariel and they hit it off immediately.

On the hour drive back to Beaufort, I gave him a synopsis of the scene at *The Bagel & I* with Frank and Ariel and me.

"Frank has been Ariel's daddy all this time?" he said, as if he couldn't believe what he heard. Then he got quiet, his anger hovering around his body as we drove. "I don't understand how that attorney could have done this to you, to Ariel...and to me."

There was no answer to that question, and I didn't want it lingering in the silent air so I switched to asking what the plans were.

"Your aunt knew what she wanted and didn't want: no viewing, no burial and no long eulogy. She wanted to be cremated; for her friends to gather to celebrate the joy of life, then after, have her ashes scattered over the Beaufort River."

"It sounds perfect. Just like Aunt Amelia."

"Only a couple of things are a bit out of order. A celebration reception is in the works right now as we speak, the hall being available today but not tomorrow. And trying to match the scattering of her ashes with a high tide meant the reception would come first."

"It still sounds perfect to me." Chatting about the details seemed to keep both of us from falling into tears.

By 4 o'clock, I entered Beaufort for the first time in ten years, this time with a daughter.

Back at their house next to Daddy's where I grew up, we only had time to drop off our bags, change clothes and freshen up before we headed off to the Baptist Church social hall. It wasn't her church anymore but a lot of her friends and clients went there. They offered the hall to Uncle Hamp.

When we walked in the side door, I found the room already packed with people and a line of others formed out the front door, waiting to sign the guest book. I recognized women putting out plates of fried chicken, platters of biscuits, bowls of potato and congealed salad, macaroni and cheese and boiled shrimp. I hadn't spoken with them in years. Once they spotted me . . . one familiar face after another came over and hugged me around the neck, offering condolences, admonitions at being away too long and surprise at how grown up I was. Then they turned to Uncle Hamp and did the same to him, only with just the condolences. Ariel stood at my side and slightly behind me, holding my hand and taking in this scene of sorrow and love.

I saw almost everyone I ever knew growing up. And they all asked the same question: why it took this long for me to come home. It was just a habit or formality because no one waited for an answer or asked anything more personal. Thank goodness; I don't know what I would have said. Southern politeness comes in handy sometimes.

Then I heard a familiar booming voice calling my name. I turned my head as Daddy stepped up right behind me. I tried not to show my surprise as I took in his full head of white hair, bags under his eyes and pronounced rounded shoulders. I never imagined him not being youthful looking and robust.

"Daddy," I said, standing erect as if in preparation to take a blow. It was an automatic response I didn't expect.

"Nadine," he repeated, more toned down this time. Then he reached out and put his hand on my shoulder, stopping short of an embrace. "Your aunt would be glad you are here."

"Just my aunt?" Daddy already crossed a threshold for him. I wanted to hear more.

"And I am happy you are here, too." He looked me in the eye, something he hadn't done in at least fifteen years; something I craved, like air or water or sleep. "Where is your husband?" He looked around behind me.

"Uh, he couldn't make it. I'm sorry. I wanted you to meet him."

"And who is this?" Daddy asked, pointing to Ariel who was still holding my hand.

"Daddy, this is Ariel Prescott." I pulled her forward. "Your granddaughter."

Daddy stepped back; his face went blank, but not his eyes. "My what?"

"Your granddaughter, my daughter." I held her hand too tight; she flinched and pulled it out enough to let me know to loosen my grip.

"Granddaughter?" he asked. "Nobody told me anything about a..." Sweat formed on his brow; his eyes appeared to droop and moisten as he stared at Ariel.

"I didn't know either. Until yesterday." I smiled at Ariel.

"Yesterday? What are you talking about? If you're the mother, there is no way you couldn't know. Isn't she yours?" Edges of his old anger started to surface and I braced again for whatever was to come next.

"I am your granddaughter and it's very nice to meet you." Ariel stepped forward as if to intercede and break the mounting tension, like she learned to do often with her mother and father. "And no, your daughter didn't know anything about this. I was adopted right after my birth." I wondered if she sounded as adult and in charge to Daddy as she did to me.

"You had a baby, put her up for adoption and didn't tell me?" His face reddened even more.

"Yes, I was pregnant and no, I didn't tell you." I straightened my back, lifted my chin and moved my feet into fifth position as if lifting a shield. I wanted to be firmly in place ready to argue this out if necessary. I was a different person from when I left and wanted him to see it. When he didn't continue with an attack, I began dropping my armor slightly. "I decided my only choice was to give the baby up for adoption and didn't tell anyone except Aunt Amelia and Uncle Hamp. I signed the papers but just before Ariel was born, I changed my mind. Right after I delivered they took her away, told me I had no rights; then, when I asked to at least see her, they told me she was stillborn."

"Stillborn? Amelia knew; Hamp knew? I can't believe this." I saw him struggle to understand. I dreaded this moment but there was no way around it, only through it.

"It's all my fault," Uncle Hamp said, as he stepped up to the three of us.

"It's not your fault, Uncle Hamp. It's nobody's fault," Ariel jumped in, taking his hand with her free one.

"What did you say your last name was?" Daddy asked.

"Prescott," she said.

"Prescott?" He turned toward me. "Wasn't that your old boy-friend's name?"

"Yes, Daddy, Frank is her father."

"Frank? But I thought you married some Yankee from up there." He pointed out into the room in the direction of north.

"I did. I am." *I left out that I hoped I stayed married.*

The conversation abruptly ended as I was suddenly pulled away by friends and extended family for the next couple of hours. But Ariel stayed with him, and soon every time I looked over, Daddy was showing off his granddaughter to whoever came by.

The next day loud crunching sounds from beneath our feet followed us as we walked over fallen oak leaves and acorns and twigs, making our way toward the designated cliff on Bay Street, one of my favorite spots. Below us flowed the Beaufort River, part of the Inland Coastal Waterway, the protected route for boats and barges traveling anywhere between Maine and Florida and back. At this point the river made a wide bend, creating a bay where sizable sandbars emerged at low tide and sail boats anchored at buoys rather than at the nearby dock. The lush marsh, now turned golden, spread twenty feet out into the river and was mirrored on the other side where the river met the gray, pocketed pluff mud.

Mama and I used to come to this same place and sit on a blanket until the sand fleas or mosquitoes chased us away.

Aunt Amelia brought many of her clients there as part of the healing work she performed, to help them to see the beauty in life all around, to help them let go of the negative tape recordings in their heads. Moving in and out of the present, I realized I needed to connect to this beauty myself. Then a shiver ran down my spine. Of course, I mused. Aunt Amelia brought me here on purpose.

Before Aunt Amelia's ashes could be cast, a Unitarian minister from Savannah offered a few words to help send her on her way. "Amelia Carter Cooper grew up Southern Baptist but as her life moved more toward the spiritual, she found most organized religions too confining. She told me of her basic feeling that mankind needed to love and respect each other as much as they loved and worshiped Jesus."

Ariel took my hand again as Uncle Hamp opened the urn and waved it back and forth over the river. Ash glided out, creating sparkles in the sun before the breeze diminished it to nothing any of us could see.

My eyes welled up but not with the kind of tears that would make me fall into sorrowful sobbing. This day of honoring my aunt went according to her plan and everyone in Beaufort who loved her most turned out for her. These were happy tears.

As we all stood in silence, when the ceremony was over something caused me to turn around, almost like I was tapped on the shoulder. I wasn't sure what it was; maybe Aunt Amelia. When no one was there, my eyes lifted and saw someone walking through the shadows of the giant oaks toward the edge of the gathering. When the person emerged into the sunlight, I saw it was Colin.

I froze, and when Ariel saw him too, she held tight to my hand. Colin came over to us and our eyes met. Then he shifted his gaze down to Ariel.

"Hi, I'm Ariel," she said, taking the lead again.

"Yes, yes, you are. Let's start over. Hello, I'm Colin Bennett."
He shook her hand and then held it with both of his.

"I have a lot to explain," I said, trying to read his thoughts.

"Father Benjamin filled me in on most of it; at least the restaurant part. Why didn't you tell me before?"

"I didn't know, Colin. Truly, I didn't know."

"I mean that you had a baby once, that you were pregnant."

"I don't know that either. I wanted to tell you but I never did.
Once I kept it from Frank and Daddy, I kept holding on to it."

Colin put his arms around me and we held each other.

"I don't want to lose you. We'll find some way to work this out,"
he said, into my neck.

"But to do that, you need to be home more. We have other
responsibilities now."

"Yes, yes, I do need to be home more."

"All right, all right." Daddy came blustering over to us. "This
must be the Yankee actor."

"Director, Daddy. Colin is a director."

"I'm Sam Barnwell. Please to meet you, son." He held out his
hand and I stood back to take in the longed or sight of my daddy
making friends with my husband.

After the ashes ceremony and a lunch of reception leftovers, I
realized I longed to see Camp Pinckney again. Without hesitation, Daddy offered to take all of us; Uncle Hamp, Daddy, Colin,
Ariel and me on his thirty-foot Scout skiff to spend the night.
We packed a couple of overnight bags while Uncle Hamp and
Daddy packed the food and drinks. Goosebumps ran down both
my arms, as I watched the flurry of activity.

As we rode through narrow and wide creeks lined with marsh
and dotted with white herons, the air filled with the smell of
the sea. Where we traveled nothing had changed in four or five

hundred years, probably longer. Those were the same waterways inhabited by the Indians and Black Beard. Mullet jumped out of the river, pods of dolphins fished in hidden schools in the murky water, and seagulls and pelicans flew in formation overhead. The wind caressed my face while the October sun warmed my sallow New York skin. I tried to glimpse Colin and Ariel's faces without being obvious or intrusive. They seemed stunned into silence by the beauty.

At the camp, Uncle Hamp prepared his signature Frogmore Stew, Aunt Amelia's favorite. I wanted to share this exceptional meal of my youth and heritage with Colin and Ariel. Cooked outside in a huge pot over a gas burner, the shrimp, corn and potatoes were sweet and fresh, and the sausage added the perfect complementary flavor. Once the shrimp was done, Uncle Hamp and Daddy lifted the heavy strainer from the cooking pot and dumped the contents over a wooden table covered in newspapers. For this meal, there was no silverware, only paper plates, cocktail sauce and rolls of paper towels. With tongs and plastic cups, we sat around the table and scooped up what we wanted from the middle, picked up the shrimp with our hands, peeled it, threw the shells into buckets and popped them in our mouths. Colin and Ariel glowed as they shoveled the food into their mouths.

As sad as it was to say goodbye to Aunt Amelia, this trip turned out to be the most wonderful few days I ever spent. Here I sat with my uncle, my daddy I lost for too long, my husband I almost lost altogether, and miracle of all miracles, my daughter. When I looked around the table, I realized I was the only one who knew them all. But everyone laughed and talked as if they knew one another for years.

"Ariel, let me give you a tour of the camp before it gets too dark," Daddy said.

"Yeah, cool. Let's go." Ariel jumped at the offer.

Colin and I moved out to the screened-in porch, just as I did almost eleven years before with Aunt Amelia.

From the splintered wood and broken cane-backed rocking chairs, sounds of animals, insects and the distant shore enveloped us, directed again, I was sure, by Aunt Amelia. We sat like that for a long time.

"So now you have to tell me," Colin said, "with just the two of us sitting here, and with no more secrets, how all of this really happened."

"If you are ready to hear it, I am ready to tell you." As I waited for the twilight chorus to lower its fevered pitch, my path to this moment came even clearer. "From the moment I knew I needed to dance in New York City; to my pregnancy; to ending up at that clinic outside of Asheville; to actually moving to New York; to responding to Ariel's letter; to where we sit tonight; these were all my choices. Nothing I did was ever meant to hurt anyone; more to protect them. But in the process I hurt everyone. My pregnancy colored all my decisions along the way. Roadblocks came where there should have been none. I thought I could handle this with only the help of Aunt Amelia and Uncle Hamp. But now I know better. She warned me often not to hold my secret inside too long. I don't know if I didn't listen or didn't hear. I couldn't face what happened, so the lies and the cover-ups came and then I couldn't face the lies I told. It seems the job of bringing all our scattered lives together and my secret to the surface was given to a ten-year old girl. Ariel is the one who stepped in and took care of this mess."

The creak of weathered wood rockers on weathered wood decking filled the space.

"Well, what now? I mean, for all of us?" Colin finally asked.

"Yes, what now for all of us?" Daddy called out from below. Back from their tour, I realized they both heard almost all of my explanation.

"I don't know. No one knows for sure, Aunt Amelia always said. But I have an idea to help us figure it out. Y'all come up here."

Daddy and Ariel joined Colin in the living room and I went to find Uncle Hamp.

A few minutes later, Uncle Hamp was carrying a tray with a large bowl filled with water and six white votive candles. I placed sheer fabric squares and a black marking pen on the tray. Between the bowl and the candles, I saw something I didn't recognize; pink tissue paper wrapped around a small object, tied with a satin ribbon.

"Go ahead, take it. It's yours now," Uncle Hamp said.

"What's mine?" I picked up the small package. As soon as it was in my hand, I knew what it was: Aunt Amelia's amulet. "But shouldn't it be with you?" I protested as I removed the tissue and held it up from its clasp.

"She wanted you to have it and I can't think of a more appropriate time to give it to you," Uncle Hamp said, as he lit the candles.

"I'm so honored." I placed it around my neck. The flickering light from the flames caught the crystals and spread a rainbow prism throughout the room, making me feel as if she was right there with us.

"Thank you," I whispered to the reflected light. Everyone laughed softly and I composed myself for what I wanted to say next.

"Now that Aunt Amelia has moved on to another plane on her journey, I feel we each need something to help take us to the next step of our own journey right here. I would like for y'all to participate with me in a version of Aunt Amelia's favorite ritual, the one she used to help guide me on the next step of my life eleven years ago." No one protested. Everyone took a seat around the table in front of the couch. As I talked, I handed each person a piece of cloth and a pen. "You should write what it is you most want to have happen next in your life. Keep it simple; a short phrase, not an essay. Then each person will say out loud what they've written. When everyone is done, we'll all put our cloths in the water at the same time, hold hands around the bowl and watch the ink disappear. This will set our desires in motion."

Daddy, Colin and Ariel looked puzzled and started to ask questions.

"Just get quiet and let it flow, ya'll," Uncle Hamp said. He smiled and closed his eyes. Then, as if falling under a spell everyone stopped talking and closed their eyes too.

When enough time passed I added, "Okay, we're ready. I don't want you to overthink this; now write."

After I finished mine, I paused, feeling something was missing. *Of course.* I picked up more pieces of cloth and composed two more.

Once everyone else was finished, I said, "I'm going to start. I've also done one for my friends," I turned toward Daddy and Uncle Hamp, "one for Father Benjamin and Taylor and one for Deni."

"For Father Benjamin and Taylor I wrote, *Permanent Parish and Restaurant.* But what I will explain is that what I want to see happen next for them is to find the perfect spot in The Village to house both the parish and the restaurant. It would be a single place where they can continue to feed the souls and the stomachs of all who seek their special loving kindness and support."

Colin grinned and nodded.

"For Deni I wrote, *Contentment and Successful Career.* What I want to say, in addition, is this is already set in motion. She will be my replacement on *Sadie Burnside.* With this, she will be able to have her own money, her own apartment and the life she always wanted, but looked for in the wrong places."

Colin chuckled and nodded again.

"Okay," I went on, "who wants to go next?"

"I've already got mine," Ariel jumped in. She just met all of us but there was nothing shy about her.

"Mine says, *A Normal Life*. What I want most, now that I've found my birth mother," she pointed to me and smiled, "and all of you," she looked at everyone else, "is for Mama and Daddy to get over it and stop arguing all the time. Maybe they won't stay together, but at least I can have a normal life and be with Daddy and Nadine and Colin in New York City. That would be so cool."

"That would indeed be so cool," I said. I loved hearing she wanted to see all of us more. "Who's next?" I asked, wiping away a slipped tear and searching each face.

"I am," Uncle Hamp said. "I wish for," he stopped to clear his throat or maybe catch himself from tearing up also, *"Amelia's Peaceful and Rapid Transition* to wherever it is we go. Then she can get back to her full-time job of watching over each of us." He laughed. "But that may be redundant because I'm sure she's doing it already. She's right here in this room with us, listening to everything we are saying." In the wavering candlelight, Uncle Hamp's face reflected deep love and sadness at the same time. I imagined my face was the same.

As if in prayer no one spoke for a full minute.

"Now, Daddy, what's yours?" I worried the mighty Sam Barnwell might not want to participate unless I made him. But I was wrong. He was ready.

"I wrote," he cleared his throat too, maybe for the same reason, *"To Not Waste More Time*. I can't change what has happened. What I want more than anything is for my beautiful daughter, successful son-in-law and amazing granddaughter to come visit me as often as possible. Maybe even have a second home here. I've got some real estate I might be persuaded to let go at a real bargain, you know."

My heart felt like it might burst with joy.

My daddy, the man I loved so deeply, so long ago, was back.

"You mean you'll give it to them, don't you, Sam?" Uncle Hamp said with arms folded across his chest, eyes directly on Daddy.

We all laughed.

"Well, whatever it takes to get Nadine back here more often. I've been fortunate. I guess I've got more than my share."

"Y'all all heard him," Uncle Hamp said. "He's gonna give you a house. Now it's up to you to hold him to it."

Colin and I turned toward each other and nodded.

"Okay, Colin, what's yours?" Daddy asked. "I did mine now you have to do yours, son."

"Mine? I'm not usually hard up for words, quite the contrary. I didn't know what to say about mine at first. But listening to everyone, I figured it out. Mostly, it's already happened, but I guess I didn't know how close it was to being taken away. What I wrote was, *Continued Bliss, but More Grace*. What I want, more than anything, is to continue the life I have with Nadine and with my career. But my career would be nothing without her to share it with. I want to develop the grace to know the balance and to not neglect what is most important."

He grabbed my hand and held it to his heart. I was mush. He couldn't have said anything more perfect.

"Now it's your turn, Nadine," Colin said, lowering my hand from his chest. I looked into the bowl of water, trying to form the right words. Then they came.

"For me, I wrote, *Dance and Trust*. You don't know about this Colin, but I've been offered a choreography job for a new dance company. Taking it will allow me to get back on my own path, back to my own work again. But what I want more than anything is to regain all of your trust." I held each person's eyes for a moment before lowering mine back to the water. "First, I thought I would not be able to live without my mother. Then I faced the same fear with Aunt Amelia. But in her passing I've been given the greatest gift of all. I now know I am nothing without each of you."

When I raised my head again, everyone's eyes glistened in the candlelight, their faces filled with peace.

"Please step forward to release your words." We all placed our fabric squares in the bowl and joined hands. With the night sounds ratcheting up their chorus again, as if to help send our wishes on their way, we watched our words dissolve from the fabric, setting in motion our next desires on our paths.

Colin squeezed my right hand and Ariel, my left. I never felt this loved and this loving. What we set in motion all those years ago was finally real. My Full-Hearted life expanded to include my husband, my daddy, my daughter and my dancing.

READER REVIEWS are important to an author.
If you would, please write one for my novel - Today.
Search *What We Set in Motion*
Amazon.com.
The length is unimportant.
Just write an honest review.
Thanks for reading and thanks for writing.
stephanie.austin.edwards@gmail.com

ACKNOWLEDGEMENTS

Writing a first novel is a daunting endeavor but the writer doesn't know the real journey until he/she gets into the process and then gets hooked. For me, the first stage is the overwhelming need to take on the task. The second stage is overcoming the fear of anyone reading what I released from my heart by asking professionals to look at the random scenes that don't yet make a whole. The third stage is when my story begins to take shape, and I boldly seek the eyes and ears of other writers to help deepen it further. By then *It's Set in Motion.* For many of us, this first one can take a long, long time. Therefore, I must give heartfelt thanks to everyone who supported and guided me to this conclusion.

My love and gratitude go to my talented and tireless writer's group members Joan Fewell Harris, Martha Weeks, Katherine Brown, Mary Hope Roseneau, Judy McCandless, Carol Lucas, Kami Kinard, and Caryl Sweet. A heartfelt thanks to the incredible editors/authors along my journey: Cheryl Lopanik, Judy Goldman, Kathie Giorgio and Gloria Singleton. A special thanks to my Beta Readers: Patsy Hand, Clay Chapman, Jan Darcy, Greta James, Anna Ellerbe, Gloria Singleton, Carol Darcy, Harriett Hilton and Joan Fewell Harris. My thank you list would not be complete without including some of the authors and writing teachers who inspired and encouraged me to keep reaching further: Pat Conroy, Mary Alice Monroe, Ron Rash, Luke Whisnant, Judy Goldman, Cassandra King Conroy and Abigail DeWitt. I thank my publicist Sharon Bialley, publishing guru Carla King, and workshop founder Judi Hill.

In addition, I believe that writer organizations play an incredible role in the authors process as well. I thank Wildacres Writers Workshop, South Carolina Writers Workshop, and the Atlanta Writers Club Conference where my novel won a Best Submission Award from St. Martins Press.

I end with my family: Thank you to my departed mother Mildred L Edwards, and to my brother Chris Edwards, sisters Jan E. Darcy and Carol E. Darcy, and my husband, Paul Coffman, Jr.

CPSIA information can be obtained at www.ICGtesting.com
Printed in the USA
LVOW08s0021310116

472820LV00002B/38/P